The
Vesuvius
Club

The Vesuvius Club

A BIT OF FLUFF

by

MARK GATISS

POCKET BOOKS

LONDON • SYDNEY • NEW YORK • TORONTO

First published in Great Britain by Simon & Schuster UK Ltd, 2004
This edition published by Pocket Books, 2005
This omnibus edition first published by Pocket Books, 2008
An imprint of Simon & Schuster UK Ltd
A CBS COMPANY

1 3 5 7 9 10 8 6 4 2

Simon & Schuster UK Ltd
1st Floor
222 Gray's Inn Road
London WC1X 8HB

Simon & Schuster Australia
Sydney

A CIP catalogue record for this book is available from the British Library

ISBN 978-0-7434-8379-7

Typeset by M Rules
Printed by CPI Cox & Wyman, Reading, Berkshire RG1 8EX

For Ian
My love, my life

ACKNOWLEDGEMENTS

Huge thanks to Ian Bass, John Jarrold (who lit the first Lucifer), Clayton Hickman, Darren Nash and my editor Ben Ball – honorary English gentleman.

I

MR LUCIFER BOX ENTERTAINS

 HAVE always been an appalling judge of character. It is my most beguiling virtue.

What, then, did I make of the Honourable Everard Supple whose likeness I was conjuring on to canvas in my studio that sultry July evening?

He was an imposing cove of sixty-odd, built like a pugilist, who had made a fortune in the diamond mines of the Cape. His declining years, he'd told me during the second sitting – when a client begins to thaw a mite – were to be devoted entirely to pleasure, principally in the gaming houses of the warmer and naughtier parts of Europe. A portrait, in his opinion (and his absence), would be just the thing to hang over the vast baronial fireplace in the vast baronial hall he had recently lavished a hundred thou' upon.

The Supples, it has to be said, were not amongst the oldest and most distinguished families in the realm. Only one generation back from the

Honourable Everard had been the less than honourable Gerald who had prospered only tolerably in a manufactory of leather thumb-braces. Son and heir had done rather better for himself and now to add to the title (of sorts) and the fake coat of arms being busily prepared across town he had his new portrait. This, he told me with a wheezy chuckle, would convey the required air of old-world veracity. And if my painting were any good (that *hurt*), perhaps I might even be interested in knocking up a few carefully aged canvases of his ancestors?

Supple blinked repeatedly, as was his habit, one lid lingering over his jade-irised glass eye (the left one) as I let myself imagine him tramping into the studio in doublet and hose, all in the name of family honour.

He cleared his throat with a grisly expectoration and I realized he'd been addressing me. I snapped out of my reverie and peeped around the side of the canvas. I've been told I peep rather well.

'I do beg your pardon, I was absorbed in the curve of your ear-lobes.'

'I was suggesting dinner, sir,' said Supple, flipping a half-hunter watch from his waistcoat. 'To celebrate the successful conclusion of me picture.'

'I should be delighted,' I lied. 'But I feel it only right to warn you that I have a peculiar horror of artichokes.'

The Honourable Everard Supple rose from the doubtful Louis Quinze into which I'd plonked him, sending a whisper of paint-flakes to the dust-sheeted floor.

'We might try me club, then,' he suggested, brushing the sleeve of his frock-coat. 'Or do you have somewhere you artistic-types favour?'

I rose and ran one of my long, bony hands through my hair. They *are* long, white and bony, I cannot deny it, but very fine. Waistcoat and face flecked with paint, I shrugged.

'As a matter of fact, I do,' I said. 'Charming little spot in Rosebery Avenue. Come back at eight and we'll drive over.' So saying, I suddenly turned the easel on its squeaking castors, revealing the portrait to the golden light washing through the skylight. 'Behold! Your immortality!'

Supple creaked forward on his expensive boots and fixed a monocle, rather unnecessarily, into the orbit of his false eye. He frowned, cocked his head to left and right and grimaced.

'Well, I suppose you get what you pay for, eh, Mr Box?'

My name is Lucifer Box, but I imagine you know that. Whether these scribblings eventually form the core of my memoirs or are found secreted in oilskin wrappers at the bottom of a lavatory cistern years after my demise, I have no doubt that, by the time you read this, I will be most terribly famous.

I handed Supple his soft kid-gloves with as much brusqueness as I could muster. 'You don't like it?'

The old fool shrugged. 'Just not sure it's terribly like me.'

I helped him into his overcoat. 'On the contrary, sir, I believe I have caught you.'

I smiled what my friends call, naturally enough, the smile of Lucifer.

Ah! London in the summertime! *Hellish*, as any resident will tell you. Even in those first few innocent years of the new century it smelled of roasting excrement. So it was with 'kerchiefs pressed to mouths that Supple and I entered the dining rooms I had selected. They were alarmingly unfashionable but, in the long light of dusk, the white-panelled plainness could have been called Vermeeresque. Not by me, you understand. A flypaper above the hearth twisted lazily, amber and black like a screw of ear-wax.

This place, I told Supple, was owned and run by a woman called Delilah whose crippled daughter I had once painted as a favour.

'She was not, perhaps, the bonniest thing,' I confided as we settled down to eat. 'Lost both hands to a wasting disease and had them replaced with wooden ones. And – oh! – her little legs were in horrid iron rings.' I shook my head despairingly. 'Ought to have been exposed at birth, her father said.'

'Nay!' cried Supple.

'Aye! But her dear mother loved the little mite. When I came to paint the portrait I did my best to make little Ida look like an angel. Prophetically enough. Though it turned out she had some pluck.'

Supple wiped soup from his pinkish lips. Sentimental old Victorian that he was, a tear sprang to his one good eye. Most probably the Death of Little Nell had been like mother's milk to him.

'Poor Ida,' I sighed, picking idly at a chicken leg. 'Grabbed from her bath-chair by a gang of dacoits and sold into bondage.'

Supple's shook his head mournfully. No doubt an image of the doe-eyed cripple had flashed into his silly old brain. His fingers tightened on the fish-knife. 'Go on. What happened?'

'She made a bolt for it, God bless her,' I continued. 'Took off across the rooftops with the fiends in hot pursuit.'

Blink-blink. The jade glass eye regarded me steadily. 'And then?'

I closed my eyes and steepled my fingers. 'She got as far as Wapping before her brittle little legs gave out. She fell through the roof of a sugar merchant's and into a vat of treacle. Of course, with those wooden hands she could get no purchase on the rim and she drowned. Very, very slowly.'

Drinking the last of an indifferent burgundy with an air of finality, I clapped my hands and turned the conversation towards more cheerful matters. Now I had Supple's trust, it was time to betray that of others. I wanted the practice.

I regaled Supple with what I know to be an inexhaustible supply of anecdotes (not many of them true, certainly not the best ones) concerning the greatish and goodish who have paid yours truly not nearly enough to be immortalized in oils.

'You are very indiscreet, sir,' laughed the old man, cheering up. 'I am glad not to have confided any of my secrets in you!'

I smiled my wide smile.

Supple, for his part, talked at length about his time in South Africa and the great adventure a young man like me might have there. He told me about his own daughter – a great joy to the old man by his account – and I nodded and smiled with the air of sagacity I like to assume for such occasions. I put on a good show of being fascinated by his colourful account of dawn over the Transvaal as I took out my watch and stared at the second hand racing over the porcelain dial. I could hear the soft action of the tiny spring.

It was midway between the fish course and the pudding, as Supple opened his mouth to begin another interminable tale, that I did the decent thing and shot him.

A stain spread across the breast of his stiff white waistcoat like poppy petals emerging through the snow. How I wish I'd had my sketch-book with me! The scene was a riot of crimson possibilities.

There, now. I've shocked you, haven't I? What the deuce can Mr Box be up to? Are customers in such abundant supply? Well, you'll just have to be patient. All good things et cetera.

Supple's face, never particularly smashing as you may have gathered, froze in an expression of pained surprise and a little bubble of red spit frolicked over his lips. He slid forward on to the table where his teeth met the rim of his pudding bowl with a shocking crack, like the knees of an out-of-practice supplicant.

I watched smoke curl from the end of the snub-barrelled pistol I'd used, then replaced the weapon under a jelly mould – silver and shaped like a sleeping hare – where it had been until recently ensconced.

Lighting a cigarette, I re-pocketed my watch and, rising, dabbed a napkin at the corners of my full-lipped mouth (it's a very pretty mouth – more of it later). Taking up a dessert spoon, I dug it into Supple's left socket and carefully removed the old fellow's glass eye. It popped out with just a little poking and lay nestled in my palm like a gull's egg. I looked at the iris and smiled. It was just the shade of green I had in mind for a new tie and now I had a match for my tailor. What a happy accident! I slipped the eye into my waistcoat and draped the napkin carelessly over the dead man's head.

A large and ugly mirror hung over the fireplace of the dark little room. I checked my appearance in it (*very* acceptable), adjusting my stance to avoid the mottled edges of the glass, which tended to obscure the wonderful cut of my best tail-coat and pulled the tatty bell-rope that hung close by.

The doors were opened almost at once by a huge woman in a daffodil-coloured frock. Her gin-flushed cheeks, abutting a long, blotchy nose gave her face the appearance of bruised knackers in a harness.

'Good evening, Delilah,' I said, with just the slightest turn from the mirror.

'Hevening, sir,' said the drudge. She shuffled a little awkwardly, glanced at the table and cleared her throat.

'Heverything in horder, sir?'

I turned, cigarette between teeth, adjusting my white tie with both hands.

'Hmm? Oh yes. The burgundy was deadly and the partridge a trifle high. Other than that a most satisfactory evening.'

Delilah nodded her massive head. 'And the hother gentleman, sir?'

'Will be leaving us now, thank you.'

Delilah thrust both mitt-like hands under the armpits of the Honourable Everard Supple and dragged the one-eyed corpse with apparent effortlessness towards the doors. I hopped athletically over the dead man's legs, sweeping up my cloak and topper from a chair.

'How's little Ida?' I asked, clapping the hat to my head.

'Very good, thankyou for hasking, sir. No doubt be seeing you soon, sir,' grunted Delilah.

'No doubt,' I replied. 'Ta, ta.'

I stepped over the threshold of the mean little dwelling and out into the sultry evening. Thinking I deserved a little treat, I hailed a hansom.

'The Pomegranate Rooms,' I said to the driver. Work was over for the moment. Time to play.

Twenty minutes later, I was dropped a short distance from said night-spot and made my way towards its mouldering wedding-cake façade. The slattern on the door opened it a crack and treated me to a quick view of her form. Poured carelessly into a garish oriental gown she had the look of a pox-ravaged sultana – both the potentess and the dried fruit.

I slipped through the grimy doorway.

'Any riff-raff in tonight, my sweet?' I enquired.

'Plenty,' she gurgled, taking my hat and cloak as persons on doors are wont to do.

'Splendid!'

The Pomegranate Rooms were small, sweltering and poorly lit by gas sconces stained tobacco-yellow, lending the whole a colour not unlike the bitter pith of the titular fruit. Rickety wooden tables littered the crimson carpets; spilled champagne formed great fizzing puddles in every shadowed corner. Each table was occupied by rather more patrons than was good for it; the majority of the sweating men in evening dress, or the remains of it, with a quantity of backless white waistcoats slung over the chairs; the women, and there were many of them, less respectably dressed, some scarcely dressed at all. It was all quite ghastly and I was very fond of it.

Such establishments erupt on to the bloated body of the capital with the unerring regularity of a clap-rash but the Pomegranate Rooms were something of a special case. A hangover from the fever-dream that had been the Naughty Nineties, I had once, within its stuffy, cigar-fume-drenched walls, espied our present monarch being 'attended to' by a French noblewoman of uncertain virtue.

I dropped into a chair at the only free table and ordered up some plonk. A fat bawd close by, rouged like an *ingénue* undertaker's first case, began at once to make eyes at me. I examined my nails until she lost interest. I cannot abide the obese and in a whore it is surely tantamount to unprofessionalism. Her chums were not much better.

I ate something to take away the taste of the champagne and then smoked a cigarette to take away the taste of the food. I tried not to make it too obvious that I was on my lonesome. It is a terrible thing to dine alone. One stinks of desperation.

With as much nonchalance as I could affect, I examined the play of the light on my champagne glass whilst surreptitiously sneaking looks at the patrons in the hope of spotting something pretty.

And then, without any ado whatsoever, a young woman glided into the seat opposite me. In a white satin dress with pearls at her throat and rather gorgeous blonde hair piled high she looked like one of Sargent's slightly elongated females. I felt a stir down below that could have been the beginnings of indigestion but probably had more to do with the way her dewy eyes were fixed on me.

I lifted the plonk bottle and my eyebrows enquiringly.

'You're rather out of place here, my dear,' I said, as I poured her a glass. 'I should say the Pomegranate Rooms rarely see the likes of you.'

She inclined her head slightly. 'Got any fags?'

A little taken aback, I nodded and took out my cigarette case. It is flat and well-polished with my initials in Gothic script upon it, yet it has never been called upon to save my life by absorbing the impact of a bullet. That's what servants are for.

'Armenian or Georgian?' I enquired.

She took out one of the long black specimens that cram the case's right-hand side and struck a match off the heel of her elegant shoe, lighting the cigarette in one rapid movement.

Her brazen behaviour delighted me.

'Lor, I was dying for that,' said the vision, taking in great gulps of smoke. 'Mind if I take one for later?'

I waved a hand. 'Be my guest.'

She scooped up a dozen or so cigarettes and stuffed them inside her corset.

'You're full of surprises,' I managed.

'Ain't I, though?' She laughed and gave a hoarse cough. 'You on your own?'

My performance had been penetrated. I poured myself another drink. 'Alas.'

She looked me up and down with what I can only describe as sauciness. 'That's a shame. You're a looker.'

I could not deny it.

'I like a tall gent,' she continued. 'You a foreigner?'

I ran a hand through my long black hair. 'My complexion owes much to my Franco-Slavic mama and little to my British papa. My waist is all my own work.'

'Hm. They must've been proud of having such a bonny babe.'

'A baroness once told me that she could cut her wrists on my cheek-bones.'

'Lot of girls died for you have they?'

'Only those who cannot live for me.'

She rested her chin on a gloved hand. 'You got cold eyes, though. Blue as poison-bottles.'

'Really, you must desist or I shall consider running away with myself.' I placed my hand on hers. 'What's your name?'

She shook her head, blowing out a cloud of smoke and smiling. 'I don't like mine. I'd much rather hear yours.'

I fiddled lightly with my cuff-link. 'Gabriel,' I said, adopting one of my *noms de guerre*. 'Gabriel Ratchitt.'

The nameless lovely took this in. 'That's an angel's name.'

'I know, my dear,' came my murmur. 'And I fear I may be falling.'

II

ON THE EFFICACY OF ASSASSINATION

OTH the night and my blood were far too hot to waste time journeying home, so I got to grips with my new acquaintance in a slimy alley at the back of the Pomegranate Rooms. I have a vivid memory of her raised skirts brushing against my chin and the feel of her very lovely bosom beneath my fine, white hands (I've mentioned them). As I plunged on, my eye caught a bill pasted haphazardly to the wet brickwork. Nellie Best was playing at the Collins Music Hall. I might just have time between this coupling and my next appointment to make the second house.

Nellie was on fine form and so was I, hearing her belt out 'Who Were You With Last Night?' as I strolled into the upstairs bar-room and topped myself up on hock. Groping for a seat and tripping irresponsibly over the fetching white ankles of a dozen young ladies, the hall became one great wonderful blur of gaseous colour and

light. I felt as though I had tumbled head-first into one of Sickert's delightfully *déclassé* canvases. The hollowed shadows enveloped me in grimy red plush, Nelly Best's canary-yellow crinolines flaring before my grinning phiz like sunbursts.

After several choruses too many of 'Oh What a Silly Place to Kiss a Girl', I tottered out into the balmy night and a cab.

'Piccadilly,' I cried, banging my cane rather unnecessarily against the roof.

Shortly afterwards, I was deposited in front of the Royal Academy of Art. By day I am naturally used to entering premises by the front door but, that night, I took care descending the treacherously corkscrew steps down to the tradesmen's entrance.

Delilah, having finished her work at the dining rooms, was there to greet me with her broken-toothed smile; she ushered me through into a corridor tiled in black and white parquet. I threw off my cloak and hooked my hat carefully on to the horns of a stuffed ibyx head, whose startled expression was not at all dissimilar to that of the late Everard Supple.

At the very end of the room was a small and awfully discreet door, inlaid, quite exquisitely, with blond marquetry in a pattern of peacock feathers. I went through the door and into a panelled hall lit by sputtering gas-jets. There had been some excitable talk about having the electricity laid on but I had used my meagre powers to veto this. I liked the atmosphere of the little journey. Somehow the flames in their bold brass stanchions felt like primitive torches in a secret tunnel. We all know the attraction of secret tunnels. When I was a boy, there was nothing in the world I wanted to discover more. It's quite rewarding finally to have one at the office.

I stuffed my hands into my trouser pockets and whistled a few bars of Nellie Best's best as I reached the end of the silent corridor. It terminated in a kind of ship's wheel, studded at the tip of each spoke with a porcelain button rather in the manner of bath taps. I tapped in a little sequence of letters corresponding to some code or other and span the wheel to the left. Another discreet door, though not nearly so prettily carved, sprang open just to my right. Why they couldn't just let me knock, I'll never know.

I passed through into a gentlemen's lavatory. Planting my rump (avec trousers, you understand) on the cold seat in one of the cubicles, I folded my arms and exhaled impatiently. It was a further five minutes before I heard the sound of footfalls and the opening and closing of the cubicle door next to mine. Finally, with a grim protesting shriek, the metal wall dividing the cubicles began to rise.

Sitting on the next po along, impeccable in frock-coat and imperial collar, was the dwarfish form of Joshua Reynolds. My boss; three foot something in his stockinged feet and ever so jolly.

'Hello, Lucifer,' trilled the little fellow. He wriggled on the seat of the lavatory and pumped my hand. His tiny patent leather shoes glistened in the gas-light.

"Evening,' I rejoined. 'Still can't run to a proper office, eh?'

Reynolds gave an impish laugh. 'No, no. You know how we like it. Cloak and dagger, my boy. That's what we thrive on. Ha-ha. Smoke and mirrors.' His eyes were bright and black in his face like raisins in dough. 'Now then,' he continued, rubbing his pudgy hands together. 'The . . . er . . . business is concluded?'

I nodded and smiled my wide smile. 'It is.'

'And the . . . er . . . package has been . . . sent to . . . Sebastopol?'

'Ye-es.'

'And was the . . . transaction . . . er . . . accomplished without undue . . .'

'If you mean have I killed old Supple, then yes, I have,' I cried. 'Shot him in the chest and watched him die like the filthy dog he was.'

The little man sniffed and nodded. He seemed to suffer an eternal cold in the head.

'A modicum of thanks would not go amiss,' I ventured.

Reynolds laughed explosively. 'What would you like me to say, my boy? That England owes you a great debt?'

'That would do to begin with. Hmm . . . "The nation will be forever and profoundly grateful." That sort of thing. But will the nation ever know it? To them the Honourable Everard will remain a gallant servant of the Empire –'

'Shot defending his own home by a vicious gang of roughs,' put in JR.

'Is that what we're saying?'

'So I gather.'

I shrugged lightly. 'Yes, he will remain every inch the gallant lad rather than the atrocious anarchist with plans to explode bombs under the foreign secretary that we know him to be. To have *been*.'

'Well, well, my boy,' said Joshua Reynolds with a twinkle. 'That is why we call it *secret* service.'

Ah, now. The cat's out of the bag. There you are, having paid your few shillings at Mr Smith's emporium at Waterloo Station (if my memoirs ever make it out of the cistern), fully expecting the entertaining ramblings of the great Lucifer Box, RA, foremost portraitist of his age (a man must have ambition) and what do you discover? That in between my little daubs I was living a double life!

It was a connection humble enough in origin. For reasons that are too painful and private to relate I'd ended up owing a favour or two to our family solicitor. Joshua Reynolds (for it was he), despite being small, turned out to be something very *big* in His Majesty's Government. Strictly behind the scenes, you understand, and most secret. I liked to flatter myself that he really couldn't manage without me.

He peered at me now with a strange expression somewhere between a smile and a grimace.

'You're looking positively consumptive, dear heart,' he said at last.

'How you wound me! The Beardsley style is *so* unfashionable.'

'Eat a little more!'

'I find it difficult to manage on the pittance you pay.'

The little man sniffed back a drop of moisture from his nostril. 'Oh, now you're being cruel. Your late papa would never forgive me if I let you starve.'

'Were I more at liberty, I could get by very well on my artistic commissions.'

He reached across and patted my hand. His own was dimpled fatly like that of an overfed baby. 'Of course, of course. But my little problems do provide a more regular salary, eh? And not too much effort required on your part.'

I smiled, admitting his point. 'Effort only in the service of pleasure.'

It may have seemed rash of them to give the job to an aberrant character like me but I cannot deny how much I relished it. The world was my studio, and they laid on the apprentices to clean the brushes. Say there was a visiting Turkish despot to be bumped off. Furnished with the dry details, the artistic part would be left to me. I'd formulate a little plan with the Domestics (Delilah, she of the daffodil frock was one of the best) and off we'd toddle. The Ottoman offender would be taking a stroll in some pleasure garden and, if the night were a dark one, a swift dagger through the ribs might be enough. I would go off on my merry way and the Domestics would move in, eradicating any trace of my presence. A day or so later, the *stabbee* would be found a hundred miles away (in, let us say, Newcastle-under-Lyme), the victim of a 'crazed malcontent'. The malcontent – usually the body of a vagrant retrieved from the local mortuary, dressed up with a dagger clasped in his rapidly stiffening digits – was sometimes found there too. Within twenty-four hours both corpses would be under-lime themselves. Oftentimes, though, something a shade more baroque was called for and Delilah and I would roll up our sleeves and embark on a coffee-fuelled plotting session that was rather cheerfully like cramming for an examination. It was all terribly well done and it lent one an immunity from even the vaguest threat of prosecution that was quite giddying. Artistic licence to kill, you might say.

Joshua Reynolds, who really was the most frightful old woman (well, no, he *really* was a dwarf, but you follow me?), glanced at me as I sank back against the cold lavatory wall and grinned at him. For once there was a flicker of something less pleasant in those bright black eyes.

'Enthusiasm is all very well, my dear Lucifer, but we mustn't get sloppy, must we? We must always remember that nasty business of the Bow Road.'

I bristled at this but held my tongue. As I say, some things are painful and private.

I was a bit done in after all the evening's excitement, but it was clear the boss had more work for me. He blew his button nose and retrieved a file from his case. As he examined its contents, I examined my fingernails. In the morning, I thought, I would take a steam bath.

'You got my note?' he said at length.

'I'm afraid I haven't checked my correspondence. I was running late, you see, what with the murdering.'

The dwarf gazed in a puzzled fashion at the contents of his handkerchief. 'Do you know Poop?'

'Poop?'

'Jocelyn Poop. Our man in Naples. We received a wire from him some days ago.'

He tossed me a square of buff paper. I read it over swiftly.

VERDIGRIS SASH. MOST URGENT.
DETAILS FOLLOW.

I looked up. 'Instructions to a curtain maker?'

'Verdigris and Sash were both highly respected scientists.'

'*Were?*'

'They died. Within a day of each other.'

'Did they indeed?' I tapped the telegram against my chin. 'And what more does Poop have to say?'

'Not a great deal. He's vanished.'

'Like me to look into it?'

Joshua Reynolds batted his eyelids. 'I'd be so grateful.'

I took a file of papers from my erstwhile employer and, with a curt nod, stepped out of the lavatory. Out of habit, I washed my hands.

Once back out into the humid night, I made my way towards Downing Street. I bade the bobby on duty outside Number Ten a cheery 'goodnight' then let myself into Number Nine.

I know, ostentatious, isn't it? But somebody has to live there.

III

THE MYSTERY OF THE TWO GEOLOGISTS

Y occupancy of Number Nine is a long and not particularly edifying story. Once upon a time, my late papa's people owned the land whereon Downing Street was built and though HMG grabbed most of it, they couldn't get their mitts on that one house which, through some stubborn whimsy of the Boxes, was to remain in the family in perpetuity. And now, as last of the line, Number Nine had come to me. More than anything I wished to be shot of the place but the terms of my inheritance were strict and so impecunious old Lucifer occupied three rooms, more or less, on the ground floor of one of the grandest houses in London. The rest of the pointlessly huge edifice was shuttered, sheeted, quietly rotting and likely to remain so unless I started to sell a lot more pictures. On the positive side it was awfully handy for town.

I awoke to find myself fully dressed and on top of the bed, surrounded by a litter of files on the missing Poop and the late Professors Sash and Verdigris. I must have drifted off in either a haze of data or a haze of hashish, I really cannot recall.

I was about to call for my man Poplar, when I remembered that he had taken a bullet in the back three weeks before on the southbound platform of a Serbian railway station (no silver cigarette case, you see). I sighed hugely. I'd certainly miss old Poplar and his passing left me in the unfortunate position of requiring a new manservant. Taking a small propelling pencil from my waistcoat pocket, I scribbled the words 'Get Help' on to my shirt cuff as an *aide memoir*. It was to be hoped that my laundress would not interpret this as the desperate plea of a kidnapped heiress hidden amongst my evening clothes.

A manservant was one of the perks of the job, yet Joshua Reynolds seemed in no great hurry to furnish me with a new one. If things didn't improve soon

I was faced with the grisly prospect of getting in Delilah to rinse out my undergarments.

I bathed in preparation for my Turkish bath and sent a note round to one of my pals expressing the desire that he join me there. The pal in question was a fiercely handsome, unfailingly cheerful lad called Christopher Miracle. To look at, you would think him one of those fellows who go stamping off around the world in a pea-coat having peninsulas named after them. In fact, he was one of the most famous portraitists in England and was said to possess an extraordinary patience and delicacy of touch. He had not been born into wealth but had *earned* it (imagine!) and the gulf that existed between our financial situations resulted in the kind of slow-burning resentment that fuels the best friend-ships. As a result of his status, he was quite staggeringly well-connected and I had a fancy he might know something of my missing professors.

The summer day was bright as a flare and stultifyingly humid. I was hard pressed to notice any change in atmosphere between the outside and the interior of the Wigmore Street baths where I later found myself.

As blond and enthusiastic as a Labrador puppy, Christopher Miracle bounced startlingly out of the wreaths of steam and thumped me on the back as a token of his affection.

'Box, old man! How are you? Looking distinctly peaky, I'd say. You getting enough nosh?'

I made a place on the warm marble beside me. 'You're not the first to speculate.'

He extended his long legs before him, the white towel around his waist pulling as taut and neat as a tablecloth.

'Is there tea?' he cried, smoothing back a lock of wet blond hair. 'I must have tea!'

He snapped his fingers with the assurance of a born team cap-tain, face already reddening in the heat, and sat with one leg up on the marble, as solid and impressive as the Velázquez Mars (having mislaid his helmet). Next to his frame, I did seem positively emaciated.

We sipped at small glasses of sweet-smelling tea brought to us by a capaciously girthed Turk and fell into happy conversation (or gossip if you prefer), denigrating the pompous and the talent-less who we felt were being preferred over us. Merely assassinating someone's *character* made for a pleasant change.

'By the way,' said Miracle suddenly. 'I'm having a party. Or a ball, if you want to be grand. In honour of the return of Persephone, goddess of the summer. Possible you could come? Or are you over-committed?'

'I collect invitations on the mantelpiece behind a bust of the late Queen. Just now I fear Her Majesty will be pitched forward into the fireplace. I'd never miss one of your parties, though, Christopher. I trust there will be a superabundance of flesh?'

'I'm counting on it. I may invite one or two from my drawing class.'

'Drawing class?'

'Didn't I tell you? Oh, I've been taking a class for ladies in one of those mechanical institutes down in Chelsea. A weekly thing. Requires little effort on my part and has several benefits. Perhaps you should give it a bash.'

I sank back on the seat and rested on my palms. 'Benefits, eh? Let me guess,' I mused. 'Firstly, hmm, yes, it keeps you in regular contact with just the kind of idle rich who are liable to commission pictures from you.'

'Excellent.'

'Further enhancing your laurel-strewn reputation,' I said gazing thoughtfully at the steam-clouded ceiling. 'Secondly, every now and then one such patron turns out to be a real stunner and game for a lark.'

Miracle laughed explosively. 'Now, really, Box.'

'Thirdly, it allows you to put a little back into society by encouraging the artistic endeavours of those less talented than yourself.'

I smiled broadly. 'I have, of course, put these benefits in order of priority.'

'Your reasoning, Box, is perfectly sound,' said Miracle with a grin. 'I allow twelve of them in at any one time,' he said. 'Probably for no better reason than it makes the occasion feel vaguely like a coven.'

'With you as the presiding daemon?'

'Naturally. They have tea and there's a little chatter and not a little swooning around yours truly, then my pupils set to work scrawling away quite appallingly with their charcoal at whatever I place in the centre of the room. It seems they have come to regard my classes as the highlights of their existence.'

I nodded to an orderly who came forward with a brass bowl of cold water. I splashed my face and ran a hand through my hair.

'What a shining light you are, Miracle!' I ejaculated. 'How come that booby Holman Hunt never did your portrait in that hideous style of his?'

Miracle chuckled.

'Speaking of pictures,' I said, 'didn't you once paint a scientist chap called Verdigris?'

Miracle thought for a moment. 'Believe I did. Great fat fellow. Eyes spaced too wide like a flat-fish. Come to think of it, I heard he's vanished. Along with some old pal of his called Sash.'

'I too had heard something of the kind.'

'Don't know much about the other. Seems they both suffered a sort of seizure. Are you digging for something?'

I shrugged. Alone amongst my friends, Miracle had some idea of my 'other life' but even then thought it no more than the hobby of an over-diligent gossip.

'Geologists, I gather,' I said at last.

Miracle nodded. 'Old Cambridge chums. Verdigris died the day after Sash. Very rum.'

'Life is full of coincidences.'

'So they say,' laughed Miracle. 'Do you think these events are connected? I'll see what I can root out.'

For a while, we sat in silence, steeped in the lethargy induced by the chamber's broiling heat. Occasionally, the mists cleared, revealing the green-and-red tiled arches of the roof. The baths hummed with human traffic; the hissing of the coals, the distant *ploosh* of patrons in the plunge pools, the heavy sighing of thickset, red-faced gents, towels wrapped like swaddling around their hard bellies.

After a time, Miracle smiled, thrust out his lower lip then patted my leg and rose. 'Shan't be a moment. Nature calls.'

I watched him stride away through the billowing steam-clouds and was so engrossed by the progress of a great heavy drop of sweat down my face that I almost failed to notice a veiny forearm suddenly clamp itself around my gullet.

With a gasp, I sank my fingers into the flesh of the arm. Struggling to stand, I found myself hauled backwards by a wild strength. My back struck the slippery marble steps and for a second or so my head swam.

'Blackguard!' hissed a voice in my ear. 'Scoundrel!'

Well, I had been called worse. I twisted my head wildly to one side, attempting to catch sight of my attacker, but the clouds of steam showed only glimpses of glistening flesh and a pair of goggling, enraged eyes beneath thick black brows. His arm tightened around my throat.

I kicked out at the brass bowl in a desperate effort to attract the attention of the attendants but, with lightning speed, my assailant began to drag me towards a neglected niche. The towel slipped from my waist and I felt my buttocks sliding over the seat.

I croaked frantically. Would one of the elderly gentlemen in their steamy shrouds notice and raise the alarm? But a ruddy hand with hairy knuckles was quickly planted over my mouth. I was completely helpless. Salty sweat stung at my eyes.

'Now, you villain! Now I have you!' The fellow's breath was stale with tobacco. I was on my haunches, my senses whirling.

Yet, at the very moment of defeat, I snatched a chance of victory. Using the brute's heaviness to my advantage, I shoved backwards against him and drove my elbow savagely into his midriff.

He gave a startled cry, fell lumpenly against the tiles and momentarily slackened his iron grip on my head and neck. It was all I needed.

Springing to my feet, I whirled around and kicked him in the throat, my leg extended with the grace of a dancer – even if I do say so myself.

His hands flew to his Adam's apple but I gave him no quarter, pummelling his face with my fists and then, after taking a handful of his wet hair, cracking his face off the wall.

'What is this?' I gasped. 'What do you want with me?'

The fellow was revealed now, a great hirsute middle-aged creature, with long, oily moustaches and a face as red as brick. Where *had* I seen the ugly bastard before? In the criminal archives of the Viennese police, perhaps? Or was he one of the brotherhood of blind assassins who had sworn revenge on me after the Affair of the Prussian Martyrs?

Those enraged eyes glared at me still. With a snarl he put his head down and charged at me. I stepped swiftly to one side but he caught me round the waist and together we stumbled back into the main chamber.

By now, of course, we had been noticed. As we whirled about, feet slithering on the wet floor, I had a confused impression of white towels and scarlet faces, mouths opened in wide 'o's of astonishment. The Turk who had brought Miracle's tea hovered around us, arms flapping, like the referee in a wrestling bout.

'Can't we . . . discuss this . . . like gentlemen?' I gasped.

He rose from my naked waist and jabbed a fist at my face. I side-stepped clumsily, feet skidding.

'*Gentleman?* You?' he spat.

The Turk was at his elbow, his face a mask of misery. 'Please! Please, sirs! If you have business, let it be concluded in the –'

He said no more, as my attacker laid him out with a swift right to the underside of his swarthy jaw and he fell to the tiles like a sack of coal.

I cracked a fist against my assailant's cheek-bone. 'Christ!' I yelled, sucking my knuckles.

He screwed up one eye in pain and jabbed at me again. 'Lucifer Box! Ha! Was ever a rascal so well named? You are the devil, sir. The very devil!'

I ducked from his fist and managed to land a serious wallop on the side of his head. He staggered and almost fell on the treacherous floor.

'Bringer of light, I assure you!' I cried. My blood was up and so were my fists as I circled the monster. 'Lucifer was the brightest and most beautiful of the angels. Till that old margery of a deity got so jealous that he cast him out!'

He snarled at this and succeeded in punching me, with sickening force, in the ribs.

Crying out in pain, I dropped, winded. My knees smacking on the floor with a snap like wish-bones.

The fellow stalked up to me and grasped a great hunk of my hair. 'Bringer of light! What have you brought to my household but misery and scandal? My God, sir, I shall thrash the life out of you before I'm done!'

I shook my head miserably. 'Who . . . who are you?'

He sneered at me, his moustaches hanging limply around his red mouth like those of a Chinaman. 'I am Pugg, sir. Major Strangeways Pugg.'

'Oh,' I said, simply.

'And it is my daughter, my sweet little Avril who you have despoiled and ruined!'

I winced as he tightened his grip on my hair. Remembrance swept over me like cold water from the Turk's brass bowl. A party, some months previously. Whey-faced poets, frayed-cuffed artists; all the splendid flotsam of bohemian London life. And a girl. A girl with a dog's name and the body of a goddess. Avril Pugg. There'd been a balcony, starlight, whispered words then something very cheeky in the rhododendrons.

Now there was a father. He raised his great fist and drew it back. I watched it swing towards me through streaming eyes.

Then there came a strange, bright clang and Pugg crashed to the floor, his addled eyes rolling up in his head like those of a doll.

I looked up and saw my friend standing over the unconscious major, a filigreed Turkish tea-urn still swinging in his right hand.

'Miracle,' I groaned.

'Too bloody right!' he cried, grasping my hand and pulling me to my feet.

IV

THE VISITOR

HAT night, still as humid as the steam-rooms, I swaddled my bruised carcass in a Japanese dressing gown patterned with embroidered sunflowers and purchased with money I should have spent on oil-paints. Or food. Or tickets to the Continent avoiding enraged fathers.

After leaving the baths, Miracle had seen me right then I had swiftly made contact with the Domestics. Delilah, always the soul of discretion, assured me that, although it didn't come quite within the purview of Joshua Reynolds's depart-ment, she would 'sort fings out' and Major Strangeways Pugg would be 'hencour-aged' to drop the matter forthwith. Well, it's pointless having power unless you can abuse it, don't you think?

I then wrapped up the portrait of the Hon. Everard Supple (a present for his grieving family) and began to ponder Chris Miracle's suggestion of giving art instruction. He was making a

killing off all these lonely old horrors in need of a little thrill to while away their afternoons. Why shouldn't I? In fact, why shouldn't I *more*. The prestigious address! The handsome young artist! The showers of sovereigns I could squeeze out of the gullible nitwits! And then I could afford to replace Poplar without waiting for Reynolds's patron-age. Of course, I'd have to do a little clearing up, but think of it!

The upshot was I placed a small advertisement in *The Times*, *Pall Mall Gazette*, *Budget* and a few other rags, making the arrangement sound thor-oughly wholesome, with just the faintest whiff of *la vie bohème* to attract those craving excitement.

I then engaged a char to spruce up Downing Street. I had intended to supervise her work but couldn't bear the looks of disapproval and endless 'tsk-tsk's as she peeled old collars and unwashed dishes from the debris of my studio, so off I went to invest money I didn't have in new curtains. I collected some interesting bric-a-brac that my pupils might find amusing to draw and added Everard Supple's glass eye to the pile as a little touch of the Gothic.

After that, with rather impressive zeal, I assumed the disguise of a dour-faced newspaperman (all it takes is a dreadful suit, bowler and false moustache) and called at the home of the late Professor Eli Verdigris in Holland Park.

It was a house plunged into mourning; black crêpe blossoming from every niche and banister, a wreath of some stinking violet flower encircling friend Miracle's rather bad portrait of the great man. He had indeed been a corpulent fellow with curious wide-apart eyes and a dimpled chin of such prominence that he resembled a Hapsburg.

Under the pretence of preparing a eulogy of the professor for the *Pall Mall Gazette* I was shown into a cluttered study for an audience.

'I'm afraid you'll have to make do with me,' said a tall young man, as fat as his father, ushering me into a chair. 'My poor mama is quite beside herself.'

'It was very unexpected, then?' I whispered, laying on the sympathy as thick as impasto.

'Entirely.' He rubbed absently at the black arm-band around his sleeve. 'My father has not had a day's illness in his life.'

I nodded and scribbled in a little note-book. 'The doctors' opinion?'

Verdigris Junior shrugged. 'They seem at something of a loss. A seizure of some kind followed by coma and . . . well . . . death.'

'Dear me. The *Gazette* offers its sincerest condolences.'

The young fellow sniffed and looked up at me. 'Everyone has been quite marvellous, though. The family. His colleagues and friends.'

'And the funeral . . . ?'

'The day before yesterday. It was . . . well . . . It is over now.'

I gave him a sad smile. 'Could you give me some idea of the nature of your father's work?'

Verdigris's mouth tugged downwards. 'Not really, I'm afraid. Frightful dunce where papa's stuff is concerned. I can root out some literature for you, if you'd care to wait.'

'That would be most helpful, sir.'

Whilst he was out, I made a quick inspection of the fire-grate and the desk. There was no evidence of anything being burnt in the grate but on the desk I spotted a large appointments diary. I flicked hastily through the pages. What was I looking for? Well, anything out of the common, I suppose. But I found nothing save evidence of Verdigris's dreary affairs and the rest of the study proved equally barren. The walls were lined with books and very indifferent landscapes in need of cleaning. I closed the diary carefully, brushed off a dusty purplish residue from the desk that had adhered to my sleeve and dashed back to my chair.

Young Verdigris came back in and handed me a thick, dust-jacketed volume. 'Here is it. Papa's magnum opus. Tried my damnedest to get into it but . . .'

I turned the book over and looked at the spine. The title was picked out in gold.

Magnetic Viscosity, I read, *with some notes on volcanic convection*. More light reading seemed on the agenda.

Sans moustache, I lunched in the domino room at the Café Royal, studying the coroner's report on the deaths of both men. There were no traces of toxins. Nothing at all to indicate that death had not been due to some freak seizure. But what connection was Poop's telegram driving at? And why had Poop himself disappeared?

I resumed my disguise as Fleet Street's finest and took an underground train to meet the wife of Professor Frederick Sash, the second of the late scientists. I had tried to make some sense of Verdigris's book but could not get on with it. It seemed terrible nonsense, or terribly clever.

Mrs Sash, a good-looking piece with a swan-like neck, received me graciously enough, although she had the infuriating habit of cutting one off in mid-sentence. As I sipped my tea, I glanced around the darkened drawing room. 'I see you have a copy of Verdigris's seminal *Magnetic Viscosity*,' I said blithely. 'Was your husband acquainted with –?'

'Oh yes. From their Cambridge days. Eli seems to have passed away the day after Frederick. What in heaven's name can it mean?'

I nodded sympathetically and scratched at my false moustache. 'Of course, there was no . . . ill feeling between –?'

Mrs Sash shook her handsome head. 'There was some rivalry, naturally, both being in the same field but no more than that. They were always on very good terms, though they had seen little of one another since their Continental adventure came to an end.'

'Continental –?'

'They once worked together in Europe for some little time.'

I scribbled in my note-book. 'No previous illness –?'

'There had been nothing out of the ordinary.'

I was hoping to persuade the lady to absent herself briefly as I had with Professor Verdigris's son, to facilitate a quick nose around the room, but my request for refreshment was answered by a delicate pull on the bell rope and the appearance of a dour-faced flunky.

I paused with my pencil hovering over the paper. 'This was your husband's –?'

'Study? No, no. He has a room on the first floor. Claimed it was too noisy down here.' She passed a hand over her face. 'He was at home all day, working up a theorem. The late post had just come when –'

She sniffed back a tear. 'You must excuse me for now, sir. We are somewhat upside-down at the moment. There is so much to do.'

'One final thing, Mrs Sash. Have I missed the funeral?'

I had. It had taken place only the previous day in Southwark.

Mrs Sash glanced down at her neat little hands. 'There again I was vexed. We were unable to use the firm my husband's family had always relied upon.'

'Firm?'

'The undertaking firm, sir. Tulip Brothers. Retired, it seems, without so much as a note! The business has been taken over. I suppose it all passed off well enough . . .'

'But?'

'But there was something a little . . . *queer* about them.'

'What makes you say that?'

She sighed. 'Well, whatever good-will they inherited has been squandered, I can tell you. It was a rather amateurish display.'

'And what is the name of this curious firm?'

Mrs Sash crossed to a small bureau and produced a black-edged card. 'I'm not saying it's necessarily worthy of a newspaper investigation,' she said, handing it over. 'But I found their attitude most peculiar. I'd be easier in my mind if someone were to do a little . . . um . . . digging.' For the first time, she smiled.

I held up the card.

TOM BOWLER. SUPERIOR FUNERALS.
188 ENGLAND'S LANE. LONDON N.W.

I had changed and was stretching a canvas in my studio that afternoon, wondering how to infiltrate an undertakers without a cadaver to present, when I heard a knock at the door.

Still expecting old Poplar to answer it, I ignored the summons for a full minute before heading through into the hallway with a muttered curse.

A singularly lovely personage stood on my doorstep, clutching a folded newspaper in her lace-gloved hand.

'Mr Box?'

'I am he.'

She stepped forward and the sunlight cast a glow over the russet-coloured dress that clung so charmingly to her figure. Tall and elfin-featured, with a tumbling fall of Mucha-like curls, she held up the newspaper and flashed me a lovely smile. 'I came in response to your advertisement.' The voice was lightly accented – Dutch? – and tinkled like a music-box.

'Advertisement? Oh! Oh, yes of course! Come in, please, Miss . . . ?'

'Pok.'

'Pok?'

'Bella Pok.' The delectable creature crossed the threshold and looked inquisitively about the hallway.

'Would you care for some tea?' I asked.

She looked me straight in the eye. 'Do you have anything stronger?'

'My dear, I daresay. Please, come through.'

'Number Nine, Downing Street,' she said, entering the drawing room. 'You have trouble with your neighbours?'

'Only once every four years.'

She smiled and took a seat by the window whilst I hurriedly looked about for refreshment. 'Such a curious place for an artist to live . . .'

'Sherry?' I offered.

'I like a little vermouth at this hour.'

I nodded, rather pleasantly shocked. 'Geographically, I am at the very beating heart of the Empire, Miss Pok. In other respects, I am as much an outcast as the greatest of my calling have been . . .' I gestured around the room. 'You must forgive my current situation but my servant is . . . *servants* are away.'

'I have learned never to judge a gentleman by the cleanliness of his doilies.'

'Then I feel we shall get on splendidly.'

I slipped through to the kitchen and began to hunt around for where the char had put clean glasses. 'Now tell me,' I said, calling through. 'What drew you to my advertisement? You have had some training in draughtsmanship?'

'Not at all,' she cried. 'It is only that I have always longed to draw and paint, Mr Box, and currently find myself with the time and the resources to fulfil my daydreams.'

'Capital!' I said, returning with two fairly respectable cut-glass vessels, a bottle of vermouth and a rather sad-looking seed cake.

'Speaking of capital,' she said, reaching for her beaded bag, 'the advertisement said a guinea per lesson.'

I held up my hand. 'Let us not concern ourselves with these bothersome details just now. Tell me a little more about yourself.'

'What could a dull little creature like me possibly have that could interest you?' she trilled. I could think of several things and made a mental note to treat Chris Miracle to dinner for his splendid suggestion.

Miss Bella Pok and I had, it transpired, a great deal in common. A mutual loathing of the frightful El Greco and veneration of the sainted Velázquez, a suspicion of Titian and an unhealthy regard for Caravaggio. As we drank our vermouth I thought how pretty and charming was my potential pupil. The sunlight pouring through the window crowned her lovely face, illumining her eyelashes as she angled it towards me.

I showed her into the studio. She crossed at once to the centre of the room and began to examine the body of a spelter Napoleonic lancer I'd picked up in a junk shop off the Edgware Road. It was a cheap thing, just a fellow in britches on horseback, but she seemed taken by it. Perhaps it was the way he brandished his lance. I rested my shoulder against the wall, one hand in contemplative attitude on my chin.

'When can I begin?' she asked brightly.

I shrugged. 'Why not at once? Will the lancer do?'

So saying, I drew up a chair and fixed a rectangle of good-quality paper to a wooden board. Miss Bella unpinned her hat and sat down. I handed her the board and some sticks of charcoal then stood behind her in silence, listening to the sound of her breathing and the sweet, liquid *tick* made by her lips as they parted.

I grinned happily to myself, deriving curious satisfaction from the quiet, methodical way she worked.

'Have you had many answers to your advertisement, Mr Box?'

The charcoal swooped and scratched over the virginal paper.

'You are the first.'

The horse's head, caught swiftly and surely. She was rather good.

'Then perhaps we can make this a . . . private arrangement.'

Steady. I felt a little flip in my heart and a distinct throb in my britches. I thought of Avril Pugg's father and the sensation lessened. A little.

'Perhaps.'

Miss Bella had caught the heavy fullness of the spelter lancer's thigh with one, decisive stroke of the charcoal. With equal boldness I now crossed the room towards her and took hold of her drawing hand. I guided it to the paper, moving myself until I was almost pressed against her back. She did not demur as I slid the charcoal over the surface of the paper, shading the lancer's legs and bottom with what I knew to be forthright sensuousness.

'You are doing very nicely, Miss Pok,' I cooed. 'You have an extraordinary grasp of military anatomy.'

I carried on with the drawing without taking my eyes from the figurine.

'A bottom is a bottom, Mr Box,' she said, 'whether a soldier's or a parlour-maid's.'

I suppressed a smile. 'True, I suppose. Tell me, are you town or country born?'

I pressed myself closer to her. There could be no mistaking the broom-handle in my trousers. With a slight dip of her lovely head Bella Pok moved away from me a little and released her hand from my grip. 'I am a farmer's daughter, Mr Box,' she murmured.

I held up my hands in supplication and backed away. *And you know a fox when you see one*, I thought.

Turning in her seat, she gave a little gasp. I looked to where she looked and saw that she was staring at the glass eye I had placed near the lancer.

'How ghoulish!' she cried, with her musical laugh.

'Isn't it?' I said. 'Shall I put it away?'

'No, no. I am not so squeamish as you might think. But it does, as they say about the *Mona Lisa*, rather follow one about the room!'

She turned back to me, grinning and presented the drawing board. 'Well, then. What is the verdict?' she said.

'Guilty!' I cried.

She gathered up her things. 'Is there any hope for me?'

I folded my arms and smiled. 'I sentence you to commence your classes on Monday next. And may the Lord have mercy upon your –'

I stopped very suddenly. My attention had become riveted on the newspaper that Miss Bella had brought through into the studio. I plucked it from her grasp. 'Mr Box?' she said with concern. 'Are you quite all right?'

In a column adjacent to my advertisement was a small item of news.

BRITISH DIPLOMAT MURDERED

Terrible discovery in Naples.

A body found in the harbour at Naples on Monday last has been positively identified as that of Jocelyn Utterson Poop of His Majesty's Diplomatic Service. Mr Poop, who was thirty-three years of age, had been stationed in the Italian city for over four years. The Neapolitan police say that the unfortunate man had been the victim of a murderous attack, leaving his skull crushed, probably by a stick or some such blunt instrument . . .

'Mr Box? *Mr Box?*' The lovely Miss Pok placed a hand on my arm.

'I'm very sorry, my dear,' I said quietly. 'The lesson is over for today.'

V

A CURIOUS UNDERTAKING

'O clue?'

Joshua Reynolds, sitting in his accustomed place on the pan, raised his little hands, palm upwards. 'The Italian police have it down as a robbery gone awry. We shall have to wait and see. The body has been packed in ice and arrives tomorrow.'

'Poor devil,' I said, leaning back against the pleasantly chill wall of the lavatory. 'Saw Naples and died, you might say.'

'So much for Poop,' said Reynolds glumly. 'Have you made any progress with the dead professors?'

I thrust my hands into my trouser pockets and kicked idly at the cubicle wall. 'Some, I think. They were both concerned with the same branch of Geological Physics and had known each other of old. In addition, there was something odd about Sash's funeral.'

Reynolds frowned. 'Not much, all told.'

'I had precious little chance to

investigate Professor Sash's effects,' I continued. 'So I plan to return for a ... root about.'

The little man gave a sigh. 'How I envy you your adventures, Lucifer. What is left for me but a dull retirement spent in the cultivation of ornamental carp?'

'One man's fish is another man's *poisson*.'

'Ye ... es. Now then, there's someone I'd like you to meet.'

So saying, he pulled at the toilet chain and, with a screeching, grinding sound, the wall behind me rose up and another lavatory bowl glided into the room.

Sitting on it was a gangling young man in quite the most horrible piece of tailoring I'd ever seen. The sleeves of his suit crept over the knuckles of slim, feminine hands with which he was kneading his hat like a widow with her rosary.

'Mr Box,' said Reynolds, pulling his handkerchief from his pocket and pressing it to his reddened nose. 'This is Mr Unmann.'

The blond man shot a hand to his crown in order to doff his hat and then remembered it was doffed already. A stupid smile made his nose crinkle in the middle.

'Sorry,' he began.

'Whatever for?' I asked.

'Oh, sorry. Don't really know why I said that. It's a great honour to meet you at last, Mr Box. Cretaceous Unmann.'

'Cretaceous?'

'Yes,' he muttered, looking down at his hands. 'Fact is, Papa was an amateur dinosaur-hunter. Never got much further than the Isle of Wight but, hey-ho. Took it upon himself to name me in honour of his favourite epoch. Sorry.'

I smiled pityingly. 'I suppose it could have been worse,' I said. 'He could have named you after his favourite dinosaur.'

'Ha, ha! Yes!' Unmann exploded in a shrill laugh. '*Iguanodon* Unmann, eh?'

Thankfully, Reynolds cut in at this juncture. 'Mr Unmann has been lined up to succeed Poop in the Naples office.'

'I see. Remarkably expeditious of you.'

'Yes. Shocking business,' bleated Unmann. 'I knew old Jocelyn. Sometimes acted as his deputy. Dreadful, dreadful.'

He looked down at his squashed hat and then put it to one side of the lavatory bowl.

The dwarf handed a buff folder to me.

'Someone fired his rooms,' said Unmann, miserably. 'But those few fragments escaped.'

'Our people in Naples sent them straight over with Mr Unmann,' said Reynolds.

I opened the file. A smell of charred paper hit me at once. A couple of documents were enclosed within, tied up neatly with waxed string. I released them and swiftly read them over.

The first was a scrap of good-quality notepaper. On it was written the legend:

K TO V.C.?

'Looks like hotel stationery,' I said. 'Shouldn't be too difficult to trace.'

The next was a long white envelope containing a sheet of slightly singed foolscap.

To Joshua Reynolds
Sir. It is important that you know all that is afoot. I am
certain I may rely on you above all persons, even poor
Unmann, bless his heart, who has been such a brick and who
means so well.

I glanced across at the young man. His face twisted into a shy smile.

If all goes well, I shall return to London as planned and there
relate to you the story of my adventures. It is a tale so fantastic
that you will scarcely credit it. I do not lie when I say it could
shake the pillars of the Empire! If I can but thwart these men's
schemes, then I will be Poop the Civil Service mouse no more
but Poop the Lion of the Foreign Office! If I am unlucky then it
will fall to others to pick up the threads. All that I know of this
affair is contained in the trunk marked with my name. I pray
you will never have to read this. JP

I folded the letter on my lap and replaced it in its envelope.

'The trunk of course, did not escape the flames,' muttered Joshua Reynolds miserably. 'Foolish youth! Such wilful egotism has more than once cost us dear. If a conspiracy is discovered then simple candour is absolutely essential!'

I could only agree. I recalled the Shanghai Balloon Incident – which so nearly did for one of our lesser PMs – and the fatal damage caused by one fellow's refusal to share what he knew with his colleagues. I should know. That fellow was me.

I tapped the envelope. 'Any suspects in the Poop murder?'

'They've rounded up the traditional pretty lot. Smashers, thugs, vitriol throwers, extortionists . . .'

'A veritable catalogue of vice!' I cried cheerily. 'Now isn't that a good idea? The kind of catalogue I'd instantly subscribe to.'

'Lucifer,' said Joshua Reynolds, warningly.

I tapped my fingers against my chin. '"Shake the pillars of the Empire", eh? What the deuce could he have meant?'

The next morning found me on a train rattling through a muggy north London. Dreary villas streamed past in a blur of hideous brightness. As soon as I reached the nearest post office, I thought, I would send a wire to Miss Bella Pok apologizing again for the hasty termination of our lesson and looking forward to another meeting soon. What would it be like to flee this baking wen of a city and run barefoot through a field of ripening green corn with that lovely girl? I pictured us laughing gaily, tumbling into the undergrowth, the cyan sky blazing above us . . .

I ran a finger under my collar and sighed, horribly stifled by my summer rig. Surely the cause of Men's Dress Reform must do most of its recruiting during the interminable London Augusts? I longed to throw my straw hat from the carriage and toss my cream waistcoat into the Thames as the Reformers are wont to do. Leafy Belsize Park was not, I reasoned, quite ready for the sight of yours truly in the buff, so I hopped from the train still fully clothed and, after contracting my business at the post office, found myself outside the offices of Mr Tom Bowler Esq. – the undertaker who had so disquieted Mrs Sash.

I began by taking a quick look around the yard at the rear of the premises. A dog-cart with a sad-looking horse in its shafts stood squarely in the centre but it was otherwise empty, save for a heap of dead flowers and wreaths that might have been the beginnings of a bonfire. I crouched down and picked through the wilted debris. Here was a wreath for the late Professor Sash. Here was a bouquet of flattened lilies, reeking dreadfully. And here – aha! A wreath for Professor Eli Verdigris! Both funerals had been taken care of by the same firm! And with a similar want of respect for the trappings of grief. I made my way around to the front.

The door was ajar and the rooms within lit. I adopted my most doleful expression and made my way inside.

It was a bare-looking suite of rooms with frosted windows and a long, dark counter that occupied half its width. Framed mezzotints of cherubs and angels crowded the green walls. There were pots of lilies everywhere and motes of orange pollen drifting from them through the dim gas-light. I wrinkled my nose at the faint smell of brackish water.

There seemed to be no one about. I rang the brass bell on the counter and, after a time, a door opened somewhere in the rear of the premises and footsteps sounded on bare boards.

Black curtains parted and out stepped a burly man with oily hair the colour of wet slate. He seemed a very jovial chap for one of his profession, grinning all over his face and, rather surprisingly, tucking into a chicken leg with gusto. Closer to, I noticed his bluey, poorly shaved chin and the spots of grease on his tie.

'Hello,' he said brightly.

I made a small bow. 'Do I have the honour of addressing Mr Bowler?'

'You do, sir!' he said, wiping his greasy fingers on his coat.

Incredibly, he dropped the chicken leg down on to the counter and rubbed his hands together. 'Now what can I do for you?'

I fiddled coyly with my tie-pin. 'I was recommended to your predecessors' excellent firm by a family friend.'

'Ah, yes! We bought the old fellows out! So, you've had a bereavement?' His brows drew together and his mouth turned down like some operatic clown. 'Aww.'

'Indeed.' I managed to hide my astonishment at his behaviour and made a quick grab for my handkerchief. 'My dear wife,' I croaked, stifling a sob.

Bowler inclined his head slightly but still smirked. 'Please accept the firm's sincere condolences, Mr . . . ?'

'Box.'

'Mr Box. I regret to say, however, that we are currently over-whelmed with . . . um . . . clients. Dying, you see, being one of the few things that never really goes out of fashion! Ha, ha!'

I blinked and returned my handkerchief to my pocket.

Bowler's gaze strayed longingly to the greasy meat he had laid on the counter and he wiped his wet mouth with the back of his hand. 'It would be rather wrong of us to take on your wife's funeral at this time.'

'Well, I'm . . . delighted to see you are prospering.'

'Very much so,' grinned Bowler. 'I can recommend another firm if you like? They're really very reasonable.'

'Expense is not the issue.'

'Of course not, sir. Ha, ha. I would further add that they are dis-creet and most respectful.'

I nodded. 'You are very kind.'

Bowler brushed a stray hair from his eyes. 'If you just wait here, I will furnish you with the details.'

I smiled weakly. He disappeared back behind the curtain.

I glanced about and then, looking down at the counter, ran a gloved finger down its length, scoring a mahogany-coloured groove in the patina of dust that covered it.

The scrape of curtain rings announced Bowler's return. He handed me a bit of paper upon which he'd written the name of another firm in a bold hand. The black ink was smudged by his greasy thumb-print.

I thanked him for his kindness.

'Not at all, sir. Good day.'

Then, without a second thought, he picked up the chicken leg and sank his teeth into it. I made my way out. Bowler watched me until I was through the door. Through the frosted pane I distinctly saw him wave.

I stepped out on to the street and crossed the road, pausing under a shady lime tree. The state of the counter alone told me that the firm of Mr Bowler was not prospering. So why had he turned down my business and recommended a rival? And, more revealingly, why had he signally failed to comment on the fact that, despite my recent 'bereavement', I was dressed head to toe in white linen?

Just then, a loud creaking close by drew my attention and I stepped closer to the tree so as to remain unobserved. I realized that I was at the entrance to the undertaker's yard. As I watched, both the rickety gates swung open and the dog-cart rattled through and on to the street. At the reins was a hard-faced fellow in a rust-coloured coat with a great scar across his nose.

In the back of the cart lay a long wooden crate of similar dimensions to a coffin. I could see that it had some kind of shipping label plastered over its planking.

I strolled from my hiding place as nonchalantly as I could and managed to get myself into the path of the cart as it clattered into the road. Scar-Face glared at me. I doffed my hat.

'I do beg your pardon. Could you direct me to the underground station?'

He scowled at me for what seemed like a full minute before grudgingly jerking his thumb over his shoulder. Whipping up the horse, the vehicle lurched ahead.

'Most kind,' I rejoined, stepping out of its path before it ran me down.

For a brief moment I was aware of nothing but the label shuddering its way into the distance.

Then I crossed to the pavement, made my way past the yard and didn't look behind me until I had reached the station. Once there, I stood with my back to the gingerbread-brown tiles, deep in thought. According to that shipping label the crate was heading for Naples.

*

That afternoon, I found myself standing on the jetty of a grimy wharf in the East End. The day remained unbearably humid and the tarry black warehouses loomed over me like overcoated giants. As I watched, another crate was hauled up from a small rowing boat.

It was a scene far from the dreamy river-scapes of old man Monet. A noxious haze drifted over the drear Thames, insinuating its way like smoke into the nearest doorway where three stout fellows and the even-stouter Delilah now dragged the crate. I followed at a distance and doffed my straw hat. Respect for the dead, do you see, because inside that narrow splintering box were the mortal remains of the unfortunate Jocelyn Poop, would-be lion of the foreign office now little more than ten stones of rapidly deteriorating flesh.

The interior of the warehouse was dim. I stepped back into the queasy green shadows of the gas-lamps as Delilah planted her feet firmly on the floor and, jemmy in hand, began to wrench the planks from the improvised coffin.

"Ave 'im hart hin just ha jiffy, sir,' she grunted, tossing broken planking over her shoulder. Her three thickset fellow Domestics, meanwhile, prepared the butcher's slab on to which Poop was to be conveyed.

Melted ice was already pooling about Delilah's boots and I heard it cracking and splintering as though in a gin-glass as the brutish female began to lift Poop's body out by the shoulders.

'Cor! What ha stink!' cackled Delilah. 'They don't know 'ow to pack hem, those bleedin' heye-ties, do they sir?'

I clamped my glove to my mouth and shook my head. The stench was vile and almost overpowering. Hastily, I gestured to the Domestics to get on with it and, within a moment or two, the dead man lay before me, his skin waxy, pockets of ice plastering the soaked fabric of his linen suit. There seemed nothing much to be gleaned from the reasonably intact torso. Poop's head, however, was quite a different matter. It was little more than a football-shaped outrage, black with congealed blood and matted with weed-like hair.

Stepping gingerly forward I peered at the gory mess and risked taking away the glove from my mouth.

'Contents of the clothing, Delilah,' I barked.

'Right haway, sir.' She returned to the wharf to collect the rest of the delivery.

I nodded towards the other Domestics. 'Get me a jug of water and a scrubbing brush.'

One of them nodded in acquiescence. By the time Delilah returned with a small leather satchel, I had cleaned up Poop's shattered noggin somewhat, exposing a hook nose and a rather unprepossessing moustache. Above the bridge of the nose, the whole of the forehead had been stoved in.

'It was more than a cosh that did this,' I mused to myself. Taking up the jug, I poured water into the wound. Particles of skin and brain matter floated away over Poop's cheeks in ghastly rivulets like congealed crusts of oil-paint.

I bent closer, holding my breath against the stench of corruption. Anticipating my needs, Delilah stepped forward with a lantern that I took from her fat hand. There was something very odd about the wound in Poop's head.

I probed with my fingers for some little time then, sucking my teeth thoughtfully, stepped away from the corpse and folded my arms.

'Delilah, I should be most awfully grateful if you could fetch me some plaster of Paris.'

'Plaster of Paris, sir?'

'Yes. Though where you'll lay your hands on some all the way out here . . .'

She smiled her dreadful smile and gave a little bow. She was back within twenty minutes. As I said the Domestics were without peer.

While the others prepared the mixture, covering themselves in floury clouds in the process, I laid out the contents of Poop's pockets that had been thoughtfully documented by the Neapolitan coppers. It was a sad little bundle. A daguerreotype of some ugly tart – probably his fiancée, two tickets to *Rigoletto* dated the night of his disappearance and a quantity of soggy paperwork, all depressingly mundane. I searched in vain for any reference to VC. What had his note said? 'K to V.C.?' Sounded like a chess move. People do play these agonizingly long-winded games over continents and decades. 'K' corresponding to 'King' . . . but to 'V.C.'? Could be an accumulation of medals. Knight of the Garter to Victoria Cross? No, no. Nonsense. Perhaps those opera tickets? *Verdi's Cabal?* Was there some link to the renowned tunesmith and his *Rigoletto?* Had Poop been done to death by a vengeful hunchback dwarf?

I decided to leave it there for the time being (a good idea as you can probably tell) and turned to the bowl of wet plaster prepared for me by the Domestics. I took off my coat, rolled up my sleeves and then carried the mixture over to the slab. With Delilah and one of her pals holding Poop's shattered head steady, I carefully poured the plaster into the great gaping wound. After setting down the bowl I smoked a cheroot and waited for the stuff to dry.

It is not a pleasant thing to make a mould from a fellow's dead bonce but between us we managed to prise the set plaster from the sticky ooze of Poop's skull. I turned the impression upwards and dragged the lantern towards it.

'Ah!' I ejaculated. 'Do you see it? Do you see it?'

Delilah ambled closer and screwed up her eyes at the plaster impression made by the object that someone had so unsportingly smashed into Jocelyn Poop's brain.

'Well, Hi'll retire to Bedlam!' breathed Delilah. 'Hit's a *face!*'

VI

THE WOMAN IN THE VEIL

 FACE it was. Clearly discernible were waves of hair above a noble brow and hollow eyes; the bridge of an aquiline nose and a suggestion of lip completing the picture. It was either the most forceful head-butt in history or the impression of some kind of bust or statue. I took a rough guess that Poop had been attacked with a relic of the grandeur that was Rome, though precise dating was beyond me. I despatched the plaster cast with the Domestics, confident of a speedy identification by one of Joshua Reynolds's other agents and also passed on a note to the little man himself recommending that a watch be kept on the strange undertaking firm of Mr Tom Bowler.

As for me, it was time for that rooting around I had promised myself.

Back at Downing Street, to change togs, I found I was in receipt of a charming note from Bella Pok. *I look forward immensely to our next assignation,* it ran. *I feel there is much we shall do together.*

Rather!

I changed into a dark costume and pumps, bundling my other clothes into a heavy bag, then waited for Delilah to arrive in a brougham.

There is a limit, you see, to what can be gleaned through what the yellow press like to call 'the proper channels'. As you can imagine, it is only the *im*proper channels that turn up matters of real interest. Having been unable to instigate a thorough search, I prepared, as promised, to have another look inside the home of Professor Frederick Sash.

I am a practised housebreaker and had done my best to look over the layout of the missing scientist's residence during my interview with his wife. I had myself dropped off a few streets away from the Sash residence and then lay skulking in a clump of hydrangeas until the lights in the place were extinguished.

It was another sweltering night, heavy with patches of unhealthy-looking mist so that the shrubberies glowed oddly like spider-webs. I slipped on a half-mask and, with a heavy jemmy in one hand and a dark-lantern in the other, padded across the lawn, keeping low until I reached the shelter of the house. Once there, I flattened myself against the brickwork and paused for breath.

The easiest point of entry to the villa, it seemed to me, was through a small, diamond-paned window in the porchway. I crept around the wall until I reached this, then began an examination of the window. I had the jemmy all ready to prise open the woodwork but then discovered that it was already ajar, no doubt left so due to the heat. I gently pushed the window open to its fullest extent and slid my terribly lithe and nimble frame through it.

The porch led straight through into the great hallway, its ceiling made up almost entirely of skylights.

I made my way stealthily past majolica pots stuffed with exotic plants and rows of walnut cabinets, crammed willy-nilly with quantities of blue china.

I examined each cabinet in turn but felt sure that it was Sash's study that I needed to explore. I made for the broad staircase, my rubber-soled pumps making not a sound as I ran swiftly upwards. A series of rooms led off a walkway that looked down directly on to the hall below.

I was making for the first door with great urgency when I heard the unmistakable creak of a floorboard.

I froze. After a moment, I edged slowly and silently back to the panelled wall, secreting myself in the shadow of yet another cabinet. I peered across the space, struggling to make out anything in the darkness. Yes there, yes! There was a shape, undoubtedly human, moving stealthily up the stairs I had come up.

It was difficult to be certain from the way it moved whether or not the stranger was an inhabitant or intent on something nefarious. Either way I was in danger. I slipped my hand into my Norfolk and pulled out my revolver, then raised the dark-lantern and prepared to slip back its metal door.

A loud cough stopped me. The figure stepped into a patch of starlight, revealing itself to be Mrs Sash, her long hair tumbled down over her neck, a glass of milk carried in one hand.

She cleared her throat again and, oblivious to my presence, moved silently along the corridor to what I presumed was her bedroom. Once the door had closed behind her, I breathed a sigh of relief and moved on.

Four doors led off the walkway. One I could now eliminate. With the utmost care, I opened the dark-lantern a crack and then, silently, the first door. Within I could make out lumpen black shapes, in all probability the sleeping forms of Sash's overfed children. One faced the ceiling and was snoring, the other had her hands tucked beneath her face like a child in a nursery picture.

I stepped back on to the landing and gently closed the door.

The next room revealed itself to be merely a linen cupboard; I made swiftly for the third. It was locked.

I bent down to the lock and rammed the jemmy into it. With a fearfully loud crack, the old door sprang open. I glanced swiftly about but no one seemed to have stirred.

Once inside, I moved to the wall and discovered it covered by thick curtains. I checked to ensure I would remain unobserved and then opened the lantern to its fullest extent. The room smelled of old leather. Books lined the walls.

This looked rather promisingly like Sash's study.

I swung the lantern around the room. The light picked out a bureau and a tall cabinet filled with curiosities. Moving on, I crossed swiftly to the bureau and pushed up the rolled top. Three or four envelopes lay there, in all probability the late post mentioned by Mrs Sash. The professor would never open them now. I opened each of the drawers in turn. Nothing of interest caught my attention – they seemed merely to contain reams of dry scientific discourse. I plunged my hand into the back of the drawers and felt about in case there were any recessed panels or buttons. Real life rarely fails to disappoint and I found no such thing.

As I turned, however, I noticed on the desk a portmanteau photograph in a tortoiseshell frame. Of the three panels, the facing
portraits were of Sash and his wife. The middle picture, though,
apparently taken some time in the sixties, showed four men standing in stiffly formal pose. I recognized two of the men at once as
younger versions of Sash, whose study I was rifling, and his colleague Verdigris whose portrait I had studied earlier. The next
man – willowy and ascetic-looking – I did not know but the fourth
seemed very familiar. Swaddled in a blanket and looking prema-
turely ancient he sat in a wheeled chair and scowled down the
decades at me.

'Aha!' I exclaimed. The man in the wheeled chair was a stranger
no more. In a flash I recognized him as none other than Sir
Emmanuel Quibble, chief fellow of the Royal Society and the
foremost scientific mind of our age. It was well known that he had
long ago retired. To, of all places, the Amalfi coast . . .

I was musing on this information when the distinctive odour of
burnt paper caught my attention. I swung the dark-lantern around
and brought its feeble light to bear on the fire-grate, which was
revealed to contain a quantity of blackened paper. Had Professor
Sash laid a fire in the middle of summer? Or had he – or one of his
family – destroyed something of a compromising nature? In my
experience nothing is ever incinerated in a grate unless it is of a
deliciously compromising nature.

I almost jumped out of my skin as the door was thrown open
and the room illuminated by the yellow glow of an oil-lamp.

'Hold hard!' yelled some burly chap, whose outline was just discernible in the gloom. At his side, Mrs Sash twittered and wailed
in distress. Clearly I would have to retake Advanced Breaking and
Entering. Without a second thought I thrust the portmanteau
photograph into my jacket, leapt towards the bookcase and
brought it crashing down between my discoverers and me. Then I
hopped nimbly on to a leather chair, smashed the study window
with my jemmy and jumped into the night, hitting the lawn in a

neat ball and rolling to my feet. As I pelted away from the place hell for leather, I could hear the household rousing but they were too tardy to catch lucky old Lucifer.

That next morning, I ran myself a bath. Really, I had to do something about replacing Poplar. The service had dug out a chambermaid to do this sort of thing but although I *am* one of those johnnies who delight in lording it over their inferiors, I've always found that one, indispensable manservant is worth a whole retinue of girls in mob-caps whose presence can only lead, in any case, to babies being left on doorsteps and photogravures in the *Police Gazette.* I lay steaming for over an hour, my hair pooling above me like weed. How Millais would have loved me then!

Reluctantly, I dragged myself from the bath and crossed the bare boards to my dressing room. Here, among my treasured wardrobe of fabulous apparel, I would prepare for the work of the day. A note from Miracle had told me he had news on my late professors. I glanced at my watch on the dresser. My appointment was for eleven. I had only two hours to dress!

I reached Miracle's studio only a few minutes late and was about to pull at the bell when I remembered that today was the day he took his drawing class. I had passed the Mechanical Institute on the way and returned to it now – a big, black ugly building, concealed behind scrubby bushes and gold-tipped railings – where stood an expensive-looking carriage with two glossy horses at its head. The creatures seemed restless, stamping at the cobbles, inching the carriage forward by degrees despite the best efforts of the groom clutching at their bridles. A sharp, ammoniac smell assailed me.

Sitting in splendid isolation against the upholstery of the carriage was a thin man, bald beneath his silk topper, his black-gloved hands bulging like burnt sausages as he gripped the head of his cane.

'Can't you keep them still?' he snapped. 'Can't you?'

The groom was profuse in his apologies. The vehicle lurched forward again and the bald man scowled. Then he took out a turnip-sized watch from his waistcoat and, looking at it, scowled again.

Just as I reached the steps to the institute, the door opened, releasing a torrent of ladies on to the street, resembling, in their feathery, chattering finery, nothing so much as the Regent's Park geese. I tipped my hat to them as they rolled by, averting their eyes and giggling. I had almost reached the door when a latecomer emerged and I had to step back to avoid careering into her.

Unlike her à la mode classmates, this lady wore a violet-coloured dress in the fashion of ten years back. A large black hat with a heavy veil, like that of a bee-keeper, completely obscured her face.

She was holding a tan-leather portfolio under her arm and her hands, in long, black evening gloves, fluttered around its handle as though she were in great distress.

'I do beg your pardon,' I murmured.

I stepped to one side to let the curious apparition pass and then turned to see that the bald man from the carriage was standing on the step beneath me, his sour face jutting towards me like that of an angry Mr Punch.

'Come,' he barked, thrusting his arm through the crook of the woman's free elbow and pulling her past me towards the carriage, shooting back poisonous glances the whole way.

'Charmed!' I cried, doffing my boater.

The double doors swung open again, revealing Miracle.

'Hullo, Box,' he cried, rubbing together his big hands. 'Come a-spying, eh?'

Without letting on how close to the mark Miracle was, I pointed my cane towards the carriage. The groom was lashing at the horses as the vehicle turned in the empty road. 'Who the devil was that?'

'Ah,' grinned Miracle. 'The veiled scribbler. She's a curiosity that one. Name of Mrs Knight. Mrs Midsomer Knight.'

'A dream, is she?'

'According to one of the ladies who caught a glimpse of her in the conveniences, more of a nightmare! Poor devil. Husband might be described as something of a brute. Never lets her out in society. She hardly says a word.'

'Why the veils? Does he beat her?'

'Burnt in a fire years back, I gather.'

My friend plunged his hands into his pockets and jutted out his lip thoughtfully. 'It's a funny thing, Box, but my teaching seems to have had an adverse effect on her.'

'What do you mean?'

Miracle shrugged. 'Only that she began well but of late her work has been shocking.'

'Hmm, perhaps school-mastering is not for you, after all. And, Miracle before you fill me in on the nefarious secrets of our missing professors, you should know that you cannot afford to be so ineffective. I took your advice. I now have a pupil of my own!'

We spent the rest of the morning ensconced in Miracle's studio drinking far too much and smoking a brace of cigars. His place was quite lovely, possessing a domed glass roof that let summer sunshine flood the pale green walls. Shadier nooks housed Miracle's super-abundance of landscapes (I abhor landscapes) and still lifes (the Frenchies call them *nature morte* and I can't think of a better description).

As the day wore on, and we began to radiate a mildly tipsy bonhomie, I allowed him to prise out of me the story of Miss Pok.

'You sly dog,' grinned Miracle. 'What is she like?'

I waved a hand extravagantly. 'A delight. Captivating. I was thinking of inviting her to your party. Hope you don't mind.'

'Mind? I cannot wait to meet this paragon.'

'You must promise to behave now, Christopher.' I smoked my cigar contentedly. 'You'll think me foolish, I know, but there is something very particular about her. Uncommon.'

'Such as?'

'Well, she drinks vermouth in the afternoons and has no fear of being in a gentleman's company unchaperoned.'

'Ten a penny at the Café Royal.'

'*Touché*. But she pays to be with me.'

'Pooh! She pays for her *lessons*, not your company!'

'Perhaps.'

'Do I detect more than the usual predatory instinct at work, Box?' cried Miracle. 'Can it be – never! You have fallen for her?'

I did not look him in the eye.

Miracle smiled. 'I shall refrain from tormenting you further. Now! It is high time to get down to something like business.'

'I suppose so,' I sighed. 'What have you to tell me?'

Miracle sat forward in his chair. 'Professors Verdigris and Sash were at the same Cambridge college between 1866 and 1869. Star pupils of their intake, it seems, along with two others.'

'Let me guess. One of them was Emmanuel Quibble?'

'Quite so! How did you –?'

'I have sources of my own,' I smiled. 'The other?'

'Chap called Morraine. Maxwell Morraine.'

I nodded thoughtfully. Was this the fourth man in the photograph?

Miracle leant back on the dark red leather. 'Their chosen field was something rather bewildering to do with the molten core of the earth. They formed some kind of research team. Went out to Italy.'

'Italy, eh? And did they call themselves anything?'

'Hm?'

'The Verdigris Collective. Something like that.'

Miracle shook his head. 'Not as far as I know.'

'Do you know what happened to . . . what-do-you-call-him? Morraine?'

'Apparently he went mad and died out there. Quibble, of course, rose to great heights.'

'Indeed. Terribly hard to get an audience with the old man, from what I hear.'

'Oh, nigh on impossible. Lives in Naples, I gather. Practically a recluse.'

'Hm. I know you won't let me down.'

Miracle gave a little laugh. 'There's a limit to what strings even I can pull, old man.'

'Nonsense. I have the utmost faith in your ability to flatter the most Doric pillars of society to their very capitals. I can be in Italy for – what shall we say? Next Thursday?'

VII

THE VERDIGRIS MAUSOLEUM

RETURNED to Downing Street to find a communication from the Domestics. The firm of Tom Bowler, Belsize Park, was apparently engaged in an unusual amount of activity at the dockside. Enquiries suggested that the firm specialized in the repatriation of Englishmen and Italians who had died abroad. Coffins were shipped over in packing crates (intrinsically valuable, it seemed, as they were returned, empty, to the point of egress, namely the port of Naples). I determined to have another nocturnal poke around, this time at the undertaker's and, after sobering myself up with a pot of coffee, put on a black suit with a waistcoat of burnt-orange to do so. I stepped out into Whitehall where Delilah was drawing up in the firm's cab. For the purpose, she had traded in her signature yellow frock for a cabby's coat and gaiters.

'Evening, Mr Box, hand where is we hoff to?'

I gave the Belsize Park address and we were away.

As we clattered along, I pressed my face to the window and closed my eyes. Night had come and the air was sickly with a yellow smog that covered the city like some monstrous slug-trail.

I tried to make sense of recent curious events. All clues pointed to Naples. Poop had died there and had foreseen catastrophic events. It was the place where that mysterious crate of Mr Bowler had been destined, the place where Sir Emmanuel Quibble, last survivor of the Cambridge Four was now in residence. But what would I find when I got there?

I was jerked from my reverie by the sudden acceleration of the cab. Rapping on the ceiling, I was answered by the Delilah's heavy features peering down at me through the hatch.

'Beg, pardon, sir,' she wheezed. 'Hi believe we his being followed.'

I pulled at the heavy leather strap of the window and peered out. I had no clear idea of where we were but could just make out the silhouette of another cab, swaying alarmingly as it juddered around the corner.

'How long has this been going on?' I demanded.

Delilah coughed into her grubby collar. I could just catch the glint of the street lamps in her eyes as she swivelled round to look back at our pursuers.

'Couple ha mile, sir. Hi've tried to throw 'im off the track but hit hain't no good.'

I dragged the window upwards with a firm tug. 'Do what you can then.'

'Righto, sir,' she answered brightly, relishing the challenge. 'I could try to – look hout!'

I was conscious of a loud report from outside the cab, as though someone had stepped heavily on the surface of a frozen pond.

'What is it?' I demanded, peering upwards.

Delilah spluttered as though mortally offended. ''E bloody well shot hat hus, sir!'

This sounded a bit much. What murderous thug had I attracted now? I pressed my nose to the glass and did a quick reconnoitre as we rattled furiously along. I thought briefly of leaping from the carriage and taking Delilah's place but instead turned my head to address her once more.

'On, then!' I cried. 'Anywhere. Lose him!'

As the hatch thumped back into place, Delilah whipped up the horse with a mixture of endearments and obscenities. We lurched forward with renewed vigour and I was flung against the dark leather. As we tottered leftwards, the cab's wheels gave an horrendous squeal and bumped twice over the kerb.

I tore off my coat and scrabbled at the lining, popping the excellent stitches (how that hurt me!) to reveal the small pistol I knew the Tailoring Domestics had concealed there.

Rocked back and forth by the motion of the carriage, I dropped on to my knees and placed the gun on the floor. In the queasy atmosphere of summer-fret and gas-light, the gun's barrel-less body glowed like a silverfish. I grabbed at my left boot and swiftly removed the long, slim tube secreted in its own compartment within the elasticated side.

As carefully as I could, the cab bucking over the cobbles, I screwed the tube on to the front of the pistol. Within moments, I was in possession of a very effective, long-range weapon.

Delilah's muffled curses and whip-cracks rang out sharply as I rammed down the window with my elbow and leaned out over the sill.

Behind us, the other cab, seemingly all of a piece with its driver, materialized like a ghostly ship. I could see nothing clearly, merely a suggestion of bowler hat and ulster. Then our pursuer's hand flew up, there came a yellowy flash and the report of a gun.

I ducked back into the cab and then levelled my own pistol, loosing off a couple of shots as we careered over a crossroads, almost colliding with a third cab. There were garbled shouts of protest, the whinny of horses, but we tore on past, street-lamps blurring like phantom dandelion clocks.

The pursuing cabman fired twice more, the *crack-crack* of his pistol swamped by the dense curtain of fog.

Suddenly, my cab smacked against the pavement and I was tossed to the floor of the carriage. I swore as my leg scraped the rough surface and I felt the fabric of my trousers rend. Struggling to right myself as we reeled ahead, I managed to get one barked knee on to the seat and, leaning up, pushed open the hatch in the ceiling.

'Try to keep us steady —' I began, then pulled myself up to peer through the hole. Delilah had sunk back, her corpulent face a mask of agony. She gripped her chest with a gloved hand.

''E got me, sir!' she gasped, then suddenly pitched sideways, diving into the fog like an uncertain swimmer into the Serpentine.

I reached out to grab her, but it was too late.

I knew I had only moments before the vehicle would career out of control. I kicked at the door and swung myself out and on to the body of the cab, hanging on for grim death.

Chancing a glance behind me, I saw the murderous driver of the other cab taking aim once again. I gained a quick foothold on the top of the door and then swung myself upwards, falling into the empty driver's seat. At once, I began lashing mercilessly at the horse, keeping my bare head low as another shot whistled past. I turned and replied with a volley of three but still the cab bore down.

We were heading down some endless, snaking high street made tunnel-like by the enshrouding smog. I had a vague impression of the blazing windows of public houses and the blank façades of shut-up shops.

Some young fellow pulled his sweetheart from our path just in time to prevent her being crushed beneath the wheels. I heard her cry out as my assailant fired again, the bullet splintering the woodwork of the vehicle just by me.

An arch of some sort loomed up on my left: two fat pillars, fringed with ivy. I had to get off the main highway to secure the general population. Between the pillars stood a pair of iron gates, thankfully open. With a lash of the whip I urged my horse through and into the gaping darkness beyond.

Looking back, I saw that my pursuer had not been discouraged and was only a hundred yards behind. As he swung through the arch, he too was lost in the black of the night. Nevertheless, I had surprised him and, as I urged the horse onwards, I tried to take stock of my situation.

All through the frantic pursuit, my mind raced. Who was behind this murderous attack? Could this have something to do with the mystery on hand? Or perhaps it was that murderous fool Major Strangeways Pugg, still set on avenging his lovely Avril.

No longer on cobbles I appeared to be travelling over some kind of muddy track or pathway. The road was as narrow as a

footpath and branches lashed at the sides of the cab as I urged it forward.

Jerking round I fired the last of my bullets behind me and then almost fell from my perch as something reared out of the Stygian gloom.

It was an angel.

I fancy my face must have been a pretty sight but I recovered quickly. An angel it was, but stone and sacred to the memory of some poor bastard as far as I could make out. I thrashed and swore at the horse. The rapid appearance of a dozen stone crosses and then a massive, ugly mausoleum confirmed that I had passed into some great municipal cemetery.

The pathway forked right and I drove the coach on, meanwhile feeling in my other boot for the clip of bullets I kept there. It was a devil of a job trying to reload the pistol and still prevent the cab from crashing into the gravestones that projected from the wet ground like scattered dragon's teeth. I had just managed it when I was startled again, this time by the sudden appearance of my enemy right *ahead* of me.

Somehow he had cut me off. Perhaps he knew this necropolis well. It was as though some hellish beast were bearing down on me, the driver's scarf flapping behind him like a pennant in a gale.

I dragged at the reins and managed to steer the cab to the left but it was too late. The two vehicles clashed like galleons and I heard the bodywork rend and protest as we ground against each other on the narrow lane.

But then suddenly I was past him and still going!

The black night exploded into unnatural light as I loosed off another two shots. My assailant seemed to stagger in his seat as his cab retreated but in an instant he had turned and fired too, taking the nose off a rather comely stone cherub in the process.

I now had some advantage in that my enemy's cab was rattling away from me in the wrong direction. There came a frantic whinny from his horse as he flogged at its flanks.

'Hyar! Hyar!'

He was turning, or attempting to. Meanwhile, my own vehicle had not slackened its pace and was thundering heedlessly through the hollows of the cemetery. Mausoleums streamed past like the town-houses of the dead.

What to do? According to the manual – or to Lady Cecely Midwinter's Espionage Academy on the Old Kent Road where yours truly had been apprenticed – I should abandon the cab and secrete myself amidst the thick gorse that enveloped the memorial stones. If my would-be assassin came back this way, I could pick him off from my hiding place among the angels.

These thoughts were flashing across my mind when suddenly the mist thinned and I saw the enormous outline of a grand building only a matter of fifty yards ahead. It was a bleak-looking chapel of some kind, its towers sparkling eerily, its great black doors securely barred against all-comers and I was heading straight for it.

Wrenching the reins until I felt the hot leather tearing at my palms, I tried to steer the carriage away from the chapel. The horse gave a great snorting cry and lurched right. I reeled from the impact as the side of the cab slammed against the old wooden doors of the building. There was a tremendous booming crash and I felt the whole cab splinter and the ground hurtle up towards me.

My chest hit the iron-hard mud and I felt the wind comprehensively knocked from me. Dazed and sick I lay on my front, staring miserably ahead as the pursuing cab drew up alongside the chapel. The figure, swathed in ulster, scarf and brown bowler, seemed smaller now as he clambered down from the driver's seat. In one gloved hand he held his pistol.

I tried to roll over but the breath was only coming back to me with agonizing slowness. Just ahead and out of reach lay my own pistol, the long barrel protruding from a clump of weeds. I flung out my arm and tried to drag myself towards it. The figure advanced remorselessly, cocking his weapon and reaching up with his other hand to pull down the scarf from his face. Was it that vengeful Fury, Pugg? There was a hole the size of a tanner in the shoulder of his cape but no sign of blood. Had I winged him or merely ruined his coat?

Lungs bursting, I tried to sit up and sling myself into cover.

'Damn it,' I gasped. 'Who are you, you ruddy maniac?'

The figure stopped and seemed to consider me.

Then, echoing across the cemetery with the eeriness of a banshee came a cry: 'Hello! What's going on? What are you doing there?'

Two men, holding yellow lamps high above their heads hove into view to my left. Their appearance had a startling effect on my attacker. Swiftly, he slipped his pistol into the folds of his ulster and raced back towards the cab, pulling himself up into the driver's perch. He whipped up the horse and rattled away.

The lamp-bearers ran towards me, as welcome as real angels. 'Good Lord, are you all right, sir?' said one. His companion, heavily bearded and mean-looking was less forgiving. 'What the blazes has been going on?' he demanded.

Ignoring him, I struggled to my feet and grabbed for my pistol. I aimed at the retreating cab, but in moments it was out of range. I turned on my heel and wrenched the lamp from the bearded man's hand.

'Here! What are you doing?'

'His number,' I hissed. 'The cab number. Can you see it?'

Nothing was clear, though, in the sickly yellow light and the cab soon vanished into the murk.

I stood for a moment, swinging the lamp round in an arc and illuminating the devastation I had wrought. My cab was almost cracked in two. The horse stood nearby, placidly chewing grass at the foot of one of those broken columns that tell of life cut off in its prime. Happily, that life had not been mine.

''Ere!' cried my bearded rescuer. 'You was bloomin' shooting! What the hell do you think you're about? This is a place of rest!'

The cemetery watchmen took me to a little cabin where I was treated to a tot of rum by the kinder of the two – Lukey by name – and furious glares from his mate, name of Bob. I assured the good burghers that all expenses would be met. In the morning I would despatch the Domestics to set about hushing things up, not least the body of the faithful Delilah who was probably still lying undiscovered with a bullet between her shoulder blades on some dreadful suburban roadway. I dragged my ragged, filthy and exhausted self to my feet and was moving towards the cabin door when a notice pinned to the wall caught my gaze.

'What is that?' I asked.

'That's the interments list, sir,' said Lukey.

'Is it, by George. And that name, fourth down . . . ?'

'The Verdigris Mausoleum, sir.'

'What a coincidence,' I mused. 'An . . . acquaintance of mine goes by that name. I wonder if it is his family tomb. Would it . . . would it be an awful imposition to ask to see that mausoleum?'

The bearded one positively glared at me and cleared his throat of a noisome expectoration that landed in a hissing green lump on the coals of the fire. 'The Verdigris? Indeed it would! After what you've been up to tonight, you're damned lucky we ain't called the bobbies!'

Lukey laid a hand on the other's arm. 'Now then, Bob. Watch that temper of your'n. You said there was summat funny about that funeral in any case.'

I adopted a sombre expression. 'Gentlemen, I am investigating certain irregularities connected with that funeral. It is more than likely that you have given invaluable service to the Crown. I need you to show me that mausoleum. At once!'

With much ill-grace Bob finally assented and a few minutes later the three of us stepped back out into the humid night.

Our feet crunched on the gravel pathways, the lantern held aloft by Bob throwing a funnel of yellow light into the oily gloom.

I was dog-tired but pressed on, unsure of what, if anything, I might find.

The Verdigris family tomb was about the size of a small cottage, done in the familiarly dreary style of Corinthian columns and arched roof. A pair of massive bronze doors were set in the centre, a thick, well-oiled padlock strung between the door handles like a fob-chain across the waistcoat of a prize-fighter.

'There,' barked Bob the lantern-carrier. 'Can we now get back to our business?'

I moved towards the mausoleum and craned my neck to make out the family name, picked out in black against the white marble.

I assumed the masterful tone that comes so easily to me. 'Quickly, man, the key!'

'Now hold on a moment –'

'Give him the key, Bob!' wailed Lukey.

Cursing, the burly fellow began to fiddle with the huge bunch of keys at his waist.

'Hurry!' I urged.

At last he selected a long, spindly specimen and, grunting with the effort, shifted his belly forward so he could insert it into the lock.

As soon as the tumblers clicked, I dragged at the chain and hauled it to the ground.

'The lantern, Bob!' I hissed. 'Give it to me!'

So saying, I grabbed the thing from his hand and, dragging open the doors, plunged into the mausoleum.

Inside the air was suffocatingly stale. The grim black oblong of a new coffin stood out boldly on its shelf against the homogenous dust-grey boxes that abutted it.

'Give me a hand,' I commanded, pulling at the head end of the coffin.

''Ere!' cried Bob, entering the building.

'No time to explain!' I cried shrilly. 'Get the coffin on the floor and get the lid off.'

'Do as he says,' said Lukey. 'He's on to something.'

Together, Lukey and myself pulled the coffin to the dust-thick floor, then I began to look about for something to prise open the lid.

'My God, if the family find out about this –' murmured Bob.

'Never mind that,' I barked. 'Hold the lantern high.'

I swung round and then stopped as my eyes alighted on half a dozen wooden chairs, stacked in the corner and presumably for use at funerals. Without hesitation I grabbed at the top chair and smashed it to pieces on the floor. From the debris I retrieved a chair leg and with this began to hammer away under the coffin lid. After ten or twelve blows, the lid gave with a nasty squeal and splintered across.

'Pull it apart!' I cried. 'Open the thing!'

Lukey stepped forward and, grasping at the wood, wrenched the lid away. Bob glided forward from out of the shadows, the queasy yellow lantern light flooding the macabre sight before us.

'Well, bless my soul!' whispered Lukey.

For within the coffin was revealed a cloth dummy, its innards stuffed with straw, its eyes and mouth merely crude stitching like that on some common scarecrow.

'Ha!' I cried triumphantly. 'Exactly what I expected to find!'

Which was a bloody lie but there you are.

VIII

THE MAN IN THE INDIGO SPECTACLES

KNOW what you're thinking. Resurrectionists! Body-snatchers once more at work in old London town! Had the good professor (and his erstwhile colleague – for a search of Sash's tomb the next day revealed the same result) been made away with by wall-eyed, whisky-breathed anatomists to be displayed and skewered at the Whitechapel Hospital? Well, no. Very probably not. At least, I shouldn't have thought so. This was the twentieth century, after all.

No, it seemed altogether more probable that Tom Bowler Esq. lay behind this bizarre enterprise. The Belsize Park premises were immediately raided but somehow the jolly mortician had avoided the Domestics and stolen away like a street-Arab in the night. I was sure I knew where to run him to earth and booked passage on the next departing vessel to Naples without waiting to hear whether Miracle had worked his charms on old Quibble. I would leave at once. Well, almost at once. There was still the little matter of Miracle's summer ball. Business, of course, as I needed to confirm my appointment with Miracle, and perhaps a little pleasure.

My friend's parties were something of a legend. In fact, Miracle's gorgeous Belgravia house had been the scene of my poking of Avril Pugg the previous December. Christmas is a time for giving, after all. I found I was looking forward to this ball immensely. It would be a welcome distraction from the problem in hand but I would also be escorting the delectable Bella Pok and could impress her with statements of the 'I fear I must away to the Continent this very night!' variety.

There had been no time for another drawing lesson but we had been in constant communication via letter and cable. I had broached the ball and she had been delighted to accept. Might I be permitted to call on her? No, she would prefer to call at Downing Street. Would eight o'clock suit?

I spent much of the late afternoon selecting a flower for my lapel. Joe Chamberlain had made orchid-growing awfully fashionable and the delicate purple flower I selected as a button-hole set off my pale complexion most appealingly. Not quite ready to admit I was still without a servant of any kind, I opened the door to Bella myself – a delirious vision in crimson – turned her round immediately and helped her back into the cab.

As we clattered along I could see how thrilled she was at the prospect of the party. Her eyes blazed and her expression was almost wild as she turned to me.

'Will I not be awfully out of place, Mr Box?'

I took her gloved hand. 'My dear, you will outshine them all.'

'And Mr Miracle. What is he like? They say he's very handsome.'

'No doubt they do. You'll like him, I'm sure.'

Curiously, though, when we arrived at Miracle's house, of our host there was no sign. Instead, the party seemed to be under the direction of Lady Constance Tutt-Haffenschafft, a friend of Miracle's and quite the old hand at throwing a function like this.

Lady Constance – of Austrian stock and the widow of someone awfully grand in trans-Atlantic telegraphy – was one of London's more unusual hostesses. She was a genuinely warm and congenial old soul who had survived the Tay Bridge disaster and, as a consequence, had developed a morbid fear of railway engines. To everyone's eternal embarrassment, she was wont to impersonate steam trains at the most inopportune moments. It was like Miracle, who didn't give a fig for convention, to take her under his wing when the rest of society had shunned her.

Glittering with jewels, Lady Constance barrelled towards us, swathed in taffeta. 'Ach! How delightful to see you, Lucifer!' she gushed. 'Do you know where young Miracle is hiding? He is not here! *Choo! Choo!* I arrive early, yes? To help in the preparations, but where is the boy? I do not know. So – *Choo! Choo!* – I have to take charge! But who is this? Who is this flower?'

'Lady Constance Tutt-Haffenschafft,' I said. 'Miss Bella Pok.'

'Miss Pok! Enchanted. En – *choo-choo*-chanted.'

Bella stepped back a little, blinking in surprise. Lady Constance gave a quick little smile. 'You are in your choice of companion most fortunate, my dear Lucifer,' she enthused in her guttural croak.

'And I in mine,' said Bella, glancing in my direction.

I glowed with pleasure.

'I had no idea you would be accompanied,' said Lady C, teeth glinting. 'Pok. An unusual name. *Choo! Choo!* You have come far?'

'Tonight, no. But I am Dutch by birth.'

'I trust you did not come to London by one of these steam trains?'

Bella shook her head. 'No. By boat.'

'Thank God! The train is the devil's play-thing! Even now I hear them! *Chuff! Chuff!*'

Lady Constance pressed her hand to her forehead for a moment then exhaled as though steam were forcing its way out of her big nostrils. The moment, it seemed, had passed.

'Forgive me. Now do go off and get yourself a little drink. I'm afraid I must make free with Mr Box for a moment.'

I bowed to Bella and, with an amused smile, she plunged off into the ballroom, soon lost to sight amongst the miasma of silken gowns and black cut-aways.

'You are very naughty,' said Lady Constance, pinching my arm.

'I am?'

'You know very well that your being London's most alluring bachelor is the principal reason why so many unattached young ladies come to Christopher's parties. *Choo!* You are meant to come alone.'

She giggled and it ran like a tremor through her portly frame.

I patted the old sow's hand indulgently. 'I am still very much unattached, my dear Lady Constance and, besides, you know there is only one woman in the world for me.'

I gave her the kind of saucy look that would keep her enthralled for another twelvemonth. Eyelids fluttering bashfully, she batted her fan lightly against the silk-faced lapels of my suit. 'Ach! You flatterer! *Choo! Choo!* You know I have purchased the most glorious new gown. Perhaps I could sit for you again . . . ?'

This was good news. I had painted her perhaps a dozen times, all for excellent remuneration. During our sittings, for some reason, the railway mania abated and she fell into glorious, blissful silence.

Looking towards the crowd in the ballroom, Lady Constance took my arm and began leading me in. 'But you have done wonderfully, Lucifer. This girl Pok. She is like a flame. So beautiful!'

'I must concur with you there.'

'And you *are* fond of her, yes? I could see it at once when the two of you stood together. I must have every detail! I am starved of gossip! *Huff!* Now, we must hurry and disengage your Miss Bella from those old goats in there before her virtue . . . *choo!* . . . is entirely compromised.'

The ballroom was hung about with paper lanterns and summer flowers. Chattering faces, reflected to the infinite by the huge quantity of gilt mirrors, looked out at me as I sauntered towards Bella. I stepped across the threshold and the old thrill lit up my innards. What did these blandly respectable folk know of me? Could they tell that beneath my crisp white gloves were fingernails that had so recently scrabbled in grave-dirt? Could they guess for even a moment that I was about to embark on a perilous mission that might save their very way of life? Of course not, but what did that matter? At that moment, the guilty pleasure that comes from leading a double life coursed through me like salts.

I caught sight of Bella once more.

She sat: a splendid curl of long scarlet silk, wrapped about with a stole of Arctic fox. An ugly young pup with unwashed hair hanging to his collar stood to her right, jabbering away.

She gave a little start as I appeared and clicked my heels.

'Bella,' I said.

The greasy fellow swung towards me with a questioning look.

'Do forgive me,' I said. 'Lucifer Box. I have come to rescue my friend Miss Pok from your miserable attentions. Shall we, my dear?'

I extended the crook of my elbow. She took it and rose with a small smile, leaving her beau blustering in fury.

'You are rather a terrible person, Lucifer,' she said.

'You're the second person to say that this evening.'

'And certain to have a bad end,' she added.

'It comes of having a bad beginning. You didn't need rescuing?'

'Of course! He was so dreary and had breath like a spaniel.'

'Well, it was my duty. And my right. You are, after all, my partner for the evening.'

She glanced towards me and the chandeliers glittered in her violet eyes. 'Indeed.'

'Then let's have some cham and then a dance. Quickly, now, I can see Lady Chuff-chuff heading our way and the band have struck up a polka.'

So, in the sweet heat of the evening, we whiled away a very pleasant hour or so, conversation and blood quickened by Mumm. Bella's gaze was locked on mine, and as we swirled effortlessly around the ballroom, I fervently wished myself free of all responsibilities. Must the dread burden of saving the Empire always fall on me?

I was standing with my back to the room when I saw Bella glance over my shoulder. A little shiver prickled up my spine and I turned and saw a queer-looking fellow standing at the hearth.

He was a very tall, barrel-chested man in spotless evening dress, standing with legs apart, thumbs tucked into the pockets of his white waistcoat, nodding and occasionally smiling tightly at some pleasantry. Thick, oily curls, streaked with white sprouted from his massive head. Perched upon his prominent nose was a pair of curious, indigo-hued spectacles. He seemed ill at ease and was constantly flipping his watch from his waistcoat.

Almost as though he sensed my looking at him, the great head flicked upwards, the light turning his spectacles a flashing white.

'Good Lord,' I said. 'Who is that?'

'That is the Duce Tiepolo,' said Lady Constance, appearing at my side with further champagne. 'I met him once before in Biarritz. I had heard he was in town.'

'Who?' I glanced almost furtively at the imposing figure by the fireplace.

'He is an Italian duke,' said Bella. 'I have read about him in the society columns.'

'One of the discoveries – *choo!* – of our oh-so-dear Mr Miracle,' trilled Lady Constance. 'How he dotes on us stray dogs.'

'Indeed,' I said. 'That's why he likes me so much. This one doesn't look like a stray dog, though.'

'Oh, he is, to Christopher, like royalty, my dear boy. Tiepolo is the last of a dying scion. His people, they fought, oh most bravely against the Garibaldi fellow back in the sixties – *chuff!* – but his family were all sent into exile when the . . . what do you call it? . . . the Rissole . . . the Risorgan . . .'

'Risorgimento,' said Bella softly.

'Yes,' said Lady Constance. 'When they came in.'

'He strikes quite a noble figure, does he not?' observed my beautiful companion.

'Oh dear,' I mused. 'Another one with a penchant for hard-luck cases.'

'You would like to meet him, yes?'

'Why not,' I said.

So we were led over and into the presence of the great man.

'Your Grace . . .'

The Duce turned slowly towards us, the deep lines at the corners of his eyes creasing together.

'Aha! Lady Constance! How delightful!'

The train-fearer was delighted to be remembered. After an exchange of pleasantries, I stepped forward and he inclined his head slightly at the sight of me. It was like being observed by some great patient snake. The lenses of the indigo spectacles prevented even a hint of his expression from being visible.

'This is Mr Lucifer Box,' said Lady Constance. 'The famous painter.'

'Oh, you flatter me,' I oiled. 'Your Grace.'

I bowed and clicked my heels. He did likewise.

'Tiepolo,' I said. 'I'm afraid I do not know the province . . .'

'One of the more ancient duchies,' he said, with a smile. The voice was quiet but assured, like a great and well-maintained engine using but a fraction of its true power.

He turned to Bella.

'Miss Bella Pok,' announced Lady Constance.

He took her hand in his great paw without hesitation. 'I'm afraid, your Grace,' she cooed, 'that I know very little of the history of your country . . .'

'Oh, my unhappy country!' said the Duce, raising his hands palms outward and smiling in mock-anguish. 'But now, here, is not the time to be remembering old sorrows. Perhaps if you would do me the honour of dining with me . . . ?'

Bella's eyes flashed.

I moved with the speed of a jealous panther. If you've ever seen one, you'll know. 'Your Grace,' I interrupted, 'I would consider it a great honour if you would consent to sit for a portrait.'

The Duce's mouth pinched in displeasure. 'This is impossible, alas. I am leaving most soon for the Continent. Besides, a *painting* . . .' He gave a little shrug. 'I was saying to our friend Mr Miracle – where is he by the way? – is not painting most . . . old-fashioned?'

Lady Constance leant forward. 'The Duce is a photographic enthusiast.'

'Is he, by George?' I said, nettled. 'Well, in that case I should hate to bother him with such a trifle as a portrait in oils.'

Bella shot me an odd look.

'You are going to the Continent, you say, your Grace?' I said airily.

'Yes.'

'Back to Italy?'

The great man's face darkened.

I put my fingers to my lips as though to hush them. 'Of course not! How silly of me! They wouldn't take too kindly to seeing anyone from the old days, would they? Where *do* you spend your exile?'

'Well, if you will excuse me, Lady Constance,' he began. 'Miss Pok...'

'I have myself some little knowledge of those days,' I interrupted. The champagne was, I fear, beginning to tell. 'My father told me all about it. Italy was in a parlous state back then, Bella. Wasn't really Italy at all, to speak of. Ruled by the Frogs, the Spanish, even the ruddy Austrians – saving your presence, Lady C.'

The Duce gazed levelly at me. 'It was a troubled time. But we could have survived as we were. If not for Signor Giuseppe Garibaldi...'

'You may know the biscuit,' I said in an undertone to Bella. 'He pulled the country together, didn't he, under King What's-his-name. Yes. I'm off there tomorrow myself, as a matter of fact. I'll send them your regards, hmm?'

The Duce's lips set into a grim line. 'You will excuse me. I must... that is, I...'

He seemed genuinely put out. Making a little bow to the ladies, he melted away into the crowd.

'Well!' said Bella.

'Hmm?'

'I thought you were rather rude to that poor wanderer.'

I flashed a cheeky smile at Lady Constance and she, giggling girlishly, waved back at me. Then I took Bella by the elbow and steered her towards the balcony. 'My dear Bella, these pompous so-called aristos are all alike. It won't do him a bit of harm to be reminded that he's the ex-Duke of an ex-duchy. He'll go home and kick his valet in all probability, but that's scarcely our concern. Now, I suggest a little air to clear away the fug of his rhetoric. Besides, I found that I didn't take to the idea at all of someone else dining with you.'

She cocked her head to one side impishly and gave me the benefit of her most devastating smile.

We walked through the French windows and out on to the warm terrace. Balustraded steps led down on either side to Miracle's vast gardens.

'It's very beautiful in the moonlight,' said Bella, gazing out at the hedges and fountains.

'Mmm,' I concurred. 'By day this place is a riot of colour. I once painted Lady Constance against the bougainvillaea over there.'

'Did she like it?'

'She was chuff-chuffed.'

Bella giggled, then shivered a little and I slipped out of my coat.

'Allow me.'

She took the coat and draped it about her shoulders. 'Perhaps you would care to paint me one day?'

'You wouldn't prefer the Duke to photograph you?'

'There's no beauty in chemicals and paper, Lucifer,' she murmured.

'Indeed not. I would . . . I would consider it a very great honour to paint you, Bella. How would you like it done?'

'Perhaps I could be Jeanne d'Arc . . . or Helen,' she said, thrusting her shoulders back and lifting up that fine, proud head.

'In Troy? Or being ravished by Zeus? Oh no, that was Leda wasn't it?'

I moved just a fraction closer to her. A tiny pulse was beating in her throat.

'I think I should like that,' she said quietly.

'To be painted or to be . . .'

'Ravished?' She laughed her charming, tinkling laugh. She did not move away as my arm brushed hers. 'Zeus was fond of all that, was he not? Forever appearing as swans or showers of gold . . .'

'I know so little about you,' I said suddenly, 'but I do not wish to pry.'

'Pry away.'

'You really are *Miss* Pok?'

'I really am. I was engaged once. To a count, would you believe?'

I looked at her in the starlight. Her eyes glittered like fragments of amethyst. I could believe princes, kings and emperors might lose their wits over her.

'I must confess that I have posed for a portrait before.'

'Oh yes?'

'Yes. The Count. He paid for a portrait.'

'How did it come out?'

'Indifferently.'

'And what about the Count? How did he come out?'

'Equally indifferently.'

'My dear,' I began, taking her hand, 'I am distressed beyond measure to have to go away.'

'To Italy?'

I nodded.

'Business or pleasure?'

I looked down and contemplated her delicate, gloved hand. 'Oh, business only. Nothing but the most vital business would take me away from you at this juncture.'

'You would rather stay in London?'

'I would rather stay with you,' I said quietly. 'And continue your . . . instruction.'

I reached out and took her hand in mine. She turned, the curve of her cheek illumined like a crescent moon. Her lips parted and I could feel the warmth of her breath.

All at once, there came the crunch of running footsteps on the gravel below and a figure lolloped towards the terrace. Both of us turned at the sight of him, his handsome face flushed, his cravat all askew. It was Christopher Miracle!

He clattered up the steps and stopped, swaying slightly, when he clapped eyes on me.

'Box!' he cried.

'Miracle! Where the devil have you been? Lady Constance has been manfully holding the fort –'

'Thank God you are here! You must help me! Dear God, it is terrible! Terrible!'

I laid a hand upon his arm. 'My dear Christopher! What is it? What has happened?'

He shot a glance at Bella.

'Miss Pok,' I said calmly, 'perhaps it would be better if you returned to the party –'

She shook her head. 'I would far rather be of assistance, if I can.'

Miracle gripped my arm. 'She's vanished and they think I have something to do with it!'

'Who has vanished?' asked Bella with a concerned frown.

'Come, Christopher. Let's get you somewhere warm. Bella, would you check there's no one observing?'

We slipped him back through into the ballroom and, by sticking close to the heavy curtains, managed to steer him into a panelled corridor without anyone seeing us.

I tried a door and we found ourselves in a darkened study.

Bella lit a lamp as I settled Miracle into a chair and pushed a tumbler of Scotch into his shaking hands.

The glass clattered against his teeth. 'They say I was the last person to see her. Now she is missing and – the police don't say it but they suspect some foul play I'm sure of it!'

'Miracle! Calm yourself! Who has gone missing?'

He looked at me with a puzzled expression. 'Have I not said? Why, Mrs Knight, of course. Mrs Midsomer Knight.'

'Who?'

'The woman I told you of. Remember? You must remember.'

'What, the veiled creature?'

Miracle nodded, his head drooping between defeated shoulders.

'Come along, sir,' said Bella gently. 'Drink up and tell us all about it.'

Miracle nodded and rubbed his tired face. 'Yesterday. It was time for my usual drawing class. I arrived early and so, for the first time, did she. Mrs Knight, that is. That spectre of a husband of hers was just dropping her off.'

I nodded. 'And then?'

'I escorted her up the steps of the Institute. She said her husband had some urgent business out of town and so had brought her before her usual time, was this acceptable? I said of course it was, as long as she didn't mind busying herself until the other ladies arrived.'

'What time was this?'

'Nine-thirty. As soon as we were inside, she excused herself and disappeared into the . . . er *conveniences*. And that was the last I saw of her, I swear it!'

'She didn't come back into your room?'

'I went about my work and forgot all about her! At ten, the other ladies came. The Misses Fullalove were at each other's throats. My mind was elsewhere . . .'

'Did none of the others notice her absence?' I asked.

He shook his head. 'No. At least, none of them remarked upon it.'

'And when did the business begin to assume a more sinister aspect?' said Bella.

'Well, at the end of the lesson when the husband arrived. Of course, I had no idea where she might be. There was the most frightful row and the police were called. A glove was then found, unquestionably belonging to Mrs Knight. A blood-stained glove, Lucifer. In the ladies' conveniences!'

'And the peelers suspect foul play?'

'We were alone in the building for half an hour before the others arrived. Knight himself saw us on the steps of the Institute. I don't know where the devil she is but I had nothing to do with it. God help me! I am sworn on my honour not to leave town.'

I exhaled noisily. 'Well, this is a pickle.'

'They've questioned me over and over and only recently released me. I have nothing to tell them!'

'But they haven't arrested you!'

'Not yet. But it can only be –'

There was some kind of commotion in the corridor beyond. Lady Constance's voice chuffed in indignation, then there were footsteps on the carpet. Bella looked at me with a fearful expression as we heard first one, then another door being opened and then firmly shut.

Miracle shuddered, his eyes wide with terror.

The door to the study opened admitting a lively little ball of a man with great shaving brushes of hair projecting from his ears and nose. The rest of his face was concealed beneath a derby hat and a pair of massive, old-fashioned Piccadilly weepers.

'Please forgive this intrusion, sir,' he said, looking at me, then at Bella. '*Miss*. Inspector Flush. Scotland Yard.'

He removed his hat and threw a very serious look at my friend Christopher.

'Mr Miracle, I'm afraid I shall have to ask you to come with me to the Yard. Certain . . . developments have come to light.'

'Developments?'

I held up a hand. 'Just a moment, Inspector. Before you haul my friend off on some spurious charge, had we not best get the facts in order? Mr Miracle was in the process of describing the events to us. You can surely show him the courtesy of allowing him to finish.'

Flush gave a triple-chinned shrug. 'That is a courtesy we should be glad to extend – at the station.'

'What developments?' cried Miracle with some asperity.

With slightly more drama than was necessary (I liked him at once), Flush removed his hat, and held it to his breast. 'We've located the missing woman.'

'Safe and well, I trust,' said Bella.

'No, miss,' said the inspector. 'Dead.'

IX

THE HORROR IN THE CARDBOARD TUBE

ELL, there it was. *Dead.* A bloated body had been pulled out of the Thames and though rats had made short work of her face, the dress, reticule and certain papers found on the corpse had led the husband to a positive identification. How tiresome it was.

The wretched Miracle had been formally charged with murder and I was allowed to visit him, giving what assurances I could. Of course, I couldn't possibly take off to Italy at a time like this, I told him. I wouldn't rest until his good name was cleared. That sort of blather.

I missed the boat to Naples and, later that day, slipped off to see the ascetic banker, Mr Midsomer Knight.

'Mr Box, have you been retained by Scotland Yard in this matter?' he positively hissed. 'Really, I cannot see what the deuce business it is of yours.'

Mr Midsomer Knight looked at me coldly as I sat across from him in his frightful, over-furnished Norwood home. I spread my hands before me in a gesture of supplication. 'It is only that I believe Mr Miracle to be entirely innocent of any crime and I wish to help in any way I can in bringing the true perpetrator of this horrid deed to justice.'

Knight gave a small nod so I continued.

'Can you tell me how your wife came to attend Mr Miracle's drawing class?'

Knight thought for a moment. 'It took some convincing, Mr Box, I don't mind telling you.' He placed his hands on the knob of his stick, leaning forward like a minister at his lectern. 'I believe a woman's place is at her husband's side. However, amongst a lady's accomplishments a little music, a little French a little . . . *drawing* are pleasant.'

'You seem to imagine your wife was in training to become a provincial governess.'

'I sought merely to protect her,' he bristled. 'Her . . . disfigurement, you understand. She could not have stood the mocking voices, the averted glances . . .'

'But finally you gave into a little, what shall we call it, female emancipation?'

Knight regarded me coldly. 'She was most insistent. I was surprised, I admit. She had never shown any facility in drawing. But, I thought that, after all, the change would do her good.' He closed his eyes. 'How foolish I was. But there is . . . there *was* . . . a streak of obstinacy in her that I made it my business to stamp out. It was a consequence of the unhealthy amount of freedom she was granted by her first husband.'

I cocked my head. 'Her *first* husband?'

'A free-thinker. It was quite a blessing for her that he passed away.'

I sighed heavily. 'As far as I can see, Mr Knight, there is nothing to suggest that your wife didn't simply leave Miracle's studio a short time after *you* left *her*.'

'And went where?'

'Wherever you prevented her from going in the past.'

Knight's pallid features coloured. 'What the devil are you suggesting?'

I waved a placating hand. 'Merely thinking aloud. Now, would it be possible – I understand how delicate must be your feelings just now – could you tell me how your wife came by her injuries?'

'The police tell me that . . . *rats* had –'

'No, no. Her old injuries.'

The banker's face was impassive. 'Fire.'

'In her younger days?'

'Yes. I believe she was seven- or eight-and-twenty at the time.'

'You did not know her then?'

'Gracious, no. We were married two or three years later. In fact, our anniversary is fast approaching.'

He fumbled in his waistcoat for a moment and produced a

small parcel of tissue paper. Spreading it out on the table before him, he revealed a pair of modestly bejewelled earrings.

'These were to have been my gift. I suppose I will be able to claim back the expense.'

He sniffed lightly and replaced them in his pocket.

I persevered. 'How did you meet?'

'When her previous husband died abroad, my firm sent me to advise her on financial affairs. We became . . . attached. One day, I asked her to marry me, and she agreed. It was a very suitable arrangement.'

I wondered whether he made bank-loans sound as appealing.

I returned home and was astonished to find Delilah waiting in a brougham outside. 'Hevening, sir. Compliments of Mr Reynolds, sir. 'E's 'eard abart Mr Miracle's spot ho' bovver, sir, and wonders hif 'e can be hof hany 'elp.'

'Most kind of him. How lovely to see you restored to health, Delilah. You did give us a turn the other day, you know.'

She clambered from the vehicle as I opened the door of Number Nine. 'Nah. Hit's well known that hi'm himmortal, sir,' she chuckled throatily. 'Unless you cut horf me 'ead and stick ha pike through me 'eart hi'll be 'ere for ha few years yet.'

We stepped inside then, a moment later, I pulled up sharply as Delilah's great thick arm suddenly barred my way. I had the door of the drawing room half open. Something was awry.

'What is it?' I whispered, eyes flashing from side to side.

Delilah stooped to pick up a cardboard tube that was lying on the cork-matting of the hallway floor. One end of it was curiously ragged, as though chewed open.

She stepped in front of me and then beckoned as we made our way silently into the room.

I stopped dead. Lying in a heap, surrounded by letters, was the body of a uniformed postman – stopped dead in a more literal fashion.

'Cor! Look hat 'is bloody face!' gasped Delilah. The skin of his face was hideously inflamed and swollen and almost as black as his boots. 'You reckon the bobby next door let 'im hin?'

I nodded. 'Must have. I was expecting something. Yes. That must be it.'

Clutched in the postman's hands – which were screwed up like rusted keys – was a squarish, brown-paper parcel. 'Get back!' I said, dropping to one knee to examine the body. 'Ah!'

There were two puncture wounds in the right wrist, the skin around them a vile, blistered mess.

'He's been bitten by something,' I whispered.

Delilah looked down at the dead man. 'Come hin this tube, you reckon?' Folding her arms, Delilah looked uneasily around the darkened room. 'Whatever hit was,' she breathed, 'his probably still hin 'ere.'

'Indubitably.'

I glanced down at the Turkey carpet. In the gloom, every shape took on a twisted serpentine form.

'Stay exactly where you are, Delilah,' I murmured. 'I'm going to cross the room and open the curtains. Then we'll get a clearer look at this thing –'

'Stay still, sir! For the love hof God, stay still!' Delilah gasped in genuine horror.

I needed no urging for I could feel a soft, appallingly ticklish movement on my trouser leg. Rooted to the spot, I managed to swivel my gaze around to get a glimpse of the creature, but in the shadows I could make out little more than a spiny shape perhaps a foot in length. It was moving inexorably up my calf.

'What shall hi do?' hissed Delilah.

I rolled my eyes. 'Get the blasted thing off me!'

Shuddering involuntarily, I struggled not to cry out as the creature undulated again and, with its horrible, creeping motion, reached my thigh.

'Light!' I whispered.

Nodding, Delilah crossed clumsily to the window and carefully raised the blinds. Milky light flooded the room.

Delilah's cry of disgust did little to assuage my fears.

I risked a look down. Clamped (there is no other word for it) to my leg was the most disgusting animal I have ever laid eyes upon. Yellowy-black in colour it was somewhere between a scorpion and a centipede, its thick carapace glinting dully like amber beads on a string. Its head – upon which were mounted the vicious pair of pincers that had undoubtedly done for the postman – was moving slowly from side to side in a ghastly, skin-crawling oscillation.

'What his it?' cried Delilah.

'Don't know! Don't care!' I managed to gurgle from between compressed lips. 'We have one advantage on our side though.'

'What's that?'

I peered for a longer moment at the insect-like abomination. Every part of me thrilled with horror at its touch. It was all I could do to stop myself from grabbing the thing and wrenching it from me.

'I think it's blind,' I hissed. 'Must avoid . . . agitating it.'

Delilah nodded slowly. 'Where's your cane? Hi could knock hit off.'

'No!' I swallowed hard, trying not to let my agitation show. 'It'll bite before you could get to it, you dolt!' The creature moved again, its swaying legs pattering hideously against the fabric of my suit.

'Come over here,' I said carefully. Delilah obeyed. 'Now . . . stand behind me . . .'

Beads of salty sweat were puddling in my eyebrows.

Delilah assumed the position, as it were, standing about ten inches behind me.

'Now what?' she said in a high, dry voice.

'Now you must take down my trousers.'

'Heh?'

I tried to steady my breathing. The creature slid further up my leg until it was practically nestling in my groin. 'Don't argue, woman,' I said at last. 'Reach around and unbutton my braces. One . . . at . . . a . . . time.'

She did as she was bidden. Her right hand reached out and slid around my waist, under the waistband of my trousers and found the first button. Her thick, ruddy hands were shaking as she tried to manoeuvre the loop of the braces from around the button.

Without a sound, she brought her left hand to bear on the problem and, after much agonizing fumbling, managed to release first one loop then the next. My trousers sagged slightly.

'Must keep them up!' I croaked. 'If they fall too soon, those fangs will be sunk in me in seconds!'

'Righto,' breathed Delilah. 'Moving to the hother side now. Can you –?'

I could. I moved my own hand down with agonizing slowness and grasped the waistband to keep the trousers taut.

Delilah was already at work on the left-hand braces. The loop slid gently from one, the other was proving more difficult.

'This one's ha bugger,' she muttered. 'Bleeding Tailoring Department and their fiddly ways. Have to go carefully hor else –'

My heart-rate accelerated sickeningly as the second button popped from its stitching with a loud snap and my trousers drooped distinctly.

The insect's head shifted and cocked almost as though it were listening. Its feelers paused in their feeling.

Delilah had moved her attention to the back buttons but I could see from the creature's activity that we had no time for such details.

'It's going to strike!' I screamed. 'Quickly, Delilah. On my word, pull them down and swamp the bloody thing!'

I seemed to draw back from my own flesh as I watched the monster's gleaming head rise, its razor-like pincers juddering and dripping . . .

'Now, Delilah, now!' I cried.

With amazing speed, Delilah whipped down my trousers and wrapped them around the insect as she dragged them to my feet. Wasting not one moment, she stamped her boot heel down hard and repeatedly on the dreadful lump in the material. I winced, despite myself.

A moment later, I had my revolver from my coat and loosed off a round between my own feet. Only as the smoke was rising from the ghastly sticky ooze did I feel able to drag the remains of my trousers over my shoes and hurl them into the corner.

A second attempt on my life! It seemed that someone was absolutely determined to prevent me getting to the heart of this baffling matter. But who?

I set Delilah to work packing my trunk and collapsed into an armchair with a glass of brandy, contemplating mortality. As the invaluable Domestic clumped about upstairs, I sifted through the less lethal portions of my correspondence. I opened the parcel and found inside, as expected, an old book, its pages brittle with age and a square of paper that read *BAIT! Appointment with Quibble – Seven-thirty. 387 Via San Fontanella. M*

Friend Miracle had not let me down. Despite being banged up he seemed still able to pull any amount of strings. He had fixed up an appointment for me with the elusive Professor Quibble and now I had something to entice the Professor into imparting secrets. I turned the book over and the soft binding flashed in the firelight.

Also in the unfortunate postman's pile was a delicately scented note from the divine Miss Bella Pok. I held it to my face and grinned like a love-struck schoolboy. It ran:

Good-bye, devilish Mr Box. Until we meet again.

I placed the note carefully amongst my shirts. The thought of returning to one such as Bella was enough to sustain me through any danger. For now, I had to try to wrap up this Miracle business as expeditiously as possible. I could not afford to miss my appointment in Naples with Quibble. I was unlikely to get a second chance.

X

WHAT KITTY BACKLASH HAD TO TELL

N hour later, Inspector Flush's fat face beamed cheerfully at me from the other side of his desk.

We were in the brown office he called home. There was a little spirit burner in the corner and a quantity of tinned food that led me to believe the inspector kept unsociable hours. Then I noticed a whitish band of flesh on his finger where once a ring must have been. Perhaps Mrs Flush had recently quit the scene.

I had called at the Yard, fully expecting to be fobbed off by some flunky in a helmet, only to find the man himself still at his post, though without a collar and nursing what I think was a mug of brandy.

'Don't you see,' I said. 'It's just as feasible to imagine poor Mrs Knight leaving the Mechanical Institute and being murdered elsewhere as it is Christopher Miracle knocking off the wretched woman in a lavatory!'

Flush made a helpless gesture. 'Mr Miracle is unable to provide us with a witness for his activities between half-past nine and ten o'clock. He could have strangled her and left her in the convenience until later.'

'And carried on an entire class without turning a hair?'

'Some killers are exceptionally cool.'

I gave an exasperated groan. 'But where's the motive, man!'

Flush gave a satisfied smile and produced a long, cream-coloured envelope from his coat. He held it before me like a lure.

'What's this?' I asked.

'It's a copy of Mrs Knight's will. Amongst numerous small bequests is the sum of five hundred pounds to her dedicated art-master, Mr Christopher Miracle.'

'What? Well, what of it? Miracle's filthy rich.'

'Many have killed for less, sir.'

I took the envelope from him and examined the contents. 'Hmm. By that argument, it could look blacker against the husband.'

'The husband?'

'Yes. She leaves him the sum of two thousand pounds, an annuity from her previous husband which ... it seems ... he was unable to control during her life-time.'

'Mr Knight was seen to drive away from the Mechanical Institute.'

'Then he could have employed someone to do it for him.'

'Mr Box –'

'You've met the man, Flush. Even if money wasn't the motive, it's obvious he disapproved of his wife having any kind of social life. When she began to grow more confident and independent he found he couldn't tolerate it and strangled her!'

Flush gave me a hard look. 'You're running away with yourself, sir. What about the glove?'

I waved my hand impatiently. 'Easy enough to steal a lady's glove! And where did this blood come from? The coroner says she was strangled, I believe.'

Flush seemed to consider this for a moment. 'Well, well. I'll bear your theories in mind, sir. Now, if you don't mind, I have rather a lot to be getting on with. I'm afraid this isn't the only case I have on hand.'

I was shown out into a dreary corridor. I thrust my hands into my pockets and walked disconsolately towards the exit, glancing half-heartedly at the walls, scarcely taking in the bills tacked to cork boards, the ugly illustrations of wanted felons, the sooty smears that marked the walls above the cracked gas-lamps. I was utterly stumped as to my next move. It was imperative I get to Naples forthwith, yet how could I leave Miracle in such peril? Would I have to put myself further into Joshua Reynolds's debt by asking him to use his influence? My musings were suddenly interrupted.

'Oh Lor!' came a hoarse shriek. 'Don't 'urt me! Don't 'urt me, please!'

I turned to the left to see a constable 'escorting' a woman from the premises. She appeared to be little more than a heap of dirty electric blue skirts, a grisly-looking drudge, hair all askew.

'You can't just sling me art!'

'You just watch me,' said the policeman.

'But what about me friend?'

The policeman pushed open the door and warm air rolled inside. 'Cor, you're sweating gin, woman! I told you. We got more important things to do than go chasing after your imaginary pals. Now, gertcha!'

He slung the creature through the doorway. As the door swung back, I just caught her croaking call. ''E done 'er in, I know that! That miracle man!'

My ears pricked up and I walked swiftly to the door, which the constable held open for me.

'Evening, sir.'

I gave him a nod and then walked out into the night.

The woman was stumbling to her feet on the steps of the station.

'Forgive me, my dear,' I said, offering my arm. 'Would you like some help?'

She shot me a suspicious glance, then grabbed at my sleeve and hauled herself up.

'We haven't been introduced.' I smiled. 'Lucifer Box.'

'Kitty,' she said, swallowing nervously. 'Kitty Backlash.'

'I couldn't help overhearing you. Something about a miracle?'

She nodded feverishly. 'It's that Mr Miracle. I read the story in the papers. 'E done 'er in!'

'Mrs Knight?'

'No! Mrs Frenzy!'

'Who?'

What was this? *Two* murders poor Miracle was fingered for?

Kitty Backlash blew air noisily from between her lips, making an unpleasantly blubbery sound. 'Couldn't stand us a drink, could you, sir? It's a ruddy long and strange tale I 'ave to tell and I've been tramping 'alfway across town today.'

'Of course. Come on.'

We found a suitably bright and rowdy pub only a street away. I lined up two glasses of gin for my guest, just enough to show I could be generous but also to ensure I got her story while she was still sober.

'Now, Miss Backlash,' I said, sitting down next to her in a corner seat. 'Pray continue.'

She sank a draught of gin and rubbed at her face with a shaking hand.

'It's 'ard to think straight, sir. Honest it is. But I'll start at the start, if you takes me meaning.'

I watched her closely, her ugly face reflecting back even uglier in the shining mirrors of the pub.

'My friend, then, is called Abigail Frenzy. She's a parlour-maid, or was. Worked for a foreign gent over Barnes way. Anyway, one day she says to me, Kitty, I've come into some good fortune. I says, ain't you a maid no more? And she laughs – I've got it easy now. A fiver just for sitting about and scribbling all day.'

I sat up at this. 'What did she mean by that?'

Kitty Backlash scratched at her chin. 'Well, I'll tell you, sir. Seems her employer comes up to her one day, months back and says how would she like to earn proper money? Now Abigail's no slut and I'm sure she thought the gentleman had improper notions, even though she ain't no spring chick, her face must've been a picture, but he says, no, it's nothing like that. Fact is, there's a lady he's sweet on but her 'usband's a terrible brute and he can never get near 'er. Only time she's left on 'er own is when she goes to an art lesson down in Chelsea.'

I leant forward, all attention. 'What is the name of your friend's employer?'

'Don't recall the name. *Foreign*. Great big chap. Eye-talian.'

'Is he, by George?' A little shiver ran through me.

Kitty Backlash drained her second glass of gin. 'Well, anyways,

I'll give you a fiver a week, he says, if you'll only swap places with this lady for an hour or two. She says, well, is she my twin? 'cos otherwise people is going to notice and he smiles and says not to worry because the poor soul's all hidden behind a veil on account of terrible burns she got when she was a gel.'

'And what did your friend Abigail say to this curious request?'

'At first she was having none of it, but then she got to thinking what a lot of money it was for so little a thing. It's always down to lucre, sir, and that's a fact.'

'I have heard it said. Go on.'

'Well, sir, she went ahead with it. Her master 'ad it all worked out. The lady in question would be dropped off by 'er 'usband. She always wore the same violet dress and veil. Soon as she was inside, she went to the lavs – pardon me for speaking so, sir – and out of the other lav would come my friend Abigail in another dress just like 'ers. One in, one out.'

'Like figures on a weather-house,' I said quietly.

'Yes, sir! Just like the pair on them little houses. Abigail'd go in and 'ave 'er lesson and the lady'd sneak away for an hour or two with her lover.'

'Miss Backlash,' I said. 'I cannot tell you how pleased I am to have met you. Now, tell me slowly, what happened next.'

The crone took a big breath and held out her empty glass. 'Difficult to talk, so parched I'm gasping!'

'All the grog you want, just go on with your fascinating story.'

'Couple of weeks back, she came to see me and poured out the 'ole tale. Fact is, she was nervous. She thought Mr Miracle was getting suspicious, on account of her being no good at drawing. Then, just this week – poof! – she vanished.'

'Did you not go to the house where she worked?'

'Yes, sir! But the foreign gent's leaving, they're shutting up the place and wouldn't give me the time of day. I hung about the studio 'oping to see Mr Miracle. Thought maybe he knew where Abigail'd got to. Then I 'eard he'd been arrested for murder and I didn't know what to do and I went to the coppers but they don't want to listen either – oh, sir!'

'All right,' I soothed. 'All right. Landlord! Another two gins here! Tell me, Kitty, did your friend have any . . . distinguishing marks on her person?'

There's nothing quite like a visit to a police mortuary to take the spring out of one's step.

The white tiles of the long, low structure glistened wetly in the gas-light as Inspector Flush led me inside. The room housed three or four long tables, their surfaces mottled with unpleasant stains like a butcher's chopping block. Only one, the furthest from the open door, was occupied.

'Now look here, Mr Box,' said the policeman in a grumbling baritone. 'We can't go exhibiting the dear departed to all and sundry just 'cos of some theory or other. Until we lay our hands on who did in Mrs Knight –'

'The woman over there, Inspector,' I said quietly, 'is not Mrs Midsomer Knight.'

That did the trick.

''Er 'usband identified her,' he protested.

'Identified a bloated corpse with its face eaten – or cut – away.'

Flush scratched his ear and shook his head. 'A 'usband would know 'is own missus.'

'Perhaps not. I didn't enquire as to details, of course, but I got the distinct impression that *relations* had in all probability never occurred between the Knights.'

Flush did not look pleased. 'Did you now? Been doing a little sleuthing have you?'

I slammed my hand on to the stained slab and immediately regretted it. My hands are delicate and shouldn't be trifled with. 'Damn it, Flush! This is important! If I'm right you have a different murdered woman in here.'

'And who might that be?'

'A Miss Abigail Frenzy.'

'Who?'

'I'll explain everything if you'll just let me see the body,' I said exasperatedly.

Flush sighed. 'Very well. But if this is some kind of prank I'll have your bloody vitals, Mr Box.'

'Lights and lungs, my dear chap, if you want them. Shall we get on?'

'I hope you ain't squeamish.'

Now I have always wondered how one gets into undertaking as a profession. Who, other than chaps who get some sort of morbid thrill from it, would want to do such a thing? Like choirmasters and their desire to improve young boys, one always suspects a sinister motive.

So it was that a goggle-eyed, deeply suspicious fellow with a thatch of ginger hair was the one who pulled back the sheet from the faceless corpse with all the gusto of a stage conjuror.

I gave him a look that told him not to enjoy himself too much and he skulked away to join a very green-looking Flush.

The body was that of a woman of about forty-five. Her torso was stained purple (by the wet dress I realized at once) and her rather fine hair matted and weed-clogged. Vermin – or a blunt blade – had indeed been busy on her face for it was little more than a gory hole. This entire case seemed to be a study in wet reds and blacks.

I stooped to examine the neck, which was livid with the bruises of the strangler's hands then turned the corpse's head slightly. It made a horrible stiff clicking sound like a bag of coral being smashed against a wall.

'You have a lens?' I barked at the goggle-eyed assistant.

He produced one. I took it and stooped to examine the ears of the corpse. 'You see?'

Flush took the lens and peered through it. 'See what?'

'The lobes are not pierced for rings.'

'So?'

'*Unlike* those of Mrs Knight,' I cried triumphantly.

'How the devil –'

'I took the liberty of having a little chat with her charming husband. He had recently purchased a pair of earrings as an anniversary present.'

Flush blushed. I pressed on.

'Whoever killed this woman was careful to destroy her face so that we would think it to be the body of Mrs Knight.'

'What? Wait,' pleaded Flush. 'What is all this? Who is this Abigail Frenzy?'

I tapped the lens against my chin. 'The point is, if this is the substitute, then where is Mrs Knight?'

I drew the sheet back over the horror on the morgue slab.

'Perhaps she is still alive!' I announced, almost to myself. 'Flush, if you will come with me to the Swan With Two Necks around the corner I will introduce you to a very interesting lady by name of Kitty Backlash. After that, I trust you will release Mr Christopher Miracle without delay!'

The upshot was that Mr Knight was sent for and Miss Kitty Backlash interviewed. Rather pleased at my virtuoso display, I waited in Flush's office for Delilah to arrive in the brougham. Kitty had given me the address of her missing friend's foreign employer. Now all I had to do was nip down there and collar him before he disappeared. Exactly who he was, I could not be absolutely certain, but suspicions were forming. Which 'great big Eye-talian' with a connection to Miracle had I recently encountered who was just preparing to shut up his house and leave for the Continent? After apprehending the Duce I felt confident I could leave this curious case in Joshua Reynolds's capable little hands while I pursued the business of the missing professors.

Brooding on this, I thumbed through Mrs Knight's particulars once more. Here was the account of the trip to Chelsea by the grim husband. Here was the last will and testament showing the annuity from the *first* husband.

'A free-thinker,' Mr Knight had said.

I glanced thoughtfully at the reams of print.

Then I saw it.

I read the words over four times before I sank back into the chair, my blood running cold.

In faded black ink was the name of Mrs Knight's first husband. The other man in the photograph of the Cambridge Four!

Maxwell Morraine.

XI

THE LIBRARY OF EMMANUEL QUIBBLE

LL the nice girls love a sailor. That they also like secret servicemen is fortunate as yours truly is no Jack tar. Some days later, while my fellow passengers took in the broad curve of Naples harbour on the prow of SS *Mandragora*, I was lying in my cabin two decks below, head wrapped in a wet towel, becoming intimate with the porcelain of the lavatory bowl.

There was a knock at the slatted wooden door and some flunky entered.

'Mr Box, sir?'

'Mmmhhmm?'

'We're here, sir. Naples, sir. Arrived safely and come to tell you, as instructed.'

'Hhhuunnhhh!'

'You just take your time, sir. I'll arrange transportation.'

The door closed behind him.

Like some valetudinarian, I was carried from my cabin and hurried into a carriage scarcely noticing my surroundings at all as my stomach continued to lurch and my head to spin in defiance of having reached terra firma. I planted a 'kerchief to my mouth – the stink of the dockside hitting me at once – and was carried the short distance to my hotel.

A sulphurous yellow building loomed before me and I caught snatched glimpses of the great hot sun and the sapphire of the sky before being ushered into the lobby. For a long moment I stood, swaying on my feet in the sudden darkness, while the concierge attended to the details but soon I was being helped into the cool lift and ferried up, up to the sanctuary of my room.

The page unlocked the door and I stumbled past him, collapsing gratefully on to the bed. As I slipped into blissful sleep, I saw him lowering the blinds over the windows and the great blocks of blinding yellow light were shut out.

Sleep came and more sleep.

I dreamt of burst-open coffins and straw men staggering from within them, of a coach-chase through the landscape paintings on Miracle's walls and of a monstrous regiment of veiled women, unwinding the stained bandages which encircled their heads in some horrid Salome-like bacchanalia.

Blinking awake what seemed like months later I found the room around me cool and dark. One of the veiled women seemed to have followed me through from my dreams, her shroud-like garments fluttering in the breeze, until I sat up on the bed and made sense of the curtains.

Feeling hugely better and absolutely ravenous, I raised the blinds and gazed out on the harbour below. Warm air as fragrant as incense washed over me. The weather – foul for most of the crossing – had cleared, revealing the most glorious blue sky and a strong, healthy sun. The wide road before my hotel was crowded with carriages and strolling couples, white parasols flaring painfully in the light. Close by loomed the ugly Castell dell'Ovo and from its rocky foundations skinny brown fisher-boys, as slippery as eels, were diving into the foam.

Dominating all, naturally enough, was the great volcano of Vesuvius, a fantastic hazy blue shape, its lower slopes verdantly fertile, its summit betraying only the faintest wisp of smoke, like a signal from the Vatican chimney.

Shading my eyes against the glare and breathing deeply, I flipped my watch from my waistcoat pocket and smiled in genuine contentment. I had a noon appointment with Cretaceous Unmann, giving me just enough time to bathe and change. I unpacked and set out my hairbrushes and cologne on the dresser. For sentimental reasons I had brought with me the spelter lancer that Bella had drawn on that memorable day. It would serve to remind me of that lovely personage until this curious case was over and I could return to her side.

I always think best in the bath. With the steam drifting about my ears, I mulled over recent events. As you may have guessed, dear reader, the Duce Tiepolo had indeed been the employer of Miss Kitty Backlash and behind the whole substitution scheme.

But Inspector Flush's men had found Tiepolo's house shuttered and empty. The whole business might have been entirely unconnected to this affair of the professors were it not for the fact that Mrs Knight had once been married to Maxwell Morraine. But how the devil was I to unravel this tangled skein?

A couple of hours later, resplendent in a new dove-grey suit, I descended and launched myself upon old Napoli.

The fresh sea air and the sun on my face were like a tonic after the foetid stink of London and I took my time strolling through the teeming city, passing the great swooping crescent of Bianchi's church before settling down at a table at the Café Gambrinus, a gorgeous beacon of extravagance to which I had become extremely attached on my previous visit. Ah, but what a callow youth I'd been in those days! I recalled the dazzling mirrored interior, fancy cakes and bitter black coffee, Guy de Maupassant arguing over his bill and, of course, the foiling of an attempted assassination of the Prince of Wales by means of a poisoned meringue that had been one of my first triumphs.

The café overlooked the opera house and a square that thrilled with bustling life. A grinning *gelati*-seller was peddling water-ices a few feet from me, his mouth packed with broken brown teeth. Filthy urchins, laughing hysterically and as bothersome as mosquitoes were pestering visitors almost to the point of distraction. The aria in rehearsal at the Opera House soared over all, a wonderful baritone that somehow blended perfectly with the smell of fresh rolls and coffee.

I took out the old book that Miracle had sent me as a lure for Professor Quibble and had just ordered a *pressé* from a fat waiter in a crisp white apron when Unmann arrived. He greeted me, stumbling over a chair and giving me a handshake as weak as a baby's. Unmann was what you might call a Natural Bland.

'Mr Box, I am so glad to see you! Joshua Reynolds wired to say you were on your way. Hot on the trail of Poop's killer, I trust?'

'Perhaps. Have you traced that notepaper?'

'Yes. "K to V.C." was written on the rather good stationery of the Vesuvio Hotel.'

'But you have a residence in the city – what was Poop doing in there?'

Unmann shrugged. 'No idea. Keeping an eye on someone, perhaps?' He rubbed his hands together excitedly. 'But you must let me be your guide here, Mr Box! I can use every scintilla of my local knowledge . . .'

'Your contacts will be essential, Unmann,' I said, sipping my *pressé*. 'I'm interested in the activities of a woman and her husband who lived here back in the seventies.'

'I see.' He took out a pocket book and pencil. 'Their names?'

'Mr and Mrs Maxwell Morraine.'

He wrote the names down with great care. 'Does this have a bearing on the death of Poop?'

'I'm not sure yet. I think, though, that whoever did for him may well be on my trail.'

'Good Lord!'

'There have been two attempts on my life,' I said with studied casualness. I gave him a quick sketch of the chase by coach that had terminated in the cemetery and the incident of the venomous centipede. I omitted the attack in the steam-rooms by Pugg.

'At first I thought them unrelated to this business but I'm not so sure now. They were not merely vulgar attacks and I'm certain they will try again, this time with even greater cunning. You too must be prepared for the gravest danger.' I set my jaw firmly.

'Great Scott,' breathed Unmann.

The poor sap swallowed such stoic babble whole. I hoped it would keep the tick out of my way. He was, of course, the kind of dependable idiot upon whom the Diplomatic is founded but, *really*, was this the best they could do these days? If the king had any inkling of the state of things he'd probably pop *another* button off his waistcoat.

'Also, I need to know if someone called the Duce Tiepolo has recently re-entered the country.'

Unmann paused in his scribbling. 'Illicitly?'

'I should think so. The new regime chucked him out. He has some curious connection to the business in hand.'

I snapped my fingers and ordered Unmann a cup of coffee. When it came he drank it in one swift gulp.

'Finally,' I continued, 'I want whatever information you can dig up about the firm of Thomas Bowler, undertaker of London and Naples.'

Unmann nodded, scratching hurriedly in his pocket-book.

'Will you stay for lunch?' I offered, stomach rumbling.

'Can't, I'm afraid,' he jabbered. 'Office in a frightful mess. Got all old Jocelyn's papers to sort through. Quite big shoes to fill. Now I'll get on to these names just as soon as I can, Mr Box. I'll cable the Santa Lucia if there's any news. Got to dash –' He glanced down at Poop's book. 'Holiday reading, eh? Might I ask –?'

'You may not. *Most* secret.' I flashed him my wide smile. 'Good day to you.'

With a nod, Unmann was gone. At length, I ordered scrambled eggs and spiced sausage and turned my attention to the book. It was some kind of novel from what I could glean. And it must be precious indeed if it were to whet the appetite of the famous Sir Emmanuel Quibble.

The venerable scholar had always been, according to my researches, an exceptionally gifted man. He had shown extraordinary facility for music and the arts before turning his mind towards scientific matters at the ripe old age of seven after conducting a remarkable experiment with a song thrush and a vacuum tube. Tragically, only a few years later, he had been thrown from a gelding, sustaining a spinal injury that kept him confined, forever after, to a wheeled-chair. Ill-health had turned into a kind of mania and now he was said to positively thrive on his allergic reaction to the nineteenth (no, I keep forgetting, the *twentieth*) century. In recent years the old fellow had withdrawn entirely from the world, moving to Italy and taking solace in his unrivalled library of arcane literature. Now I was being granted the rare privilege of entry to this inner sanctum. What would I find there?

I sat for a while with eyes closed, listening to the muffled aria that thrilled through the sunshine. How I loved Italy! The heat assuaged by salty air, bright with dragon-flies humming over starched white tablecloths. I caught sight of a woman a few tables from me. She had her back to me and I took the opportunity to drink in the details of her exquisite carriage.

She wore a splendid canary-yellow creation with a high, transparent collar, tight against her throat and her hair was hidden beneath the brim of a huge oval hat. Of course, there are few things in life more deceptive than a person's back view. How many times have you yourself spotted someone at the theatre or on the underground whose magnificent bearing and gorgeous, swan-like neck have lured you into a state of unconditional lust? Only to discover, as they bend to read, to adjust a shoe or step off the staircase, that they have a face like a Transylvanian fish-wife.

I ordered tea with lemon and sat with my chin on my hand, surveying the lovely, graceful woman before me who would, any moment now, turn and reveal herself to be a gorgon.

The woman seemed to be listening to the aria as well. Her head was cocked attentively. I imagined she was smiling. At last she shifted in her seat and the sunshine illumined her face.

My teacup clattered on to its saucer.

The woman was Bella Pok.

I rose and, raising my hat, stepped into her line of sight. Shading her eyes, she smiled sweetly at me as though we had simply run into one another at the Café Royal.

'Lucifer!' she cried. 'I'm so delighted. I had anticipated traipsing all over Naples to find you and yet here you are, large as life.'

She gestured to a chair and I sank into it. 'I don't suppose this is a coincidence?'

'Not a bit,' she said with a grin. 'You really can't expect a girl to return to her drab little existence after becoming involved in Mr Miracle's adventure! Whatever's going on, I yearn to be part of it. Please say you'll have me!'

Which is the sort of invitation one longs to hear from such as Mademoiselle Pok.

I shook my head, however. 'There is nothing going on. As I told you, I have business here in Naples which I hope to combine with a little sketching. You know it is vital for we daubers to refresh ourselves now and then.'

She looked hard at me.

'Don't be so disappointing,' she said.

I sighed. 'I'm afraid I must escort you back to your hotel, Miss Pok,' I said, 'and then put you on the first boat back to England.'

'You certainly shan't put *me* anywhere.'

'Bella –'

'I want to be at your side, Lucifer!'

'On no account!' I snapped.

'But if there's nothing to fear, then why ever not? Am I such an embarrassment?'

'Of course not.'

'Well then.'

She sighed and sat back in her chair, the brim of her hat eclipsing the dazzling disc of the sun. 'Whatever can I do to persuade you?'

Well, she didn't have to do much in the end. Fact is, I was fearfully besotted with her and her boldness in following me to Naples had only endeared her more to me. Over a kir or three, she cajoled and argued until all I could think of was the glow of her lovely face and the wide, inviting mouth I so longed to kiss.

'Very well,' I said at last. 'If you mean to stay then you are

welcome. But this is no holiday for me. You must excuse me if I
have to . . . dash off at the most inopportune moments.'

'Of course.'

'May I see you to your hotel?'

She was staying, appropriately enough, at the Vesuvio. We made
an appointment to meet there the next day and I walked back to
the Santa Lucia, *whistling* if you don't mind.

Well, she would certainly help take my mind off the business in
hand. The danger was that she would do so too effectively. I had
work to do in Naples. This was not a honeymoon.

After dressing for dinner I hailed a cab and barked out
Quibble's address in my ever-so-good Italian. I am, naturally, a
master of languages. I have, in addition to robust Eye-tie, a little
French, a little German and some particularly filthy Latin. I am
also quite good at American.

Stooping to conquer with a '*Pronto!*', I was ferried away up the
steep slopes of the old city towards Capodimonte.

The weather had deteriorated into a stinker of an evening.
Sweaty mist hung in great miasmic wreaths around the jumble of
crumbling stucco, my carriage cutting a coffin-shaped swathe
through it as we climbed ever higher. The humidity was so thick
that the traffic seemed scarcely to move at all. I could hear the soft
clop of horseshoes on the cobbles, muffled by the atmosphere as
though for a funeral.

As we ascended the mountain, the mist cleared slightly to reveal
verdant countryside thick with dark olive groves until, at last, the
carriage drew to a halt. Six or seven lonely cottages clustered
around the edifice of a mansion like mournful piglets around a
long-dead sow.

It must have been a grim place at the best of times, but on an
oppressive evening like this one, I felt positively mournful as I
bid the driver wait and made my way up the weed-throttled
gravel to the gates. Thick creepers were enmeshed in every part
of the ironwork, as though a mob trying to get in had been

turned, by some spell, into a jungle of rain-rotted vegetation.

I pulled at the bell and ran a finger under my stiff collar.

Presently, the gates juddered open, squealing as they were hauled over ground thick with a sediment of dead leaves.

'Good evening,' I said to the ancient butler who emerged around the edge of the gate.

'Good evening, sir. Mr Box, is it? Sir Emmanuel is expecting you, sir.'

'You're English?'

'Naturally, sir. As are the entire staff. My name is Stint. Might I advise you to loosen your garments, sir?'

'Beg pardon?'

'It is a trifle warm within, sir,' he wheezed.

He was like a column of smoke in livery. Pale eyes, pale face, wispy white hair and whiskers. To my very great surprise he appeared to be shirt-less beneath his threadbare uniform.

Stint kicked the front door to open it, so swollen was the woodwork. Once inside, he ushered me down a stifling corridor, the once-bright blooms of its wallpaper faded into bleak greys. Piled high in heaps all along the walls, their cloth bindings waxy with age, were hundreds of books.

'It's very . . . um . . . dark, Stint,' I said at last, removing my coat.

'No lamps, sir.' He shook his white head mournfully. 'Sir Emmanuel does not care for the light, you see. I have been trying to persuade him as to the virtues of the electricity. But that, as they say, will be the day.'

The room I now entered was fat with books. They lined the walls, covered the floor, hung around in tottering heaps in the shadowed corners. The combined mass of ruddy old leather and faded gilt should have lent the room a jolly air, but the fire blazing in the hearth made the place like a hot-house.

The firelight illuminated the figure of Emmanuel Quibble, swathed in black like some behemothal spider. The impression was reinforced by a number of mahogany reading-stands that

projected from his chair on telescopic appendages thus allowing him to consult as many as eight or nine volumes at any one time.

He wheeled himself forward with one china-blue hand. The other, inevitably, clutched a book over his blanket-covered lap. He was probably sixty-odd yet contrived to look twice that. What little hair he had was of an almost translucent blond, as though old straw had been carelessly applied to his scalp with gum. Forever in the habit of licking his lips, an angry red halo had developed around them and his eyes were nigh on invisible behind a pair of ancient, filthy, thickly lensed pince-nez.

Chuckling at the sight of me, he held out his hand and I gingerly gripped the perished-apple knuckles.

'Sir Emmanuel,' I cooed. 'It is indeed an honour.'

'Of course it is! Lucifer Box, eh? Can't say I've heard of you. You're some sort of painter, I gather. I do not normally grant interviews but I was told you had something that might interest me,' he said, adjusting his spectacles. 'Well, pray be seated. Do not mind those volumes. Move them along. There is a very pretty space there by Bleasdale's *Tales of Surgical Misadventure*. There now!'

I squeezed myself into a chair by the roaring fire.

'Are you cold?' he asked, suddenly.

I was already perspiring horribly. 'Quite comfortable, thank you.'

Quibble shook his head mournfully. 'It is like a tomb in here. I can never get warm. The servants complain that I stifle them but how can they object to a fire in December!'

'It is July, sir,' I said carefully.

'Is it?' He began a high cackling sound, exposing tiny peg-like teeth. 'Perhaps I am too cold-blooded. My doctors tell me I have a thin hide.'

I smiled indulgently. 'I wonder you don't have yourself dust-jacketed.'

'What's that?' He cupped a withered hand around his ear.

'You ought to equip yourself with a dust-jacket, Sir Emmanuel,' I shouted. 'Like one of your famous collection.'

He liked that and cackled some more. 'Capital idea! I know just the men for the job. Grindrod and Spicer of Camden Town. Let me see. Hmm.' He extended his stick-like arms before him and looked them up and down as though contemplating the measurement of a suit. 'Yes, blue card with calf-skin end-boards. I think I should go very well just above your head, Mr Box, between *Patterson's Pathology of the Goitre* and *Rabelaisianism*. Can I tempt you with a Madeira? No? Then perhaps we shall eat.'

He rang a little glass bell. I lifted my Gladstone and took out the book that Miracle had sent me. Quibble eyed it hungrily.

'What is it? Let me see!'

I lifted the volume and held it up to the firelight. The title glinted like gold in a stream.

Quibble let out a little cry and wheeled himself towards me with feverish speed.

'It isn't? Can it be? *Daniel Liquorice!*'

'It is.'

I placed the book in his shaking hands. 'I believe it is somewhat scarce,' I said blithely.

'Scarce?' Quibble almost shook with pleasure. 'It is practically unique. *Daniel Liquorice!* In my hands!'

With great care he opened the book and raised it close to his bespectacled face. '"Being an account of the journey of an itinerant gentleman in His Majesty's East Indies",' he read. 'Heggessey Todd's lost masterpiece! Where did you find it, Mr Box? Where?'

He wriggled in his chair like a wormy baby, his tongue flashing around his raw mouth in a little circle.

'I have my sources,' I said, tantalizingly. 'Perhaps we can come to terms over dinner.'

'Yes, yes! Naturally. You must be fed!'

He rang the bell again with renewed urgency. A servant came to the door. Quibble barked orders at him then turned again to me.

'Mr Box, would you mind?'

He waved a skinny hand at his wheeled-chair. I rose and began to push him through into the dining room.

Paintings of what appeared to be Quibble's ancestors were just visible behind yet more staggered heaps of books, varnished eyes staring out in mute appeal, as though their owners were drowning in yellowed paper.

I pushed the wizened man to the head of the table where he sat cradling *Daniel Liquorice* as though it were a child. 'Name your price, my dear sir. I have dreamed of owning this book since –'

'It's not money I want, Sir Emmanuel,' I murmured. 'But information.'

'Information?'

I walked to the opposite end of the table where I found my chair being pulled out by another servant. Dressed, like Stint, in rather mouldering livery, a patina of dust covered his dulled silver buttons and epaulettes. He was a tall young lad with a pebble-smooth face and close-cropped hair. His eyes were very blue under dark brows as bold as strokes of charcoal.

He turned to the soup tureen and placed the lid gently at my side, fixing me with a look I can only describe as impudent. He smiled.

'Evening, sir,' he said, ladling beetroot soup into the dish before me. The voice was throaty from tobacco. Another relic from Blighty, it seemed.

'Good evening,' I said.

He bent low, suddenly, till his face was right by mine. He smelled of honey. 'Charles Jackpot, sir.'

Then, bless me if he didn't wink. 'But you can call me Charlie.'

XII

A LONDON DERRIÈRE

SAID nothing and turned my attention to the beetroot soup.

The nosh was dusty but passable. The soup was followed by a kind of salmon pastry and, after my new acquaintance, Mr Jackpot, had cleared this away, by an absolutely magnificent goose. Quibble clearly remained insulated against Italian notions of cuisine.

Eschewing the grimy napkin, I sucked the grease from my fingers as the servant cradled the dishes in his arms. He didn't speak, merely fixing me with the same impudent gaze. In the glow of the fire he had the face of a Renaissance saint. It was most unnerving.

Clearing my throat, I wiped the dust from Quibble's best crystal and poured myself a generous glass of plonk. I watched Charlie Jackpot as he loped back, with what I can only call a swagger, towards the kitchens.

Quibble turned a page in the book. 'Now, sir. May we get to business? I cannot rest easy until I know this volume to be mine. Time and tide, you know. They wait for no man.'

He craned his neck and peered back into the other room, as though it pained him to be separated from his library for more than a few moments.

'If you should like to know precisely how long they *do* wait, I have a volume on the subject. I believe it is over there between *On the Dangers of Bicycling* and *Coprolites of the Permian*.' Quibble licked his lips till his spittle glistened on their flaking surface.

I felt inside my coat and produced the photograph I had taken from Professor Sash's study. I slid it down the table towards the invalid and watched Quibble carefully as he lifted the photograph and held it about an inch from his spectacles. He coughed throatily. It was a sound like brown paper crackling in an oven.

'Where . . . where did you get this?'

'It was among the . . . er . . . personal effects of Professor Frederick Sash.'

Quibble's head snapped up. 'Effects? He's not dead, is he? Sash isn't dead?'

I nodded. 'And his body stolen. Along with another of the gentlemen in that photograph. Eli Verdigris.'

'Verdigris too? *How?*'

'That remains a mystery. I am investigating the matter, sir, and believe you can be of material assistance.'

Quibble heaved a heavy sigh. 'I hear nothing out here you see. Sometimes I think it was folly to leave the old country but I could get nothing done. The constant distractions! My great burden is work – so much that I am called upon to do!' His tongue flashed around the wet hole of his puckered mouth in great agitation.

'What of the other man in the photograph, Maxwell Morraine?'

'*Morraine?*'

'Yes. I'm sure you know he died out here some years ago.'

The old man suddenly fixed me with a malevolent stare. 'Who are you? What do you mean by bringing this volume here as though I were some horse-trader? What is the real reason for your visit, hm?'

He waved the photograph at me, his shrivelled mouth turning down into a snarl. 'You want to bring all *that* up again!' he yelled. 'Well, it won't wash, d'you hear me? Let the dead rest in peace!'

'All what, sir?'

'Get out, sir! Out! Stint!'

He grabbed at the glass bell and rang it until I feared it would shatter.

I shot to my feet. 'Forgive me, Sir Emmanuel, but I am convinced you are in grave danger –'

'*Stint!*'

The doors sprang open and the pale servant was framed there. 'Sir?'

Quibble writhed in his chair, shaking his bulbous head till

cowlicks of sparse hair tumbled from behind his ears and his book-tentacles rattled. 'Show this *person* out! You are never to admit him into my house again.'

'Sir Emmanuel, please –' I began.

Stint was at my elbow. 'If you wouldn't mind, sir?'

'I believe that a long-buried secret is threatening your life, sir, and that of a very noble friend of mine. Please, help me to find –'

'*Out!*'

I was escorted through the gloomy corridors and shown out into the muggy night.

Well, that hadn't gone very well at all, had it?

Old Stint shook his head mournfully. 'I do beg your pardon, sir. I've never seen the master so upset.'

'Stint,' I said earnestly. 'I have serious reason to believe Sir Emmanuel to be in danger of losing his life. Watch him carefully and contact me should you notice anything suspicious. Do you understand?'

He nodded.

'I am staying at the Hotel Santa Lucia. *Anything* suspicious, mind. And tell your master that the book is a gift. A gesture of my good faith.'

I pushed open the protesting gate and made my way back on to the drive. Grateful for the comparative cool, I stretched and took a deep breath before setting off for the carriage.

As I moved off, however, there came the sound of a match being struck and then a tiny point of amber light glowed in the shadows as someone inhaled greedily on a cigarette.

Sidling up to the gates once more I was somehow unsurprised to find the servant Jackpot loitering there. He smiled and the cigarette in his lips poked upwards, the curling smoke causing him to narrow his very blue eyes.

'Hullo,' he muttered.

I touched my fingers to the brim of my hat and began to move off back towards the road.

Suddenly the boy pushed his face to the railings and, after briefly looking about, spoke in an urgent whisper.

'If you wanna see something of importance, Mr Box, meet me in town. Tomorrow. Midnight.'

'Meet *you*? Why ever should I do that?'

'Via Santa Maria di Costantinopoli. The house with the crimson light. You won't regret it.'

Now it was my turn to smile. 'Won't I? And what could you possibly have that would interest me?'

His answer shocked me for a moment or two. For, stepping back a little from the railings, he suddenly thrust two fingers up at me.

Before I had time to react, he curled two fingers of his other hand into a semicircle and banged them against his palm. The penny dropped. Here was a 'V' and now a 'C'.

I nodded.

The servant flicked his cigarette into the shadows. 'Midnight tomorrow.'

And with that he was gone.

Next day, as arranged, I called on Miss Bella Pok at her hotel. The sunshine had completely deserted us and there was a squally feel to the weather, combined with a high, keening wind echoing banshee-like over the land. After breakfast, at Bella's insistence, we took a two-wheeler along the coastal road until we reached the outlying plains of the great volcano, its peak scarcely visible in the yellowy fog. She had a yen, you see, to travel on the famous funicular railway that had been constructed with great ingenuity (and no little bravery) right up the slopes of the grumbling peak, terminating just short of the cone itself.

'I'm sure there are more interesting ways of passing the time,' I said, smiling my wide smile.

Bella touched a gloved hand to my arm. 'But aren't you fascinated by it, Lucifer? The boiling energy beneath our very feet? The fiery lava just waiting to erupt?'

Well, I was, of course. But just then it wasn't Vesuvius's fiery lava that was on my mind.

There was a station on the lower slopes that resembled nothing so much as a small desert fort, its flat roof thick with grey volcanic dust. I bought the tickets and we watched as the wind whipped balls of dust and old newspaper to worry at the feet of us travellers. A big clock struck two and we got aboard the cramped train carriage, watching the bleary sunlight glinting off the cable wires that stretched ahead up the slopes of the volcano.

The carriage – a curious thing built in a stepped arrangement like a mobile block of steps – was half-empty. Bella sat down on one of the steps, staring with animated curiosity out of the filthy windows. Next to us was an old woman with a bag of knitting and a couple of American boys in offensively loud checked suits and wide-awake hats, already loudly proclaiming the mountain's incredible majesty, though all we could see so far was greasy ash. As we crawled up the sheer slope, great filthy clouds of sulphur billowed over the roof of the train, condensing on the windows like poisonous teardrops.

I suddenly noticed a young man sitting on the step above me. I received a quick impression of neat black suit and long auburn hair. His eyes were huge and brown, his nose slightly snubbed as though he had gently pressed it to a window-pane. He lifted his hat and smiled dazzlingly.

'You are impressed?' he asked.

I didn't know if he meant by the volcano or himself.

'Very,' I said.

Bella glanced up and the stranger smiled.

'Please forgive me, you are Signor Box, yes?'

I nodded.

'My name is Victor,' he said, holding out his gloved hand. I gripped it firmly and introduced Bella.

He took Bella's hand and kissed it gently. 'Our mutual friend, Signor Unmann,' Victor continued, 'expresses his regrets and begs that you accepted me as your guide in his stead.'

'Ah,' I said, losing all hope of useful information from my supposed man in the field.

'You know the mountain well?' asked Bella.

The young man took a deep breath of the frankly noxious air. 'For me, Vesuvius is like a drug. I cannot help but travel up these slopes whenever I have the chance – even though I live here in Napoli.'

'Yes,' I coughed. 'Intoxicating. Known Mr Unmann long have you?'

'Oh we are old . . . how do you say? *Chums*. Yes. Old chums. Now tell me, after we have been up and down the great Vesuvius – like the Grand Old Duke, yes? – what would you like to see? Naples is such a thrilling city.'

Bella began at once to itemise every last church in the place and I was slightly relieved when the guard called out '*Destinazione!*' and our carriage creaked and wheezed its way into the upper station.

Victor got nimbly to his feet and ushered us out of the train into a cloud of ash-filled steam. I wasn't sure I wanted this little Eyetie crowding my afternoon with Bella and made plans to get shot of him just as soon as we returned to the Funicular station.

We set foot on black volcanic soil. Bella looked down at her feet and lifted her boots.

'Are you all right, my dear?' I asked.

She grinned. 'Just checking that they hadn't begun to spontaneously combust.'

Only three hundred yards from where we stood, the immense caldera of the volcano glowed an intense orange, plumes of white smoke belching from the sizzling rock. The heat was so intense I could feel the tiny hairs on my hands shrinking. I wished I'd worn gloves. Exposure to the Neopolitan sunshine was already threatening to tan me like a navvy.

I turned my face away from the oven-like heat. Victor stood his ground and shook his head in wonderment. 'What a magnificent thing she is!'

'Been quiet for a while has it?' I asked.

He grinned. 'A sleeping giant.'

'But not likely to turn over in her sleep any time soon?'

'You never can tell,' chirped Victor gaily. 'Come, let us go closer.'

He led the way forward. It was easy to spot the fairly fresh lava flows that lay in petrified streams all about us and I shielded my eyes against the glare from the boiling ground.

Victor closed his eyes. Smoke curled over and about his slim frame like ghostly vipers and we stood for a few silent moments amongst the blackened landscape. Bella clambered onto a great square boulder of volcanic rock and pointed down at the verdant plain. 'What is that?'

Far below us lay a collection of whitish buildings, scattered like child's blocks in the greenery.

'That is Pompeii,' said the youth. 'Look there if you wish to see what fearful power the Earth truly has within her.'

We lingered on top of the volcano for some little time with our new acquaintance chatting amiably throughout. Bella seemed quite taken with him but I felt curiously out of sorts. Perhaps it was the impending appointment with the mysterious servant Jackpot. At any rate, I was grateful to get back into the funicular and begin the descent.

Bella noticed how preoccupied I'd become.

'You seem troubled, Lucifer,' she said, crossing to where I stood by the misted window.

I patted her hand. 'Forgive me, my dear. Not quite comfortable in my own skin today, if you see what I mean.'

She nodded, smiled. 'It seems a shame. It's such a bonny skin.'

Our eyes locked for a moment, blue to green. We had the whole evening yet. Was this an invitation . . . ?

All thoughts of a jolly tumble with the divine Miss Pok were temporarily banished, however. As the funicular pulled into the station, I happened to glance through the milling crowds at the exit. At once a huge, barrel-chested figure caught my gaze, dressed in a heavy black coat and hat, his indigo-coloured spectacles lending his face a skull-like air.

'My God!' I breathed. 'Tiepolo!'

I raced to the exit door of the carriage and banged the heel of my hand against the woodwork as the vehicle clanked with painful tardiness into the station.

'What is it?' cried Bella concernedly.

I craned my neck to see the Duce Tiepolo's bear-like figure receding into the crowd.

'Forgive me, Bella,' I yelled, wrenching open the door. I turned and addressed the young man, Victor. 'Sir, would you be kind enough to escort this lady back to the Vesuvio Hotel? Can't explain now!'

I was just aware of Bella's vaguely baffled expression and young Victor raising his hat as I tore from the funicular and out into the station. Barging through the crowd of tourists, I clattered down towards the plain, just in time to see Tiepolo slip into the back of an expensive-looking motorcar which chugged away in a cloud of yellow dust.

I returned to my hotel and changed into evening dress for my appointment with Jackpot, dashing off a note of apology to Bella. I found a pleasant café by the quayside where I downed a few kirs. The Duce Tiepolo was here in Naples! And to risk recapture he must have a very good reason. But what connection did he have to Mrs Knight, her first husband, Morraine, and, by extension, to the professors? That old Quibble was in danger I was now certain but why, if Naples were the locus of this mystery, had he not already been done away with? Perhaps he was the *source* of the danger! Yet his reaction to the deaths of his old colleagues had been genuine enough. Quibble was no dissembler. 'You want to bring all that up again,' he had raged. All what? There had been no word from Unmann regarding the import/export business of the curious undertakers but here, at last, was a lead of sorts. This young man Charlie Jackpot appeared to know something. I clapped my topper to my head and set off for the ancient heart of the city.

The steady chirrup of insects kept me company as I walked the gas-lit avenues of Decumano Maggiore, its cobbles worn into ruts by the traffic of the centuries.

The premises on Via Santa Maria di Costantinopoli were distinguishable from their low and unhealthy-looking neighbours only by the ruby-red light above the lintel. The gas-flame behind the cheaply stained shade shuddered like a rheumy, winking eye.

I made my way softly down the steps to the door. It bore no knocker, nor number of any kind. I had raised my hand when it groaned open, seemingly of its own accord. Shudder not, reader, this is not a spook story! Whatever agency lay behind the door was most assuredly human.

Actually, I must immediately qualify that remark as what lay behind the door appeared to be a monkey. In the light of the sallow gas-jets I could make out poorly papered walls weeping with damp and the stooped figure of whom I spoke: a curious man with very long arms, dressed in green velvet plush. His hair, scraped from a centre parting *en brosse*, stank of oil.

He cocked his pallid face to one side by way of an interrogative. What should I say? Was his master at home?

I took off my top hat with as much nonchalance as I could muster and decided to be bold. 'I understand that a young man of my acquaintance is expecting me. We're old pals and I haven't spoken to him for some time. I wonder –'

The little creature seemed uninterested in my story, however. He moved to the back of the dismal hallway, nodding absently, and drew aside a disreputable-looking curtain.

The monkey-man smiled grimly, his mouth like a wound. '*Si, si. Uno ragazzo.*'

I was spared any more of his charming conversation, however, by the sudden appearance of Mr Jackpot himself from behind the drawn curtain. He was wearing a slovenly jacket and trousers, both too big for him, the pantaloons held to his hips by a thick brown belt and a good two inches shy of his stripe-socked shins. In stark contrast, his collarless shirt seemed clean and there was a white rosebud in his lapel.

'Hullo,' he said.

I gave a little bow.

Jackpot smiled lop-sidedly, his large lips sending dimpled echoes over his cheek. 'Won't you come in, sir?'

He gestured into the darkness. I followed without a word. The tiny doorman melted away into the gloom – for all I knew, he had gone back into the wallpaper from which he had sprung.

I was ushered into a small, square chamber, underlit and over-heated. Perhaps Jackpot had become accustomed to his master's tastes. The décor seemed all of a piece with the grisly entranceway; there was a brass-framed bed containing a stained mattress, and a jug and wash-bowl on a spindly table. On a Turkey rug sat a drab *chaise-longue* of surpassing vileness. A miserable fire sputtered in the grate, damp sea-coal popping and spitting against faded Dutch tiles.

'How nice,' I said at last.

The boy closed the door behind me and took my hat, coat and gloves like the good and faithful servant he was.

I lit a cigarette to disguise the smell and tossed one to Jackpot who ignited his from the fire. Moving to the sofa, I flapped aside the tails of my coat, prior to sitting. I stopped with my rear end halfway to the upholstery. 'May I?'

'Of course, sir,' said Charlie. He hovered by the door a moment, wiping his hands over the greasy fabric of his jacket. Then: 'Might I join you, sir?'

I was already lounging back as if I owned the place. I waved a hand and bid him do so.

As he sat down next to me, I pushed him sideways with my leg and, grabbing at his cropped hair, pulled back his head until he yelled in pain. His fag dropped to the dirty floor.

I smiled. 'I believe you have something to tell me.'

Charlie scowled and fixed me with a penetrating and vaguely unnerving stare. I tugged his head back still further but he had stopped yelling. 'That won't get you anywhere,' he murmured in a low voice.

'Then perhaps this will,' I cried, grabbing my pearl-handled revolver from beneath my shirt. I pressed the cold barrel to the youth's temple and glared at him. 'Now. What precisely do the initials VC mean to you?'

But still he seemed unmoved. I watched as his Adam's apple bobbed slowly up and down.

Charlie Jackpot just smiled.

Irritated by my failure to intimidate him, I moved the revolver slowly down his smooth face and pushed the barrel between his lips. Charlie's very blue eyes regarded me levelly over the glinting gunmetal.

I withdrew the pistol from his mouth with ill-grace.

'There now,' said Charlie with a smirk. 'Isn't this nicer?'

Mr Jackpot turned his huge eyes on me in a kind of mute enquiry. A moment later he put his hand on my thigh.

Well, what was I to do? For the well-bred gentleman there was surely only one recourse. I fucked him.

XIII

L. B. TO V. C.

HARLIE Jackpot had that annoying knack of looking ravishing even in sleep. He lay stretched over the burst stuffing of the chaise, starkers except for his striped socks. Whatever these had once possessed by way of elastic had long since perished and they hung slackly over his white shins like discarded caterpillar pupae.

For myself, I sat on a creaking chair, also in the buff, relishing the gorgeous glow of the fire as I contemplated this most recent act of naughtiness. You are shocked, are you not? Or, perhaps, reading this in some distant and unimaginably utopian future like that funny little man Mr Wells would  have us believe in, you are not shocked at all! Fact is, Lucky Lucifer here has still more secrets. My arsenal is formidable – a sentence which comes across more interestingly in a French accent.

As you know, there is no service I am unprepared to render for King and country, and I am not averse to a pretty face and a pretty rump, whether they be man's or woman's (I draw the line at beasts, unlike at least one member of the Cabinet). It is the prerogative of the secret agent to be (and to have!) whatever he fancies, don't you agree? This is not a privilege extended to the population at large, as I found when I was discovered in a house off the Bow Road – the incident that brought me to the attention of Joshua Reynolds. The old dear helped extricate me from that spot of bother but saw it as a very useful way of getting me on to his payroll. In the yellow-backed novels it is known as *blackmail*.

You must remember that London was in a bit of a panic, with the recent exigencies of Mr O.F.O'F.W. Wilde so fresh in the memory, and J.R. had me by the unmentionables. The compensation was that my divers assassinations took me all over the globe where the love that dared not speak its name was positively encouraged to bellow from the rooftops. Such as in old Napoli, it seemed.

Still, it was a dangerous game and I was in no great hurry to do two years' hard labour just for a frolic with some dolly renter.

Charlie opened a sleepy eye (exhausted, poor thing) and smiled his simian smile. Reaching over to my discarded coat, I retrieved my cigarette case and lit a fag for myself and then for him, padding naked over the cheap carpet to the *chaise* and delicately inserting the cigarette between his kiss-crushed lips. Charlie sucked in the smoke as though his life depended on it and let it rise over his mouth like the curly tips of a ghostly moustache.

'Ta,' he said softly.

'How much do I owe you?'

'Owe me?'

'For services rendered.'

The boy dragged on the cigarette. 'My pleasure.'

I bowed my head. 'Then, tomorrow, you must at least allow me to buy you a bun.'

Charlie draped himself across my lap with his knees up. Gazing into my face he idly scratched his balls. I could feel his hot feet against my thigh. "Spect you're wondering why I was so forward with you,' he said at last.

'Forward?'

'You know. This evening at the old fella's place.'

I blew smoke into his face.

'Young men often throw themselves at me. I've come to regard it as something of a burden.'

'I'd seen you before.' He grinned.

'Really? At Ascot? Windsor? I was in Mentone last summer, perhaps we met there?'

He scowled again, rather pleasingly, and wiped at his nose. 'Do you know where you are?'

'Yes. A filthy knocking shop for undiscerning tourists.'

Charlie got to his feet and perched on the edge of the table, crossing one foot over the other. 'No, no. There's a little more to it than meets the eye.'

I grunted sceptically. In my experience there's very rarely more to these places than meets the eye.

'This one's different,' he said quickly. 'Better even than that big yellow house in Islington.'

That was where he'd first spotted me! A Hallowe'en Masque held by a very pretty couple called Flora and Walter Paste. I had come as the Prince of Darkness (of course) and come *across* a fetching Succubus in very tight fleshings. It had been a night of grand indiscretion. Lawks. No wonder Jackpot been so damned impudent at Quibble's.

'It's supposed to be strictly members only but I know a trick or two. Get your togs on.'

'I am not in the habit of obeying orders.'

'All right. But it's the only way you're gonna find out about the VC.'

I pulled up my braces. 'Very well. Shall we get on?'

Charlie dressed quickly with the abandon of one who cares little for his appearance. Curbing my natural instinct to spend at least an hour getting back into my clothes I graciously allowed Charlie to help me with my collar studs and cuffs. I shrugged on my cut-away and, moments later, looking only a little the worse for wear, followed him back out into the corridor.

Several identical doors studded the shoddy walls, plaster hanging like rotten cloth in the spaces in between. The place reeked of damp. There was no sign of the ape-like doorman.

Charlie walked on ahead, ignoring these doors, all of which undoubtedly led to similar bleakly furnished rooms.

As we advanced I became aware that we seemed to be moving almost imperceptibly but inexorably *downwards*. Also, the corridor's decoration stabilized so that smooth expanses of crimson wall began to emerge, as though we were travelling along an artery and had left behind some morbid and diseased junction.

I flipped my watch from my waistcoat. Nearly two o'clock in the morning. From ahead of us came a curious subdued hubbub. Music. Chatter. What I can only call *carousing*.

We had come to the end of our journey. Before us stood a massive set of ebony doors. They looked very old indeed, banded in iron and carved into grotesque, leering faces.

Charlie gave me a strange smile and then hammered on the doors, like some scruffy Black Rod. The doors shuddered open. I caught a vague impression of a hulking doorman with whom Charlie exchanged either words or a kiss. Then I was ushered through.

Beyond the doors was a vision of Hell.

Don't fret. It is Lucifer's domain, after all.

The chamber we had entered was very large and lit by dim gaslight. A series of swooping arches stretched away into the darkness and I realized, dimly, that we must be in some kind of adapted tunnel system running right under the roadway above. The walls were expensively rendered in a brilliant display of the *art nouveau*, black and gold tendrils curling like some monstrous plant from floor to ceiling.

Tapestries and great swathes of scarlet cloth billowed overhead like the skirts of a giantess. Upon them was wrought, in (well, exquisite is not quite the word) well-observed detail, classical pornography of the most astonishing variety. Priapic old lechers pursued virgins with a passion around a witches' sabbat, dominated by a frightening goat-headed Devil. Girlish youths and Rubensesque ladies formed a frame around scenes of Caligulan excess, where satyrs had their way with women deprived of their togas, and centaurs carried off drunken revellers.

The embroidered shenanigans, however, were as nothing to what was being enacted beneath them.

Flashes of colour rose up out of the gloom; male and female faces fixed in orgasmic relish, oil-slicked hair bobbing over a sea of unbuttoned britches, silken knickerbockers flung up from the mêlée like flags of surrender. The stench of absinthe and tobacco was overwhelming.

I glanced at Charlie Jackpot but his expression was unreadable in the murk. Of course my overwhelming emotion was one of horror. Not at the extraordinary outrages being committed in the name of love all about me, of course, but at the dreadful, unarguable fact that such a place existed and it would take me four days throwing up over the side of a steamer to get to it! What price my poor Pomegranate Rooms now?

Charlie pushed his way through the fleshy miasma, kicking aside copulating couples, until he found us a kind of ottoman. The pair he dislodged from this with the toe of his boot rolled off on to the floor with hardly a murmur, locked together like the jaws of a ferret.

I leaned back against the cushioned velvet. Charlie disappeared for a moment and then returned with a battered silver tray, bottles and glasses crammed upon it up to its tarnished edge. Pouring me some kind of hideous brandy, he gulped down most of a pint of porter and wiped his lips with the back of his hand.

'You work in shifts, then?' I pondered.

'How's that?'

'I was just wondering how you find time to look after Sir Emmanuel. It must be exhausting to wash dishes and then come on to this place.'

He giggled. 'I like my work.'

I drank the brandy as swiftly as I could so it didn't have time to touch the inside of my mouth.

Charlie leaned closer until his lips brushed my ear. 'I'll tell you it all, Mr Box. But you have to promise to get me out of here. Set me up.'

'I can make no assurances,' I said, my attention distracted momentarily by the sight of a Negro youth in a guardsman's uniform merrily tossing himself off over the patrons to our left. 'Not unless you have something of real import to impart.'

'That I do. See, I hear things,' murmured Charlie, darkly. 'They don't know that I work up at the house as well as here.'

'Who are *they*?'

There was a swish of skirts close by. I was conscious of a scent of mimosa and suddenly someone was standing right at my elbow.

'*Buonasera*, Charlie.'

The low voice belonged to a girl of middling height, exceptionally slim, wearing only an ivory corset and mustard-coloured stockings. Her long auburn hair was piled high and interlaced with flowers, crowning a face of surpassing loveliness; almond-shaped eyes heavily lined in kohl.

'Venus!' cried Charlie delightedly. He pulled the girl on to his lap and kissed her fiercely, running his hand up and down her stockinged leg. She adjusted herself in his embrace and cast a furtive glance to me.

'Who ees this?' she asked in the same seductive whisper. Her accent was as thick as tomato sauce.

Charlie grinned. 'This is Mr Box. Mr Box, meet Venus.'

I gave a little bow. Venus proffered a painted hand. I kissed the middle knuckles, taking care to let the tip of my tongue linger a moment. It seemed the form in these environs.

Venus's gaudily rouged lips puckered and she looked down, all abashed, the little minx. I had the queerest feeling that we'd met before.

'You like-a ma place, Signor Box?' she said with a half-smile.

My eyes widened. '*Your* place, my dear? Well, you do surprise me. Yes. Yes, it's quite something. What do you call it?'

It was Charlie who answered, fixing me with a meaningful stare and taking a plug of his porter. 'This? This is the Vesuvius Club.'

Well, of course I *noticed*. Vesuvius Club. V.C.! Not the Verdigris Collective, not the Verdi Cabal, not the Victoria Cross and not the bloody Venomous Centipede. The Vesuvius Club! K to V.C. Poor old Poop must have known of this place!

'Is-a something wrong, Signor Box?' cooed Venus.

I shook my head to clear it. 'Not a bit, my dear. It's just that Mr Jackpot and myself have some . . . business to conclude . . .'

Venus put one hand on her hip and smiled. 'I never stand in thee way of custom, eh? Perhaps you would be more comfortable in ma private quarters?'

I glanced at Charlie and he nodded.

'How kind,' I cooed. 'Will you lead the way?'

The delightful girl batted her kohl-rimmed eyes and swept off into the crowd. Charlie drained the last of his pint and followed with me bringing up the rear. Wary of stepping into a bear-trap (as this much honey might turn out to be), I walked with hands clasped behind me to feel the reassuring presence of the pearl-handled revolver strapped to the small of my back.

Venus led us through the roaring mêlée and through a side door into a cooler, darkened room that smelled of rose-petals. She lit the lamps, revealing a scarlet boudoir of impressive proportions, divided by silk curtains and scattered about with fat oriental cushions. A dressing mirror dominated the far wall.

'Please make-a yourselves at home,' said Venus, sitting down on the dresser and crossing her legs. Her mustard stockings flashed in the half-light.

'Most obliging of you, miss,' I said.

Venus cocked her head again. 'Charlie and I . . . we are old friends . . . yes? And any friend of his . . .'

Charlie grinned at her and, picking up a bottle of cham, wrenched out the cork. He poured three glasses. Venus drained hers in one go, span her champagne glass between her delicate fingers and fixed me with a slightly intimidating stare. What had those fiery eyes seen in their few years? She made me feel positively callow.

'I hope-a to see much more of *you*,' she said. With that, she swept past us both, paused to kiss Charlie briefly on the cheek and then was gone.

'Christ, ain't she something!' cried Charlie. He lifted the champagne bottle to his lips and guzzled down more plonk.

'That she is. Are you two –?'

'Some chance!' laughed Charlie. 'Even if I were that way inclined. No. She's got a fella, the real boss. She runs this place for him.'

Charlie threw himself down on to a cushion.

'But you want to know about a man called Poop.'

I sat up. 'Go on.'

'Well, he came in here a while ago, asking questions. Thought he was a punter. He stood me a drink but he weren't interested in getting, you know, *friendly*. He just give me some moolah to keep me eyes open. Said he was on to some kind of racket.'

I frowned. 'Racket?'

Charlie nodded. 'Treasure. Seems that he'd had some kind of nark sniffing around but he'd gone missing. Wondered if I'd be interested in taking up where the nark left off –'

The boy stopped dead.

'What is it?' I cried.

'Dunno. Can you smell something?'

Charlie coughed. His hand flew to his throat and he coughed again, more raggedly. Then it was my turn. The air had somehow turned too stifling to breathe, like being in an overheated steam bath.

I turned and saw the thread of some strange, purplish smoke drifting towards us. Feeling suddenly sick, tears sprang to my eyes and I too began to cough uncontrollably.

I tried to reach out to Charlie but suddenly found my limbs weighed down as though they were statuary. Scarcely able to move, I half-stumbled, half-fell to the floor. Through a mist of stinging tears, I could just make out Charlie's broad back. He tumbled to the floor, scrabbling at the air as though it were attacking him. With a titanic effort I hauled myself on to one knee and peered blearily about the room. What devilry was this? A Venus fly trap – and us the flies! Clutching at the oriental cushions, I staggered to my feet and tried to head towards the door.

Every step seemed to take an eternity. It was as though I had a diver's lead shoes upon my feet. Coughing constantly I put my hands to my face and slapped myself in an attempt to clear my befuddled brain. My mind seemed to be swirling and tumbling and swimming madly, as though I'd drunk a quart of absinthe.

Reeling around, I found I had lost the door. It was as though I'd been transported to some other room, so strange and alien did Venus's boudoir appear. The dressing table stretched crazily before me on stilt-like legs. Great heaven! The furniture appeared to be moving! The drawers of the dresser gaped open like hungry maws, snapping at my legs as I lurched and stumbled across the floor.

The oil-lamp loomed largest of all. It was then, with my eyes almost popping from my bursting head that I saw that the lamp was the source of my terror. For, gushing from the shade like a spectre or genie was a billowing quantity of some noxious gas, mauve in colour, settling heavily on the floorboards and sending me into near-convulsions.

I reached for the lamp but the closer I got the more dreadful were its effects. My fingers seemed to bend and stretch like the talons of a terrible bird as I groped at empty air, the image of the lamp blurring and multiplying before my exhausted eyes. I looked wildly about for Charlie but could make out nothing in the greasy smoke.

With one last attempt at clear thought I grabbed hold of the lamp's iron base and picked it up. Perhaps I intended to smother the damned thing or hurl it into a dark corner but, in truth, I do not know. My senses whirled, a great blanket of mauve darkness enveloped me and I was falling, falling, falling into an abyss . . .

XIV

THE PALE MAN

N the distance, a clock struck four. I stirred and found myself lying prone on cold stone. Shifting a little, I cracked open stinging eyes, peered blearily about, coughed and opened my mothball-stale mouth. I tried to sit up but sank back at once on to the chilly floor, skull throbbing as though it were fixed about with a tight iron band.

Where the hell was I?

I raised my head again, widening my eyes in a last-ditch attempt at wakefulness. I was in some kind of cell, window-less and cramped. Slimy straw lay all about me and there was a pervasive odour of ammonia.

Head splitting, I somehow managed to stumble to my feet and then sank back against the wet bricks. Looking down at myself, I saw that I was in full evening dress, my shirt-front torn and the lapels of my coat plastered with mud.

I could recall nothing at all. Never mind where was I! *Who* was I?

I hammered my fist against my forehead and screwed up my eyes. Something about a box. A box with a centipede in it. No. That wasn't right. Perhaps it was a book. A book in a box. Daniel Liquorice! Was that my name? No. A Jack in a box? Jack Box? Jackpot? That was someone else entirely, I felt sure. *My name is Box.* Ah! *Lucifer Box. Yes. Yes.* I placed the flat of my hands against the chilly wall and willed myself to remain calm. *Lucifer Box. Of Downing Street, London.* I shook my head over and over. I must concentrate. *Where was I? Italy. Italy, of course. Naples! But why? Why?* I snapped open my eyes and struggled to focus on the cell door. It looked depressingly solid.

Bending down, I peered through the rusted keyhole. I could just make out a suggestion of a gloomy corridor beyond.

I sank down against the wall then leant forward as I became aware of something poking into my back. I had a dim remembrance of a similar feeling, connected to a yellow villa in Islington but this was not quite the same. Exploring under the tail of my ruined shirt my fingers closed upon the warm, reassuring presence of my revolver, still strapped in the hollow above my buttocks that nature almost seemed to have provided for the express purpose.

I took it out, opened the chamber and span it.

'That won't help you,' came a whispered voice from the darkness.

I started and whirled round, brandishing the pistol.

Nothing.

'Who's there?' I demanded.

A hissing chuckle sounded close by. I crept towards the far wall. Just about visible was a tiny, barred window, evidently connecting to the cell next door. I pressed my face to it, making out a crouched figure in the gloom beyond. He turned his face towards me but little detail was visible in the filthy mass of hair and beard.

'Oh . . .' I cried. 'Hullo.'

'Good evening. Or is it morning? I no longer know.'

'My name is Box.'

'And mine's the Count of Monte Cristo! Hee-hee!'

I pulled back from the window slightly, alarmed at the fellow's crazed laughter. He fixed me with a wild eye and shuffled across the floor of his cell. 'As I say, that weapon of yours won't do you any good. They don't feel pain. They don't feel anything!'

'Who don't?'

'They came for me, you see. I was getting too close. Too close to the truth. Mr Poop – he was on to them.'

My ears pricked up. 'Poop! What do you know of Poop?'

The strange old man coughed noisily. 'Looting they was! Stripping the excavations bare and flogging the stuff to keep this wretched place going!'

'Excavations?'

'They've forgotten me now. Hee-hee! Thrown away the key. Maybe you'll rot here too!'

As if in response, a key rattled in the lock and my door was thrown open. A strange figure was framed there; very tall, clad in black and wearing what appeared to be some kind of brass helmet. I rubbed at my eyes. Was this still part of my strange purple dream? Had the notion of a lead-shoed diver sprung to life before me?

My neighbour in the next cell jumped to his feet and pressed his grimy face to the bars.

'Look out! They've come for you! Don't resist! They don't feel anything! Hee-hee!'

The extraordinary helmeted figure stumped across the cell towards me and opened his great arms as though offering an embrace.

I thrust the revolver into my pocket and backed away. Pale as death, the man's jaw hung slackly open, a strand of drool dangling from his lips. His eyes, staring blankly ahead, were a horrible yellowy grey like the yolks of over-boiled eggs.

My gaze was drawn, however, to the strange brass thing that covered the top part of his face. On the closer inspection I was now afforded, I could see it was like a Norman helmet, though the upper part was made of glass and glowing a weird, sickly purple. Great brass screws were inset at the temples, effectively clamping the helmet to his head.

Stepping quickly to one side, I raced towards the door, bargaining that the brute's sluggish gait would count against him.

'No good!' croaked my neighbour through the barred window. 'He'll get you!'

At once the creature changed direction and cut me off, his eyes rolling in his head, arms outstretched in deadly intent.

I resorted to my pistol but he swung at me, knocking the weapon flying. As I moved to retrieve it, his sweaty hands jerked forward and clamped about my throat.

I staggered backwards, gasping at the terrible pressure.

'Hee-hee!' cried my neighbour. 'Now you're done for!'

The fiend's bloated white face was right by mine and I could see directly into the glass section of his strange headgear. Inside seemed to float a purplish miasma.

I dug my nails into the flesh of his throttling hands but he did not even react, forcing me backwards as I beat and pounded at his face. My head felt as though it would explode at any second. Desperately, I thrust my thumbs into his eyes and pushed with all my strength. The soft flesh gave sickeningly but still I pressed on, digging into the very sockets and forcing my thumbs upwards.

No scream did he make, nor sign that he felt even a scintilla of pain.

'Told you! Told you so! They feel nothing! The devils!' cackled my fellow prisoner.

I hammered my fists against my attacker's chest but his great weight forced me to my knees. I groped wildly about in the straw. The revolver!

Rolling us both over with a supreme effort, I grasped at the pearl handle of the gun, aimed desperately and loosed off a bullet into the brute's chest.

He was knocked back as though plucked by a giant hand, staggered and slumped against the wall. I groped at my throat and rubbed my crushed wind-pipe, struggling to draw ragged, whooping breaths.

Suddenly the helmeted monster was on his feet again, seemingly oblivious to the wound in his chest. He surged forward, his great hands flexing, intent on rejoining battle at once. Though dazed and exhausted, I scrabbled to my feet and made a dash for the door. The fellow threw himself forward and grabbed at my ankles, succeeding in getting both hands around one of them and bringing me down on the floor. I swivelled on my rump and planted my boot in the middle of his face, kicking savagely until I felt his nose crack and bright blood fountain on to my trouser leg.

I tried to take aim again but the lumbering giant gripped my other ankle and shook me about like a rag-doll. The pistol went off but was sent clattering against the wall.

With a cry I shuffled forward and managed to get my fingers under the edge of the helmet. I tugged violently, desperately.

Swarming forward with one last effort and gripping the helmet for dear life, I kicked the fellow in the throat sending him vaulting backwards. I was left clutching the brass helmet in both hands.

And now he began to scream. A dreadful tortured gurgle it was as his suddenly bare head was exposed to the world. There were huge gory gouges in his temples where the attaching screws had been ripped out and he raised his hands to them, gasping in pain and shock.

'Lor! You done for him! How did you manage that?' hissed my hairy cellmate in amazement.

I glanced down at the helmet. The strange, gaseous substance still swirled within the glass enclosure but I could now see that thin, delicate pipes led from it into the screws that been affixed to my attacker's temples. A tarry liquid began to leak from inside and its dark mauve colour was at once familiar. And then I remembered. I felt my overtaxed brain making connections like points changing on a railway. It was the same stuff that had nearly done for me and Charlie.

Charlie! Of course! The boy had been on the point of telling me something of vital import. When . . .

I looked down at the strange helmet again. Piped directly into its poor owner's blood-stream the mauve stuff had rendered him little more than a zombie!

Putting the helmet carefully aside, I scrabbled for my revolver and levelled it at the prone figure.

The man had begun to weep from his gory eyes, great heavy tears mixing with the drool and blood plastered over his dead-white face. He tried to raise himself up on one hand but sank back to the floor with a great cry. I suddenly realized there wasn't much time.

Scuttling across to him on my knees, I managed to raise the fellow's head up, cradling it in the crook of my arm. It was like the Death of bloody Nelson.

'Tell me,' I whispered. 'Who did this to you?'

The mauve fluid was trickling out of the wounds in his temples. Great rasping gulps began to sound from the fellow's blood-caked mouth and then, with a dreadful, rattling gurgle, he pitched back into my arms, quite dead.

I got to my feet. The fellow had been sent to collect me or to kill me. Either way, it was wise to get moving.

'Wait! Wait!' cried my neighbour. 'What about me?'

I paused on the threshold. 'You're no use to me in this babbling state.'

I slipped through the open door and out in to the darkened corridor.

As I passed the adjacent cell, the old fellow thrust towards me desperately. 'Please! I'll tell you. Just let me out!'

I took a chance and shot the lock off. He raced out into the corridor but I covered him warily. He seemed just the type to leap for my throat.

'All right,' I muttered, backing away from the stink he gave off. 'Where are we?'

He pushed his long grey hair from his eyes. 'Why, the Vesuvius Club, of course!'

'Still? Good. That's good. Now tell me more about Poop and these looted treasures.'

I gestured with the pistol and we began to creep off up the corridor, keeping our voices low.

'I knew Mr Poop. Did a lot of work for him. I know my way about this city, you see.'

'You're an informant?'

The old man cackled. 'I keeps my ear to the ground.'

'Go on.'

'Well, Signor Poop was on to some sort of racket in stolen stuff.

Old statues and that sort of thing, hocked off to the best Chelsea drawing rooms and nobs' offices. He reckoned that's how Venus's fella got the V Club up and running. They was smuggling stuff out of Naples in coffins, pretending it was bodies, then smuggling the moolah back in. We was getting close to nabbing them when . . . well . . .'

I nodded slowly. 'You got your ear a little too close to the ground, eh?'

This must be the fellow Charlie had mentioned. I scratched my chin. Where was Charlie now? It was vital that I find him and pump him (for information, you understand).

We emerged suddenly into a curtained area and there, sitting on a stool with his back towards us was the curious ape-like chap who had greeted me when I first arrived. I gestured to my bearded friend that he should make for the front door and scarper. He nodded and gave me a little bow then I cleared my throat noisily and the monkey-man turned on his stool.

Out of the corner of my eye I saw Poop's informant steal towards the exit and, silently, slip through it to freedom.

My head still ached appallingly from the mauve gas but I thrust my hands into my trouser pockets and looked about with a casual air. 'Hello again! Got a little lost in all these damned corridors. Had a little adventure, but found my way back. Not to worry.'

With a merry wave, I strode off down the long corridor. When finally I stood once more before the great doors I paused to make myself presentable. Magnified by the gasping gas-jets, my shadow leapt hugely over the walls. Once again, the sweet sounds of debauchery bled from under them.

Raising my fist, I hammered twice on the black surface.

Almost immediately, the doors rasped open and a flickering red light washed over me. I stepped inside but felt my way barred at once by a great bear-like shape.

Membership was clearly an exclusive affair.

Charlie, of course, had previously gained us ingress and I suddenly realized that it might be a little more difficult alone.

'Yes?' came a thick voice from the dimness.

I was damned if I was going to say 'May I come in, please?' so instead I ordered 'Stand aside' with all the boldness I could muster.

There was movement in the darkness which I realized must be the fellow shaking his fat head. 'Can't do that, sir. You have to give the signal.'

I nodded and shrugged as though cursing my own stupidity. 'The signal! Of course!'

I rubbed my hands together and laughed lightly. What signal?

The impressive shape shifted on its feet. I patted my pockets as though the solution might be found in there. Why hadn't I observed more closely when Charlie had stood in this position? Had he given a password of some kind? No, the doorman would have said so. It was a *signal* he was after.

The shape began to move towards me with some menace. I knew I would be put out on the wrong side of the door within seconds. A signal? Something to do with the Vesuvius Club. Something simple and recognizable.

Then a notion popped into my head. I took a chance and thrust my fingers up before his nose in a 'V' shape.

He stopped his inexorable progress. I curved my hand and formed a 'C' that I slapped against my palm as I had seen Charlie do. The creature stepped aside. 'Have a very good evening, sir,' he growled.

'Thank you. I intend to.' I breathed with relief, moving swiftly past him and into the heaving chamber beyond.

The room was still what you might call a *pornucopia*.

My ragged appearance excited no comment and I proceeded to a couch, occupied solely by a mournful-looking youth with terrible acne. I sat down as far from him as possible and stuck out my long legs before me. He began at once to cast shy glances at my loveliness but I studiously ignored the hideous bugger, content instead to watch the activities of two splendidly naked ladies who were cavorting on the floor with their bums in the air.

A rough-looking waiter sauntered past with a tray of drinks and I grabbed him by his skinny wrist. He thrust a shot glass into my hand and moved off into the crowd. I turned back and discovered I was still under the scrutiny of the grisly youth perched at the other end of the sofa. I raised my glass and toasted him. His cheeks, angry with blemishes, burned redder still.

'I am Ricardo,' he mumbled.

'And I'm . . .' I threw him a pitying look. 'I'm afraid you're terribly ugly.'

His whole frame sank with shame.

'*Buonasera*, Venus!'

I turned at the cry. It had come from a thickset fellow far to my left who was wiping beer from the wet stalactites of his moustache.

Venus! She had fetched up more respectably this time in a dress of dazzling crimson, one hand on her shapely hip, in the approved style, the other clutching a long amber cigarette-holder. She was exchanging gossip and laughter with her clientele, her kohl-rimmed eyes shining with mirth. Charlie had said she was the paramour of the villain who owned this place. Had she been complicit in lighting the lamp with its strange mauve poison or was she merely an unwilling pawn?

Either way, I had to hide. Without a second thought, I reached across the sofa, grabbed the spotted Dick by his tweedy lapels and pulled him to me.

'On the other hand,' I said, moving him round to screen me, 'I've always had a penchant for ugly boys.'

Master Ricardo set to with a vengeance, his pinkish lips slapping against my mouth in a squid-like action that was most disagreeable. To my astonishment, an albino in a beret then toddled towards us as though the kiss had been some general call to arms. He began fiddling with my fly-button as my eyes goggled above the pitted curve of acne-boy's cheek. As soon as Venus had moved away, I repelled all boarders with a disgusted cry, pushing young Ricardo to the filthy floor and kicking the albino in the solar plexus.

He flopped like a bag of wet washing and I stooped at once as though to help him, all the time keeping an eye on Venus as she made her halting progress through the chamber, wreathed in the bluish smoke of her cheroot.

At the end of the long, mirrored bar was a door inset with a frosted pane. Venus glided towards the door and then, glancing swiftly around, passed through into the darkness beyond.

I rolled the albino into a corner and then swiftly followed Venus, threading through knotted limbs conjoined in shameless excess. Turning the handle, I opened the door and slipped silently through.

The sudden quiet startled me. Torches sputtered in gold stanchions, revealing the curve of a broad corridor disappearing into gloom. I smiled to myself. Now this really was a secret tunnel!

I could hear the tat-tat of Venus's elegant heels on the stone floor ahead. Pulling off my boots as quietly as I could and, clutching them to my chest, I followed her.

Padding along, I kept myself snug to the wall until I came to a branch in the tunnel. It continued to my left. To my right I could make out the top of a spiral stairwell. Only the first three of the worn stone steps were visible as they descended into darkness.

Unsure as to which route Venus had taken, my attention was momentarily caught by a heavy tapestry that was fixed to the brickwork. In the flickering torchlight, its threads leapt out in golds, reds and purples. It was clearly very old and seemed to show the broad sweep of a harbour, dominated by the great hulk of a black mountain. I moved closer. The weave was disintegrating but I could just make out that a pillar of smoke was escaping from the embroidered summit. Vesuvius!

XV

INTO THE CRIMSON CHAMBER

HERE were footsteps in the tunnel. Caught in the open corridor, I rapidly rifled through my options. Only one. Lifting the edge of the tapestry, I tucked myself in behind it, and pressed myself flat against the wall which had a distinct curve I had not previously noted. I listened attentively as several pairs of feet passed by and began to descend the spiral stair, accompanied by a rustling sound.

As I stood with my back to the wall, I noticed a point of bright yellow light emerging just above my left shoulder. As soon as I was sure the passers-by had gone I turned around and put my eye to the hole in the crumbling mortar.

What I saw was a strange, circular room that, like everywhere else in that place, was the colour of flame. This time, however, the decoration actually imitated the pit of Hell or, more probably, the crater of a boiling volcano. Painted fire licked the round room,

twisting into orange shapes like barley-sugar canes and merging into patterns of deep crimson lava.

The room was dominated by a massive round table with four ornately carved chairs set about it. In them had been placed straw figures, exactly like the one I had found in Professor Verdigris's coffin.

The air seemed heavy with oily incense. Its foggy weight hung under the ceiling, swirling like a nest of serpents as it was disturbed by draughts from the crumbling walls.

As I watched, a yellow door opened and an extraordinary procession came in: three figures, resplendent in red velvet robes, decorated all over in blazes of gold and silver sunbursts. All three wore what looked like masks from the Venice Carnival, exquisitely rendered in similar hues, the cruel, snarling features picked out in white. Not for the first time in that bizarre place, I wished I'd had my sketchbook. Though this was, perhaps, a rare occasion where the

Duce Tiepolo's photographic apparatus might have been handier! Without it, who would believe such a sight? My thoughts dwelled on the Duce for a moment. Could he be the paramour of Venus? The organizing brain behind this whole enterprise?

One of the robed figures, slight in build, took up a gavel that lay at his right hand and rapped it on the table.

'I, Vesuvius, summon thee,' he said.

The next figure, altogether more imposing, bowed his head saying, 'I, Stromboli, answer.' This could be Tiepolo. His build was similar.

The third, tall and thin, bowed too. 'Etna answers thee,' he squeaked.

My eye widened as I pressed closer to the spy-hole.

Now I've been around a bit, as you can imagine, and I knew at once that this was more than a knocking shop's AGM. Few go about their business in motley and even fewer adopt names stranger than 'Mister Chairman' as their monikers.

No, this was rummer than a baba.

More torches had been lit and now I could see that there were maps and what appeared to be charts pinned to the walls. I looked more closely at the four chairs. Bizarrely, the straw figures had been shackled to their seats, as though to prevent their escape.

Vesuvius set aside the gavel and spread his hands wide, looking for all the world like a sinister masked version of the Messiah from Da Vinci's *Last Supper*. A queer, piercing note began to rise in his throat. After a moment the sound was taken up by his two fellow volcanoes who moved swiftly to apparently pre-appointed positions around the circular chamber.

I narrowed my eye in an effort to see more. Now I realized that the place was littered with curious paraphernalia, scattered about like grave goods in a plundered tomb. There were great brass bowls filled with what looked like spice standing on piles of glittering rock. Red candles were held in tightly bound bundles atop a mahogany rail that ran right around the room.

Still the shrill note continued. As I watched, they picked up the brass bowls and carried them over to the centre of the table. Stromboli's robed chest rose and fell visibly as he began to scoop out handfuls of mauve-coloured powder – a colour that was beginning to make me uneasy.

Vesuvius turned his masked head and, just for a moment, I had the curious sensation that his fixed features were moving, glowering. The painted mask gave him a strange pagan appearance and behind the diamond-shaped slits, his eyes were merely black hollows.

Stromboli handed him a brass goblet, into which the mauve powders were rapidly poured, then placed two of the black rocks into his outstretched hands. I saw now that they were chunks of raw flint.

'O Vulcan!' bellowed Stromboli. 'Son of Jupiter and Juno! Forger of Creation! Labourer beneath the slopes of great Etna. Smith of the Gods!'

'Vulcan!' cried the assembly.

I strained to hear.

The intonation rose ever higher. 'Builder of the brass houses,' thundered Stromboli. 'Shoer of the golden shoes with which the gods trod on wind or water.'

Something about wind?

'Ye who shod the mighty steeds of Jove's chariot! We honour thee!'

What was that? Cobblers?

'Vulcan! We honour thee!'

Stromboli brought his hands together with a great crack as he smashed the flints against themselves. At once, they sparked and in the blink of an eye, the ruddy powder that lay piled high in the goblet caught and flared up with a glorious purple flame. Yet the smoke did not seem to choke the assembly as it had with Charlie and me. Rather they seem to relish it, swaying gently as though in the grip of some powerful drug.

The hem of his velvet robes rustling over the flagged floor, Stromboli strode towards the wall.

'Now! In honour of the mighty volcano of Vesuvius, we offer our sacrifice!'

With great precision he took hold of one of the torch-sconces and pulled it toward him.

At once unseen gears began to clatter into life. Then, to my astonishment, the great round table began to hinge open like the lid of some titanic coffee-pot revealing, beneath it, the top of a stone-faced well. A waft of dank air came flooding towards me. It reminded me of the bottom-of-the-vase stink of Tom Bowler's office. Then, with the sound of further machinery, the whole roof began to open, as though some baleful eye was set there. What I first took for a puppet began to droop downwards. In the guttering torch-light I could see bare feet and legs, then, with a crunch of gears, a whole body flopped into view, suspended by its arms above the hole in the floor.

It was Charlie Jackpot!

He had been beaten, manacled at the wrists and hung from chains, clad only in a pair of grisly grey undergarments.

'Oh Christ!' he groaned. 'What do you want with me? Let me go!'

Stromboli was standing with hands on hips, surveying his nefarious handiwork. With a great clank like the moving hand of a town-hall clock, Charlie fell another few inches.

'Please!' he begged. 'Don't hurt me!'

'Our gift to Neptune!' For the first time, the pomposity of the ceremony was broken as Stromboli burst into throaty laughter.

Clunk!

Charlie's chained form descended a foot further towards the well. The boy cried out but the figures remained unmoved.

'So much for traitors,' hissed Vesuvius.

Then, with a snap of his fingers, he turned on his heel and marched out with Stromboli, Etna scurrying behind them. The yellow door slammed shut.

Footfalls on the spiral stair told me that these strange apostles of the volcano, were passing right by my hiding place. I waited until their steps had receded and then, taking a chance, I slipped out from behind the tapestry and dashed down the spiral stair towards the door of the round chamber.

With a quick look around, I pulled it open and nipped inside.

The air was still thick and unhealthy. Above me, Charlie, eyes closed, was groaning softly to himself. The strange system of cogs and pulleys that suspended him juddered again and his bound body descended another inch.

'Hello, Charlie,' I said, leaning against the edge of the well.

His eyes flicked open and he stared wildly down at me.

'Oh thank God! Mr Box!'

I, in turn, looked down into the dark water below. It was moving – either a sewer or an underground river of some sort. Either way it would be enough to dunk Charlie to death like a human madeleine cake.

'Glad to see you hale and hearty. Now where were we? You were, I believe, about to tell me something rather important.'

'Mr Box! Please. You got to get me out of here!'

I shrugged casually, jumped up on to the lip of the well and grabbed at one of the boy's shoulders but only succeeded in setting him swaying to and fro in a fashion that endangered us both. The mechanism dropped again; it seemed to have increased its speed. Charlie groaned pitiably.

'Can you move your hands at all?' I cried.

'No,' he gasped.

With a great creaking shudder, he dropped a whole foot into the well and gave a little yell.

I shook my head. 'If I can't stop this infernal device of theirs then you'll drown for sure.'

'Thanks a million.'

Again, Charlie's chained form dropped alarmingly. Now his head, hair stiff with sweat and grime, was level with the lip of the hole. Rushing to the wall, I scrabbled about amongst the maps and charts that littered the wooden rail. One, its colours gleaming darkly in the torch-light, was some kind of tough paper stretched between two cream-coloured tubes of metal. Snapping the thing together I moved quickly to the lip of the well and thrust it up towards the mechanism. On cue, the great cogs turned again and Charlie disappeared into the hole. Only his manacled arms projected now.

I strained on tip-toe but finally managed to shove the tube into the gears. At once the cogs seized, although it was obvious I hadn't bought Charlie much time. The oily teeth of the machine were already squeezing and crushing the thin metal of the map-tube.

Throwing myself over the stones of the well I pulled Charlie's arms towards me with one hand and tore the knife from my watch-chain with the other.

Feverishly, I pierced the lock of the manacles with the thin blade and rattled it about inside.

'Quickly, sir!' squealed Charlie, his voice a hollow echo. 'Oh, quickly!'

The lock snapped open. I slipped the blade between my teeth and, forcing the metal cuffs apart, I dragged Charlie from the hole just as the map tube was ground into pieces and the cogs resumed their inexorable round.

Little pieces of the destroyed chart fluttered like dead leaves all about us. Panting for breath, I found myself on the floor with my arms around Charlie as the now-empty manacles continued their descent into the depths.

'Well, Mr Box,' grinned Charlie. 'It seems you can't keep your hands off me after all.'

'You are very impudent, young man,' I replied. 'It will get you a long way. Now, let's get out of here.'

Just at that moment the yellow door was flung open, crashing back against the painted brick. Our hearts, I feel sure, stopped at the same moment.

Stromboli stormed in. The mask still disguised his eyes but it seemed a fair guess that he was staring down at Charlie and me as we lay in an undignified heap on the floor.

'What's this?' he thundered in Italian. 'The club has increased its membership somewhat unexpectedly, ah?' His masked head inclined a fraction as he looked at me.

I'm pretty nifty at thinking on my feet, even when I'm actually sitting down with a renter in my embrace, but this fellow's sudden appearance had me more than a little stumped.

With as much dignity as I could muster, I extricated myself from Charlie and got up.

'Do forgive the intrusion,' I said, twiddling with my cuff-link. In one swift terribly well-rehearsed movement I had my revolver out and levelled squarely at Stromboli. 'But please don't move.'

The tall man held up his hands but seemed quite calm. 'What is your business here, signor? Are you a . . . customer?'

'This boy,' I said, indicating Charlie, 'is . . . my valet. I received word that he was being held here against his will.'

'So you came here to bring him home?'

'Correct. My laundry, you see, is in a frightful state.'

Stromboli shrugged. 'Well, my dear sir. We need detain you no longer. There has evidently been some . . . misunderstanding. Your valet has been employed in this establishment and it appears that one of our gentlemen's . . . er . . . games . . .' He pointed to the chains hanging from the ceiling. 'Took on a logic of its own. If you were to let this little matter blow over, I'm sure no more need be said.' He indicated my revolver with a casual swing of his arm. 'There is really no need for these . . . histrionics.'

I glanced quickly about. Could we really get out of here without the alarm being raised? I was armed, of course, but these people were evidently fanatics and knew that Charlie had betrayed them. What punishment had they meant for me, I wondered?

'Well, this is all most irregular, sir,' I said, reaching down and hauling Charlie to his feet. 'I am not in the habit of rescuing my servants from dens of unnatural vice and then letting the matter pass.'

My indignity was, in all probability, a mite unconvincing.

'Given my pressing need for fresh linen, however, I am prepared to go no further with this. But I should like to know who I have the honour of addressing.'

The tall man laughed lightly and dropped his hands a fraction. With a jerk of the revolver, I indicated he should get them up again, sharpish.

Instead, three black-coated and very well-armed thugs emerged from behind their master.

Stromboli's arm shot out towards me. 'Kill him!' he yelled.

Oh lor.

One of the thugs dropped at once to his knee, assumed the position and prepared to fire his pistol. I shot him through the forehead and took a grim satisfaction from watching his brains slide across the wall like clay-slip.

Charlie rolled over and hid himself behind the lip of the well. Stromboli and another thug took cover behind the great raised table as I fired again. My report was answered with two shots of the thugs' own. We were effectively pinned down, cut off from the only door.

'Bloody hell!' whispered Charlie. 'This is a fix, Mr Box. What're we going to do?'

I levelled my revolver on the stone facing of the well and tried to get Stromboli's masked head in my sights. Frustratingly, it bobbed up and down like a shooting gallery target.

'You are trapped, my friend,' he called. 'We had been saving you for our next . . . *rehearsal*. But now I fear we must put a swift end to this sport.'

I was breathing hard. There seemed no way out. Bullets sang off the stonework that was our only cover. I held up my arm to shield myself from the splinters of masonry. There was a cry to my left and I saw that Charlie had been hit by the debris. He crumpled to the floor at my side.

'Take them!' roared Stromboli. 'Take them even if you have to die in the attempt! Forward, you scum!'

Obediently, the remaining thugs dashed forward. I looked around desperately. Only one bullet remained in my pearl-handled life-saver. No options presented themselves.

Except one.

I glanced down at the well.

Peeking over my stone barricade, I fired my last bullet. One black-coat was hit in the eye but the other was undeterred. Grabbing Charlie by the arm, and rolling over the lip of the well with a great unwilling cry, Lucifer descended into the pit and into the stinking darkness.

XVI

A DESPERATE FLIGHT

TRIED to grab at the chains that Charlie had hung from but we fell into nothingness: a sickening, awful lurch that felt like the hangman's drop. I was conscious only of my arms holding on to Charlie for grim death and my stomach flipping and my head spinning as we were precipitated downwards. If this was The Fall then I understood why my namesake came out so ill-tempered.

All of a sudden we were in water; warm, brackish, filthy water that seemed all around us, though I was hardly aware of a splash.

I swallowed a pint and then felt myself rushing towards the surface. Charlie was like a dead weight in my arms. Our heads broke the surface and I shook mine, blinking furiously as I tried to get my bearings in that horrible blackness.

Treading water, I managed to tuck Charlie's head in the crook of my elbow and wipe the slime from my stinging eyes. We were in some sort of tunnel, as expected, though whether this was a sewer or the course of an ancient river was impossible to tell. That there was a form of current was unmistakable, however.

I glanced upwards quickly. Above us, I saw the surviving thug's white face looking down at us as through the wrong way down a telescope. Would Stromboli order his man to jump after us? I gave in to the current. Charlie, oblivious it seemed to everything, was swept along with me.

In seconds we were moving swiftly away, borne like corks upon the effluent. As yet, no one seemed rash enough to follow us down.

After a little time, I became aware that the tunnel broadened out and I craned my neck from the water's embrace.

We had reached a confluence where three tunnels met and merged. A great iron grille barred further progress. The current took us up to this barrier and I clung on to the slime-strewn metal with one hand while cradling the unconscious Charlie in the other.

I peered through the grille. The river sluiced through it and plunged down into further darkness. It was a man-made waterfall of some kind, though not the type that Blondin would ever have chosen to cross.

Charlie opened his eyes. He stared at me for a few moments, then his bruised face broke into a grin. He seemed entirely unaware of his circumstances.

'Hullo,' he breathed.

I nodded. 'How're you feeling?'

He glanced down and his eyes widened as he found he was almost totally immersed in black water. His face suddenly creased in pain. 'Been better, Mr Box. Where the hell are we, if you don't mind me asking?'

I manoeuvred him towards the grille and unhooked my arm from beneath his jaw.

'Hang on to that,' I ordered. 'Need a rest.'

He managed to push his fingers through the holes of the wet metalwork and clung on, though I could see the pain in his stretched arms was returning with a vengeance.

I struggled out of my lovely tail-coat. It was nothing but a saturated encumbrance now and I pushed it away into the frothing water. Its immaculate tailoring ballooned briefly on the surface and then disappeared.

'There doesn't appear to be any exit this way,' I said at last. 'So we'll probably have to swim back against the current. Are you up to it?'

He didn't look it but he said yes.

I shook the grille with my hand but it was solid despite the corrosion on its surface.

'Where's the light coming from?' said Charlie.

'Where indeed?' I said, hauling myself up the grille and peering through the murk. A glow-worm phosphorescence was visible somewhere past it to the right of the waterfall.

'There's another tunnel through there,' I muttered.

Charlie shook his head. 'No. I meant *that* light.'

He raised his arm from the water and pointed back the way we had come.

Bobbing in the darkness were the unmistakable outlines of men in the water, the searing white light of flares hissing in their upraised hands.

I looked around wildly. The livid new light threw huge jagged shadows against the grille before us. I looked it up and down, thinking frantically, then pushed myself off from the tunnel side, took a huge breath and plunged down into the river. It was utterly disorientating.

Thrusting forward, I immediately felt for the grille in front of me. It was impossible to see a thing in the murky brine so I ran my hands over the surface of the submerged metal, groping for any change in the structure. Somewhere at the back of my mind I could picture one such sewer construction; a vast gated thing perhaps glimpsed as a child on a school-visit to one of Joseph Bazalgette's shit-sifting palaces.

For a few seconds, I groped blindly in the disgusting water, feeling nothing but the same repeated pattern of slimy iron bars. Then, yes! At last! My hands met space and I was dragged forward by the tug of an undoubtedly faster current. There had to be room for first Charlie and then me to push ourselves through.

I kicked off from the grille and raced to the surface. Shaking the water from my hair I briefly glimpsed a flotilla of flares bearing down on Charlie then, without a second thought, I grabbed him, pushed his head under the water, took another breath, and followed.

Bubbles rushed along the lines of our soaked bodies as we reached the hole in the grille and I forced us through.

All at once we were tumbling down, down, half-emerging into the air, then immersed again in the falling water, finally crashing into the tunnel on the other side and freedom.

Well, freedom of a kind. It wouldn't take those thugs long to discover what we had done and plunge through after us.

Charlie was taking in huge gulps of the foetid air.

'All right?' I quizzed. He nodded exhaustedly.

I swam ahead a little. There was now a clearer view of the strange light source. Not far from where we were floating there was a small hole in the tunnel wall. Half a dozen or so rotten bricks had tumbled through revealing a chamber beyond. I swam quickly towards the breach, gained it and managed to scramble up to get a better look. Before I slid down into the water again I saw, strung over the salt-corrupted walls like Christmas decorations, the unmistakable glow of electric light!

Relief flooded through me. Weak as he was, I knew that Charlie would rally at the sight of dry land and the chance of a rapid escape from our pursuers.

When I swam back to him, however, I could see that our recent exertions had taken their toll. His head was lolling back in the water and his eyes were showing white.

'Charlie!' I hissed. 'Wake up! There's a way out ahead. Just hold on a little longer.'

He fell forward and attempted to focus on me. He smiled stupidly and closed his eyes.

With a heavy sigh, I began to drag him onwards. The water in this new tunnel was much more shallow and I could feel the sediment-covered bottom squelching beneath my shoes as I threaded my arm under Charlie's and staggered towards the hole in the wall.

Meanwhile, a series of cries and oaths told me that our pursuers had worked out our method of escape through the grille.

When we reached the breach in the tunnel, I pushed Charlie through it and into the room beyond. Normally, the feel of strong buttocks in wet trousers might have made my thoughts wander but I shoved Charlie on without a second glance. As soon as he had fallen forward into a crumpled heap, I leaped up and pulled myself through.

I lay dazed for a long moment. Then, as my eyes adjusted to the light, I saw that we were surrounded by packing cases and ladders, black against the garish flare of the electric light. Charlie stirred and opened an eye experimentally.

'Some sort of warehouse,' I said, getting up and testing the windows. One creaked open on a hinged pane and moments later, we had clambered out on to the street. Perhaps it was not surprising that even in Naples we had some trouble finding a cab, given our state. Eventually, we gave up and managed to drag ourselves back down towards the harbour and finally into the reassuring warmth of the Hotel Santa Lucia.

The next day dawned blazing hot. Through the half-drawn blinds, I could see Naples sparkling almost painfully in the searing sun, as if in celebration that my life had been spared (one gets these fancies now and then). Perhaps I would go for a constitutional? A walk by the sea on this glorious morning would clear my head and lift my spirits! I drew the blinds shut and, shambling back to bed, lit a cigarette. Sod that.

Charlie Jackpot, whose tired face and dark-ringed eyes still somehow conspired to make him a corker, lay sprawled on the bed next to me. In the mess of sheets his form showed pale and flawless as a marble tomb effigy.

I slapped at his buttocks and he grudgingly emerged from sleep. 'Good morning, Charles.'

He grunted and burrowed further into the sheets.

'Let us return to our previous conversation,' I said brightly. 'The one so rudely interrupted by the noxious oil-lamp. What's going on in the Vesuvius Club?'

Charlie rubbed at his hair and groaned. 'Not now. I'm half-dead.'

'And thanks to me, only half.' I examined my bare knee. It was barked and bloodied. 'As I recall, you were trying to interest me in a little bargain.'

He raised himself up on one elbow and yawned. 'That's right.'

'You want a leg-up, yes? A way out of your sordid little existence?'

Charlie hugged himself and shivered. 'I just want to get a start in life, Mr Box. In return for what I know. Don't seem too unfair from where I'm lying.'

I nodded. A notion was forming in my early morning brain. 'Mr Jackpot, I currently find myself in the position of requiring a valet.'

The lad's face fell. 'What?'

'Don't answer me back like that, you little villain. Just listen –'

'Not *service*!' he moaned. 'That's what I want to get away from. I meant get *set up*! You know. Like a gentleman.'

'Dear me, we are ambitious, aren't we? What do you fancy? A villa in Broadstairs and two hundred a year?'

He frowned sulkily.

'If you don't wish to be pitched into the street I suggest you shut your pretty little mouth and pay attention.' I drew deeply on my cigarette. 'Your duties will be fairly light. Valeting, as I say. Cleaning. A little cooking. Running my baths. Saving Britain from mortal peril. That sort of thing.'

Charlie looked nonplussed. 'What . . . what happened to your old valet?'

'Shot,' I said blithely. 'You see Charles, I'm in a rather specialized line of work. If you're genuinely interested, my *firm* will take you on.'

'Who do you work for?'

'His Majesty's Government.' I reached across him to stub out my cigarette on the marble table. 'I'm a spy, Charlie. An agent. An assassin. A sharp instrument of the powers that be. And I need an assistant. What do you say? It's not a bad life and you will have King Edward's undying gratitude.'

He frowned. 'I dunno.'

'"Don't seem too unfair from where I'm lying",' I threw back at him. 'There'll be a nominal wage. Just think! You'll be a pepper-corn renter!'

Charlie patted his bruised eye tenderly. 'What do you mean *nominal*?'

I snorted. 'You're on approval, my boy. There can be no question of a decent salary until I am quite satisfied as to the depravity of your character.'

'Bloody hell!'

'Cheer up,' I murmured. 'I'm sure we'll rub along together very well.'

There came a knock at the door. Cursing, I jumped from the bed, slipped into a dressing gown and padded to the door.

A uniformed telegraph boy bowed to me. He was a stringy thing wearing the insolent slouch of the adolescent like a badge of pride.

'Signor Box?'

I nodded and he placed the wire into my hand. I scrabbled at the envelope. *Sir Emmanuel vanished*, I read. *Come at once. Thos Stint (Butler)*.

The boy cocked his head. 'You answer, signor?'

'No. No answer.' I closed the door.

Charlie had risen and was struggling into his frightful grey knickers and striped socks. 'What is it?'

'Your former master has disappeared, Charles. We must make our way there forthwith. You can continue your interrupted tale as we go.'

I dressed in a whirlwind, reloaded my pistol and, as I followed Charlie to the door, passed the pile of clothes I had discarded from the previous night's adventures. I pulled up sharp. Something shiny was projecting from the damp-mottled cloth of my destroyed waistcoat.

Stooping, I pulled it out. It was a fragment of chart that I must have salvaged from the round room. It showed some kind of cross-section, coloured in various lurid inks. It was impossible to make out much detail and I realized at once that I must consult some literature on the subject.

'Two birds with one stone,' I muttered to myself with a smile.

'Eh?' said Charlie.

'Nothing. Come on.'

We raced down the quayside and found a cab. The driver, an old fellow with eyebrows like white sea-urchins, propelled us northwards with gratifying expedition.

Rocked from side to side as we sat in the dingy carriage, Charlie continued his story.

'Well, I kept me eyes and ears open, like Mr Poop'd said to do. I didn't pick up anything for ages –'

'Not like you.'

'Then one night I overheard a bit of talk. It concerned some old geezers back in Blighty and one over here. Well, my ears pricked up because the one over 'ere was his nibs – Sir Emmanuel. My bleedin' employer. Hello, I thinks, what're they up to?'

'And did you find out?'

'Not exactly. But I 'eard them saying there was a woman to be brought across too. Party called Knight.'

I gave a satisfied grunt. 'K to V.C. Go on.'

'Well, I told all this to Mr Poop but then he never come back.'

I looked out of the window and frowned. 'No, he wouldn't have. They were on to him, Charlie. They smashed his brains in with one of their quaint antiquities. Anything else? It seems to me your precious information is rather thin.'

Charlie shrugged. 'Listen, I've risked everything to throw my lot in with you. I tried to hear more but I weren't allowed in. Venus's fella –'

'You've seen him?'

'Just the back of 'im.'

'Big fellow? Broad back?'

Charlie shook his head. 'No. Not at all. Slight, really. He had a hat and cloak on but he looked pretty slight to me.'

'Oh I see. Well, you were saying?'

'Don't know if I should tell you, seeing as how you set so little store by my "precious information".'

I sighed. '*Please* go on.'

Charlie gave a small smile. 'All I know is, Venus's fella has something to do with the House of the Lightning Tree, the biggest den in Naples.'

'Den?'

'Opium, Mr Box.'

I was pondering this when I was jerked forward as the cab drew to a halt. 'Ah! We're here!'

We were outside the crumbling manor house. I jumped from the cab and positively wrenched the bell from its housing as I summoned the butler.

The old retainer came stumbling out and pulled open the gates. He glared at Charlie.

'Where the devil 've you been, young man?'

'Never mind that now,' I interrupted him. 'What's happened? We came as soon as −'

The servant was shaking his head mournfully. 'He's gone, sir. Vanished!'

'Anything unusual in his behaviour?'

Stint ushered us towards the door, casting venomous glances at Charlie. 'No, sir. Not at thing. I brought him the post as usual at a quarter to nine. I returned at ten to bring him his morning coffee but found the library locked. When there was no reply to my knocking I had the door broken open.'

We had stopped at the library door and saw the lock was shattered. Stint pushed it open. 'The library was empty.'

I looked over at the wheeled-chair − the imprint of the ex-occupant's arse plain in its faded orange cushion − and then at his desk. Nothing leapt out as being particular although the atmosphere of the room was unusually stifling even allowing for the weather and Quibble's infernal over-heating. Moreover the windows were open . . .

'The question being then, how does a crippled man escape via the French windows?'

'It is unthinkable, sir. That the windows were open at all is most singular given Sir Emmanuel's horror of cold.'

I nodded absently. 'The post you brought. Of what did it consist?'

Stint pointed towards the desk. 'There they are, sir.'

I looked down. Spread out on the blotter were a quantity of envelopes. I reached towards them and then, thinking better of it, took out my handkerchief and, covering my hand, spread them out in a fan.

'Nine, all told,' I mused. 'But only four have been opened.' Bending down, I peered at the opened letters. 'Invitations all, it seems. Hello! What's this?'

Almost obscured by the blotter was a tenth envelope, a tell-tale mauve in colour and edged in black. I picked up the letter knife and worried it from its hiding place.

'Addressed to Sir Emmanuel,' I said, flipping it over.

Stint moved closer to the desk. 'But no enclosure, sir?'

I shook my head. 'Where did you find your master?'

'He was over there by that bookshelf. Between *Decline of the Procreative Urge* by H. H. Nunstead and Pothan's *On the Efficacy of Tarmacadam*.'

I looked up at him.

'Hard not pick up the master's habits, sir,' he said with a sniff.

I crossed to the bookshelf and took the place occupied by the late scientist. I glanced over at the cold, empty grate of the fire.

'There was, of course, a fire burning?'

'Of course, sir.'

'Over here! Mr Box!'

I turned at Charlie's cry and moved swiftly to where he stood, swinging one of the French windows open and shut. He stepped outside and pointed to the exterior lock. A swift examination told me all I needed to know.

Striding to the fireplace I again folded my handkerchief over my hand and began to root about in the blackened embers.

'Ah!' I cried, my fingers fastening upon a small fragment of charred mauve paper. '*Here* is that enclosure, Stint. Or what remains of it.'

I held the scrap of paper close to my face. A strong odour at once assailed me. It was pungent and familiar.

'D'you smell that, Charlie?' I cried, waving it under the boy's nose. 'I'd say ... I'd say this paper has been impregnated. Impregnated with a chemical with which you and I have had some little acquaintance!'

'Good grief!' gasped Stint. 'You mean you are addicted to some *drug?*'

'Eh? No, no!' I stood up straight. 'This is what I believe happened here this morning. The letter in the mauve envelope was a lure, containing some bogus message and instructions that it was to be burnt upon receipt. Your master did as he was told and was then overcome by the noxious substance in which the letter had been soaked.'

Stint bit his lip anxiously. 'And then he threw open the windows in an effort to clear the fumes?'

'Nay, for the windows have been forced open from the outside as Mr Jackpot here discovered! Whoever sent this letter lay out there in wait. When they saw that their plans were working they broke open the windows and grabbed Sir Emmanuel. They then left the windows ajar to allow the toxin to escape.'

'But who, sir? Who would do such a thing?'

The odour of that vile chemical contained in the mauve letter was unmistakable. The purplish dust on Verdigris's desk! The charred paper in Sash's grate! All three must have received a mauve envelope. Whatever had been written therein must also have contained instructions to burn its deadly enclosure.

Now I knew how – just not by whom.

It was time to test just what Stint had absorbed. I took the scrap from my waistcoat pocket. 'What do you make of that, Stint?'

The butler peered at it.

I thrust my hands into my pockets. 'A cross-section of some kind. I wonder if you could point us to a volume or two on the structures of modern machines?'

Stint shook his head. 'Oh no, sir.'

'No? Why not?'

'It's not a machine, sir. It is a volcano,' he said.

XVII

THE LAIR OF MR LEE

S it, by George!'
I looked over his shoulder and indicated a double line that had been inked into the shape on the chart. 'And this?'

'I believe it is known as a vent, sir. A fissure in the rock through which the magma flows to the surface.'

Charlie took the fragment from him. A series of arrows had been drawn by hand inside the lines. 'Then why are these arrows pointing towards the *inside* of the volcano?'

'I really cannot say,' sniffed the butler.

We advanced towards the book shelves. 'Tell me, Stint. Do you think, by any chance, we could track down the particular volcano?'

A smile fluttered over his pale lips. 'Every chance, I should think, sir. I'm sure Sir Emmanuel would be very happy to know his collection is being put to good use. I believe we shall need the steps, sir, if you'd be so kind.'

Charlie pulled the revolving library steps from their shadowy niche. Before I could protest, he had mounted the steps and began pushing his way along the shelves. The steps' wheels squealed appallingly.

'Hmmph,' said Stint, disapprovingly. 'Now then,' he said and pointed upwards. 'Third shelf. What do you see?'

In the feeble light Charlie passed treatise after dreary treatise. There were atlases, text-books . . .

'*Manlove's Tectonic Activity*,' Charlie read. '*Vulcanism in the Pacific Rim . . . The Lava Bomb . . .*'

'We're getting warmer, you might say.'

Charlie had stopped with one hand on the shelf, preparing to push himself off again when a hefty book in a cloth-bound cover seemed to catch his attention. '*Magnetic Viscosity?*' he called hopefully.

'That's the one,' said Stint.

'Maxwell Morraine,' I cried.

Stint looked over at me. 'Yes, sir? What of him?'

'It never occurred to me to ask *you*, Stint. What do *you* know of your late master's colleague, Morraine? He threw me out of the house at the very mention of his name.'

Stint shrugged. He seemed suddenly weary. Charlie came down the steps and stood by him, handing him the book. Stint began to flick through it as he spoke. 'You are far too young to remember, sir, but it was quite a tragedy. Professor Morraine went . . . funny.'

'Funny?'

'In the head, sir. They do say it was on account of his wife running off with some gent but Sir Emmanuel told me Mr Morraine had always been a little touched. Even when they were students together.'

'Yes. I had heard they attended the same college. And they came out here, didn't they, to work?'

Stint nodded vigorously, then paused, comparing the fragment of chart with an illustration within the great book. 'Sir Emmanuel's father had this house and he always loved the Italian countryside. Seemed like a natural place to pursue their researches. All Greek or Italian to you and me, I suppose, sir, but Professor Morraine had theories about the massive potential energy contained within the lava, within the very stuff of the earth's core! But it all came to naught. Then there was the fire and poor Mrs Morraine . . . well. Aha! I have found the volcano, sir.'

He held the book aloft, the piece of chart pressed against the relevant page. To no one's great surprise, it was a cross-section of Mount Vesuvius.

Emmanuel Quibble's extraordinary library was proving to be invaluable. Following the positive identification of the geological chart, we began digging for a clue as to the identity of the strange chemical used on the old man.

Charlie sat down and put his feet up on the desk, pulled off his boots and began to pick at his toes, earning fierce stares from Stint.

'Make yourself useful,' I ordered, tossing him a copy of *Arsenical Poisoning and its Causes.*

'I am. Being useful, I mean. I'm thinking.'

'Ha! I am on His Majesty's service. You are on mine.'

He put his hands behind his head. Is it possible to swagger whilst sitting down?

'Seems to me there is a connection between this purple stuff and what I told you about Venus's fella.'

'What about him?'

'The House of the Lightning Tree. Remember?'

His face dimpled into a cock-eyed smile.

'Opium?' I cried.

And within a very few minutes, thanks to Stint's cross-referencing, we had it. 'A distillation of the seeds of the manganese poppy,' I read, tracing a finger over the delicate colour-plate showing the flower.

'Never heard of it.'

'I don't doubt it. Grows only in certain parts of the Himalayas. Now, get your boots on, Charlie, you're going back out.'

'I am?'

'Yes. Arrange some transport for our visit to this den. We'll reconvene in the lobby of the Santa Lucia at ten.'

'Righto, chief.' Charlie got up and struggled into his boots, holding the door frame for support.

'Oh, and Charlie?'

'Yes?'

'Do mind out for yourself. I fear you are becoming indispensable.'

The boy smiled and I felt a curious twinge as he closed the door after him. I thought at first it must be some undigested fancy from the Café Gambrinus but I finally recognized it as an almost alien emotion. *Fondness.*

I took my leave of Stint and returned to the hotel. Quibble, Verdigris, Bella, Reynolds, Charlie – my head was spinning. After a long bath I soon felt more like myself. I felt myself so much, in fact, that I ended up having one off the wrist, imagining the wondrous Bella wrapped in my fevered embrace.

We dined together that evening and Miss Pok looked more glorious than ever, I thought, glowing like a moonbeam in the gilded shadows of the restaurant. I apologized again for the unseemly hastiness of my departure from the funicular.

'There's really no need,' she said lightly. 'You did warn me you might have to . . . pop off a little hastily now and then.'

'Did that Italian chap see you back all right?'

'Oh yes. He was quite charming.'

She smiled and raised her glass. 'To you, Lucifer.'

I responded, clinking my crystal against hers. 'No, to us.'

'You have not though, been entirely frank with me,' she said after sipping her wine.

'No?'

'No. Unless you felt a pressing need to sketch the crowd, it did look very much like you were *chasing* someone.'

'Ah,' I said. 'Umm . . .'

She held up her hand. 'Don't say anything. I know you would tell me if you were able. There are matters of great import on hand, are there not?'

I nodded slowly.

'And this business with Mr Miracle is somehow part of it.'

'Indeed.'

She nodded. 'Then one day, perhaps, you will tell me about it.'

I liked the sound of that. It promised a *future*. Together.

We said goodnight at her hotel room door and, for the first time, I was allowed a kiss on her smooth cheek.

Ah, me!

Anticipating a night's work, I returned to my own room and changed into a Norfolk jacket, nautical sweater and light but sensible tweed trousers. On the stroke of ten, I slipped down to the lobby and found Charlie waiting for me.

I looked about for a four-wheeler but Charlie pulled at my sleeve. 'No carriages. They'll hear us coming a mile off.'

To my amazement, he pulled aside a quantity of canvas that lay in a bundle in the street. Beneath it, at an angle to the wall, was a tandem bicycle.

'Is that the best you could do?' I cried.

'Needs must,' he grinned. 'I nicked it.'

I have never been a, shall we say, *fan de cycle*, and was not in the best of moods for mounting one. However, Charlie was right – it would be a far less conspicuous way of approaching Naples' premier opium den than a cab. I grudgingly acquiesced and dragged the machine from its hiding place. Together we managed to mount it. After a few wobbly moments, we mastered the thing and began peddling feverishly up the slopes to Capodimonte, following Charlie's directions. I was grateful, at last, for all those bone-shaker lessons my governess forced me to take.

At length, we turned into some kind of rookery, a shambolic collection of semi-ruined villas adjacent to a vast olive grove. The rotten plasterwork of the structures was visible even in the starlight; the eaves of the buildings practically merged into one another like a line of guardsmen toppling on the parade ground.

I hopped off the bicycle and held it steady so that Charlie too could dismount. Then we began to push it quietly along the road. Before us was a large and disreputable-looking building with a blackened, twisted olive tree dominating its façade.

'That looks like it,' whispered Charlie.

I nodded – even in this town of curiosities, what else could it be? – and indicated that we should lay down the bicycle on the parched earth.

I felt glad of my reloaded revolver as we advanced into that filthy hole.

Torches burned in sconces on the fronts of some of the dwellings and it was possible to see figures huddled in the shadowed gloom.

That they meant us ill was obvious and I raised the gun and cocked it in as blatant a fashion as I could.

'Stay close by me, Charlie,' I hissed.

The shadows fell back a little but we hurried briskly along past walls of blotched green plaster.

Charlie hammered repeatedly on the door of the big house.

I slipped into a shadowed niche, watching as the figures that surrounded us grew bolder. I distinctly saw a great bear of a man with a kerchief knotted around his head grinning at me in the flickering torch-light. In his hand he carried a thick cudgel and he was slapping it repeatedly into his palm.

'Let's cut along, eh, Charlie?' I said quietly.

Suddenly, the door creaked open and an indisputably Chinese face loomed out of the darkness.

'What you want?' squawked the newcomer, his scantily bearded face appearing as a strip of red flesh in the torch-light.

I surged forward through the door and pushed him backwards. Charlie bounded inside, darted past him and slammed the door shut behind us.

'What you do? What you do? You cannot come in here!' barked the little man. He was round as a pudding and clad in a filthy muslin robe.

I levelled the revolver at him. 'I think this will do as my passport,' I hissed in his face.

'No need for this!' cried the Chinaman in a hoarse whisper. 'Why you come like this? We all friends here. You want pipe?'

'No. Yes. Let's get inside,' I urged.

We followed the Chinaman through a warren of rubbish-strewn corridors, emerging eventually into a large chamber that might once have been a sitting room. The walls were festooned with cobwebs and damp-blossoms. What was visible of the floor showed naked and broken floor-boards leading to some noisome cellar beneath.

The prevailing impression, however, was of a terrible fug, a poisonous atmosphere rich in the unmistakable scent of the poppy. Opium smoke hung in wreaths over the heads of the multitude that crammed the room, their slack jaws and rolling eyes speaking of days and weeks lost to the pipe. Like so many sacks, the addicts lay strewn over the floor, gurgling happily as they sucked, the shining black beads of opium glowing like fireflies.

Don't get me wrong. I'm no prude and like a pipe as much as the next man. But all things in moderation, as Genghis Khan used to say.

Our Chinese host was threading his way through the heaps of human detritus, lantern in hand. 'My name Mr Lee. You fine gentlemen. I have office. We talk there.'

The 'office' was at least clean. Two chairs and a table comprised the only furniture. I sat in one and Charlie sat down heavily on the other. Lee set the lantern on the table and giggled most unpleasantly.

'I have extra fine poppy for you, English. Very cheap –'

'No thank you. I have very expensive tastes. I want some of the purple poppy.'

Lee's blinked then laughed. 'I not understand. House of Lightning Tree have many pipes. But no purple poppy. Come. Relax.'

I stood up, seized him by his filthy robe and pushed him up against the wall. 'My friend and I are in something of a rush, do you see? We need to know to whom you supply the *purple* poppy?'

His fat face flushed in alarm and he shot an appealing look over my shoulder at Charlie.

'You crazy! You crazy! Please!'

Charlie got to his feet. 'I can't help you,' he said to Lee. 'This fella's a painter. He'll as like bite your ear off unless you tell him what he wants to know.'

Lee gave a gulp and his chins wobbled. 'I know nothing.'

I slammed him against the rotten plaster. 'Tell me, you glorified tobacconist.'

'There no such thing as purple poppy!' he squealed.

I nudged the barrel of the pistol into the folds of fat around his wet mouth. 'Believe me, I will take a professional interest in seeing the red of your blood running against the yellow of your skin.'

Lee looked at us desperately, wringing his chubby hands. 'I tell you! I tell you!'

Shaking with terror, Lee sank back against the rotten plaster. His pin-prick eyes closed momentarily. 'Purple poppy come over especial from Shanghai. Most rare. Most precious. It is much dangerous. It has many faces. Up, down, forget some, even kill you. Must be very, very careful. Needs expert. No good for you nice gentlemen!'

'I see,' I said quietly. 'And you've been supplying this filthy stuff to someone, haven't you? To what end?'

'I cannot tell you . . .'

I pressed the pistol further into his face. Sweat was streaming over his oily skin. 'Please! Please! I know only my instructions! I deliver purple poppy and I hear no more.'

I stepped away from the perspiring fat man while still keeping him covered with the pistol. 'Deliver it where, exactly?'

Lee smiled his fat smile. 'I can give you address, but it is impossible for me to leave these premises, my business, you understand –'

I levelled my revolver at his nethers. 'You will take us there, Lee. Or the Neapolitan castrati will be acquiring a new member.'

The darkness was thickening as I commandeered a dog-cart and set off with Charlie and the reluctant Chinee into the sleeping streets. We must have made a pretty sight, lashing away at the skinny steeds but then Naples is accustomed to strange sights; half-mad city that it is.

Lee spoke little but contented himself with pointing and urging as we clattered through the narrow alleys, ducking wet washing that was strung between the houses and shops.

We clattered out of the city and along the coastal road.

'Now look where we're heading,' observed Charlie with a grunt. It was no great surprise to see the great volcano looming before us, its fiery crown smoking like a beacon. After an hour or so, we rolled on into an area of broad parkland. A strange collection of buildings formed a squared 'C' shape around the perimeter. In the ruined isolation of the C's centre stood a blackened villa, its windows fogged with soot.

'This place,' said Lee. 'Place where I bring poppy.'

I jumped from the cart and swung my pistol round to cover Lee. 'Come on, out!'

The Chinaman shook his head. 'Please. Do not make me. I not want to go in there.'

'What's the matter?' cried Charlie, clambering out and lighting a lantern. 'We'll look after you.'

Lee did not appear to be reassured and shook his head violently, eyes glittering like jet. 'Not that. I never see anybody when I come. But . . . house haunted.'

'Pah!' I ejaculated.

'No, no!' protested Lee. 'Is the truth, sirs! Please let poor Lee go home now.'

I shook my head. 'I fear not, old man. Don't worry your top-knot, though. Any spooks will get a blast of this.' I cocked the revolver and the three of us began to make our way stealthily across the grass.

A dim light shone in the lower floor of a neighbouring house. We slipped into the shadows so as to remain invisible. I looked about. A pair of old, blistered black doors were visible at the base of the building. The coal cellar.

'Where did you bring the poppies, Lee? To this cellar?'

Lee shook his nervous head. 'No, no. Through front. Come, come.'

We moved silently forward to the blackened edifice of the villa and crept over the gravel to the porch. The front door seemed intact but all the windows that were visible had been boarded up. I reasoned it was wiser not to advertise our presence so, in a very few moments, I had pulled down some of the splintering wood and exposed a smoke-blackened window-pane. I took off my muffler and, wrapping it around my fist, smashed the glass. It gave with only a faint tinkling.

The three of us clambered inside, our feet sinking slightly into a carpet of glass and debris, Lee whimpering and squealing like a nervous child.

The atmosphere was at once oppressive with decay. The lantern showed fire-damaged furniture, their varnished surfaces blistered and cracked.

I turned to Charlie. 'Seems quiet enough.'

'As the grave.'

Lee wailed softly. I grabbed him by his robe. 'Where did you leave the opium?'

The Chinaman was looking about in terror. 'Here in hallway. Not want to stay longer than need to.'

The dusty floor of the entranceway had clearly been disturbed. Charlie held up his lamp revealing a series of trails, as though sleds had cut swathes through the dust.

I tapped him on the shoulder. 'You explore the house, Charlie,' I whispered, lighting my own lantern. 'Mr Lee and I will take the cellar.'

'Righto.'

I watched him heading for the mouldering staircase then began swinging the lantern about in search of the entrance to the coal cellar. I found what I was looking for in a recessed corner beneath the stairs.

'Please, sir,' whimpered Lee. 'Let us go now. This place bad.'

I felt for a door handle. It was big and carved into a hexagonal shape. To my very great surprise, it turned easily and the door creaked softly open.

Gingerly we stepped down on to a poorly lit wooden stair. The smell of damp assailed me at once but my attention was riveted on the curious sight before me.

The coal cellar appeared to have been adapted into some kind of laboratory. The remains of tubes, flasks and retorts littered benches and there were fragments of geological charts pinned to the wall. Fragments, merely, as the place now resembled the flue of some great chimney. The broken walls were soot-streaked and wet. Glass lay twisted into fantastic shapes on the remains of benches and cupboards. In the corner was a broad, fat-legged table and on it burned a single candle.

There was someone else in this house.

Just as the thought crossed my mind, I heard a terrible moaning.

For a moment I took it to be Lee but the fat creature was jibbering with fear right by me, his eyes clamped shut. I glanced over my shoulder and back the way we had come. The sound was coming from up the stairs, an awful, wretched groan, followed by a burst of ragged sobbing.

'Charlie!' I cried. 'Is that you?'

At once the noise ceased. I felt the hairs on the back of my neck rise.

'Charlie?'

I jammed the pistol in Lee's back and quickly we mounted the cellar steps, pushed open the door and stepped back into the hallway.

I held the lantern high above my head but could see no one.

Then the moaning began again, as though a soul were in torment. It seemed to be coming from upstairs. I swung the lantern in that direction and, just for an instant, caught a glimpse of something white on the landing above. It seemed to flutter into the shadows like a great bird. I started. Lee absolutely yelled in shock.

'Shut up, you fat fool!' I spat then, and, urging him forward with the revolver, made for the staircase.

The creak of our feet on the rotten stair seemed to halt the sobbing once more. We pressed on, ascending swiftly.

I called out for Charlie, then swung the lantern round as I caught sight of the whitish shape again, still above us on the staircase. It was a figure, dressed in some sort of billowing white gown. Or shroud, I thought dully.

I strode towards the phantom shape, determined not to be rattled.

'Who's there?' I demanded. 'Show yourself!'

With Lee almost hysterical at my side, I reached the top of the staircase and was confronted by a door. Gingerly, I reached out a hand and took hold of the knob.

I swallowed, nervous in spite of myself, and began to turn it.

A hand reached out of the shadows and clasped my arm. I pulled back in undisguised alarm, thrusting the lamp aloft and shining a light down on the frightened face of Charlie Jackpot.

'Bloody hell, Mr Box! Did you see it? Did you see it?'

I nodded, a little too quickly. 'I saw it!'

'The face!' he whispered. 'Did you see its face?'

All at once, the door in front of us flew open and the figure in white seemed to swarm upon us.

I yelled in stark terror and batted at the thing with both hands. Lee took to his heels and pounded down the rotten stairway. Charlie threw himself behind me and we sank back against the wall as the spectre went hurtling down the stairs after the Chinaman, screaming and sobbing as though it were a denizen of Hell itself.

'Christ Almighty!' I gasped, after we had picked ourselves up off the landing. 'What was it?'

Charlie shook his head. 'It went . . . it went towards the cellar.'

I stood up and opened the lantern to its fullest extent.

Slowly and silently, we descended the stairs and approached the door to the cellar.

There was no sign of Lee.

I opened the door, taking care that it should not creak, and then took a few tentative steps downwards.

I lifted the lamp. Behind me, Charlie gasped and clapped a hand to his mouth.

Sitting in a fire-charred chair was the ruin of a woman. Dressed in a stained and tattered white robe, her hair hung about her shoulders in great, knotted clumps. It was her face, though, which drew all our attention. The eyes looked out from a skull-like visage from which the flesh seemed to have been boiled away. Great blistered lumps of skin hung like candle-wax from the jaw and cheek-bones.

'Good God,' whispered Charlie.

The woman looked at me wildly, those dreadful eyes glistening in the lantern-light. Then she began to moan once more, her whole body shuddering as though a disinterred mummy had been brought to some foul simulacrum of life.

And all at once I knew her.

'Mrs Knight?' I cried. 'Mrs Midsomer Knight?'

'Yes,' said the voice of Lee behind us. 'Most regrettable that you will never have chance to meet her properly.'

He was brandishing a Colt in his pudgy hand.

'Please to stay still. I can certainly kill one of you before you have chance to overpower me.' The Chinee turned his narrow black eyes upon me and smiled. 'Drop gun.'

With a sigh, I dropped my revolver to the tiled floor.

Lee levelled his own gun at me, a horrible snarling grin flickering over his lips as he bent down to retrieve mine. He thrust it inside his robes. 'You have done well, Mr Box. But it is time to stop toying with you. You dangle like child's puppet. So sorry.'

He advanced on the wretched woman before us. He plucked a hypodermic syringe from somewhere in his robes, and with practised efficiency plunged it into her forearm. With a groan, she slumped forward. 'Now, please to escort lady from cellar.'

He gestured with the Colt and Charlie and I manhandled Mrs Knight up the stairs and back into the hallway. Thanks to the nameless drug – no doubt the purple poppy in one of its many guises – she was the very opposite of a ghost. She weighed a ton.

Lee ushered us through the house, into a large, gloomy room dominated by a pair of disreputable-looking French windows. Its floor was an inch-thick in dust but clearly visible in its centre were four coffins, dragged in from the hallway.

Three of the coffins were sealed, the fourth open. Lee smiled. 'One bird fly. She not have enough of purple poppy. Now she sleep better. Please to put her in.'

Reluctantly, Charlie and I lowered the woman into the empty coffin, its satin lining rustling in a peculiarly horrible fashion.

'Let us check on others,' said Lee with a smile. 'Please to open coffins.'

Gingerly, Charlie knelt down and lifted the lid from the first of the grisly boxes.

'Raise lantern please, Mr Box,' said Lee with infuriating politeness.

Within the coffin was what appeared to be the corpse of a man, his skin waxen and deathly pale. He was of large build and had a very prominent chin. His eyes were spaced wide apart. Professor Eli Verdigris.

The remaining coffins revealed, as expected, Professors Sash and Quibble. All of them lived on. Lived on in some ghastly, drug-induced coma.

'So all is ready. The party is complete.'

'What the hell is all this for, Lee?' I demanded.

Lee said nothing but indicated that we should move towards the French windows. Charlie pushed at the rotten woodwork until the doors groaned open.

Beyond lay an extraordinary landscape, lit by flaming torches – a vista of shattered stonework, tree-lined avenues and ancient, rutted roadways. I stepped out on to the flagged ground and gasped.

'What is this place?' cried Charlie.

'You not know?' said Lee with a horrid smile.

'I know,' I breathed. 'It is Pompeii!'

The torches illumined the ruins in a fearful relief, the hazy black hump of Vesuvius rearing over the lost city like the back of some dreadful beast.

'And now,' said Lee, hissing with laughter and brandishing both pistols. 'It is time for you to die.'

For an instant, I despaired, letting my hands drop to my sides. But in that moment, Charlie jumped out in front of me and hurled his lantern at the Chinaman. It hit him full in the chest, there was a satisfying splintering of glass and as the startled Lee looked down in surprise, his foul gown burst alight, and he was enveloped in flame.

I darted forward and brought my own lantern crashing down on Lee's head. He staggered and fell forward on to his knees, dropping a pistol and battering desperately at his blazing robe with his free hand.

Despite his panic and his hideous shrieks of pain, Lee raised a shaking hand and aimed a pistol at me. Roaring like an enraged tiger I ran at him full force and planted my fist in his throat. I felt the flesh give sickeningly and he toppled to the flagstones, smacking his cheek against the crumbling masonry.

Charlie was at my side in an instant. He whipped off his jacket and succeeded in putting out the flames.

'Well done, Charlie,' I said, breathlessly. 'Let's get the fat lump inside. Once he's recovered his senses, he can tell us what the hell's going on.'

Charlie looked down at Lee and shook his head, ''Fraid not, sir. You don't know your own strength. He's a gonner.'

I turned the Chinaman over. His wind-pipe was crushed and he was quite still.

'Bugger,' I said eloquently.

Exhaling heavily, Charlie sat down on the flagstones and looked at me. 'Now what?'

I peered into the fiery gloom. 'Now, Mr Jackpot, we wait. Sooner or later, someone is going to come and collect those coffins.'

XVIII

NECROPOLIS

OR what seemed like hours, there was no sign of activity. We passed the time exploring this relic of the ancient world – a frozen, grey world, stopped in a moment by the power of the great volcano. The ruins that littered the gardens of the villa did not seem to form part of the main excavation, and were unattended – a private monument. Charlie came across what appeared to be the entrance to a tunnel but it proved to be merely an ancient well. Neither of us felt further inclined to mess with wells.

I recalled my previous visit to the ruin and how, despite the loathsome press of gawping day-trippers, I had found Pompeii quite magnificent; its frescoed villas, its filthy pictures, its roads still rutted with the tracks of ancient carts. Yet it also wears a melancholy aspect, for here are laid bare past lives, here is the shattered grandeur that was the Roman Empire, here lie the actual folk themselves, or casts of their tortured remains – *the skeletons still within* – so that teeth show horribly in rictus grins from shapeless lumps of plaster.

In the flickering torchlight now, undisturbed by the goggling crowds, it was possible to feel one had actually slipped back in time. I explored the villa while Charlie walked about the grounds. The black and gold murals I found looked fresh and vivid, the ancient scribblings on the walls outside as though the graffitist had only lately quit the scene. When Charlie returned from his recce, I half expected his silhouetted form to resolve itself in toga and sandals.

I gazed over his shoulder at the smoking summit of the volcano.

'Look at her, Charlie,' I whispered. 'Vesuvius looks down upon Pompeii as if to say "I have destroyed you once. How dare you show your face?" One day it'll make good its threat and cover all this up again.'

'Then people could come and stare at us,' chimed in Charlie.

'Not a pleasant thought is it?' I replied. 'I'd hate to have some hairy fool poking a stick at my petrified bum.'

We laughed. Charlie sat down next to me as I stretched out over the flagstones, enjoying my fag. Above us the stars packed the black sky.

'What are you thinking, Mr Box?' said Charlie gently.

I continued to stare at the sky. 'Only that a night such as this should not be spent in the contemplation of mortal danger but of love.'

The boy lay down next to me. In the soft silence I could hear his quick breathing. I suppose I knew that he wanted me to place my hand on his, to turn him towards me and kiss him with all the fever that that sulphurous atmosphere demanded. Instead I flicked my cigarette away and heaved a sigh.

'But business before pleasure,' I said, sitting up. 'Miss Bella Pok will have to wait.'

'Who?' said Charlie sharply.

'A rather singular young lady of my acquaintance. Perhaps when all this is over . . .'

The boy's face fell. Aren't I a rotter?

Before Charlie could say something he might regret I stayed him with an outstretched hand. Just visible in the distant gloom was a curious purplish glow.

Charlie had already moved away and I could see him straining to listen. Soon I became aware of the sound of trudging feet on stone and, a little afterwards, seven or eight unnaturally tall men lumbered into our line of sight. Charlie gasped and I too wondered briefly whether they were some kind of phantasm. The queasy mauve light above their heads told its own story, however; the poor wretches wore the same brass helmets as my attacker from the Vesuvius Club.

They clumped in single file towards the villa and I beckoned Charlie to duck behind the cover of the opened windows. As the strange procession trooped past us and into the villa, we stood stock still, aware solely of the warm breeze in the great dark trees.

With effortful grunting, the helmeted zombies trudged back into the garden, carrying the four coffins between them. We waited as long as we dared and then set off in pursuit.

The unearthly glow from the brass helmets functioned like the Israelites' pillar of fire and so Charlie and I were able to shadow the funereal procession with some deftness. Appropriately enough we were making our way through the city's ancient cemetery, the rather charmingly named Via delle Tombe. Passing through the old town gateway, we soon reached what seemed to be a massive earthworks. The zombified men put down the coffins and stood stock still, as immobile as the tombstones that surrounded them.

Crouching low, I peered across the earthworks. A thin strip of yellowy light was just visible.

'Where's that coming from?' gasped Charlie.

'I do believe,' I said, getting to my feet, 'from under the ground.'

Charlie began to rise also but stopped, half-crouched. 'Sir?'

'Hmm?'

'You hear that?'

I listened. Very, very faintly, I could hear a curious susurration.

'What is it?' said Charlie.

It was indeed a strange sound, somewhere between the wheeze of a bellows and the whir of a motorcar engine. Suddenly one of the helmeted men jerked into life like a wound-up automaton and bent down towards the ground. The strip of light widened as, with a rending squeal, he opened some kind of hatch set into the rubble. With surprising dexterity, the others then began to lower the coffins through the hatch, clambering down after them. We gave it a minute or so after the metal door had finally swung to before we advanced across the excavation.

With the quiet concentration of a professional, I got to work on the hatch and within a few minutes I had levered the thing open. Despite my best efforts, it creaked loudly as I pulled it back on its hinges.

I peered down into the hole beyond. A shaft led steeply

downwards, its sides studded with small electric lights. I could just make out the top of a metal ladder.

'Down?' queried Charlie.

'Down.'

Leading the way, I swung myself over the lip of the shaft and began to clamber down the ladder, the rungs sharp with the blood-like smell of warm iron. We seemed to have been descending for a full five minutes when I paused for breath and reached out a hand for Charlie's ankle on the rung above me in order to stop him clambering on to my head.

He crouched down and tried to peer past me into the gloom. 'Seems to me someone's been doing quite a bit of digging.'

The helmeted automata could have only manhandled the coffins down here with inhuman strength. We recommenced our descent, and after a further minute or so we reached a layer of soft volcanic rock where the shaft abruptly flattened out, stretching ahead in a kind of dreary, dusty grey corridor. Again, electric lights had been strung from the walls, coiled wire looped between them like strange umbilical appendages.

'That sound's much louder now,' commented Charlie as we advanced.

I nodded. 'Perhaps some kind of air-pump.'

After a time, the loose, shale-like rock began to give way to the familiar sight of a Roman pavement. Seemingly we were now in the unexcavated bowels of Pompeii, amongst structures no man had seen for almost two thousand years. No man save those we now sought. The road branched off to the right almost immediately, giving on to a wonderfully preserved archway. The light was brighter here and clearly getting brighter still as the whole structure was suffused in a great ball of luminescence.

Charlie stumbled slightly on the pavement and I looked down to see that the stone floor was concave, a great grooved channel having been excavated in its centre. I glanced around swiftly then noticed the distinctive decoration that covered the walls in a series of serried niches, each containing a yellowy electric bulb.

'That appears to be Neptune,' I cried, pointing at the carving's twisting tail and powerful muscled torso. 'This must have been a bath house.'

Charlie nodded indifferently. 'What is it *now*, though? That's what we have to worry about.'

There seemed to be no one about, so we pressed on. The first chamber we entered, again decorated with the motif of the sea-god, had been only partially excavated from the rock. A series of chair-like niches, not unlike church vestibules, occupied each wall. Here the Pompeiians had evidently changed out of their togas and gone skinny-dipping in the plunge pools. One such pool, now half full of the rain water which streamed in from above, still stood close by.

Charlie gave a sharp gasp and I turned on my heel.

'It's all right,' he breathed, steadying himself. 'Just didn't expect *that*.'

He brought the torch-beam to bear on one of the vestibules where lay sprawled a complete skeleton, its arms flung wide, its jaw grotesquely open. The soft grey rock still swathed half of its carcass like a volcanic robe.

'Come on,' I urged.

We passed through the ancient changing rooms into a much larger chamber, supported by more of the Neptune columns and boasting a grand, domed roof. Within was a frankly fantastic sight.

One might have been forgiven for thinking some *nouveau riche* tradesman had decided to desert his aspidistra-stuffed environs and move into the old Roman fort down the road. Every inch of that great chamber was crammed with a weird combination of domestic contemporary furniture and looted ancient treasures. A headless nymph stood next to a huge armchair. Magnificent glass-ware shared table space with fruit bowls and a Napoleon-hat clock. The whole place was steeped in a curiously pellucid green light, as though the baths were still active.

At the far end of the room stood a huge fountain shaped like a round table with a raised edge to contain the forgotten waterstream. One great crack marred its flawless surface yet it had been altered by newer and stranger additions. Papers and charts were strewn across it, together with a quantity of queer-looking machinery. At the centre of the fountain a three-dimensional cutaway model of the volcano was hooked up to some sort of Wimshurst-device. Wires spilled from the stonework, and huge pipes had been erected against the walls. From these emanated the strange, wheezing whirring we had encountered on the surface.

Charlie stepped gingerly into the room, his mouth agape. He held up a hand towards the great fat pipes, then looked back towards me, smiling delightedly.

'Feel them, Mr Box!' he cried. 'They're warm.'

It was true. Whatever strange machinery had been erected here, it brought light and heat to the dead ruins.

'Quite something, ain't it?' said Charlie.

A footstep. Then the voice, familiar to me yet strangely elusive.

'Isn't it just?' said the voice from the shadows.

Both Charlie and I turned towards the sound.

Framed in the doorway stood a beautiful figure, resplendent in a crimson velvet gown. Her auburn hair was piled up and her dark-eyes lined with kohl as I had first seen them that night in the Vesuvius Club.

'Venus!' cried Charlie.

'Good evening, my dear,' I said mildly.

The gorgeous creature inclined her head slightly. 'Charlie. Signor Box. Such a pleasure to meet you again,' she said gaily, clapping her hands together and advancing into the room. 'Let us have wine! Despite the improvements, it is still chill down here and one feels the damp.' The Italian accent seemed to have gone west.

Venus strode to a fat-legged mahogany table and poured three glasses of wine rather carelessly.

'What's going on, Venus?' said Charlie plaintively. 'That fella of yours has gone too far this time. You've got to throw your lot in with us.'

Venus smiled. 'He's gone too far, has he, Charlie?'

She offered me a glass but I shook my head.

'We've supped, thanks,' I said curtly. 'Now, if you come quietly, I swear I will do what I can for you.'

Venus paused with a crystal goblet of dark wine halfway to her lips and began to chuckle, her laugh filling the ancient room. 'You will do what you can for me?' she roared. 'Where? When?'

'At your trial,' I said evenly.

'My trial?'

'Yours and that of the villain you call your lover.'

'My dear sir, you are quite comical. For what should . . . we . . . stand trial?'

'For the attempted murders of Professors Sash, Verdigris and Quibble.'

'Pooh! They are alive! What have I done but give them a little trip abroad, gratis.'

'And for the abduction of Mrs Midsomer Knight.'

'Safe and well and here also.'

'Well then, for the murder of Jocelyn Poop of His Majesty's Diplomatic.'

'Ah well,' said a new voice. 'I'm afraid I must plead guilty to that one.'

A man walked into the room, also dressed in crimson robes, his face covered by one of the masks I had seen at the Vesuvius Club.

Venus took his hand and kissed it. He removed his mask with the other hand and smiled. 'Good evening, Mr Box,' said Cretaceous Unmann, raising a pistol.

'I'll take that drink now, if I may,' I said quietly.

I sank a goblet of wine in one draft. 'Won't you join me?' I asked Unmann, proffering a glass. 'It's really very fine.'

Unmann shook his head, a sly smile playing over his lips.

'Well then,' I said, 'Perhaps you'd like to tell me what the blazes you're doing burrowing beneath Pompeii and who it is that you're both working for.'

Unmann smiled again and cocked an eyebrow at Venus. 'Shall I explain?'

'No,' she replied. 'Let us allow that honour to pass to the genius behind this whole scheme. A greater mind, even, than his sainted father who the world so cruelly wronged. Please say *buonasera* once more, Mr Box, to the man you know only as Signor Victor. Signor Victor *Morraine!*'

I turned instinctively, expecting to see the slim, striking young man from the funicular railway entering the cavern but there was no sign of anyone. I turned back when I heard a faint rustling sound.

Venus was untying her hair so that it fell in heavy, auburn loops about her neck. With a jerk of her hand, the hair flopped to the floor. A wig! She stared at me, grinning wildly, her dark, dark eyes ablaze with triumph, then hoisted up her crimson skirts, exposing bare, muscular legs and what we doctors call a cock and balls.

'Christ Almighty!' was all I had to say.

'Venus!' gasped Charlie. 'You're a boy!'

XIX

THE ENGINES OF VULCAN

ND so 'she' was. The beautiful Venus was the youth I had been introduced to as Victor. But Victor Morraine! This was almost more extraordinary. The dazzling creature inclined his head and moved towards my manservant, skirts swishing over the cold stone floor. 'Oh, Charlie. If only you had been true to me!'

The boy was staring at him, open-mouthed. Venus flopped down in the armchair. Unmann continued to cover Charlie and me with the pistol.

'I suppose it takes all sorts,' I said philosophically. 'Really, Unmann, I can't see what you can gain by helping this . . . *person* with whatever pathetic revenge he's planning.'

Unmann laughed, no longer the silly ass. His composure was quite chilling. 'You can have no conception of the scale of Venus's ambition. But you're right in one respect, Mr Box. It *is* revenge that he seeks.'

I twiddled the stem of the goblet between my fingers. 'Do tell.' In my experience, that's all it takes.

Venus's eyes blazed. 'Yes! I want revenge! Revenge on those treacherous men who earned their reputations from my father's work yet had not the brains to complete it! Revenge against the woman who betrayed him and broke his fragile mind. They shall all suffer.'

I cocked my head to one side and waved a hand around me. 'But this is all very elaborate, isn't it? What exactly  do you have in mind for this "suffering"?'

Venus's face set into a hard mask as though he were gazing back through the years. 'My father was a great man – a visionary. He lacked only the discipline to see his work through to its logical conclusion. Fortunately his genius was passed on to me! And I have completed his work.'

I felt suddenly cold. 'Completed? You mean that's what all this is?'

'It is. Heat and light from the immense power of the volcano.'

'Very commendable,' I said levelly. 'I presume you intend to help the world?'

Unmann chuckled. 'Yes – to understand its mistakes.'

I sighed. 'I imagine you intend to hold civilization to ransom or something equally dreary.'

Venus rose and held out his arms wide, so that the velvet hung down from his marble-white flesh like the wings of a monstrous bird. 'We stand in the ruins of a once-teeming city. A city destroyed by the might of the great volcano, by the wrath of the very earth herself! But consider for a moment, Signor Box, the geology of this great country. From north to south, she is encircled by a ring of fire, a network of volcanoes erupting like sores on her beautiful form. Etna, Stromboli, Ischia, Vulcano –'

'Campi Flegri! Cimino! Vulsini!' chimed in Unmann.

'And greatest of all,' cried Venus breathlessly. 'Vesuvius!'

I blinked. Thought a little. Thought a little more. 'What are you saying?'

'An immense explosive device placed within her very bowels . . .' whispered Venus. 'A weapon of such incalculable power that the world will shudder at the very thought of it!'

'And when the bomb goes off . . .' I cried, appalled, 'a chain reaction!'

'A stupendous river of fire will erupt,' crowed Venus. 'Tearing apart the rock, consuming the seas, plunging this kingdom into oblivion for ever!'

'My God!'

'You're out of your bloody mind!' cried Charlie.

'But what do you gain from such an act?' I demanded. 'The destruction of your entire country? Centuries of culture?'

Venus's eyes grew brighter yet. 'I owe this country nothing! It was the arena for my father's dissolution and ruin. I only know that I must show those traitors that Maxwell Morraine was the greatest scientist the world has ever seen! They, and all this sordid land, shall perish in the flames of my vengeance.'

I shot a wild glance at Unmann. 'And you want this too?'

'I want what Venus wants,' said the young man simply.

'And you'd condone the destruction of all Italy, the deaths of millions, just to slake your thirst for retribution?'

'Why not?' He shrugged.

'I must inform you that I cannot permit that.'

Unmann laughed. 'It seems to me, Lucifer Box, that you have very little say in the matter.'

Venus crossed to the great round table and pressed an ivory button on the machinery that had been clamped on to it. There was a loud squawking sound and within seconds four huge, helmeted thugs had slipped silently into the room.

I was rapidly searched and my precious revolver confiscated. I found myself pinioned with my arms behind my back by Venus's creatures, Charlie likewise and, together, we were 'escorted' from the bath house.

My question remained unanswered. I caught one more glimpse of Venus's scowling face and then we were being pushed out into another of the grey corridors.

Charlie seemed to be in something of a state of shock. 'Bloody hell,' he muttered. 'If I'd only known her fella was *her* all the time!'

'Well, you certainly missed out on a rare frolic, Charlie boy, but you mustn't get sentimental. Remember it was he who tried to drown you in the sewer. And God alone knows what he means for us now.'

The helmeted thugs pushed us on until we came to a set of doors, incongruously shiny in the blank grey walls. One of them wrenched back the grille that covered them and I realized that some kind of elementary lift had been constructed. For a horrible moment, I thought they meant to do us in there and then by hurling us into the empty shaft but, no, there were brass doors behind the grille and, at the touch of a button they squealed open.

The tiny cabinet beyond could scarcely contain us, but all four thugs duly squeezed inside, their meaty hands clasped tightly about our arms.

One of them rotated a handle and the lift began to judder downwards; the temperature constantly rising and the sound of clanking, grinding machinery beginning to throb from all around.

Finally, the lift shuddered to a halt. There was a pause and then the doors sprang open into a dismal tunnel. The very air seemed heavy with steam as though we had entered an atmosphere only fit for the Titans to breathe.

A jab in the back told me to get moving. As we walked I saw that one whole side of this tunnel had been panelled with crystal as though to provide a viewing platform and I strained to peer through it. Such was the quantity of steam that had built up, however, the crystal window was totally fogged. What devilry lay beyond?

'Chin up, Charlie,' I called.

'Will do, sir,' he responded with more cheeriness than I expect he was feeling. 'You reckon these gorillas speak English?'

'I'm rather relying on them not to,' I said, casting a quick look and grin at my captors. Their only response was another shove in the small of the back.

'Got any ideas?'

'Well,' I sighed. 'It's a very pretty mess. We are dealing with a lunatic. There's no way to reason with him because he wants nothing but destruction.' I pulled up suddenly. 'Hello, what's this?'

We had approached another lift inset in the blank wall. The doors were open and two more of the helmeted zombies were engaged in curious activity within. The lift cabinet itself appeared to have been halted one floor below so that the two men actually stood on its roof. One was holding the thick, oily chains from which it was suspended whilst his fellow busily sawed away at them.

'What're they up to?' hissed Charlie.

'I don't understand it,' I whispered. 'They seem to be cutting off all escape routes. Including their own. If he keeps sawing like that . . .'

But perhaps these zombified husks had no concept of personal mortality any more. I tried to see more but was shoved onwards. I just glimpsed a series of metal rungs sunk into the lift-shaft, glinting in the sallow electric light and extending towards the surface.

We had reached the end of our frog-marching and stopped outside the door of some kind of cell. One of the thugs jerked his thumb at Charlie and, when he failed to move, the others grabbed him and began to haul him away.

'Charlie!' I cried. 'You fiends! Get your ruddy hands off him!'

I was then bundled unceremoniously into the total blackness of the cell. The clang of the door behind me was like the Last Trump.

I sank to the floor and wiped the streaming sweat from my face. How far below the ground I was I could not tell but the heat was almost unbearable. And all the time came the constant *thrum-thrum* of mighty engines.

I crawled over to the wall and blindly examined the structure of my confinement. There was no hope of escape. The walls were of solid rock and the floor, though softer, was hardly less impenetrable. I could only wait until they came for me and then attempt to flee. If they came at all. Perhaps they meant me to boil alive in here as the great volcano erupted!

I was left alone in the pitch-black cell for perhaps an hour and my head was nodding on my breast in the stuffy darkness when, at last, there came footsteps. The light from the corridor flooded the cell and I shielded my eyes as the door swung open and Venus stood before me, his swarthy face wet with perspiration, his dark eyes shining malevolently.

'Very sorry to have kept you, Signor Box,' he said with palms outstretched. 'But now all is prepared.'

'All *what* is prepared?'

'I wish you to see my little project. I would not have you die in ignorance.'

'Not today, thank you,' I cried cheerfully and turned my back on him.

'It is important to me that you appreciate the sheer scale of my achievement,' insisted the deadly beauty.

'Is it? Well, yes, I can see that from your point of view it probably looks that way but, forgive me, what's in it for me? I mean, surely, after the shilling tour, you're going to bump me off.'

'Not I. I have very little quarrel with you, Mr Box. In fact, I have enjoyed our brief association immensely. I only wish we could have known each other better.'

'There's still time!' I cried, turning to face him. 'What say we find somewhere nice and cool and have a little lie down, hm?'

But Venus evidently didn't take to my kind of flippancy. That smooth hand cracked me nastily across the kisser. 'It is my associate Mr Unmann who will do the deed. I believe he has something particularly unpleasant in mind.'

He threw back his head haughtily, and gestured to the corridor beyond. The guards dragged me from the cell and we retraced our steps up the corridor. Venus paused and leant across to the crystalline window, wiping away the condensed steam that clouded it with one delicate hand. Evidently satisfied, he pulled open an iron door. As I was about to be pushed through, I strained at my captors' hold and jerked my head back.

'What's going on there, *Mr* Morraine? Your lackeys are sabotaging the lifts. Are we all to die in this great revenge of yours?'

Venus merely smiled and I was hurled through the door into what I can only describe as a mechanical cathedral.

It was a vast chamber, hewn from the very rock, perhaps half a mile across and so high that its upper portion was obscured by clouds of steam. Behemothal brass and copper pipes as thick as tree-trunks fanned from a central, organ-like structure resembling tentacles on some giant metal squid. Said pipes had been channeled into the glistening rock-walls, leading, I imagined, deep into the very heart of Vesuvius. Vast pistons slammed into one another, sending up great clouds of super-heated steam and flooding the floor with gobbets of black grease. Above all this wonder had been erected a network of spindly galleries and platforms, all connected by row after row of spiral staircases. Helmeted zombies swarmed everywhere, monitoring switches and levers and cranks, attending to the minutiae of Armageddon.

Seated in four chairs near us, their wrists and ankles securely bound, were Mrs Knight and Professors Sash, Verdigris and Quibble. The effects of the purple poppy seemed to be gradually abating. All four were stirring slightly in their bonds.

'I always need an audience to bring out the best in me,' trilled Venus.

One figure detached itself from the crowd of helmeted work-men and came towards us. It was wearing some kind of protective clothing, fashioned from rubber and a helmet with square glass eye-holes. He removed the mask revealing himself to be none other than Mr Tom Bowler of Belsize Park. Or Stromboli, as I now realised he must be.

'You!' I hissed.

'Me. Hullo, Mr Box. So sorry I couldn't help you with your bereavement. I promise to be very attentive, though, when it comes to your own interment.' He flashed a horrible smile and turned to Venus. 'We are almost ready to begin the ceremony.'

'Wonderful!' enthused Venus. 'But first we must show Mr Box our little toy.'

I stared at Bowler. 'Great God, man!' I shrieked. 'Why are you doing this? What hold does this creature have over you?'

He wiped at the sweat that was pouring into his eyes. 'This is the future, Mr Box! A new world of machines and engines! We shall control the magma flows of this entire planet and once the world witnesses the destruction of Naples, they will give us any-thing we want!'

Something about Bowler's tone gave me pause. He obviously had plans beyond this day of destruction. The destruction of

Naples was to be a grand demonstration, not a suicidal act of revenge that would consume all Italy. I seized upon this chance. 'There's more to it than the end of Naples!' I yelled above the clanking din. 'You don't know, do you?'

'Silence him!' cried Venus.

'Tell him, Venus! Tell him about the chain reac –'

I felt a rough gag being fastened over my mouth. In the filthy, steaming heat it was a desperate struggle to breathe.

I was dragged back (which is better than being dragged up, like mein host).

Bowler gave me a strange look then shook his head and returned to his diabolical work.

Venus grabbed me by my shirt-front and pulled me towards the centre of that soaring chamber. At the heart of the forest of boiling pipes stood a curious round structure, riveted together in brass panels like the segments of an orange. Steps led to it and Venus dragged me up them until we were looking down on the brass globe. A glass panel occupied its upper surface and Venus forced my head down so that I could see inside.

Within, surrounded by a mass of wiring was what I knew must be the convection bomb. The whole interior of the thing sparkled with power.

And stuffed in like a rag-doll beside it, his eyes wide and terrified, was Charlie Jackpot.

Venus rose to his full height on the steps, held out both his arms wide, then began spinning about, like a giddy child. His peculiar chuckle merged with the pounding *thrum-thrum* of the colossal machines as he gloated in the midst of his infernal creation.

'Behold!' he thundered. 'Behold the Engines of Vulcan!'

He stood in a frock, I stood in mute impotence, the thugs restraining me as those fearful contraptions hammered and shuddered all around. What was I to do? I could feel the veins throbbing sickeningly in my head.

Venus began to grow calmer and then, with a jerk of his head, indicated that I was to be taken away.

'To Signor Unmann,' he cried, flashing me a dreadful grin.

Protesting and stumbling I was hauled from the room. I managed at least to shoot one last pleading glance at Bowler.

After the hellish atmosphere in the bomb-chamber, the grey featureless corridors came as something of a relief. It was to be a temporary respite only, however, as I was hauled into another room, one dominated by a huge iron pipe, in which Cretaceous Unmann awaited my convenience.

Unmann, holding the fearsome mask – that of Etna – regarded me impassively as I was hurled to the rocky floor, and then rattled out an order. I was pulled up on to my bloodied knees and securely bound hand and foot. Finally satisfied that I posed no immediate threat, Unmann indicated that we should be left alone.

'Where is your oh-so elegant poise now, Mr Box?' he taunted.

Filthy and gagged, I was in no position to reply.

I tried to assume an air of nonchalance. Terribly difficult when held captive by lunatics beneath an active volcano, I'm sure you'll agree.

'How you patronized me!' hissed Unmann. 'Took me for a shambling fool. Yet now it is you that kneels before me!'

He paused. Perhaps realizing that a one-sided rant is nowhere near as interesting as a taunt-based dialogue, he crossed the floor towards me and pulled down my gag.

'Much obliged,' I panted. 'Listen, old man. I've no doubt I misjudged you but you did put on such a good display of playing the fool. Now, can't we talk this over like gentlemen?'

If I'd hoped to appeal to our national sense of decency I was sorely disabused.

'Gentlemen?' he spat. 'How trivial you are, Box, when there are matters of the greatest moment on hand.'

He seemed to require prompting. 'Will you not at least tell me,' I said wearily, 'how the blazes you got caught up in all this nonsense?'

Unmann chuckled to himself. 'There's little to tell. But, after all, why not? Venus was abandoned by that Medea of a mother of his and drifted into crime where I was already happily billeted though the Service knew nothing of it. We began our little enterprise by founding the Vesuvius Club. It paid awfully well. At first it catered purely to, shall we say, the more straightforward desires but there is always a ready market for those of our persuasion, eh Mr Box?'

'I'll thank you not to lump me in with you two,' I muttered. 'I find frock-coats more convenient than petticoats.'

Unmann scowled at me. 'Venus is Victor Morraine's true self. The self he retreated into when his life was torn apart. The self who has schemed and plotted all these years to avenge his father's humiliation.'

'Yes, yes,' I cried. 'But why kill Poop?'

Unmann shrugged. 'We have been relieving Pompeii of its treasures in order to finance the glorious technology you see about you.'

I nodded slowly. 'And that poor sap Poop stumbled upon the truth?'

'He barely glimpsed the truth! But that, sadly for him, was enough. I lured him out to the harbour and bashed in his brains.'

I sighed exhaustedly. Unmann seemed to have stalled again. 'And what of your plans for the professors and Mrs Knight?'

'They will witness the end of all Italy as they are consumed in the fire. It will be a quick death. I think Venus is being immoderately merciful. Not a courtesy I will be extending to you, Mr Box.'

Sweat was trickling down my back. Unmann rapped hard on the door and bellowed for the guards.

The door flew open and the thugs entered. They seemed to know what was required, pulling me up by the arms and pushing me towards the great iron pipe.

Unmann slipped his fingers around a small handle and pulled at it. With a metallic screech some species of hatch was revealed. I struggled to take in the details, my eyes awash with sweat – a grilled section was fitted across the pipe and its twin was positioned directly above, so that a small cage was effectively formed, allowing a man to crawl inside and inspect the interior, albeit with some difficulty.

I knew at once that I was to be that man.

'Hey-ho,' cooed Unmann.

I was lifted bodily and thrust into the pipe.

'It will not be comfortable for you, I'm afraid.' Unmann smiled. 'It is somewhat akin to the medieval torture I believe they called "Little Ease". But whereas those unfortunates were kept crook-backed for years your time inside will be brief.'

The grille supported my weight, neatly caging me.

'This pipe acts as an exhaust from the steam-pumps. Every few hours, a vast jet of surplus steam is channelled through here and out on to the surface.'

He let the implications of this sink in.

'I had considered all manner of delightful demises for you. But time is pressing and I really cannot imagine anything much worse than having the flesh boiled from your bones by a stream of super-heated steam!'

Nor, for that matter, could I.

'Oh fuck!' was all I could manage. So much for last words.

'Close the hatch,' he said, his face settling back into a mask of impassivity.

One of the guards eased the hatch back into place.

'*Ciao!*' I heard Unmann cry over the rending creak of the iron shutter.

Then all was hot, unbearable darkness.

XX

DEATH BY STEAM

LTHOUGH dear Mr Unmann hadn't furnished me with a precise time, I knew I wouldn't have to wait long, stuffed like a plug of tobacco in an iron pipe, for my end to come. I also knew that it was ludicrous to think of shinning my way upwards. Even if I could get out of the bonds that imprisoned me, it was clearly a very long way to the surface. No, I had one chance and that was to get down the pipe and into the bomb-chamber.

All this flashed through my head as I sat there, my lungs burning in the airless tube, my head throbbing appallingly as I fought down the urge to panic.

I am no escapologist but had taken the very basic step (heaven bless my tutoring at Lady Cecely Midwinter's!) of expanding the sinews of my forearms and ankles as much as possible so that, when relaxed, there was at least a little give in the ropes.

I tested that give now and found that it was inexpressibly comforting.

I would not be saved from being boiled alive like a crab in a kettle by having my hands and feet free, however. My immediate priority was to break through the grille upon which I was perched.

Conscious that Unmann and his thugs might still be in the room I began to press down as silently but as hard as I could on the meshed surface. Cramped by the identical grille above me it was almost impossible to get any kind of momentum going but I struggled on, sweat coursing down my body, occasional jets of steam warning me of the horror to come.

I brought both feet down harder and harder on the grille yet it seemed scarcely to yield an inch. Now caring not a whit that my actions might be overheard, I slammed my whole bodyweight on to the grille, grunting in frustration and pain as the heated metal bit into my flesh.

At last I felt a tiny movement. The grille had drooped at one edge. I felt with soaking fingers and touched bare, sharp metal. Elated, I moved my hands towards the break and began to rub my bonds rapidly over it.

From deep below came an ominous rumble.

I had to escape at once! *The bonds were tearing.* If I didn't, then I was doomed. *They seemed about to give!* If only I could get a chance to talk to Bowler. His mania – *one rope gone* – seemed only for power – *a second bond snapped* – not the wanton destruction of the whole of Italy – *Free!*

I manoeuvred myself round in that tiny space and wrenched at the broken grille with my hands. The deep, disquieting rumble, like a giant clearing its phlegm-choked throat, sounded again.

As I forced the grille back upon itself, it sent out a dreadful shriek of tortured metal. Without a second thought I wriggled like a caterpillar into the shaft beneath it and let go.

Under different circumstances it might have proved exhilarating but my head was pounding sickeningly, my arms and legs ached and bled and I was still in imminent danger of tumbling straight into the bowels of that infernal machine.

As it was, I skittered pell-mell through the great iron pipe until I crashed, feet-first into another grille. I sank back and yelled in pain as my knees cracked on impact. A great trembling began in the pipe and red-hot vapour began to bleed upwards through the grille. The steam! The steam was coming!

Where there was another grille there had to be another inspection hatch. I began to kick frantically at the grille beneath me. If I could only get through it and into the next of these cramped chambers, I might effect an escape through the side of the pipe. It mattered not that I might find myself amongst the enemy, that I might even flop out at Venus's feet, if I didn't get out of there in minutes I was doomed.

I kicked again and again and still the temperature rose. Sweat seemed to gush from my face and arms as I rolled on to my back and rammed my feet against the metal floor for all I was worth.

Then! A gap! I squeezed myself through, the wire tearing at my flesh and immediately pressed my palms to the hatch. With a shove, the latch broke and the door crashed open. I tumbled through into light.

The cooler air hit me like an Arctic front. I dragged myself out of the pipe and slammed shut the hatch just as a colossal blast of steam came soaring upwards.

Falling to the floor, I pressed the door closed with my feet. I watched the pipe tremble and bulge and rattle, and even through the soles of my shoes I felt a terrible heat rise, then all was quiet.

Scarcely able to believe I was alive, I took stock of my situation. I looked up and saw the pipe extended upwards as far as I could see. Below, through clouds of steam and some kind of gantry I was standing on, I could make out the great volcanic chamber and, at its heart, the convection bomb.

I was on one of the catwalks that criss-crossed the upper levels of that vast, rocky chamber. Incredibly, because of the tremendous noise and confusion all around, I had not been observed.

Reduced to a sodden wreck in shirt-sleeves, I crept along the gantry, stealing occasional glances over the railing at the scene below.

Helmeted men were milling everywhere, checking gauges, monitoring the great motors, affixing God knew what to the great brass globe in which poor Charlie lay. I spotted Bowler, hard at work inside some strange brass and mahogany panel shaped like a church pew. And there were the berobed Venus and Unmann, crossing the floor of the chamber arm in arm, like Bertie and Alexandra on a blasted state visit. They approached the imprisoned quartet of Mrs Knight and the professors and there was some talk and mocking laughter, though I could make out nothing specific above the din. With a final flourish, Venus and Unmann put on their grotesque ritual masks and separated, Unmann towards my side of the cavern, Venus up a spiral staircase and into a small hut that projected from the rock walls like a wasps' nest.

I kept well-hidden and watched as Unmann quit the chamber through the iron door. I glanced down at the hapless hostages and then over towards the curious hut. Unarmed, I had little chance of blustering my way into it and ending Venus's deranged plans. But if I could get to Bowler there was just a chance I could convince him of his folly.

And, of course, there was Charlie Jackpot who seemed to require rescuing six times before breakfast.

I sped down the spiral staircase, round and round and round until I emerged, giddy and breathless in the shadowy perimeter of the great cavern. I looked about cautiously then took my chance, sprinting over to the central machine and clambering as silently as possible up on to the dais where the brass globe stood. I spread my hands over the glass panel and peered inside. Charlie caught my eye at once and reached up to bang his fist against the glass. I stayed him with a hushing finger to my mouth then sank down and attempted to hide myself in the lee-side of the object.

I looked quickly about but no one seemed to have detected me. Making an instant examination of the bolts that held the device together, I knew I'd require some kind of tool if I were to release Charlie.

I got to my feet once again, tapped on the glass panel and gestured to Charlie to have patience. Then, I slipped away down the steps and looked about for some method of opening the sphere.

A burly helmeted fellow with a 'kerchief wrapped around his mouth and a rifle around his shoulder was the closest person to me. In a broad brown belt around his ample waist I spotted tools including spanner, screwdrivers and knives.

Noiselessly, I crept up behind him, pulled the spanner from his belt and cracked him over the back of the neck with it. If I had expected him merely to sink to the floor like any reasonable thug I was disappointed. I had forgotten about their immunity to pain. I tried again, even harder but the spanner merely thwacked over his bull-like neck as he turned sluggishly toward me. I really didn't have time for this. I dropped to the floor, pulled a knife from his belt and, sliced away his hamstrings in one graceful roll. He dropped like a stone. Grabbing the belt, I dragged him over towards the sphere and then planted the knife into his chest as though staking a vampire.

That was the end of him. Sometimes one must be direct.

Relieved, I picked up the spanner and turned towards the sphere.

Bowler was waiting for me.

I raised the spanner above my head and the shocked undertaker ducked. At once, I locked my arm around his throat and dragged him back towards the hissing machines.

'You're mad!' he cried. 'I will be missed!'

'I'll smash your bloody head to pulp if you don't listen to me and keep quiet!' I ordered.

Cowed, he held up his hands to the level of his ears and shrugged. 'You're too late anyway, Box. The ceremony will begin in minutes.'

I tossed the spanner to him and poked the end of the guard's knife into his nose. 'Unscrew that thing and get the boy out of there.'

Bowler got to his feet and began to unscrew the glass panel slowly.

'Hurry! Or you'll be seeing the inside of a pine box damned sooner than me.' I jabbed the knife toward him and his actions grew noticeably quicker. 'Now listen to me, Bowler. Venus has lied to you. This bomb will start a chain-reaction that will cause all of Italy's volcanoes to erupt. It will destroy the entire country.'

'Ha!' Bowler unscrewed another nut and tossed it to the floor. 'He would never –'

'Wouldn't he? Now tell me what your evacuation plans are.'

Bowler shrugged. 'At the climax of the ceremony, the process will begin and we will be ferried back to the surface.'

I shook my head. 'In what? Venus's trained zombies have been making short work of the lifts, Bowler. There's no way out for anybody. He wants you all to remain here with him. For his ultimate revenge.'

Bowler took this in and then shook his perspiring head. 'Why should I believe you, Box? Venus is an honourable . . . person, terribly wronged. He will lead us out of the fire and towards glory!'

The panel was off and Bowler lifted it carefully to the floor. Keeping him covered I looked down into the device.

'Charlie!'

Looking tired and ill, the youth began to clamber out of the sphere. 'Put it on my tab, Mr Box. Thanks. What do we do now?'

I swung back towards Bowler. 'Now we're going to pay a little call.'

It took only moments for Charlie to change into the dead guard's clothes and to disguise his face with the sweaty 'kerchief. I tossed him the rifle.

'Lead the way, Mr Bowler. I'm your prisoner.'

I raised my hands and encouraged Charlie to make a good show of threatening me with the rifle. With a deep sigh, Bowler led the way and the three of us advanced through the steaming mess of pipes and machines towards the spiral staircase.

Bowler took out his watch from the pocket of his oil-stained coat. 'This is senseless. The countdown will have begun. You are too late.'

'Shut up and move.'

We ascended rapidly and approached the metal landing on which the observation room stood. A solitary guard stood outside the door. Bowler gestured to me and the guard stepped aside. The undertaker knocked and opened the door. Charlie pushed me through in a show of aggression and suddenly we were inside.

The chamber was rather curiously like a signal-box on some suburban railway line. The window was fogged so that the only light in the dim little room came from the multitude of panels and switches that covered the far wall. Sitting in a swivelling red chair was Venus, resplendent in the scarlet robes he had adopted in the Vesuvius Club for that little 'rehearsal' I had witnessed.

His delicate white hands were busy at the controls and he glanced over at us absently. 'So, Bowler! You have brought us a little present. It seems my dear Cretaceous was not able to finish you off, Signor Box.'

'He very nearly poached me,' I said, taking the rifle from Charlie and advancing on him. 'But I'm a resourceful fellow. As you can see.'

Venus's face fell. 'You are too late. The –'

'Yes, yes, the countdown has started. I know. But you can stop it from here. Very carefully but very quickly.'

'Or what?' hissed Venus. 'You think I fear death? I embrace it! It is my destiny!'

I looked at Bowler. 'You see, man? He's utterly deranged. He has no intention that any of you should leave the volcano.'

Bowler gave a strained laugh. 'You're pathetic! Do you really think that . . .' He tailed off and his gaze became fixed on Venus who had a strange, messianic smile on his fine features. 'Is . . . is this true?'

Venus threw back his head and laughed. 'It will be a glorious end, Signor Bowler. We shall take all of Italy with us!'

Bowler's hand flew to his mouth. 'Oh my God!'

He raced towards the door. Charlie caught him. 'Oi! You're going nowhere, mate.'

Charlie hauled him back into the room. Bowler's chin was trembling. 'But we've got to get out of here!'

'We shall *stay*,' I commanded. 'And stop the countdown. All of Italy is at stake. Mr Morraine, will you oblige?'

For answer, Venus merely folded his arms.

'Then if you will not, I shall!' cried Bowler. 'You cannot be allowed to destroy us all.'

So saying he dashed across the cabin and began to wrench wires from the machinery. With a roar of rage, Venus was upon him, pummelling Bowler's face and chest with surprising force. I wasted no more time and shot at the flashing scarlet form. The first bullet hit Venus in the arm and he staggered back. The second tore through the fabric of his robes and bit into the wall.

Clutching his injured flesh, Venus powered past me and, knocking Charlie to the floor, flung open the door and was gone.

'Quickly!' called Bowler, pulling more of the complicated mass of wiring. 'The device. If he reaches it, he could still set it off!'

I needed no further encouragement.

'Come on, Charlie!' I urged and we raced from the hut. Charlie took the rifle and shot the helmeted guard dead without breaking his stride. I leant over the staircase and could see Venus's slim figure flitting through the steam-shrouded pipes towards the sphere. I grabbed the rifle from Charlie, rested it on the iron banister and loosed off a volley of shots.

Venus emerged from the steam with a large group of his opium-sodden drones. He pointed up at us.

'Kill them!' he howled. 'Kill them!'

With their curious, sluggish movements, the helmeted fiends began to fire back at us. Charlie picked up the rifle from the dead guard and we careered down the spiral staircase at a fearsome pace, dodging bullets and responding in kind.

'We have to stop him getting to the bomb!' I cried as we reached the base of the steps. We ran in a frenzy across the floor of the chamber until we reached the brass sphere. Venus was nowhere to be seen.

'Mr Box!' gasped Charlie. 'Look!'

I noticed in that moment that the glass panel was no longer where Bowler had left it. It was being screwed back into place from *within* the sphere. His slender frame squashed visibly, Venus lay crouched inside, grinning madly.

He raised his hand and smiled. The crazy fool was waving at us.

Then there came a strange ratcheting sound and the sphere rolled forward like a billiard ball, vanishing into the great bronze pipe.

Despite the noise and the heat and approaching thugs it felt suddenly as if a great hush had descended.

'We've failed,' I said quietly.

XXI

ASCENT TO PERIL

HARLIE grabbed me by the shoulder. 'We're not beaten yet, sir! The fella in the hut knows where that pipe leads. There must be some way to stop the bomb.'

I nodded quickly. 'You're right.'

We clattered back up the spiral staircase, picking off the last few zombies lumbering towards us as we did so, and threw open the door of the observation room. Bowler was still there, poring over reams of documents and plans.

'Betrayed!' he groaned, hammering his fist at his forehead. His hair hung in a great black slap over his pale forehead. 'Betrayed at every turn! To think I could have trusted that monster!'

I pulled him round. 'There's still time to make amends, Bowler. The bomb has been launched. Where is it heading?'

He shook his head mournfully. 'Into the belly of the volcano. There is a weakness in the crust. The bomb will blast it away and the magma will erupt!'

'How do we stop it?'

The undertaker put his head in his hands. 'We cannot. We shall die in the flames. Die at any moment!'

Not what we wanted to hear, naturally.

'There must be a way!' I thundered, grabbing him by the lapels. 'Think, man. You know everything about this blasted scheme!'

'Yes! And we were clever! We allowed for every eventuality.'

Charlie came over and sifted through the blueprints. 'What sort of eventuality? What could go wrong?'

I nodded furiously. 'You're right, Charlie. We will sabotage one of the fail-safes.'

Bowler looked at me as if I were mad and then smiled. 'There . . . there may be something in what you say. There is a junction. I knew it was dangerous but the rock-formation made it unavoidable. It's where the steam shaft crosses the bond pipe. The two chutes join for a moment and then continue on their way.'

'And is there any way of closing off the junction?'

Bowler dashed to the wall where a screen of some kind indicated where the bomb had got to.

'Yes! If I repair some of the damage I managed to inflict, I can control it from here.'

He sucked at his knuckles anxiously. 'The bomb has reached *this* level.' He jabbed his finger at the curious display. 'The junction is some way below.'

'Then there's still time.'

Bowler was practically gnawing his fist. 'But if we close the pipe and trap Venus there, the bomb will still explode. It will be close enough to cause an eruption!'

It was my turn to ponder. I looked quickly at the plans and then at the display. 'And if you shut off the steam-pipe, what then?'

He shrugged. 'The steam-pressure will build.'

'Dangerously?'

'Of course. The system is designed as a safety valve. If the pressure is not released . . .'

'That's it!' I cried delightedly. 'Bowler, close the hatch on the steam pipe.'

'But why?'

'Just do it!'

He dragged Venus's great leather chair to the console and began furiously punching at buttons and pulling levers. Then he dropped beneath the display and began frantically rewiring the machinery. For a few anxious minutes he fiddled and pulled at the complex copper circuitry, swore several oaths and then, with a great cry, sat back. A coloured disc slid into place on the display before us.

'It's done! The steam pressure is building.'

'Now, tell me when Venus and the bomb are almost at the junction. How accurate is this thing?'

'Pretty accurate.' He rubbed his hands and licked his dry lips. 'Level Eight. Achieved. Level Nine . . .'

'He must be boiling alive inside that thing,' said Charlie.

I nodded. 'Just what he'd intended for you. He doesn't give a damn now. He must see this thing through.'

'Achieved,' continued Bowler. 'Level Ten . . . approaching junction . . .'

'Prepare to open the hatch!' I cried.

'Level Ten achieved!'

'Open it!'

The disc slid out of its housing, revealing blank space. 'It's done,' said Bowler simply.

'What is?' queried Charlie.

I held up my hand. 'Wait, wait . . .'

From deep beneath us we heard it. A deep, booming, clattering roar. The floor of the room began to shake with massive violence.

'What . . . exactly have we done?' said Charlie.

'Projected a huge body of steam at the sphere, Charlie! If I'm right then –'

'Then it should be forced right back up!'

'Exactly!'

The three of us stood there in an agony of suspense as the hut and the great chamber itself trembled. I glanced over at Charlie. His face was white and he had sunk his teeth into his lower lip. Bowler was smoothing his hair down in a repeated gesture as though comforting himself. If, *if* we got out of this insane situation, how were we to escape? There would be seven of us all told, including the captives. My thoughts raced back to the lift-shafts and the men who had sabotaged them. Of course! The chains had been severed but the iron rungs set into the wall must survive. It would be a hell of a climb but it was surely our only chance.

I was yanked back to the present when a tremendous, shattering roar came from the chamber beyond. Charlie, Bowler and I raced out of the hut and looked down. The great brass sphere had come tearing back through the bronze pipe, shredding its end in the process and slamming into the walls of the cavern. Its impact

fractured a number of the huge iron pipes and steam began to flood the chamber.

'We did it!' cried Charlie.

'Yes – we've brought the bomb back. To us!'

The undertaker looked worried. 'The bomb won't go off now, the steam pressure is still building. The pipes are ruptured.'

'But there'll be no eruption?'

'Not as Venus planned, no. But the explosion could still damage the magma shell higher up. There's no time to be lost!'

'First we have to free Mrs Knight and the professors.'

'What?' wailed Bowler. 'To hell with them! We have to get out!'

I trained the rifle on the reluctant mortician. 'You have much to make up for, Mr Bowler. I suggest you get down those stairs and help them. Forthwith.'

With a scowl, he ran pell-mell down the stairway, Charlie and I close behind. As we picked our way across the floor, I glanced over to where the sphere lay embedded in the wall, crushed like a spoiled fruit, the glass panel shattered. Hanging half out of it was the body of Venus; his scarlet robes plastered to his body like a shroud, his once-beautiful face set in a crazed rictus grin, the sinews exposed red raw by the heat that had boiled away his flesh. His eyeballs goggled at us in a macabre, steam-palled death-stare.

'Come on!' I urged. I turned my attentions to the captives in their chairs and was at once confronted by the not-too-dissimilar features of the unfortunate Mrs Knight.

'Are you all right?' I enquired. She merely groaned in reply. Charlie was already hacking away her restraints. Despite their weakness, Verdigris and Sash were able to make some sense of the situation and once free pulled themselves up the gantries towards the next level. I helped support Mrs Knight, who had been more recently stupefied and Charlie and Bowler carried the crippled Quibble between them. The old man groaned pitiably as we clattered up the steps towards the next level.

Of a sudden, there came an ear-splitting crack and the floor of the cavern began to shift and undulate. With a horrible, belching roar, molten lava began, inexorably, to force its way through the gap.

We needed no more encouragement to tumble through the door and bolt it behind us, falling gasping into the corridor beyond.

'The lifts!' I yelled. 'Quickly!'

Charlie let out an exhausted sigh, then all seven of us staggered off up the corridor, the way we had been brought what seemed like half a lifetime ago. We reached the lift doors, closed now, and Charlie and Bowler lowered Quibble to the floor. I stabbed at the controls but the blasted things refused to open. Mrs Knight appeared to have fallen into a faint.

'Professor Sash!' I barked. 'Are you fit enough to help open these doors? Verdigris – you too? Charlie, Bowler, give them both a hand. I'll see to our invalids.'

It is not in my nature to slap a woman, especially when she looks like a boiled hog's head, but now was not the time for subtlety. I batted as kindly as I could at the poor soul's ruined cheeks until she became once more sensible of her surroundings.

'We have to climb, Mrs Knight,' I hissed. 'All of us. You too, Professor Quibble. It's our only hope.'

'What?' he gasped from his resting place on the shuddering floor. 'What is all this?'

'We're inside Vesuvius, Professor. I know it's hard to credit but Maxwell Morraine's deranged son has developed his theories into practical form and a great big bloody bomb has set off an eruption. You understand?'

He peered at me myopically and opened his mouth to protest.

'You want me to leave you here?'

Quibble's rat-trap mouth closed firmly.

From deep below us came a fearful rumble. I glanced feverishly about.

'They're moving!' gasped Charlie, his fingernails jammed into the crack between the lift doors. 'Come on! Put your backs into it!'

Slowly, the doors began to screech apart. Around us the electric lights studding the walls had begun to spark and sizzle. All at once, the doors gave and Charlie, Bowler, Verdigris and Sash hauled them apart. Inside there was only empty space.

I gazed up at the shaft, the chains from which the lift had been suspended swung uselessly, stirred by the hot winds from below.

'We have to get on to those rungs,' I cried. 'Charlie, you go first. We'll get Quibble up after you and I'll push the bugger. Got that?'

Charlie nodded and swung himself up on to the first rung as another tremor hit and the shaft visibly rocked.

'Keep going!' I urged. Charlie, hanging by one arm, helped me to launch the shaking Quibble on to the rungs. Behind me came Verdigris and Sash, doing the same for the still-enfeebled Mrs Knight; the penitent Bowler brought up the rear. We climbed and climbed but Quibble's ruined body became heavier and heavier. I pushed as best I could but his withered hands were struggling to support him on the hot iron rungs. My own arms ached fearsomely.

Chest heaving, I struggled on, Quibble's useless legs dangling before me like empty stockings. 'Must . . . get out, Professor,' I gasped. 'Can't rest . . . *Move!*'

The old man was certainly game. Somehow, incredibly, we made progress. I craned my neck to see above.

'Charlie!' I called. 'How far?'

'We're getting there!' he cried.

Suddenly the lift-shaft shook again and there came a bizarre sucking, grumbling sound.

'Don't stop!' I shouted. 'All of you! Keep climbing.'

But I sneaked a peek down the deep shaft and saw that instead of the darkness we had left, there was now a dreadful fiery red.

'My God!' I cried hoarsely. 'The lava! It's rising!'

Far below (thank the Lord Harry), crowned by flame and smoke, a vast plug of molten rock was surging up towards us.

I swung my head up to yell at Charlie to help drag Quibble up but the words died in my mouth. The top of the lift shaft was only ten feet or so above us and looking down, holding my revolver, was Cretaceous Unmann.

'You have a choice, Mr Box,' he called down. 'Jump down into the lava or be picked off by me.'

'What the hell do you mean?' I cried.

He loosed off a shot that sang off the ladder with a screeching clang. I heard Mrs Knight squeal in terror.

'What I say. I offer you a choice of demises.'

'Listen, you mad fool,' I shouted diplomatically. 'If we don't all get to the surface in the next few minutes we're going to fry! Is that what you want?'

'You think I wouldn't do it?' he yelled. 'You think I don't have it in me to shoot you down?'

'I have no doubt you have it in you.' I cast a quick look downwards at the rising tide of lava. The figures of Sash, Verdigris, Mrs Knight and Bowler were silhouetted starkly against a curtain of blood-orange.

'I'm only saying you will die as surely as the rest of us if you don't move right now!'

'But that's what Venus wants! Death! Destruction! Annihilation! Ha, ha, ha!'

Another shot rang out and I heard Bowler scream. I looked down and saw him swaying on the rungs below, blood pouring from his throat. Then the poor fool was gone, spiralling down, down, down into the blistering lava flow.

'Choose, Mr Box!' screeched Unmann, his ripped robes flopping forward over the lip of the shaft.

The whole edifice shuddered again and I felt Professor Quibble begin to topple backwards on to me. I thrust out a hand and pushed him back but the walls were shaking so violently now that it was almost impossible to get any purchase on him.

I looked up and saw Unmann levelling the pistol at me. I was a sitting duck.

Quibble's withered head turned to look down at me and a strange look flitted over his pallid features. I suddenly knew what he was going to do. I pulled myself tight to the rungs in order to present as small a target as possible and flinched as I heard Unmann's shot blast out. At the same instant, Quibble let go of the rungs and fell back into the void, taking the bullet that was meant for me. As he spiralled noiselessly down the shaft, all was confusion. I tried to clamber the last few feet towards the top of the shaft before Unmann had a chance to recover but was suddenly aware that Charlie, with a great bellow of rage had taken hold of the ripped fabric of Unmann's robe that hung streamer-like over the lip of the shaft and pulled on it for all he was worth.

With a great disbelieving gasp, the lethal diplomat toppled forwards.

I caught a glimpse of his startled face as he sailed past me and then he was just a ball of swirling scarlet, plummeting down the shaft after the noble Quibble into the pulsating stream of molten rock.

Just before he hit, though, there was a bright flash and pain seared through my shoulder. I gasped and looked down at where Unmann's parting shot had penetrated my flesh. I swayed on the iron rungs.

In a second, Charlie's strong arms were under mine.

'Hang on, sir. I've got you!'

Waves of nausea began to pulse through me and I felt my senses swim. Charlie grasped at my shirt and heaved me out of the lift shaft. I staggered to my feet as the invaluable valet helped the others out and then we staggered as one unit through the volcanic tunnels towards the Pompeiian bath house.

As we emerged into that strange room, the pellucid lights were flickering and the ancient walls shuddering under the impact of the eruption. I was only dimly aware of all this as Charlie plunged on, dragging me with him, my whole body shot with pain. The others were merely a dim blur behind me.

Somehow he got me to the ladder and, weak as a kitten, I managed to pull myself up and up, every step an agony. Surely there must be an end to this climbing? All at once we were at the hatch and tumbling into the bleary dawn.

Of course, we were not yet safe. The livid sky told us what we already knew. Vesuvius was erupting and, whilst it was not the cataclysm Venus had hoped for, it was still not wise to hang about.

I chanced a look back as Charlie lugged me out through the Pompeiian ruins the way we had come. Above us, the great black hump of the mountain was belching smoke and a thin river of livid red was dribbling from the cone like Gorgon's blood.

And then the five of us were part of a great fleeing mob. I received a confused impression of voices and smells and it was suddenly as though I were back there in ancient Pompeii. The dawn sky overheard was blackening with ash and the world was disappearing in a vortex of reds, ochres and yellows. My eyes fluttered and the canopy of my lids was a cool green. The blood flowing from my shoulder looked almost black, flowing in a stream over the snowy whiteness of my exposed arm. How strange, I thought, to die in such a terribly beautiful palette.

XXII

END GAME

ND yet, gentle reader, (as I'm sure you've gathered) I did not die! A long week later and the great shuddering roar of that eruption was like a strange dream to me. After the removal of Unmann's bullet from my shoulder and much rest I had been re-established in my room at the Santa Lucia where I was at least able to sketch a little. An easel was optimistically set up but I found myself quickly exhausted and it was far easier to drift off into sleep after some of Charlie's nourishing soup than to work. It was fully a fortnight before I was able to receive visitors.

First came Joshua Reynolds, on a rare foreign trip, bearing the profound thanks of HMG and whispers of medals, which I nobly refused for fully two minutes until he started taking me seriously and I had to beg for them.

The next day brought the newly liberated Christopher Miracle. He looked a little drawn (but not badly drawn,

ho-ho), as well he might and he beamed at me with what looked suspiciously like renewed respect.

'I owe it all to you, old man,' he said with a catch in his voice. 'Flush would have strung me up if you hadn't intervened. I'm most awfully grateful.'

I gave a heroic but modest smile. 'We still don't know quite what happened that day, do we?'

'Ah, yes,' said Miracle. 'We do. If you're not too tired, dear Lucifer, there's another guest who is most anxious to speak to you.'

Charlie showed in the extraordinary apparition that was Mrs Midsomer Knight, once more swathed in veils and sporting a rather splendid new gown of deepest emerald. She took a seat by my blanketed form and inclined her head in greeting.

'Mr Box, how do I begin to thank you?'

'Please don't even try,' I said manfully. In truth I didn't have the strength to be gushed over. 'It's reward enough to know that my friend here is exonerated and that you and the professors – well, a quorum of them at least – are out of danger. That and the fact that a dangerous lunatic's plans have come to nought.'

'Ah yes,' mused Mrs Knight. 'My unfortunate son.'

I sat up on one elbow, wincing slightly. 'It would please me greatly, however, if you could clear up one or two points in connection with this matter.'

'Anything.'

'Perhaps I can help you there,' came a booming voice from the doorway. The massive frame of the Duce Tiepolo emerged from the shadows.

'Your Grace,' I said quietly. 'I fear I have done you a grave disservice. For I thought you behind this whole mad scheme.'

'I *am* guilty,' said the great man. 'Guilty of a mad love. For this wonderful woman.'

He took Mrs Knight's hand in his. 'It was so long ago,' he croaked. 'It is not an easy thing, Signor Box, to know that you have been born into wealth and privilege then see all that swept away. I was a hunted man. One day I arrived in Naples and I met a girl. She was only sixteen or so, and a little frightened of me. But I knew at once that I loved her . . . Loved her!'

'But she was married.'

The Duce nodded bitterly. 'With a child. The husband, Morraine, was a good man, an honest man, but we could not help ourselves, could we, my dear? It was like a fire, the passion that burned within us!'

Mrs Knight sighed. 'At first it was easy to see each other in secret. My husband, Maxwell, thought only of his work. He and his colleagues laboured from dawn to dusk. But finally our secret was betrayed! Maxwell was mad with jealousy. I went to see him. To tell him I must leave him . . . I found him in his laboratory. Told him that the Duce and I were in love. At first he seemed not to hear me. He was burning his papers after some scientific disappointment. He threw more and more paper on to the fire until suddenly it was out of control and . . .'

Mrs Knight pressed her hand to her mouth and sobbed. 'It took away my youth, my beauty . . .'

The Duce clamped his huge arm around the delicate woman's shoulders. 'And I knew nothing of this for years. The authorities caught me and I was deported. I found out about the fire and believed Kate to be dead. How was I to know that she had been spirited away from Naples and was back in England? Years passed. I never expected to see my lover again.'

'But you did.' I drawled, taking a slow drag on my cigarette.

'I did! Can you imagine it, Signor Box? After all that time? I have roamed Europe like a vagrant. I was passing through London and, one day, as I was walking through the park, you saw me, didn't you, my pet?'

He turned to his lost love, his weathered face wreathed in smiles.

Mrs Knight continued. 'Even after all these years I knew him at once.'

'And you felt the same?' I asked the Duce.

'Once I knew it was her, of course! What did I care for her scars? Her "ugliness"? She was my darling girl. Restored to me when I thought her long dead.'

The Duce's noble head bobbed low on his breast, then he raised it again, tears welling in his rheumy eyes. 'I bought the silence of my companion and we spent the whole afternoon together. There were secret letters, stolen moments. And then I hit upon the drawing-class scheme. We planned to elope. Elope! Like star-crossed lovers!'

'That night, the night of Miracle's ball, she was meant to steal away and meet me in the gardens. But she did not come! And then I heard about the body – oh! A second time she was taken from me!'

He groaned like a wounded beast. 'And so I came here. Home. To Naples. In secret, of course, and seeking – who knows what? Peace?'

I pulled myself up on the pillows. 'And what of that day in the Mechanical Institute, Mrs Knight? I gather you had already suspected you were under observation?'

The veiled woman placed her hands in her lap and sighed. 'That I had. But I thought they were sent by my husband, and that our scheme was impenetrable. I little thought what they might have in mind until that day. Miss Frenzy and I had just switched places when two men burst into the lavatory. At once they grabbed poor Miss Frenzy but she fought valiantly, biting one of them upon the hand.

'Of course I could not simply hide in the cubicle and leave Abigail to her fate but their faces were a pretty sight when they were suddenly confronted by two identically dressed women! As time was obviously of the essence, they bundled us both from the place and took us to some low lodging house where the truth was forced from us. One of them, a man called Bowler, decided that fate had put in his way a serendipitous event. They had come to abduct me, how much better if I were thought to be dead!'

She tailed off and gave a little sob. 'From that moment poor Abigail's fate was sealed. I was quite unable to protest as they gave me the first of those hideous injections and I was scarcely sensible from that day on.'

Tiepolo laid his big hand over hers. 'It is over now,' he said in a reassuring tone.

I sank back. 'And what will you do now, my dear? If you'll take the advice of an impecunious artist . . .'

'Thank you, Mr Box, but I do not need it! I am resolved to change my life while there's still time.'

The Duce Tiepolo grunted his approval.

Miracle frowned. 'And what of your husband?'

'I'm afraid he shall have to get used to it,' trilled Mrs Knight, almost girlishly. 'For the Duce and I are . . . well . . . eloping tonight.'

I wished them both well, confident that, in the fullness of time, I might receive massive financial reward for services rendered.

Miracle ushered them out then returned to my side.

'Well?' he demanded. 'Have you heard from her?'

'Heard from whom?' I said, all innocence.

'Why from Miss Bella Pok, of course! You have been in here fully two weeks! Has she not been to visit you?'

I shrugged lightly. 'I have received a note or two enquiring after my health.'

Miracle leaned forward in his chair. 'And when do you see her?'

I laughed sharply, making my injured shoulder twinge, unable to keep up the pretence a moment more. 'Tomorrow morning! But now I am most awfully tired, Chris. You must let me get my strength up for the great occasion!'

He left me, promising dinner at Maxim's, showers of gold and all the tea in China once I was fully recovered.

A happy peace had settled over my routine. Charlie had turned himself into an excellent nurse and his bedside manner was more than admirable.

That night I slept heavily, my head seeming to pound in time to the eruption of Vesuvius as I found myself back there, the sky behind me a strange, lurid red. But suddenly I knew it was not the sky at all but the canopy of my own eyelids. I blinked once. Twice. And the pounding roar of the volcano resolved itself into an urgent knocking at the door of my hotel room.

I glanced down at the bed. Naked, Charlie lay sound asleep at my side, his bruised body lightly covered by the cool cotton sheets. Suddenly I remembered.

'Bella!' I cried.

I jumped to my feet, immediately regretted it and flopped back on the bed. I looked wildly about.

'Up!' I hissed, slapping Charlie on the side. 'Up!'

He half opened his very blue eyes. 'What?'

'Get yourself up, Charlie boy. We have company.'

He groaned and shook his head. 'Tell them to sling theirs. *I'm* your company.'

I leant down and pinched him savagely on the nipple. 'Get yourself up, Mr Jackpot or you'll be sorry.'

Yelping in pain, the boy sat up and flapped his hands at mine. 'All right, all right, you swine!'

Still befuddled by sleep, he looked dumbly at his nakedness and began to get dressed.

'Quickly!' I hissed. 'It is Miss Pok.'

He struggled swiftly into his trousers and threw on his shirt.

'Now, after you've shown the lady in, you must make yourself scarce.'

'You ashamed of me?'

I sighed. 'You're my servant, Jackpot. It's time you started behaving like one instead of bleating away like the Little Match Girl.'

'Lucifer?' came Bella's muffled voice from beyond the door.

'All right,' said Charlie, sloping sullenly off towards the door. He dragged it open and ushered Bella inside with ill-concealed contempt.

'Miss Bella Pok,' he muttered.

'Thank you, Charles,' I said between gritted teeth. 'You may take the rest of the day off.'

'Oh!' he cried, clasping his hands to his bosom. 'May I, sir? Oh, how kind of you, sir.'

'That will be all, Charles,' I said firmly. He went out and slammed the door.

'Bella! How wonderful to see you! Pray accept my apologies for him. It is so devilishly hard to find good servants these days that one accepts even the most rough-edged and bothersome.'

'I thought he was rather sweet,' she said sunnily.

I was slightly breathless and my head ached. 'Well, well, no doubt that is your pleasant disposition. I fear I do not appear at my best . . .'

She took in my tousled appearance and sleep-shocked hair and waved away my apologies with a yellow-gloved hand. I took it and kissed it fervently.

'You are safe! That is all that matters!'

'You got my note, then? It was a foolish thing I did. To risk my life when I had so much to look forward to.'

Smiling indulgently, she lifted the white veil from her face. I felt my pulse quicken at this renewed view of her beauty. 'You are very bold, Lucifer,' she said quietly.

'I have offended you!' I groaned. 'It is only that I had hoped so much that when I got back to England we might . . .'

She sat next to the bed and took my hand in hers. 'Rest assured, dear Lucifer, that I have not forgotten you.'

I smiled happily.

'Now,' she said, settling herself. 'How on earth did you come by these dreadful injuries? I want to hear all about your adventures!'

'Oh?' I said wearily. 'Really?'

Impressions of the extraordinary events of the past weeks began to crowd my brain, all of them tinged in a volcanic glow. I thought of coming up with an entirely neutral version of events, concerned with sketching trips and abandoned canvases and amusingly dreadful restaurant fare but Bella deserved better than that. She knew I had some dark secret.

'Lucifer?'

I opened my eyes. 'Was I drifting?'

'So it seems,' she said concernedly. 'Are you quite well?'

I winced suddenly and she moved to my side, noticing, beneath my dressing gown, the bandages that swaddled my chest.

'Oh you poor, poor darling.'

I made a stoic face. 'It's nothing, really.'

She shook her head. 'I shall fetch you a drink.'

'Well, it is the hour for vermouth,' I smiled.

She took my hand and squeezed it. Moments later she had returned with two glasses.

I took the one she proffered gratefully.

The glass was almost at my lips when I suddenly felt curiously uneasy. It was not the ache in my shoulder, nor the fatigue of having so many visitors, nor even the effort of my recent tumble with young Charlie. It was a strange, indefinable something and it caused me to set the glass down on the counterpane. 'Think I'll save it for a moment. Don't want it to go to my head.'

Bella shrugged. 'As you please.'

I looked at her steadily and nodded towards the glass. 'Aren't you joining me?' I said lightly.

The young woman shook her head. 'No, thank you.'

She seemed to become aware that I was staring at her. Bella's pale, slender throat made a noticeable undulation and she looked down at me, smiling. Then her face changed with the suddenness of a mask falling away. She balled her hand into a fist and punched me hard directly in my wound.

I gasped in pain and shock and fell back against the pillows. At once, Bella had picked up the whisky glass and was prising my mouth open. My head swam with nausea as I felt her fingers stealing into my mouth and the edge of the glass tapping against my teeth.

'Drink it!' she hissed. 'Drink it, you bastard!'

There was nothing but steel in her voice now and the lovely eyes had turned cold.

I pushed at her but I was so weak that she forced me back on the bed. Risking some kind of fearsome rupture, I rolled off the bed and fell to the floor.

Bella at once stalked towards me, holding the glass in both hands.

'What the hell are you doing?' I screeched. 'Are you mad?'

'Drink it, my dear. It is prussic acid. There will be a little pain but soon you will be insensate.'

'Bella!' I cried, trying desperately to stand. 'What is wrong? It is I, Lucifer Box!'

'*Pauvre petite*,' she murmured. 'You pursued me like a goat from the day we met, didn't you? And never once did you guess at the truth.'

'Truth? What truth?'

She put down the glass and from her dress produced a dainty pistol which she levelled at my chest. She laughed. It was that gay, musical laugh I had grown so fond of. 'You remember a chase by coach through London?'

'Of course.'

'I drove that coach! I! I sent the venomous insect to your home! I did it all, to get my revenge on *you*!'

'On me?' I said, all innocence.

'I believe I once told you I am Dutch by birth. That is not quite true. I am Afrikaans. I lived in Pretoria till I was nine. Just me and my beloved father. Everard Supple!'

I shook my head desperately. '*Who?*'

'Can you have forgotten so soon? The man you gunned down in cold blood! I know, Mr Lucifer Box, I know all!'

Everard Supple? Everard Supple! It seemed incredible. The old fool I'd killed all those weeks ago as a routine assignment. But how could she have found out? This was just the sort of thing Joshua Reynolds was meant to protect me against!

'Supple was your father?'

'Yes! A great man. A man whose feet you were not worthy to kiss!'

I wasn't having this. I struggled to my feet, tears of agony springing to my eyes. 'A dangerous anarchist!' I yelled. 'I despatched him because he planned to assassinate the foreign secretary!'

Bella's eyes blazed in fury. 'I will not listen to your lies! I only know that I have spent these last weeks planning how best to despatch *you*, Box. I was not sure, at first, despite my information, that you were responsible.'

'Information?'

'My father's *diplomatic* contacts.'

'Ah,' I gasped. 'Spies.'

'I had no idea how I might engineer a meeting and then your little advertisement came along. It was too perfect. I came to your studio and I confess I could not believe you to be a killer. And then . . .'

'Then?'

'There, amongst the paints and brushes, I saw it. My father's glass eye!'

'Ah –'

'And then my heart hardened, Mr Box. I swore I would destroy you!'

'You didn't manage very well, did you?' I piped up, eyeing the door. Despite my weakened state I was going to make a break for it. Fool! Why had I sent Charlie away? There were hotel staff about. But could I make it in time? If I could but raise the alarm . . .

'Unlike you, Mr Box, I am not a professional murderer.'

I looked at her with as much stoicism as I could muster. 'What do you want me to do?' I asked. 'Beg for my life? I won't do it, my dear. You must know me well enough by now. I may be a cad but I'm not a coward. I stand by what I did to your father. I should do it again.'

'Ha!'

'You must understand, that I am a servant of His Majesty's Government. I never kill without taking the greatest pains to ensure that what I'm doing is right! Of course I feel for you and your loss but you must believe me when I say your father was a dangerous fanatic.'

'And what does that make you! The fêted artist, the dashing dandy. But by night – philanderer, sodomite and assassin!'

As a thumbnail sketch of me that wasn't half bad.

Bella aimed the revolver at my face and cocked it. 'And so . . . farewell . . .'

Then things moved very quickly. I sprang forward, throwing the deadly contents of the whisky glass towards Bella's face. Her arm shot up defensively and the liquid splashed harmlessly over the sleeve of her gown. An instant later she fired the revolver, but I had already thrown myself to the floor and, gasping in pain, rolled over and behind my easel.

Bella skittered towards me. I grabbed at a pot of brushes and flung it at her. The glass shattered against the wall and the pistol spat fire again.

I scrambled under a chair, the pain of my wound making me giddy, and struggled to think. I would never make it across the room alive.

'Come out, come out wherever you are!' cried Bella with a kind of dreadful gaiety.

She dragged the easel aside on its squealing castors and my ludicrous hiding place was exposed.

'What an ignominious end, Mr Box!' she crowed. 'Now, Papa! You shall be revenged –'

All at once, and to my utter astonishment, the bedroom door flew open and Charlie launched himself on to Bella's back.

The two of them careered around like a carousel, Bella's skirts sending painting materials flying. She bellowed alarmingly and began to twist her arm from Charlie's grip so that she might get a clear shot at him.

'Lucifer!' cried Charlie. 'Quick!'

I needed no prompting. I dashed out from under the chair, grabbed at a half-finished canvas and cracked Bella viciously under the jaw with it. She toppled backwards and Charlie fell from her, the gun grasped in one hand. He threw the weapon to me and I had raised it ready to fire when I stopped dead.

Bella had fallen back against the dresser and now stood stock still. Her shaking hands flew to her back and came away bloody. She sank to her knees, seemed to pause for a moment, and then pitched forward on to her face with an awful gurgling moan.

Stuck in her back was the lance of that frightful spelter statue she had drawn so prettily on the first day of our acquaintance.

Charlie dashed to my side and lifted my head on to his knee. Fatigue and nausea were washing over me. 'Charlie . . .'

We both watched as a torrent of blood as red as lava began to flow from Bella's back, drenching her gown. Then her eyes turned glassy and she lay still.

'This is meant to be my day off,' said Charlie. 'Who do I talk to about overtime?'

I looked him directly in the eye and managed a smile. 'Charlie, what can I say?'

He stroked my hair with uncommon gentleness. 'All part of the service.'

'Well, I'm glad you mentioned that, Charlie,' I murmured, managing to prop myself up on one elbow. 'You know, my pal Beardsley always said that his indisposition made him frightfully horny. No doubt one is not quite in control of oneself when one's glands are up.'

I smiled what my friends call, naturally enough, the smile of Lucifer.

**Have you read these other titles
in the Bunsen Book Club?**

WITH VINEGAR AND
BROWN PAPER
by Ariadne Oliver

When newly-wed couple Silly and Sausage decide their lives need a little
spicing up, they get more than they bargained for! The odious Colonel
Fleming is found stabbed through the ears on a golf links and only our
intrepid twosome stand between local simpleton Tommy Wideawake
and the gallows . . .

HELLO, MR QUARMBY!
by Todd Wakefield

Twelve mysteries from the acclaimed author of "Really, Mr Quarmby!",
"Stop that, Mr Quarmby!" and "Mr Quarmby Runs Riot". Readers will
welcome these new tales featuring the deaf, dumb and blind Welsh
detective as he once again pits his wits against the most devious of
criminals and the irascible Scotland Yard Detective, Inspector Pump.

LEAN BROWN
by Sandy Maltravers

Five years after his explosive introduction in "Clean Grit", Ronald Stride
finds himself pitch-forked into a one-man campaign against a crazed
troupe of Prussian snorkellers hell-bent on resurrecting the Kaiser's
cause and planting the German flag in Parliament Square. It's a tight spot
for Stride but, as his mentor "Baba" Carrington puts it: "He was shut up
at Mafeking with Baden-Powell and knows a thing or two." Together,
Stride, Carrington and the lanky American agent Teddy W. Greatorex get
athwart of the enemy's plotting and are soon set fair for a final
confrontation with a grotesque Count Von Stummup.

"TERRIER" MASTERSON HITS OUT
by "Slapper"

Re-enter Tom "Terrier" Masterson! The hero of "The Darkie Gang" is once more bored with civilian life and determined to give the enemies of the Empire a good kicking. But will "Terrier" and his two fists be enough to foil the machinations of sinister mastermind "The Scallywog"? Another terrific "shocker" from the author of "That Hat Means Murder".

THEY WORE DARK TROUSERS
by Tenacious Beatme

Plucked from semi-retirement by a desperate British Government on the eve of the Battle of the Somme, the Comte de Cointreau must re-unite his old pals for one last desperate venture that takes them to the very heart of the German war-machine! Can bluff Randy Robinson, wily Sacha Goldilox and the Comte himself outwit the combined forces of the Wilhelmstrasse and the heathen magic of the fabled lost continent of Atlantis? Another rattling tale of sorcery, flogging, high-adventure, whipping, facial disfigurement and spanking from the author of "The Bad Black", Das Ist Verboten", "Strange Document" and "Satan's Succubus".

UP PLUTO'S CORE
by Edward Fleisch-Cutter

The planet Pluto hollow? Absurd? Or so the world's scientists believed until Professor Potty and his chum Douglas Strongarm turned their gigantic space-rocket-cum-drill towards it! Burrowing deep below the Plutonian dust, the intrepid adventurers happen upon the long-lost kingdom of Longlostikar – a land where Pluto-dinosaurs still roam and Pluto-men with a thousand heads and blue thighs battle for dominance! Part of the thrilling "Pluto" sequence that includes "King of Pluto", "Ulnomia, Queen of Pluto", "Lord Mayor of Pluto" and " Dirty Pluto".

THE DEVIL IN AMBER

A "SHOCKER" BY

MARK GATISS

POCKET
BOOKS

LONDON • SYDNEY • NEW YORK • TORONTO

First published in Great Britain by Simon & Schuster UK Ltd, 2006
First published by Pocket Books, 2007
This omnibus edition first published by Pocket Books, 2008
An imprint of Simon & Schuster UK Ltd
A CBS COMPANY

1 3 5 7 9 10 8 6 4 2

Simon & Schuster UK Ltd
1st Floor
222 Gray's Inn Road
London WC1X 8HB

www.simonsays.co.uk

Simon & Schuster Australia
Sydney

A CIP catalogue record for this book is available
from the British Library

ISBN 978-0-7434-8380-3

Typeset in Caslon by M Rules
Printed by CPI Cox & Wyman, Reading, Berkshire RG1 8EX

For Winnie – 'Gather the rose of love whilst yet is time'

Acknowledgements

Thanks to Ian Bass, Caroline Chignell, Edward Fitzwilliam Hedley, Jon Plowman, Martin and Tim Stainthorpe, Nigel Stoneman, Rochelle Venables (for devilish editing) and to Ian, as ever, with all my love.

'If you value your souls, don't look in its eyes.'

1

Fallen Idle

He was an American, so it seemed only fair to shoot him.

I'd already winged the beggar once – somewhere in the region of his flabby calves – and was now in hot pursuit with the tenacity for which I'm mildly famous. For reasons too dreary to dwell on, I found myself clinging to the running board of a motor car, wind whipping at my face, positively pelting through the choked streets of Manhattan. Ahead of me loomed the gorgeous elegance of the new Chrysler Building, thrusting like a sword into the cold, brilliant blue sky. Ice and sun glinted off its exterior; sharp as a pin in the eye.

For those of you not in the know (dear me, where have you *been*?), my name is Lucifer Box: painter, occasional memoir-scribbler and agent (most secret) for His Majesty's Government. Sad it is to relate that my artistic career was somewhat in the doldrums. Fashion, that gay but inconstant dog, had moved on and I was regarded with some suspicion by the bright lads of the new school. Passé, old-hat, pre-War (the Great one, you understand: although there'd been nothing

particularly great about it from my point of view). Between the Surrealists and the Cubists and the Whatsists, there seemed precious little demand for a spectacularly good portrait painter such as yours truly. Oh, don't protest! Modesty is for *amateurs*.

Even the landed gentry who had once positively drenched me in commissions seemed in thrall to the damned new religion of photography, and were busy cramming the green-damask walls of their country piles with horrid daguerreotypes of their scarcely smiling selves. And so here was I, the gorgeous butterfly of King Bertie's reign: middle-aged and rather neglected, my hair shorter and greying – though my figure still as trim as a boy's, thank you very much.

Crouched low against the cold metal of the motor, I peered at my distorted reflection in the window. Still a head-turner, no doubt about it, and those eyes no less blue, no less cold and clear.

So much for Art! Happily I had other interests and when not exhibiting my daubs to an increasingly bored public, I was engaged, as I've said, doling out death and violence as gleefully as I did Crimson Alizarin or Mars Yellow. Every man should have a hobby.

Trouble was, of late the glee had rather gone out of this too. But I mustn't get ahead of myself.

The chap I'd been assigned to bump off on this charming December day was called Hubbard. Hubbard the Cupboard, don't you know (the Colonials like their schoolyard nick-names), his curious moniker coming not only from his ungainly shape but from his being a dealer in stolen goods. It was said Hubbard's cupboard was never bare.

The fat fool, however, had strayed somewhat from his usual territory of filched diamanté and crudely forged Demuths, being the brains, it was said, behind an influx of cheap cocaine that was currently drowning New York's nightspots. So, before the hooters of all the hoofers were irretrievably rotted, Hubbard was to be removed from the scene forthwith.

I was in town, tying up the loose ends of another job (the start-ling history of the Sumatran Automata will have to wait for another day), and, at its conclusion, had been hastily shunted off in pursuit of this nefarious drug baron.

I kept my head low as the car slowed down. The fat man's blood was visible in the snow, trailing in neat crimson curlicues as if fallen from a leaking paint tin. If I could finish him off by lunchtime, I knew a place down in the Bowery that did a smashing shad-roe-caviar club sarnie.

Dropping from the running board, I flattened myself against the grimy wall of the nearest brownstone and watched as the flivver chugged off with a backfire like a Lewis gun.

Inclining my trilby at a rakish angle, I paused a moment, know-ing I cut quite a dash. I'm afraid I rather fancied myself – but then everyone else did, so why should I be left out of the fun?

The trail led off the pavement – or 'sidewalk' as I suppose I must call it – and I moved off, my breath billowing like exhaust before me. The air was heavy with the stink of Polish cooking and uncollected rubbish.

Hurrying through the churned-up, brown drifts and following the trail as it swung right, I found myself in a light-starved court-yard. At its centre, smothered in snow, stood a quaint little clapboard church, fragile and unremarkable – save for the polka-dot pattern of bright blood on the steps. The door to the church was slightly ajar. I had him.

As quietly as possible, I slipped inside, taking a moment to adjust to the musty darkness with its familiar odour of incense and damp. Rapidly I made out shadowy pews, a pulpit like a ship's fo'c's'le, a narrow spiral stair leading to the bell tower.

My gloved hand closed around my Webley. As I reached the well of the stair, there was movement above and a little rivulet of dust cascaded onto the brim of my hat. Stealing upwards, I emerged into a beam-ceilinged chamber where two great copper-green bells hung

in their housings. The hunched figure of a man was silhouetted against the flat light pouring through an arched window. I raised my pistol and he swung towards me, his face a picture of fear. But unless Hubbard had hastily taken holy orders, this was not my quarry.

The priest's face fell as he glanced over my shoulder.

I span on my heel, hearing the scrape of shoe leather on wood and realizing at once that Hubbard was right behind me. Suddenly there was something startlingly cold at my flesh and every instinct thrilled as I felt a coil of piano wire loop about my throat. Without a moment's hesitation, my hand flew to my collar just as the wire tightened, allowing vital room for manoeuvre. I gasped as the deadly lasso bit into the leather of my glove.

Hubbard's sickly breath hissed into my face as he crushed me in a bear-like embrace. I own I was in a pretty blue funk. Trying frantically to turn about and aim the Webley, I felt instead my wrist savagely twisted and the pistol went crashing down the stair-well.

Still the noose tightened. Jerking my elbow repeatedly backwards, I met only empty air as Hubbard the Cupboard swung clear. There was a cold, bright *zing* as the razor wire sliced cleanly through my glove and ripped at the flesh of my hand.

Yelling in agony, I dropped to my knees and reached desperately behind me, clawing at the rotten woodwork of the floor, striving to find purchase on my assailant's ankle. The cold wire sawed into my palm.

'Help me!' I cried to the priest. 'Help me, for Christ's sake!'

But divine intervention came there none, the holy fool merely whimpering and wringing his hands.

Again I cried out in pain but then my fingers closed on the turn-up of Hubbard's trouser leg. It was wet with blood and I realized at once that this was where I'd already wounded the fiend. Frenziedly, I scrabbled at the floorboards till my fingers found the rusty end of a

bent nail. Croaking with effort, I prised the nail from the planking and managed to ram it with main force into the wound on my enemy's leg.

Hubbard screamed, stumbled forwards and suddenly the wire noose slackened. I rolled away, nursing my damaged hand, then, leaping to my feet, finally came face to face with him.

He was broad as a meat locker and swaddled in a cheap fur-collared overcoat such as an actor-manager might have left out for the moths. His eyes – buttons in the burst upholstery of his ugly face – glinted black and tiny. I'd never met Hubbard, only shot him, so by way of an introduction I kicked him in his lardy throat, sending the brute flying backwards into the bells. At once, the great shapes rolled in their housing.

He tried desperately to right himself, but the bells moved like quicksand beneath him, clappers ringing off the ancient bronze. He clawed at their surfaces, nails scoring grooves in the thick verdigris; sliding, gasping, out of control.

'This ain't right!' he squawked in a grisly Brooklyn accent, already slipping through the gap between the bells. 'It's a set-up!'

I scowled at him, cradling my wounded hand, totally unmoved by his imminent demise. 'Tell it to the marines.'

Hubbard gasped as he fought to keep from falling, his little feet scrabbling comically at the wooden housing. 'I'm a patsy!' he screeched.

'Cornish?'

'A *patsy!*' he cried. 'Oh, God!'

The corpulent cur knew he was a goner and something nasty flashed in those black eyes. One hand flew to his overcoat, and in an instant a small snub-nosed revolver was in his chubby hand. He wasn't intending to go down alone.

I stood powerless, my heart racing in time with the blood thudding onto the boards from my wet glove. Still the wretched priest did nothing, standing by in saintly inaction.

When the shot rang out I was surprised to feel no pain whatsoever. It took me a while to realize that this was intimately bound up with the fact that Hubbard now boasted a capacious and gory hole in his temple from which startlingly papal white smoke was pouring.

Hubbard gurgled most unpleasantly and then made his final foray between the bells, tumbling to the church floor below and setting the wretched things pealing gaily as though for Christmas Mass.

A cold sweat prickled all over me as I turned to greet my rescuer. He stood at the top of the stairs, still holding the weapon he had used on the ill-famed dealer in stolen goods.

'You're getting slow, old boy,' said the lean, brown newcomer, stepping into the light.

'Hullo, Percy,' I said lightly. '*Thanks.*'

Percy Flarge grinned his infuriating grin, pocketed his pistol and tipped his hat onto the back of his head, setting his blond fringe bouncing. 'Least I can do to help out a chum in his hour of need.' He peered at my hand. 'I say! You *have* been in the wars.'

I stepped away from him. 'I'll take things from here.'

Flarge shook his head. 'Wouldn't dream of letting you, old love. You should really put your feet up! Least I can do, as I say, for the great Lucifer Box.'

The great Lucifer Box suddenly felt a clammy sickness grip him and chose that moment to collapse onto the planking in a dead faint.

I awoke to a biting pain in my hand. I was stretched out on a pew, back in the main body of the church and sat up, blinking for a moment. The light had that strange, vivid quality as before a thunderstorm. The place was abuzz with what I knew to be Domestics – those terribly useful folk who clean up after chaps like me have been splattering haemoglobin all over the furniture – but there was no sign of Flarge.

I shook my head, groggily. My wound had been neatly and expertly stitched and was now being bandaged by a little ferret-faced chap in a short coat and yellow gloves. This was 'Twice' Daley – one of Flarge's favourites. Unlike my own dear Delilah (presently cook, valet, general factotum, bodyguard and thug) back in Blighty, he was a local man of no particular distinction.

'Hi there, Mr Box!' he cried.

I nodded weakly. 'You'll forgive me if I don't shake hands.'

He gave a short, barking laugh and tied off the bandage with his nimble fingers.

I flexed my own digits to assess the damage. 'Thanks for the repair job, Daley. Everything cleared up here?'

He nodded, his rheumy eyes scanning the church. '*Shoo-wer*. We paid off the pastor with enough rubes to make a new roof, and the Cupboard'll soon be doing the breaststroke in the Hudson – face down, if you takes my meaning.'

I did. 'I have orders to bring back everything he had on him. I trust you took care to—'

'Mr Flarge done all that,' he interrupted.

'Did he now?'

'Oh, yeah. Nice and regular. He's very *per-spik-ay-shee-us*, is Mr Flarge. He saved your ass too and no mistake.'

I ignored Daley's taunting and looked towards the back of the church. 'Is the body still here?'

'*Shoo-wer*. You wanna pay your last respects?' He grinned nastily, exposing tiny neat teeth like those of a deep-sea fish.

'Why not?'

Outside, freezing night was creeping on. Daley handed me a pocket torch and led me into the yard, where a tumbledown out-house had been pressed into service as a temporary morgue. Snowflakes as big as chrysanthemums were floating down from the drear sky and I bent down and scooped up a handful to assuage the awful throbbing in my hand.

Daley shuddered open the outhouse door and the body of Hubbard was revealed in the beam of the torch. We went inside.

'What exactly did Mr Flarge take away?' I asked, peering down at the powder-blackened hole in Hubbard's head.

'Whole bunch of stuff,' said Daley, taking the stub of a fat black cigar from his waistcoat pocket. 'Mr Flarge had a big carpet bag on him. Filled it with papers, mostly, and, you know, some merchandise.'

'Cocaine?'

'Uh-huh.'

Well, that seemed to confirm the theories. I nodded absently, and began to search Hubbard's body. Flarge had certainly been thorough. There was nothing in the big man's ghastly suit. No wallet, no identification, no driver's licence.

More than anything, I wanted to spot something that young pup had missed, and Daley knew it. He smoked his spit-wetted cigar and watched my fruitless activity with obvious glee. I'd almost given up when something caught my eye.

It was Hubbard's handkerchief. In sharp contrast to the dead man's vile tailoring, the wipe was made of an exquisite ivory-coloured silk of obvious antiquity. It was folded into three neat triangles, like a miniature mountain range, and there seemed to be some sort of exotic pattern on it. It might be a mere trifle, but trifles ain't to be sniffed at when you've not even been invited to the party . . .

Daley was watching me closely. I cleared my throat and straightened up as though satisfied.

'Very well. There's nothing more to be done here,' I said. 'Thanks for your help.'

Daley gave a little bow. I gasped suddenly, as though in pain, and dropped the torch, which rolled under the table.

'Sorry!' I managed through gritted teeth. 'Damned wound!'

Daley bent down to retrieve the torch and I swiftly whipped the

handkerchief from Hubbard's breast pocket, stuffing it into my trousers just as the Domestic bobbed back up.

'You get yourself to bed now, Mr Box, you hear?' he said with a horrible grin. 'Then maybe get on the boat back home to Eng-ur-land, huh? What with Christmas coming and all.'

I smiled tightly and stalked off into the gathering snowstorm, the silken rag tucked firmly into my pocket.

2

You Might As Well Live

Those who have followed these incoherent memoirs may recall that my long and rather lovely hands are not to be trifled with. A youth of my acquaintance once compared them to Our Lord's as depicted in Caravaggio's *Ecce Homo*. I was, naturally, immensely flattered, though my digits had been engaged in singularly un-Christ-like activity at the time.

Now, as blaring taxi cabs crawled around me in the sickly electric-yellow glow of the evening, I feebly raised my injured fingers and hailed one such, muttered the address of my hotel and slid inside the motor, avoiding the driver's invective by studiously pretending sleep. The soft, wet patter of snow against the windows lulled me and I placed my bandaged hand on the wonderfully cold glass. The pain was somewhat tempered.

I've dealt with Art and its shortcomings. Now, as promised, we shall examine the state of my other pursuit, namely espionage. Once again, for the newcomers (Keep up! Keep up!), I must devote a short passage to the Royal Academy of Arts, that bastion of the

Establishment in London's Piccadilly (where *else's* Piccadilly? Must I address you like simpletons?). Fact is, the RA is not what it seems. For strip away the facade of Burlington House – you *can* do that, you know. The whole Palladian front descends into a specially dug trench in case of mortar attack. No, *really* – and you'll uncover a seething hotbed of plotting, counter-plotting and assassination. Of course, that's what you'd expect to find in a building full of artists, but this is a different business altogether. For the RA is the true face of His Majesty's Secret Service. Not that other lot of whom you may have vaguely heard: the blighters who go around destabilizing per-fectly friendly democracies in Bolivia or knocking off the Nabob of Whatchamacallit. No, we're the real thing: the ones who oil the wheels of the great machines of state; the ones who make it possi-ble for you to sit down in Lyon's Corner House with a cup of rosie and the 'Thunderer' without some greasy foreigner taking a pop at you with a Walther PP. 7.65.

As I've said, to me it was always the merest hobby of a dilettante, a little like collecting stamps or mounting Red Admirals – but my exploits amongst the Russian navy will have to wait for another day. No, from my youthful adventures at the tail end of the old Queen's reign to my ill-starred work against the Bosch during the last big show, I reckoned myself one of the brightest and best of the Academicians; trotting merrily from continent to continent; cutting, thrusting, derring and doing.

Now, though, the game seemed to be full of arrogant young-bloods like the odious Percy Flarge, an athletic Cambridge Blue of little discernible charm. If there's one thing I cannot abide, it's a smart alec. Unless that smart alec is me. And Percy Flarge was, from the crown of his trilby to the tips of his absurd coffee-and-cream brogues, smart as paint.

At first I'd taken him for one of the legion of doe-eyed admirers who have crossed my path over the years. My *fan-club*, I suppose you would call them. Like so many others, he'd cornered me on the

grand staircase of the Academy, brimming with energy and stuffed with tales of my famous cases. The spectacular matter of the Spitzbergen Mammoth! That nasty business with the Italian volcanoes! The explosive urinals of Armitage Shankz and the colourful revenge of the Man with the Wooden Wig! (I've never written that one down, have I?). He was a looker too, which never hurts, forever bobbing aside his silly blond fringe and batting his lashes like a flapper at a Valentino flicker. I was absurdly flattered and rather let down my guard.

Then came a change of regime at the top (more of that later) and Flarge's attitude began, subtly at first, to alter. Sly jibes here, stifled giggles there. Surely old Boxy was past his best? Time for younger talents to take the lead. Of course what really rankled was the fear that the loathsome creature was right. Hubbard the Cupboard, for instance, should have presented scant challenge for the great Lucifer Box but the bounder had almost bested me, had almost *derringered* me into oblivion, and if it hadn't been for that deplorably wiry and sunburnt colleague of mine, he would have succeeded.

I was startled by the blast of the taxi's horn and realized I had indeed flaked out on the cracked leather upholstery. At last we shushed through the filthy drifts and pulled up outside the snow-flecked frontage of my hotel. I felt light-headed still and the darkness, coupled with the ugly illumination of headlamps, conspired to make me giddy. Pressing a couple of dollars into the driver's hairy hand, I clambered out into the cold, rubbing my neck and swiftly making my way into the December-dark lobby. Palm fronds poked out from tobacco-fogged niches where old men, already dressed for dinner, gleefully scanned the obituary columns.

Exhausted, and anxious to take a proper look at the 'handkerchief', I crossed to the lifts and jabbed impatiently at the button. Above my head, a gilded arrow on illumined green glass crawled slowly round. I sank against the wall and sighed heavily. A dull

ache was banging behind my eyes and my hand hurt like billy-o. I'd had hell's time that day.

When at last the lift arrived and the heavy lattice screen was dragged back, I stepped inside without looking up. The interior was all walnut.

'Fifteen, ain't it, Mr Box?'

I glanced over, and my scowl melted instantly away. It was a bell-hop I'd noticed only that morning, red-headed and pale as a Tudor portrait, noticing *me* from under long-lashed eyes.

Now he held his head on one side, as though trying to dislodge a marble from his ear, one of those silly round hats at an acute angle on his well-oiled hair. He had huge green eyes and lips as red as raspberries.

'Do we know each other?' I asked at last.

He seemed flustered by this and looked away. 'Um . . . old Van Buren – that is, *Mr* Van Buren, the manager, sir. He told me your name. There's a package come for you and he said, "Rex, you be sure and take that up to Mr Box when he comes back." And I says, "Is Mr Box that tall, refined-looking gentleman—"'

'Yes, all right. Just bring me the parcel, *Rex*.' I stepped out of the lift and looked him directly in his emerald eyes as the grille closed over his face. 'Room Fifteen-o-eight.'

Smiling a little to myself and feeling much better, I let myself into said room. It was large and well appointed, a big white divan cover on the bed, cream-coloured leather armchairs in each corner. The warm aura from discreet lamps prevented the whiteness from appearing too stark and I found it immensely comforting after the privations of the outside world.

Throwing off coat and hat, I reached into my trousers, pulled out Hubbard's silken rag and carefully unfolded it on one of the pillows.

Though roughly handkerchief-shaped, it had clearly been torn from a much larger piece of material. Two of the edges were ragged and bore crabbed text in what looked like some species of Latin.

The bottom corners were highly decorated with coloured emblems, a picture of a mountain and dragon's heads. There was a sort of fiery motif, embroidered rather beautifully, the flames licking over what looked like an animal on a spit.

I examined the thing until my vision swam then decided to abandon it for the night. After all, I was almost certainly clutching at straws. Perhaps Percy Flarge hadn't bothered with it because it was nothing more than a snotty rag.

Pulling off my shoes, I padded to the bathroom and ran a tub. It was a huge relief to strip off the sweat-drenched togs and I stood naked for a moment, letting my bare feet sink into the deep white pile of the carpet, before plunging into the bath. The heat made me feel raw. I closed heavy lids and rested my injured hand on the soap dish.

That I'd failed pretty spectacularly at my mission to rub out Hubbard was scarcely in question. Also, I'd been somewhat humiliated by friend Flarge. But worse things happened at sea, as I knew from that funny old night on the *Lusitania*. And Hubbard was at least dead, so perhaps I was exaggerating the calamity. Come on, old man, I told myself. Chin up. I was sound in wind and limb and, most importantly, *alive*.

Something about this matter, though, didn't add up. Why were my superiors so keen to bump off small fry like Hubbard? The dreary narcotics trade was surely a police matter. What did it have to do with the RA? And why hadn't a local been pressed into service?

Yours not to reason why, Box old chum, you might well say. The doing or dying bit is what counts. But I suddenly didn't feel like doing much doing – and certainly not dying – if I was being kept in the dark by my superiors.

Dimly, through the woodwork of the bathroom, I heard a knock at the main door.

I sighed and ignored it but the caller was insistent.

'Come!' I bellowed, causing a minor avalanche in the foam that covered my naked bod.

A creak from without and then a second knock – this time at the bathroom door.

'Yes, yes,' I barked. 'Why don't you come in?'

A muffled voice: 'Um . . . Mr Box?'

I stood up in the tub, reached across for the handle and wrenched at it. 'Don't stand on ceremony. I've had a bloody day and I'm in no mood for – oh!'

I'd forgotten about the bellhop.

At the sight of him, the venting of my spleen was very much halted. The lovely red-head looked straight down at my pendulous tackle and blushed. Averting his face, he thrust a brown-paper parcel towards me.

I frowned at it, sat back into the water, then pulled at the ribbon that was wrapped like liquorice bootlace around the parcel. Inside was a little purple box and inside that, a block of whitish stuff.

'Soap,' I mused.

'Sir?' The bellhop was still standing there, his pretty face cast into shadow by the opalescent bulb above.

'It's a bar of soap,' I explained. 'Smelling of – yes – violets and bearing the imprinted word *"DISSOLVE"*.'

'OK, sir,' said the boy for no apparent reason. He cleared his throat. 'Any answer?'

I looked up, twinkling naughtily. 'What was the question?'

He gulped and looked down at his shiny shoes. He seemed new to this lark but was evidently game and just needed a gentle push in the right direction.

'The question, sir? Um . . .' He lifted his eyes and looked coyly at me from under his lashes. Nice technique. He'd undoubtedly go far. 'Might I come in, sir?' he asked at last.

'The very question I hoped you'd ask. Yes. Come in, won't you? Shut the door. That's it. What did you say your name was?'

'Rex, sir.'

'Well, Rex, what do you make of it?' I said, sliding lower under the foam and noticing how very tight and snug were my new friend's blue trews. 'Ever heard of a brand of soap called "Dissolve"?'

'Can't say that I have, sir,' said Rex, his big Adam's apple bobbing nervously.

'No, no. Most odd. The manufacturers usually favour something more fragrant,' I continued, then looked sharply at him. '*Take off your shoes.*'

The boy licked his lips and slipped off his patent-leathers.

'"Dissolve",' I murmured, then flicked my gaze back to him. 'Trousers – erm – *pants*, if you please. Could it be an instruction to knock about the remainder of our English monasteries? *Shirt*. Seems most unlikely, Rex, don't you think? *Underthings.*'

'I guess,' said the charming youth, slipping out of the last of his clothes until he stood in only his white socks on the wet mat before me. His toes were outlined in black from the new leather like the brass rubbing of a crusader's tomb.

'Happily, I think I know its secret,' I said, dropping the soap into the bathwater. The foam began to bubble and froth and then the whole bar liquefied, spreading a broad purple stain across the water. And lying there on the surface, as though scrawled with a magic wand, was a message.

Rex gawped and read aloud. 'Moscow Tea Rooms. 10 a.m. tomorrow. Joshua Reynolds.'

I wafted my uninjured hand through the water and the message vanished, drifting in inky strands to the enamelled bottom.

'Message from the office,' I said quietly. 'I'd've been happy with a telegram.' I glanced up at Rex. 'Better take your socks off, hmm?'

The youth hopped from one foot to the other as he divested himself of the last of his clobber, then I took his hand and helped him into the hot bath with me.

His long legs slid through the fading violet residue of the secret message. He had a smashing smile and shook his red-head wonderingly. 'Gosh! I ain't seen nothing like that before!'

A moment or two later, I presented him with an even nicer surprise.

3

A Trip to Neverland

At eight the next morning, I left the cosy embrace of young Rex (sucked off and buggered if you must know) to keep my appointment with the boss.

I'd had an uneasy night – once my eyes closed – caught in a nightmarish New York of the future, all sky-scraping apartment blocks and rocket ships, as in those unpleasant German films. The dream-me, wearing only queerly tight underwear with President Coolidge's name embroidered about the waist, sauntered past the Algonquin, the pavement transformed into a howling white tunnel of cocaine. Overhead, Hubbard the Cupboard was performing dazzling aerobatics like Lucky Lindy, but the smoke trailing from his rocket-ship transformed into narcotics too, falling on my shoulders like snow. As his machine roared past, I distinctly saw bright rivulets of blood pouring from the aviator's nostrils and the dead man laughing at me, fit to burst.

Later, out in the real street, I darted between the yellow flashes of the taxi cabs, my brogues tramping through the drifts of mud-coloured

slush. Despite the temperature, New York teemed with Christmas activity, the scents of coffee and perfume as vivid as incense. Shopping was approaching fever pitch and I found myself shouldering through crowds like a three-quarter in a greatcoat.

I was mentally preparing myself for the meeting that the soapy message had foisted on me. Joshua Reynolds awaited my pleasure.

He was not, alas, the dwarfish chap whom you may have encountered before: the cheeky fellah with the vivid little eyes who'd steered me through countless adventures too numerous or scandalous to mention.

No, he'd gone the way of all flesh, his titchy heart giving out just one month into the retirement he'd always craved. The name was then passed on like a title – I never did find out the dwarf's real moniker – and a very different personage had ascended to the top of the Royal Academy's secret staff.

We were about of an age but whereas I had taken strenuous efforts to maintain my superlative physique this new J.R. had run to fat. He had the look of a minor bishop – a colonial one, perhaps, always perspiring into his purple and wishing they'd given him the See of Leicester (or something just as dreadful). As I peered in through the window of the tea rooms I could see his rumpled, disappointed face glowing whitely in the gloom like the moon behind clouds in an Atkinson Grimshaw.

I had a hand on the door knob when I caught sight of a chap on the opposite side of the road. Tallish and well built, I noted a suggestion of tousled curls and pocked skin, briefly brightened by the flare of a match. He drew on his cigar and glanced briefly at me. Did I flatter myself that a flash of *something* passed between us?

Then he was gone, swallowed up in the great mass of humanity that surged down the canyon-like roadway.

I stood aside for a plump dowager in silver furs, then slipped inside the tea rooms. The din from outside was immediately replaced by reassuringly elegant chatter and the gentle tinkling of a

grand piano. Waiters moved swift and silent as eels through the mahogany dimness.

Joshua Reynolds scarcely looked up as he stirred his coffee, ladling sticky wedges of brown sugar into its creamy depths.

'Morning,' I said brightly, unwinding my scarf. 'I didn't know you made house calls. Or are you here Christmas shopping?'

'Sit down, Box,' he muttered, gesturing towards the plump green velvet.

'I say, public meetings in the Moscow Tea Rooms. Whatever next! Your illustrious predecessor was far fonder of the shadow and the whispered word . . .'

Reynolds's fat face snapped upwards, the flesh wobbling slightly like the skin on cocoa.

'Times have moved on, Box,' he said, the voice oily and self-satisfied. 'You'd do well to remember that. We live in a rapidly changing world. Everything's *faster*. Motor cars, aeroplanes, even the Prince of Wales.'

This might have been a joke. I didn't risk a smile. A waiter brought me a polished silver teapot which tinsel-glinted wonderfully in the dark.

'As it happens,' said Reynolds at last, 'the business of the Academy has brought me this side of the Atlantic. A wretched crossing. I shall do my best never to repeat the experience. How do you find it?'

I allowed a pleasant memory of the bell-hop's bum to surface for the moment. 'Oh tolerable, tolerable.'

'Speaking of speed,' continued Reynolds, returning to his earlier theme, the suggestion of a sneer creeping onto his lips. 'That chap Flarge, he's certainly fast. Particularly when getting up the stairs of belfries, eh?'

'Yes. Very nimble,' I said dryly.

Unconsciously, my hand drifted to my breast pocket, where Hubbard the Cupboard's curious hankie was safely stowed. Flarge

wouldn't be getting his mitts on that in a hurry. It might be important or it might be the airiest nothing but it was the only advantage over my rival I currently possessed. I'd hoped to have the thing deciphered and presented like prep to the boss, but the charming Rex had taken up all my spare time.

'Flarge saved your bacon, by all accounts,' continued the fat man. 'Plays a straight game. Best man we have in the show. Clean. Lean. Healthy. Kind of chap the Royal Academy needs more of, eh?'

I took a sip of tea. 'Is that a roundabout way of saying you need *less* of chaps like me?'

Reynolds smiled. 'If you like.'

I shook my head. 'I don't like.'

He took a great slurp of his coffee and set the cup down so heavily that it rang off the saucer. 'Look here, Box. I'll not pussyfoot around. You're getting too old for this game. No doubt you once had some flair for it all—'

'I'm the best,' I said coolly.

Reynolds harrumphed into his fat-knotted tie. 'Not being hidebound by friendship or misplaced loyalty, however, I judge only by results.'

He glanced down at some papers on the table before him. Was this it, then? The great cashiering? I looked about, wanting to fix this moment in my mind's eye, but a big-eared diner's braying laugh cut through the chatter and I roused myself.

Reynolds mouth turned down, as though someone had stuffed a lemon in it. 'Frankly, if it were up to me you'd be back on the boat and daubing your way into your dotage by now but it seems you still have some friends in positions of influence.'

'How reassuring.'

Said friends he dismissed with a casual wave of his flipper-like hand. 'There's a job of sorts come up. Nothing too taxing. Just the thing for you to bow out on.' He smiled and it was like a candle flaring into life behind a Hallowe'en mask.

I sighed. That it should end like this! Trailing a paltry little crook like Hubbard had been demeaning enough. What was this final mission to be? Vetting recruits for evidence of transvestism? Checking the collar studs on King George's shirt-fronts for miniature arsenical capsules?

'F.A.U.S.T.,' said Reynolds at last.

'The opera?'

'The *organization*. Heard of it?'

I brushed biscuit crumbs from my napkin. 'Can't say I have.'

'Out of touch again. Never mind, never mind. F.A.U.S.T. stands for the Fascist Anglo-United States Tribune.'

I laughed. 'An acronym so tortuous it can only be sinister.'

Reynolds looked down at his file. 'That is, I suppose, the thinking of our superiors. This lot want to create closer ties between the fascist movements on both sides of the Atlantic, as the name implies. For myself, I'm not too vexed by these johnnies. Broadly right on the Jews, of course, and you must admit Mussolini's turned Italy round.'

'Always presupposing that it needed turning,' I ventured, smiling. 'Who's in charge?'

Reynolds shifted in his seat, his rump making the leather parp like the horn of a motor. 'Fellah called Olympus Mons. Bit of a swaggerer.'

'Have to be with a name like that. I like him already.'

'Yankee-born, Balliol-educated. Anglophile. Sees himself as the fascist Messiah. His acolytes call themselves amber-shirts.'

'You want me to kill him?'

Reynolds's guffaw almost knocked over his coffee pot. 'I'm afraid such a task will, in future, be left in safer hands. No, you're merely to observe his activities. If you're still capable of doing so.' He shot me a nasty look. 'We've a lead of sorts. One of Mons's amber-shirts seems to have grave doubts about his leader. Wants to tell all.'

'Where do I meet him?'

Reynolds drained the last of his coffee and smacked his lips unpleasantly. 'This is all we have.'

He tossed over a slip of paper. On it was a neatly typed message: 'You: Robespierre. Me: Peter Pan. "99". 8.30'.

Reynolds wiped his hands on the tablecloth. 'No idea what it means. Just that he'll find you there. Tonight. I'm afraid you might have to do a little work, Box, and find out for yourself. Think you can manage that?'

With a flick of the wrist, I was dismissed into the bleak December day.

I looked about, hoping to catch sight of my cigar-smoking friend, but sign of him was there none, so I took a cab back to the hotel and sought out my own couch until lunchtime.

Night-time found me motoring up-state dressed as the renowned French Revolutionary. I was grateful the message hadn't suggested Marat as I wouldn't have been able to fit the bathtub into the Cadillac. As I barrelled along near-deserted roads fringed by pine trees, their boughs weighed down with snow, gas stations and houses loomed out of the darkness, Christmas decorations glittering around their eaves. I swung left down a drift-covered road, passing a pile of the Lloyd-Wright Californian school jutting from a hillside like a great tithe barn, all glass and dressed stone with an imposing tiled roof.

I pulled up at a red light and let the engine chug. Soft, wet snow coated the bonnet. Tugging at my britches (they kept getting caught up in the gear-stick), I mused over my situation. It hadn't taken long to establish the meaning of the message from Olympus Mons's disaffected colleague. A quick word with dear Rex the bellhop (what a useful boy he was) furnished me with all the necessaries and I was now heading towards the mysterious "99" and an encounter, it was to be hoped, with Peter Pan. Odds on that the fellah nursed a grievance against his boss – over lack of advancement, probably – and was

now prepared to stick in the knife with gay abandon. With any luck, Mons was involved in some lurid sexual scandal the details of which we at the Royal Academy could store up for future use. Sordid, I know, but it's a living.

The light changed and I threw the Cadillac into first gear. The wipers thrummed back and forth, smearing the snow into bleary triangles. Ahead, projecting from the flat fields, were half a dozen parabolic buildings, pewter-grey and rusty with age. A mesh fence ringed the place, and as I bounced the car along the track, stones spitting up against the wheel rims, a lopsided 'keep out' sign became visible.

A bundled-up figure – all scarf and goggles – stomped towards me and knocked on the jalopy window. With some difficulty, I managed to hinge the glass open. Snow whirled inside, settling on the dark leather.

'Can I help you, bud?' said the newcomer, through his moth-nibbled muffler.

'I have a ticket to Rio,' I said crisply. 'No baggage.' Which is what Rex had told me I must say. Frankly, I've always found passwords and codes a little tiresome. Say what you mean, is my adage. Unless it's 'I love you', of course.

The insulated man gave an affirmative grunt and dragged the protesting gates open. I slid the Cadillac through.

The aerodrome – for such it was – was a sad sight. Through the falling snow, weeds were visible, erupting through the long-disused potholed landing strips. But though the curved buildings were dark and silent, a streak of livid yellow light blazed from under the huge doors of the main hangar.

There were already thirty or so other cars parked up in front of it, and as I clambered out of the motor I saw Genghis Khan and what could have been the Empress Josephine getting better acquainted in the moonlight. Their faces were masked and I slipped on my own, covering me as far as the bridge of my nose. Settling a periwig onto

my head, I walked to the hangar and without further challenge, was let inside.

All was light. A wave of warmth hit me like a brick. By way of introduction, I was greeted by the elongated honk of a trombone and the rasped strains of 'I'll Be Glad When You're Dead, You Rascal You!'.

Glancing at once to my right, I saw a septet of jazz musicians attacking their syncopated tune with ferocious relish, limbs blurring in a frenzy of polished brass and banjo, oiled hair falling forward and sticking to their sweating foreheads.

A wonderful room had been constructed within the hangar, a kind of cat's cradle of girders and struts with gantries up a height leading to a series of neat compartments. Great sheets of canvas encompassed the whole like gigantic drapes, surrounding fat sea-shell-shaped easy chairs in exquisitely tooled white leather and a vast glass table.

Dotted about were various items of ephemera: a mirrored cock-tail cabinet, a huge map of the world, a small wood and chrome ship's wheel and a massive Union Flag. It was, do you see, the wreckage of the R-99, the splendid airship that had gone down over Martha's Vineyard some two years previously, happily without loss of life and without exploding in an inferno of hydrogen as they are wont to do.

The fixtures and fittings were so damnably pretty, so the thinking had gone, that it seemed only right to turn them to good use. Now the "99" was New York's swellest speakeasy and clearly the place to be seen – albeit in fancy dress.

The somewhat arctic style of the ruined airship was currently offset by the astonishing blaze of colour provided by the costumed guests. Coloured streamers poured from the roof girders, mingling giddily with explosions of taffeta, silk and velvet, got up in every form of uniform, toga and frock. It's marvellous how stylish duds can transform even the most commonplace person, and perhaps

even more marvellous how a simple half-mask of black or white can render the must lumpen of features strangely romantic.

I swept as gracefully as I could through the carousing throng, passing Cleopatras, Abraham Lincolns and a variety of gorgeously frocked queens (of the divorced, beheaded and died variety, you understand), all gyrating wildly to the strains of the jazz band. There was a frenzied air to their enjoyment and the grins visible under the masks had a fixed, rictus quality that was almost alarming. Perhaps I was just feeling jealous of their youth.

I'm always trying to recapture my youth – but he keeps on *escaping*.

Standing with one bandaged hand on tricoleur-sashed hip, cigarette in the other, I waited until a flunkey in a turban deigned to offer me some pink champagne.

The face of our informant, 'Peter Pan', was unknown but I kept my lovely eyes peeled for such a vision, or even his independent shadow shuffling along the skirting boards. All manner of fairies, nymphets and dryads pirouetted before me, the shimmering of cut-glass chandeliers speckling their lithesome young bodies like sunlight through forest leaves – but there was no sign of any denizen of Neverland.

A giddy couple – Adam and Eve by their state of déshabillé – stumbled past me.

'None of your beeswax!' cried the girl, slurping her cocktail. 'It's just some caper he's got on and – Oh . . . *hi!*'

She laid a friendly hand on my sleeve and giggled. 'Hey. Have you seen Raphael?'

I blew a languid smoke-cloud through my nose. 'The Urbino Master?'

'The *guy*. You *know*. Raphael! Hey, Leonard. Butt me, would ya?'

Her companion leant in and popped a slim cigarillo between her lips. I gave her a light from my own. She clasped my hand as she bent down, glancing up at me with saucy eyes.

'Thanks. Hey, you wanna dance?'

'Aren't you looking for Raphael? And what about Adam?'

But the Biblical first-hubbie was engaged in a frantic Charleston with a dime-store Pola Negri in a bad wig. Eve dismissed him with a curt shake of her lovely head.

She was certainly a stunner in her fleshings, a cleverly embroidered fig leaf covering both her breasts and her unmentionables. Had fate not intervened, I might well have asked her to give me a little tour of the Tree of Knowledge, but just then someone knocked into me, sloshing pop onto my silken sleeve and dragging Eve away. Of course, she forgot me at once and disappeared into the throng.

Tutting, I reached into my pantaloons and pulled out my handkerchief.

'Where'd you get that?'

I glanced up. A small white-blond fellow, togged up as Julius Caesar, was peering at my wipe. Looking down, I realized I'd pulled out Hubbard's curious relic by mistake.

The noblest Roman jabbed out a fat, hairless hand. 'May I see?'

There was a curious timbre to his voice, a kind of faintly hysterical edge as though he was fighting to control his emotions. I waited a moment, not sure how to play the situation, then dropped the ragged silk into his palm. His quick eyes – bespectacled beneath the slits of his half-mask – scanned the relic with hungry eagerness. 'My, my,' he cooed, blinking lashes pale as straw. 'It's *very* old. Medieval, at a guess. Northern European. Quite a miraculous survival.'

He cleared his throat twice and beamed at me. 'Where'd you get it?'

I can recognize affected nonchalance when I see it. For the second time, I ignored the question. 'Do you know what all that writing means?' I asked.

A faint smile broke the small man's impassivity. 'Ah, now.' Cough-cough. 'That's the question.'

I took a sip of champagne. 'You have some . . . expertise?' I ventured.

'A little, yes,' he said mildly. 'Name's Reiss-Mueller. Professor Reiss-Mueller. I work at the Metropolitan Museum. Down in the bowels. Drop by some time. I can give you my honest opinion on it.'

'In return for what?'

The little man hooked a finger over his lower lip, like a child contemplating what it might want for Christmas.

Then, suddenly, there was a low brown Yankee voice in my ear. 'How goes the Revolution?'

It was so close to my flesh and pitched so low that I shivered, then swivelled about on my high-heeled velveteen shoes.

'Not so bad. Are you a friend of Tinkerbell's?' I cried, tucking the handkerchief into my trousers.

Peter Pan was revealed, not the puckish individual I was expecting, but a rather strapping fellow in a challengingly short green tunic and matching tights. A feathered cap looked rather dainty on his expensively cut chestnut hair. Beneath the white half mask, large brown eyes burned intensely.

I turned back to Reiss-Mueller but the little man had melted away into the seething, chattering crowd.

4

I Move In Bad Company

Returning my full attention to the newcomer, I found myself somewhat distracted by the impressive bulk of his thighs. Clearing my throat embarrassedly, I looked Peter Pan full in the face. He had a rather heroic jaw with that indefinably attractive just-shaved glow, only some rather bad pocking spoiling the otherwise flawless effect of his skin. He gripped my arm and pulled me aside. 'Sal Volatile's the name. We gotta talk.'

I took a long drag on my cigarette. 'So I gather. You have some information to impart?'

'Uh-huh.' The brown eyes darted about inside the slitted hollows of the mask. 'Secrets.'

I smiled my wide smile. 'Secrets, eh? Well, you're the boy who never grows old. I beg you to blab.'

His face (or half of it) fell. 'This is serious.'

'I'm sure it is. How much do you want?'

His chin suddenly lunged so close to mine that I recoiled. 'I don't want money!' he hissed. 'Jesus! You think I'd risk it all for . . .'

He glanced away and I followed his gaze. Anne of Cleves and one of the Abraham Lincolns were busily chopping up lines of cocaine with a razor blade. They sat on opposite sides of the glass table, chatting merrily like children divvying up sherbet. The woman inhaled a vast quantity and then shook herself all over like a dog emerging from a pond. Her eyes grew glassy for an instant and then she giggled uncontrollably, her hand flying to her mouth and a little dribble of colourless mucus forming on her upper lip.

'Do you believe in Evil, Mr Box?' said my companion, grinding his jaw and looking at the couple with unfeigned contempt.

'Only on Wednesdays.'

The jest was not appreciated. 'Evil, sir. Old as the Earth. Seductive as a lover's promise. Patient, watchful Evil . . .'

'If you're referring to the narcotics, my boy, then I consider there are greater perils threatening the globe just now.'

'How right you are.'

I sighed. 'Look here, Mr Volatile. I dislike riddles. Has all this cryptic blether got anything to do with F.A.U.S.T.?'

A curiously mad grin suddenly lit up his features. 'Ha! More than you know, sir. More than you know.'

'You're doing it again! Are we going to come to some accommodation or am I wasting my time? These Froggy shoes are awful uncomfortable, don't you know, and I'm hankering for my bed.'

He swung back in my direction and suddenly lifted up his mask.

I took a step backwards. It was the curly-haired chap who'd shadowed me outside the Moscow Tea Rooms! His cheeks looked even more pitted in the curiously lurid light but his whole face blazed with a fierce intelligence. 'If I'm being careful, sir, it's because I'm playing a very dangerous game. I'm going to tell you everything. I swear. About the Lamb. About the Prayer. But first you need to see what you're up against. Come with me.'

'Wait!' I cried. 'What lamb? What prayer?'

For answer, he led me through the thrashing, giddy throng to a

little anteroom, much chillier than the main chamber and constructed from corrugated iron.

I hung back, suspecting a trap, but he beckoned urgently to me and something about his manner (or his smashing legs) made me throw caution to the wind and step inside.

He reached across me to close the door and I caught a strong whiff of cologne with an undercurrent of sweat. The racket from the costume party was instantly shut off, lingering only as a throbbing background beat. Without a moment's hesitation, Volatile began to strip, shrugging off his tunic, revealing the curve of muscular shoulders as big as over-ripe oranges. Was this what I was to be, well, *up against*? I felt a lovely rush in my gut as though someone were roasting chestnuts inside me.

Somewhat to my chagrin, he peeled off his tights, bent down into the darkened corner and then threw a bundle of clothes at me. 'Get these on,' he said smoothly, unfolding a silk shirt for himself.

As I changed out of my finery, I thought what a damned shame that matters were clearly too pressing for any extracurricular fun. But was this Lost Boy of my persuasion? Hard to tell. He was so aggressively masculine, though, that I had very grave suspicions.

In a few minutes we were both dressed alike in jodhpur-like black trousers, boots that glistened wetly like chewed liquorice and tailored silk shirts of a rather gorgeous amber hue. I began to get the picture.

'Another costume party?' I said.

'In a manner of speaking,' said my new friend, smiling thinly. 'You got a car?'

The Cadillac roared back towards Manhattan, a freezing wind, peppered with snowflakes, whipping over the bonnet. Sal Volatile was almost completely silent throughout the journey, muttering occasional directions as we crossed silent bridges or swung past another block of looming apartments.

He stiffened as we cruised down a broad avenue somewhere off

Fourteenth Street then nodded almost imperceptibly. 'We're here.'

A spectacular kinema in the Art Deco style blazed, floodlit, from the darkness, a vast votive angel spreading its stony wings over the entranceway. The gangster talkie normally showing five times a day had been temporarily replaced by another spectacle, and as we drove past the entrance we watched hundreds of over-coated figures streaming into the lobby.

Parking around the back of the picture palace, we stepped into a landscape of filthy snow and dustbins, great spouts of steam issuing from the indented drains. Volatile reached into his trouser pocket and produced something that looked like a library card. He handed it to me and I strained to make out the tiny print. 'F.O.I.F.?'

This case was a study in acronyms.

'Friends of International Fascism,' muttered my new ally. 'That's who you represent tonight. We're going to a F.A.U.S.T. rally.'

I shuddered as the wind whistled down the alley, setting the lids of the bins rattling. 'How thrilling. I shall fix a suitably manic gleam into my baby blues.'

Volatile grunted. I didn't honestly anticipate any awkward questions as these rallies, like New Year sales, tend to lean more towards fevered screeching and hysteria than closely reasoned argument.

We joined the crush of delegates streaming into the cinema and divested ourselves of our steaming outdoor wear. The cloakroom attendants were kept as busy as coolies.

Stripped of their fedoras and long coats, I now saw the assembly in all their glory. As a breed they were predominantly men and women of healthy aspect; fine boned and lustrous of hair (scraped back from the forehead for the boys, set in finger waves for the girls). Each and every one of them was dressed as were we in the F.A.U.S.T. uniform.

We queued dutifully and followed the others through into the main auditorium, the smell of damp wool immediately overwhelmed by the charged odour of a thousand light bulbs. The place glowed

like a grotto, the interior done out in shades of Italian ice cream, galleries and seats in patterns of repeated ovals. A safety curtain had been drawn down over the kinema screen and an elaborate lectern installed before it. Dominating the whole thing was a vast black flag, draped from ceiling to stage. In its centre, a design in blazing orange showed two flashes of arrow-headed lightning – the symbol of the movement.

We took our seats in a row of excited amber-shirts, faces aglow with anticipation, gossiping as though they'd come to see the hit show of the season.

'All right, Mr Volatile,' I said quietly. 'Now we're snug. What was all that about back at the party? What's the lamb?'

Volatile glanced quickly over his shoulder, then put a finger to his lips.

On cue, a muffled drumbeat began to sound and the audience hissed themselves into silence. The drumbeat slowed into a self-consciously momentous *thrum-thrum-thrum* and unseen cornets shrieked out in fanfare. As one mass, the crowd's heads turned back as dazzling spotlights crackled into life.

'Here he comes,' whispered Volatile.

The spotlights snapped off and then back on again, revealing, with almost magical timing, a phalanx of amber-shirts in a V-formation. The crowd gasped in excitement.

The newcomers were indistinguishable in dress from the rest of the adoring mob but they had the indefinable whiff of glamour about them. They were not the tallest, most muscular, not even the blondest of these Übermenschen but they were the stars of the show and they knew it.

One was a pudgy, balding chap with wispy moustache and horn-rimmed spectacles, another a great horsy woman with her ginger hair in cartoonish Valkyrie braids. I scanned the elite, hoping to catch my first glimpse of Olympus Mons, the great leader. As the spotlights shut off once again, I got a quick impression of a tall, muscular figure

with luxuriant black moustaches. Then, as the music rose in a shattering crescendo, the phalanx began to march towards the platform.

Seats banged up like Tommy-gun fire as the assembled crowd rose to its feet, raising their arms in that damn-fool salute we've all seen on the newsreels when the Eyeties slobber over their Duce.

Now more spotlights burst into life as the top dogs of F.A.U.S.T. took their places on the platform and, cheered to the rafters, Olympus Mons made his way to the podium.

Somewhere in the early forties, he was under six feet but carried himself with an athlete's easy grace. There was a great scar running from his broken nose to his chin, so that his lip curled up in a most unpleasant fashion, permanently exposing the right dog tooth. He was handsome – in a thuggish way – but his dark eyes were hooded like those of some reptile. Hooded, that is, until, smoothing back brilliantined hair, Mons smiled his million-watt smile. Then the eyes seemed to grow huge, like ink spreading on a blotter, taking in the whole audience in their hypnotic range. It was as though a powerful searchlight was scanning the auditorium, and each amber-shirt must have felt, as I suddenly did, that the Leader was looking directly at *them*.

Mons stood in silence for a long moment, bathed in white light like a heavenly messenger, the silken folds of his shirt clinging to his impressive physique. Then, with a tiny gesture of his hands, he bade them be seated.

The multitude sat down in a chorus of coughs and whispers as Mons took up his stance before his adoring public, one hand clenched behind his back, the other at his side. The microphone in front of him whistled briefly and then he spoke.

'My friends,' he whispered. 'What a thrill it is for me to stand before you, knowing that, at the close of the year, efforts to strengthen our movement internationally have met with such resounding success.'

The voice was curiously light and had a Yankee twang of no

definable origin. 'For the old order is passing away,' he continued, volume increasing. 'The ancient fault lines of party politics replaced by a new model.' *Louder now.* 'Mankind reborn: vigorous!' *Louder yet.* 'Forward-looking!' *Yelling.* 'In step with a new world order!' *Positively screaming.*

The crowd roared their approval. I shuddered at the ecstatic glitter in their wide eyes.

'The misnamed system known as . . . *democracy*,' continued Mons, his voice dripping with contempt, 'based on antediluvian parliamentary systems, is on its way out! The People want a new system of government. The People have spoken. The People can no longer be IGNORED!'

The People, or the thousand or so amber-shirts buffoons who imagined themselves to be their representatives, set up a deafening cheer that rang back at Volatile and me from the stuccoed roof of the kinema.

For himself, Volatile seemed to shrink from the great man's presence, his face a picture of disgust, as though he'd smelled something that'd been knocked down in the road.

Mons seemed to feed off the throng's energy, his eyes, momentarily closed, now blazing blackly again like the lamp of some mythical lighthouse.

International Jewry, of course, was next on the agenda. 'We in F.A.U.S.T. do not seek to persecute the Jew on account of his religion – for our credo is complete religious toleration. We do not persecute him on account of his race. For do we not seek to conjoin with the British Empire? An empire that counts a dozen races amongst its citizens? No. Our quarrel with the Jews is that they have set themselves up as a nation within our great nations. Now we offer a solution! A final solution. They have always sought a promised land. We shall give it to them. A separate country where they can all live in peace – and cease to bother us!'

This got a shrill, hysterical laugh. The Jew, it seemed, was at the

back of almost every bit of mischief from Whitechapel to Wisconsin.

I glanced behind me again, more than a little frightened by the sight of all those flushed faces turned towards their leader like seals awaiting supper.

There was more such simplistic tosh from Mons, laying into the Bolsheviks and the capitalists, larding praise on Mussolini, that Austrian fellah, old Uncle Tom Mosley and all. I found it positively vulgar.

Nevertheless, I yelled appreciation and shouted huzzahs with the rest, marvelling at the strength of Mons's rhetoric. The man was utterly hypnotic, isolated in that burning circle of white light. But was he a real threat, as my superiors at the RA seemed to fear, or simply another third-rate crackpot dreaming of power?

He was speaking now in ever shorter bursts, each ending with a brilliantly judged appeal to the basest instincts of his slavering audience. I was very aware of the throbbing of my injured hand, and its steady beat, along with Mons's voice, the staccato hollering of the crowd, and the stuffy atmosphere of the hall, began to make my head spin. I sought refuge in focusing on the amber-shirted figures in the shadows behind the leader.

Then one face leapt out at me, my head grew suddenly clear and I caught my breath in absolute astonishment.

It was a woman near my own age with neatly bobbed black hair. Despite the fine angularity of her features there was something hatchet-like and cold about them, rather as though a skilled draughtsman, having designed a great beauty, had forgotten to rub out his working.

It was her eyes that drew me, though. Of a peculiar, piercing blue, they were every bit as gorgeous as my own. Not surprising in the least when you consider that the woman sitting there in her neat amber-coloured shirt, gazing up at Mons with unfeigned adoration, was my sister.

5

Sibling Devilry

You may picture me in an ice-shrouded Central Park next morning, lost in remembrance, contemplating sluggish pond water surrounded by wind-ravaged trees that clattered together like sticks of charcoal in a pot.

Pandora! My sister! After all these years.

Fact is, the old sis and I had never got on. Like all the best family spats, its origins were humble enough, stretching back to the dark days when Mama had announced, in solemn yet excited tones, that the three-year-old me was to be blessed with a little friend.

I was a serious child, coddled somewhat by my parents and ever so pale and Victorian, with my neatly brushed cow-lick hair and knickerbocker suit.

I had set my heart on a brother (what boy would not?) and so, when dear Pandora arrived in her swaddling clothes, trailing the scent of my Mama's lavender water, I fixed her with a resentful stare over my wooden fort and made a secret vow. She *had* to go.

All manner of plans were hatched, mostly involving the stoving in of baby's head with an alphabet block or the pitching of baby's perambulator into the Serpentine with Nanny getting the blame. A career in homicide, do you see, was already beckoning.

As time went by, though, and we grew up together within the dreary boundaries of the olive-walled nursery, I got used to the brat. Sadly, as my murderous instincts lessened, Pandora's seemed to grow. Despite also being a looker, she seemed to feel herself to be in my shadow. I couldn't see it myself. As far as I was concerned, my parents meted out their love in equal proportion. That is, they gave us none of it. Each.

For myself I took this as licence to blossom on my own terms, working my way through chemistry sets and the dissection of frogs, learning to scribble, growing faint when glancing at a postcard of the Michelangelo pietà and, later, getting into scandals with the wife of Mr Bleasdale the grocer.

Pandora, by contrast, grew into a very queer fish. Outwardly prim, her hair excessively neat, her dolls stacked in order of height, her bedroom as sterile as a hospital ward; there was always about her something rather frighteningly detached, as though she was waiting, with infinite patience, for the opportunity to strike.

She had remained unmarried and began throwing herself, with bewildering intensity, behind one lunatic cause or another, ranging from the abolition of Christmas to the compulsory introduction of a fruit-only diet.

We had drifted ever further apart as the years rolled by, not helped by my inheriting the family home at Number Nine, Downing Street (one is only disturbed when the hustings are on). There was a brief reunion after a bizarre tragedy engulfed our family (that's another story), but otherwise we remained strangers. These days, I knew little of Pan's life save that she lived by the sea, eking out her meagre inheritance and writing pamphlets on the importance of a thrice-daily bowel movement.

Seeing her again in such unexpected circumstances had left me in a state of shock and I'd half-stumbled from the F.A.U.S.T. rally, numbly arranging to meet Volatile the next evening and, at length, prising my sister's address from a party lackey.

I glanced up now from the bench as over-coated figures slipped by, bent over against the snow that fell as heavy and as thick as blossom onto their bowed shoulders.

And now, suddenly, there was Pandora, looking rather smart in black, her long legs scissoring through the drifts.

I stood, raising a quizzical eyebrow. Pandora stopped dead, and for a long moment there was only the shushing patter of snowflakes.

'Oh, Lord,' came the well-remembered drawl.

'Pan!' I cried heartily. 'You look awfully well, dear heart.' I kissed her twice on the cheeks. 'This fascist brotherhood of yours obviously agrees with you more than a fruitarian diet.'

She seemed astonished at this. 'How do you—?'

'I saw you,' I said. 'At the rally last night. I say, it's freezing out here, fancy a spot of Java?'

'What do you want, Lucifer?' Her accusatory blue eyes – a mite larger than mine – swivelled in my direction over the powdered curve of her cheek.

'Can't I pay a call on my own sister?'

A faint smile puckered her heavily rouged lips. 'No.' She pressed her shiny black shoe into a drift and contemplated the print it left. 'Don't pretend you're getting sentimental.'

'Perhaps a little,' I lied. 'I find myself thinking with some longing about the old days. We were all so happy then . . .'

'I was never happy,' she snapped. 'I had a wretched childhood, as well you know. Principally due to your tormenting.'

'Was I really so rotten? Well, that was ages ago. Listen, since we're both in town, why don't we have some lunch—?'

'Too busy,' she cut across me. 'The business of F.A.U.S.T. occupies me constantly.'

'Yes! I'm sure it does. Rather a surprise, eh, you being interested in the old movement too?'

'I'm party secretary. It's rather more than an interest,' she withered. 'What were you doing at the rally? You want to join?'

'Sympathizer, shall we say? I must say that chap Mons is an interesting cove. I'd love to have a chin-wag with him.'

Pandora looked me directly in the eye. 'Listen. If you're genuinely interested in the Tribune, brother mine, then I may be prepared to forget about the past.' She looked suddenly worried. 'You're not working for a newspaper now or anything like that?'

'The wolves of Fleet Street have never found a welcome at Number Nine.'

She glanced down and gave a little shiver. 'Olympus . . . that is, *Mr Mons* . . . he's, well, he's had some little bother with the press.'

'Poor fellow. I know what they're like. Build you up only to knock you down. I dare say they hate the fact that he's a success.'

'No!' cried Pandora with unsettling ferocity. 'Material wealth doesn't concern *him*! They're frightened because he speaks the truth. He knows that the old order has had its day. All across Europe, capitalism is failing. And the only bulwark we have against the Bolshevik tide is World Fascism!'

'Oh, absolutely,' I said blithely.

'Only by working together can the fascist movements of the world unite to create a better world. An ordered, strong, clean world fit for a better breed of humanity!'

Her breath smoked in the freezing air so that she positively appeared to have steam coming out of her. I gave her an encouraging smile. Lord, but she'd swallowed this stuff hook, line and sinker.

'Any chance of arranging a meeting?'

'Why are you here?' she said suddenly.

'Business,' I lied. 'An art dealer on Fifth Avenue is interested in my work.'

'New work?'

'Not exactly.' I shivered inside my overcoat. 'Apparently there's something of a nostalgia for all things Edwardian just now.'

'Poor Lucy—'

'Don't call me that!' I said through gritted teeth. Then, more mildly: 'Please. You know I hate it when you call me that.'

Pandora's red mouth widened just a fraction. 'A relic of the old days, eh?'

'Seems like it. I must be careful not to be swept aside in this new world order of yours.'

She nodded towards my bandaged hand. 'Had an accident?'

'I picked a fight with an engraving tool. It won.'

Suddenly a smile flickered over her sombre face. Somehow or other I seemed to have touched a soft spot in Pandora's formidable hide. Wrapping her stole tightly about her throat she lit a black cigarillo and was soon wreathed in its smoke. 'Perhaps tomorrow. Mr Mons has some business down by the docks. If you give me your number I'll see what I can do.'

'How splendid! Look, sis, I'm very grateful—'

'I said, I'll see what I can do.'

She took my hastily scribbled number and walked off, her face all but swallowed up by the voluminous collar of her astrakhan coat.

I watched her until she diminished into the whiteness then stamped my frozen feet. What a spot of luck! Pandora was too wily to believe I'd suddenly become a doting brother so I'd been right to appeal to this crazy new fad of hers. And now I had a direct line of contact to Mons!

I began to stomp off through the drifts then gradually slowed to a halt. The wind was getting up again, whipping snow in my face and sending an eerie susurration through the bare branches of the trees. I had the uncanny feeling that something was watching me from the undergrowth.

Sal Volatile's words seemed to echo in my mind. *Evil, Mr Box. Patient, watchful Evil.*

I felt suddenly glad to turn my back upon the park and head for Fifth Avenue.

'A pleasure to see you again,' said Professor Reiss-Mueller. 'I didn't know if you'd come.'

I was deep in the ill-lit basements of the Metropolitan Museum, flanked by shelf upon shelf of labelled cardboard boxes. Behind a desk, illuminated only by a shell-shaded lamp, the white-blond, bespectacled fellow from the "99", was once again examining Hubbard's handkerchief. The desk was covered all over with his scribbled notes.

'You were, I recall,' continued the pallid creature, 'about to promise me something in return for my expert opinion.'

I shrugged. 'What do you want?'

'Absolute frankness.'

'I'm not sure I'm at liberty—'

'You see,' he whined, none too convincingly stifling a yawn, 'it's not much of a life down here. I live amongst the relics of the dead. Dust is my meat and drink, you might say. So it pleases me to hear a little of the life that goes on above me on those crowded sidewalks.'

He coughed twice again, a tic that was already driving me a little crazy. The lamplight flashed off one lens of his spectacles, turning him into a mildly smiling, electric Cyclops.

'You seemed lively enough at the "99",' I countered.

Reiss-Mueller chuckled. 'Mere bread and circuses, my friend. This little beauty,' he cried, waving the hankie, 'promises much more.'

'Does it?'

Again I was conscious that he knew slightly more than he was letting on. Sweat stood out on his chalk-white forehead and yet the gloomy basement was as chill as an ice-house.

'Okey-dokey,' I said, trying to adopt the house style (not without

'The lamplight flashed off one lens of his spectacles.'

discomfort, as I'm sure you can imagine). 'I retrieved that square of silk from the body of a stolen-goods receiver whose brains a colleague of mine had recently blown out. I'm feeling horribly threatened by said colleague – some years younger than me – and am mightily pleased that he managed to miss this piece of evidence. I'd very much like to present it to my superiors so that they'll think me ever so clever and worthy of praise and give the young whippersnapper a ticking off. So, whether it's a clue to the whereabouts of the True Cross or merely Henry of Navarre's laundry list, I'd be most awfully grateful if you'd translate it.'

Reiss-Mueller gave a stuttering laugh. 'How thrilling. All that *violence*.' A little tremor of excitement ran through him. He held the relic close to his face and was silent for some minutes, his breath coming in quick little bursts. 'Trouble is,' he said at last, 'I can't.' Cough-cough. 'In short, though the artefact appears wholly genuine, the language is gibberish. It's *almost* Latin. Then takes another turn to become like Hebrew, then Aramaic. But the words make very little sense.'

'A code?'

'I think not. There's no obvious pattern.'

'Wouldn't be much of a code if there was.'

Another smile, two more coughs. 'Quite. Some of it's a ritual. Other parts . . . how can I put it? *Directions*. See, this part with the picture of the mountain. It's like a map. The ragged edges show it's the bottom corner of a larger piece of material.'

He let the silk droop in his hand. With a disappointed sigh, I reached for it but Reiss-Mueller snatched it back. 'I haven't quite finished.'

He pointed to the images on the ragged edge of the silk. 'These markings. They're Cabbalistic.'

'Black magic?'

'Uh-huh.' He gave an amused smile and coughed twice behind his hand. 'Quite my line of country, don't you know. That little

fellow—' He pointed to a barely discernible goatish-looking creature sitting cross-legged in one embroidered corner. 'That fellow could be Banebdjed.'

'Bane—?'

'The soul of the god Osiris. His Ba. It's a ram-headed deity.'

'A Ba-lamb?'

Reiss-Mueller chuckled. 'It's all mixed up with the composite pagan idols worshipped by the Knights Templar,' he said, gleefully patronizing. 'Speaking of violence. Oh, boy. Those fellows knew how to party.'

He pointed a milk-white finger at some of the dense text. 'These could be the names of various demons – Moloch, Belial, Thentus and so forth – but, like I say, the language is kind of garbled. Still, if you let me study it for a while, I might make some headway. I know all about the arts of the left-hand path.'

'Perhaps.'

I watched his plump fingers almost caressing the silk. 'There are some words here that are very clear, though as to what they mean. . .'

'What do they say?'

Reiss-Mueller held up the hankie close to his face and read from it. '"There will come one who is spoken of. All unknowing he will come. And only he that makes himself alone in the world can defeat the Beast".'

'Meaning?'

'Don't have a clue!' he chirped.

'What about this?' I continued, indicating the four-legged animal roasting on a spit in the embroidered flames.

The little man shrugged. 'Some sort of sacrifice? A sheep? A goat?'

I suddenly remembered Volatile's words. 'Or a *lamb*?' I mused. 'So. An educated guess. Is it a map? A ritual? What?'

He glanced up again and smiled. 'How remiss of me. I'd suggest

47

it's some bastardized version of the Clavicule of Solomon. Or maybe the Grimoire of Pope Honorius. One way or another, it's an invocation.'

'What kind of invocation?'

The light caught his spectacles again so that for an instant he appeared to have huge, blind white eyes. 'Why, for summoning the Devil, of course.'

6

An Attempt On Mount Olympus

Waking to the steady throbbing of my injured hand, I lay for a moment on the cool pillow-case that still bore the imprint of Rex's head. We'd become a bit of an item (I crave diversion constantly) but the boy had risen early to attend to his tedious duties so I was once more alone.

I stretched out my legs under the sheets then reached across to the little bedside table and retrieved my cigarette case from beneath the white Bakelite of the telephone.

Watching the smoke curl lazily to the ceiling, I reached for the handkerchief and, producing a lens, made an effort to peer closer at some of the embroidered pictures – the letters being all Greek (or, in fact, everything but) to me. The mountain, picked out in faded blue and white, was surrounded by dense text that did indeed appear to be some species of directions. There were numbers and repeated symbols and a sort of outlined range of hills that seemed to be an indication of where to find this particular peak.

I suddenly felt a curious prickling at the back of my neck. There

was something oddly familiar about that mountain and, for a moment, I almost caught at the remembrance. But it tantalised only briefly and was gone, like the odour of Thomas's *lad's love*, 'leaving only an avenue dark, nameless, without end'.

Further down the relic, towards the embroidered corner bearing dragons' heads and the queer composite demon that my friend in the museum had identified as Banebdjed, was the image of the four-legged animal roasting over flames. Could this be the lamb that Volatile had spoken of? In which case, were the late Hubbard and Olympus Mons somehow connected?

I got up, showered and dressed, then changed the dressing on my wound – it was weeping in rather grisly fashion – and I was slipping into a snug three-piece grey tweed when the telephone rang.

'Yes?' I cradled the tulip-like receiver under my chin as I buttoned my waistcoat.

'Pier Thirty-Nine,' said Pandora's voice curtly. 'Forty-five minutes from now.'

'Pan! Thanks, sis. I'm immensely indebted—'

There was a hiss and a click and the line went dead. Hastily, I finished dressing, folded the silken rag and popped it into my pocket as though it were indeed nothing but a handkerchief, and took the lift down to the lobby.

Another yellow cab took me down to the docks, the outside world only visible through a hastily rubbed circle in the frost-rimed glass. Vignettes of brownstone blocks, diners and spindly towers flashed past.

I realized that in my haste to meet Mons, I didn't actually have a clue what I was going to say to him.

By the time the car drew up at the pier, I'd pretty much resolved to play the silly ass and come across simply as Pandora's mildly famous artist brother, fed up with the way the world was drifting and keen to, *you know*, do my bit.

Peering through the fogged-up window, I saw that a big grey-

wheeled Daimler was already parked there, empty save for its peak-capped chauffeur.

I paid off the cabbie and slipped outside onto rotted wooden planks, my freshly shaved face stung at once by the bitter cold. The waters of the great river, visible far beneath me, were frozen hard, several sheets of ice toppling over each other like tectonic plates.

Further from the pier the frozen surface was thinner, and the black waters of the Hudson were lapping and churning around the hull of a disreputable old tub called the *Stiffkey*, its once gay livery faded, rust from its ancient rivets dribbling like old blood and staining the surrounding water.

I spotted Pandora at the far end of the gangway, a cloche hat framing her powdered face. Mons, in greatcoat and trilby, was deep in conversation with a big, disordered sailor with matted white hair and a face blossoming with the signs of heavy drinking. The sailor's clothes were weather-beaten and greasy and a massive ugly watch chain, extending from his top pocket to his hip, seemed to rein him together.

As I approached, Pandora looked up, said something to Mons and the great leader dismissed the sailor with a curt nod, clattering down the gangway towards me, hand extended.

His hooded eyes grew wide again. This close I noticed that they were almost all black pupil, only a narrow halo of white visible, like the corona of the sun during an eclipse.

'Why, Mr Lucifer Box!' he oozed in his oddly light American voice. 'How utterly delightful. I had no idea Pandora here had such an illustrious sibling.'

His hand was warm and dry and he held onto mine just a little too long, fixing me with those extraordinary orbs of his.

'Pleasure to meet you too, sir,' I enthused. 'Dashed impressed by your performance at the rally the other night.'

'Oh, one does one's best.' He looked down, bashfully, and the black suns diminished: the reptile's membranous eyelids, as it were,

flicking back into place. Then he smiled and his scarred lip curled up further over the exposed dog tooth. 'Interesting you choose that word. *Performance*. I fear my public expect new tricks of me all the time and I fail to deliver.'

'That's nonsense!' chimed in Pandora. 'You give them everything they want and more—'

Mons held up a black-gloved hand in an impatient silencing gesture.

Pandora's mouth clapped shut as though she'd been struck. A brief flicker of annoyance passed over Mons's face. Then he was all smiles again.

'Your sister has become absolutely indispensable to me, Mr Box.'

'Call me Lucifer, please.'

Mons gave a low chuckle, stroking the end of his thickly waxed moustaches. 'It's a wonderful name. Not much used these days.'

'Lucifer, Jesus, Judas . . .' I cried. 'All the best people have the best names.'

'And Olympus?' speculated the great leader.

'How appropriate for a Greek god!' gushed Pandora, her hand immediately flying to her rouged lips as though to hush them.

Mons smiled patiently, wearily. 'Your sister is very kind but has a somewhat exaggerated view of my talents.'

I shivered within my suit. 'I doubt it, sir. You're the man to get the world out of the fix it's stumbled into. It seems to me, half the population's stuck in the distant past, the other half's too idle to look to the future. They need guidance. They need a man with an iron will. They need *you*.'

Mons flushed with pleasure. He began to walk away slowly from the *Stiffkey*'s gangway, hands clasped behind his back, and I trotted after him, Pandora keeping a safe distance behind.

'I know I have it in me to do great things, *tremendous* things,' he murmured. 'I can mould the people of this world into one wonder-

ful, shining whole. But to achieve great things we must be prepared to take great risks, don't you agree, Lucifer?'

'*Rather*,' I said, grinning like an idiot.

Mons looked me up and down again, perhaps not sure what to make of me. 'You like risk, Lucifer?' His eyes flashed wide again and, with a giggle, he simply stepped over the side of the pier.

Pandora gave a little yelp. 'Olympus! Don't!'

I gasped and leaned over the edge to see what had happened but Mons had landed neatly in a crouching position on the frozen river below. The ice made a weird percussive noise beneath his shoes.

He stared down at the dark water, swirling inches below the ice, then gestured upwards. 'Join me!'

I looked at my sister, shrugged and then jumped lightly over the side. The ice shuddered, took my weight and I walked swiftly and confidently to Mons's side. He rubbed his hands together and began to stride further and further away from the safety of the pier.

'I've always had my own way, you see,' he continued in a low murmur. 'My Pop always said I was born with a silver spoon in my mouth. Silver plated with gold, garnished with platinum.'

'How marvellous for you.' I looked down. The waters of the Hudson pressed and swirled at the ice as though protesting at their imprisonment.

'You think so?' said Mons. 'I'll let you into a secret, Lucifer.'

'Please do.'

'My enemy is not the Bolshevik hordes.'

'No?'

'No. It is ennui. It is the staleness of the commonplace. Life becomes very empty when it's nothing but parties and booze and sex.'

I nodded vigorously. 'Oh, Lord, yes. Couldn't agree more. Though I dare say you'd have a job convincing other people of that!'

Mons put a gloved hand on my shoulder and squeezed it painfully. I think he liked me. 'So I looked for other distractions,' he said cryptically. The inky eyes bored into mine.

'Distractions?' I asked, all innocence.

Mons looked over my shoulder into the middle distance. 'Racing motor cars. Aeroplanes. Eventually I found politics. For a time, the yawning hole within me was filled.'

An expression of utter blankness stole over him now, and for a moment he seemed nothing more than a bored little boy, tired of his toys.

'For a time?' I hazarded.

'Everything becomes flat eventually,' he said bleakly. Then the eyes began to blaze again and a mischievous smile danced around his curled lip. 'Well, *almost* everything.'

Slowly at first, he began to rock on his heels. Again, the strange booming sound of ice under pressure began to reverberate around us. I risked a nervous glance down.

Mons was laughing now, swaying back and forth in his expensive shoes, harder and harder and harder.

Finally, as I knew it would, a narrow fracture opened up in the ice. Black water immediately frothed over the gap, like spittle expelled from a palsied mouth, and the break in the ice grew wider, zig-zagging towards us at worrying speed. Mons looked about, his exposed tooth glittering like a vampire's fang. 'Risk, my dear Lucifer! What's life without it?'

So saying, he pelted back towards the pier, his laughter, picked up by the weird acoustic of the frozen bay, ringing behind him.

The ice began to splinter all around us. I needed no prompting and hared after Mons, feet sinking into the liquefying surface, shoes filling with freezing water, stumbling and unbalancing until we both made the safety of a wooden ladder, its rungs spongy with rot.

Mons pulled up sharp at the bottom so that I actually began to sink into the waters. Trying hard to appear nonchalant, I lurched and bobbed behind him. He flashed a crazed look over his shoulder, teeth flashing like knives, then, in one swift move, pulled himself up to safety.

I followed in an instant, toppling over the bent rungs and affecting a blasé chuckle as though the whole thing had been a childish game.

Mons looked down at me and clapped a hand on my shoulder. 'Let's talk again,' he rapped, then strode towards the Daimler and clambered inside.

Pandora rushed after him, her heels clocking on the sodden planks.

'Happy now?' she called, a faint smile twitching on those very red lips.

She only just managed to haul open the door of the big car and slip inside before it roared off into the traffic.

So much for Olympus Mons! Mad as a March hare, that much was obvious. I squelched back towards the road and hailed a cab.

Rex was waiting for me when I entered the hotel lobby.

'Gentleman to see you,' he cooed, brushing his hand against my thigh in a none-too professional fashion. 'I get off at three.'

'What?' I carefully detached the boy from my side. We were in company, after all.

'Three. I thought maybe we could take in a show and—'

'I mean what gentleman?'

Rex shrugged grumpily. 'Said "Delilah" sent him.'

I frowned, but allowed Rex to show me into the smoking room before dismissing him with a curt nod. He slunk off like a jilted schoolgirl.

Within the warm, panelled room, a big man in flannels was tapping a thick cane against his foot and staring into the fire. Upon sight of him, I immediately relaxed. He had broadened in the waist and his face was ruddy with too much drinking but the handsome features were unmistakeable. A hesitant blond moustache almost covered a ragged scar. He looked up and smiled warmly.

'Hullo, Box, old man,' cried Christopher Miracle.

I gripped my fellow dauber's hand with all the manliness his presence warranted. 'It's been too long, Chris,' I said, with feeling. Sincerity rarely passes these pretty lips of mine so you must get it while you can.

Miracle nodded, laid his stick aside and retrieved a sheaf of papers from inside his jacket.

'Your charming friend Miss Delilah telephoned.'

'Ah.'

'She knew I was here pursuing my usual rootless existence,' continued Miracle. 'Said you wanted all the gossip on one Olympus Mons.'

I nodded. This was a terrific idea of Delilah's. Through family and a wide circle of friends, Miracle had always been the best-connected bloke a fellow could wish to call upon. Though his circumstances had changed greatly since the halcyon days of our friendship, if there was any man who could fill in some background on the shadowy Mons, it was he.

Miracle glanced down at the documents and grunted. 'Interesting blighter. Money to burn, it seems.'

'I don't doubt it. Has all the hallmarks of a spoilt brat who doesn't know what to do with himself.'

Miracle looked up. 'Was like that myself. Once.'

His watery blue eyes grew momentarily dim. He threw a glance towards the crackling fire, then cleared his throat and shrugged as though embarrassed by his admission.

'Olympus Mons. Born in Iowa of wealthy farming stock. Sent to some of the best schools the States can offer – although between you and me that's not saying much – but expelled from the lot.'

'Any particular reason?' I queried, offering Miracle a cigar.

'Refusal to conform. Bully. You know the form. Anyway, he was eventually rusticated so often they packed him off to England where he seems finally to have settled down. Took a fancy to Blighty and the notion of Empire in particular. Inherited pots from his father's

death and enjoyed the playboy life until a holiday in Italy got him all steamed up about Mussolini.'

I nodded, blowing smoke rings towards the ceiling. 'So far, so public record. What's the gossip?'

Miracle grunted mischievously, clipped the end of his cigar and popped it into his mouth. 'Well. . .my sources tell me that he created a good deal of resentment when he muscled in on the American fascist movement. Took the whole thing over in six months as though it was his destiny. Usual grumblings from those who'd served their time and done all the foot-soldiering. . .'

This made sense. Sal Volatile, I presumed, was one such. 'Go on,' I urged.

Miracle took a moment to encourage his smoke into life then raised his brows. 'The word is, the true believers reckon this whole F.A.U.S.T. thing is no more than another fad for him. That he'll soon tire of it and move onto some other craze to stave off boredom.'

'Excellent,' I cried. 'Dissension in the ranks. Divide and conquer. Should be a doddle.'

Miracle waved his hand, suggesting more, the tip of his cigar glowing through a veil of bluey smoke. 'The reason they think this, it seems, is that he's been sinking all his moolah into a schloss.'

'A what?'

'A castle. In Switzerland. Despite his Yankee roots and British pretensions, that's apparently where he's happiest.'

'Switzerland, eh?'

'I'm reliably informed there's been a tremendous amount of activity thereabouts for quite a while.'

'What kind of activity?'

'Digging. Under the castle. Apparently he's been pressing the local labour force into service for months.'

I chuckled. 'Is there gold in them thar hills?'

Miracle's mouth turned down. 'Dashed unlikely, I'd say. What there is, is talk.'

'What do you mean?'

'All rot, of course, but those funny Swiss beggars think the place is haunted or something. They reckon Mons is trying to do something unholy.'

My hand stole to my pocket, where Hubbard's silken rag nestled. 'They may not be far wrong.'

I snapped out of my reverie and rose from my chair. 'Thanks for your help, Chris. You want some lunch?'

Miracle held up his hand. 'There's something else, Lucifer, I think you should know before you. . .go any further with this matter.'

I sank back onto the green leather. 'Go on.'

Miracle took a long draw on his cigar and flicked an inch-thick chunk of grey ash into the chromium plate at his side. 'Mons's castle. It's just across the border from France. Little place called Lit-de-Diable.'

Despite the cheery fire crackling in the gate, I grew cold and suddenly knew why the mountain embroidered on the occult relic had looked so familiar.

Miracle's eyes locked with mine for a moment and bleak remembrance was writ large in them.

'Thanks,' I said at last. 'Forewarned is forearmed, eh?'

Miracle stubbed out his cigar and raised himself up with some difficulty. 'I'd better be off.'

I plastered on a cheery smile. 'Busy afternoon?'

Miracle managed the same, his scarred face twisting slightly. 'You know me.'

We shook hands and I had a sudden, vivid impression of him in that gold-leaf summer of '13, arms akimbo, the scents of warm, wind-blown hay in the air, announcing that he was off at once to join up, give Jerry a fat lip and be home for Boxing Day.

The reality of course, had been somewhat different. Every bit as gallant and heroic as one would have expected from such a massive

personality, Miracle had sailed through the War unscathed until one night, late in the conflict, when we'd found ourselves working together on a dangerous mission on the Franco-Swiss border. For once, the machinations of the Royal Academy and the more solid business of the British Army had found common purpose: namely the annihilation of Baron Gustavus Feldmann, the most dangerous man in Europe.

Feldmann's deadly plot, centred around the airstrip at Lit-de-Diable, was the Hun's final, desperate gamble and he'd very nearly carried it off. We'd bested him at the last, of course, though at horrific cost to our side. My unit had been utterly smashed and Miracle was found wandering about on the border, whey-faced and talking nonsense, blood pouring from the wounds in his leg and gloriously handsome face.

Once so hale and full of life, poor Chris had never been the same man again.

I saw my old friend to the revolving door and he turned up his collar against the biting wind. With heavy heart, I watched his stooped form until he disappeared amid the cabs and the crowds.

7

I Strike Damned Queer Country

In my experience, if a chap hangs on to secret knowledge he tends to wind up very dead, taking said knowledge with him. I'd fervently hoped, then, that my new contact, Sal Volatile, would spill the beans in the aftermath of the F.A.U.S.T. rally and not delay the final moment.

Volatile was insistent, however. His plans were not yet in place and so, in properly covert style, I was to linger in the bitter weather on the corner of Twenty-third and Fifth. I was there at the appointed time but of my chestnut-haired chum there was no sign.

Sleet slapped against my face as I sheltered in the porchway of the chichi drugstore he'd nominated as our rendezvous, huge display bottles of red and green liquid giving it an unintentionally festive air.

I scanned the street for him, watching umbrella-wielding figures slipping between the motors that crawled alongside.

Suddenly there was a hand on my elbow and I was swung round to find myself looking straight into Volatile's handsome face. His hat

was pulled down low but there was no mistaking the fear in his eyes.

'Gotta be careful, pal. Real careful,' he muttered.

'All right.'

He nodded towards the drugstore. 'We can talk in here.'

Despite having chosen the venue, he seemed to reconsider his choice for fully thirty seconds, looking over his shoulder and then peering through the plate glass of the window. The red liquid in the giant bottle gave his pocked face a hellish tint. Finally, he nodded and let go of my arm.

I pushed at the door, setting the 'open' sign swinging, and we swept inside into a mercifully warm interior.

A long bar, studded with stools that had the appearance of upholstered mushrooms, took up the whole of one side of the place. On the opposite wall hung a huge rectangular mirror all stuck over with postcards of Florida.

A fat soda-jerk in a white coat and silly white hat beamed at us over his siphons. I ordered two cups of coffee and the fellah set to work, skilfully brewing the java without even glancing up from his sports magazine.

Volatile gulped down his.

'Well,' I said. 'As they say in the flickers: shoot.'

He threw a wary glance outside. 'I'm hoping I can trust you, Mr Box. I *need* to trust you.'

'Go on.'

'Mons is crazy. He's turned the whole organization into his personal fan-club. It wasn't like that before. We had good intentions, I can assure you.'

I nodded encouragingly, though I knew full well the sort of bigoted trash of which his good intentions consisted.

'You contacted us because you have something on Mons,' I queried. 'What is it? You said something about a prayer? And a lamb?'

Volatile leant forward, eyes wide. 'I found the Lamb!' he whispered,

as though I should know what he was talking about. 'Right under their noses! Mons is going crazy looking for it. He thinks he's on the right track but he'll find the bird flown!'

A curious, hissing laugh spluttered from between his teeth. I was beginning to worry that everyone around me was a little unbalanced.

Volatile's mood switched back abruptly. He jumped to his feet, crossed swiftly to the door and, shading his eyes, looked out onto the snowy sidewalk. Either he was paranoid to the point of delusion or he was convinced he was being followed.

I glanced across at the soda-jerk but he was absorbed in his baseball literature.

Eventually, Volatile sat down again, rubbing his weary face with long, nervous fingers. 'There's only one place I'll be safe. In a church.'

I almost laughed but managed to disguise my outburst by taking a gulp of coffee. 'Sanctuary?'

Volatile bit his lip and the bristles on his unshaven chin curved upwards. 'Well, not a church, at all really. The Convent of St Bede. It's in England. I've got a passage booked out of here. Got an understanding with the captain. Pier Thirty-Nine. Tonight at midnight. Boat called the *Stiffkey*.'

'The captain being a big, square fellah. Boozy face, long watch chain?'

'That's the guy. Name of Corpusty. Know him?'

'Saw him. He didn't see much of me, though.'

'That's good.'

'Why?'

Volatile leant even closer. 'I want you to go instead of me. The trip's a blind. I've got other means of getting to England. You'll act as a decoy.'

He handed me a sheaf of shipping documents. I looked them over.

'Charming. And what do I get out of all this? Am I to expect company? Company with stout boots and tommy guns?'

'I'll tell you it all!' cried Volatile. 'I've got the inside track on the whole damn thing. How Mons gets his cash. What he's got planned for the Lamb. It's evil, sir! *Diabolical.*'

'So you said.'

'And if I can get safely to the convent—'

'More coffee?' The fat soda-jerk was looming over us, coffee pot in hand, beaming through the steam that poured from its pitted lid.

'No, thanks. Look,' I turned back to Volatile, 'tell me about this "lamb". And what's this alternative escape route of yours? If something goes wrong I'll need to find you—'

'I'll get in touch,' he muttered. 'Soon as we're both in England.'

'No more coffee?' The soda-jerk was grinning stupidly, the steam from the pot fogging his owlish glasses.

'NO! Thank you!' I hissed.

But the fellow pushed back his spectacles from the bridge of his flat nose and shook his head. 'I insist!'

Suddenly he'd upended the pot and scalding black fluid was raining down onto Volatile's hand. Volatile yelled and jumped from his stool. In a flash, the soda-jerk had pulled a snub-nosed revolver from his apron and the dim interior of the drugstore flashed yellow as a bullet spat out. Volatile was hit in the knee and flung backwards into the far wall, shattering the mirror, snapshot images of Key West and Orlando fluttering about him like confetti.

All this I observed as I grabbed Volatile's shipping documents, dropped to the floor, rolled over – my coat skirts dragging in the pool of spilled coffee – and reached for my Webley. It was out of my pocket in an instant and replying to the soda-jerk in kind. Two sang off the counter and the fat man ducked behind a cardboard advertisement for stomach-acid relief.

I looked rapidly about, my bandaged hand throbbing appallingly. There was no way I'd make it into the back room, my only chance

was the door to the outside world. Letting fly another bullet, I scuttled over Volatile's prone, groaning form and reached a hand towards the glass door. The big display bottle immediately to my right exploded with a nerve-jangling smash as, once again, the villain blasted at me. Red liquid like diluted blood hung in the air for a moment before splashing down onto the tiled floor and into my eyes.

I let fly another bullet as I rubbed at my lovely face, praying the stuff from the bottle wasn't toxic.

With an ugly grunt such as I imagine water buffaloes give, the soda-jerk heaved his bulk over the counter and landed before me, kicking the gun from my hand as I floundered about.

'Now just stay calm, like a good boy!' he cried, settling himself on the slippery floor and casting a quick glance at the semi-conscious Volatile.

'What do you want?' I moaned miserably, rubbing the red stuff from my dazzling optics.

He dropped to one knee and frisked me very thoroughly, batting my hands apart with the barrel of his revolver and sending my Webley skittering across the tiles with another well-aimed kick. Swinging his pistol towards me again, he aimed it squarely in the centre of my forehead. Naturally, I put up my hands.

'Just tell me what you want!' I cried in a shamefully panicky fashion. 'I can be very accommodating.'

'So I heard,' chuckled the brute in a whiskey-soaked rasp. 'Now get up.'

I sighed, my gaze flicking about for any sign of advantage. 'Who are you? Why did you plug that poor sap?'

He scowled and kicked me hard in the solar plexus. I flopped to the floor, wincing in pain.

'Just keep your mouth shut!'

He lashed out again but this time I twisted onto my side and grabbed hold of his shoe, wrenching his foot over into an unnatural

angle. He screeched in pain and tumbled onto me, knocking the breath from my lungs. For a moment, my face was flattened against the cold white tiles, red fluid pooling into my hair, overpowered by the sweaty stink from the barman's grease-splashed crotch. Then I managed to rise to a crouching position, jerking my elbow out and into the rolls of fat that encompassed his gut.

He groaned in pain and fury. I jumped to my feet and slammed the heel of my shoe onto his hand. There was a sound like kindling crackling in a fire and, screaming, he let go of the revolver.

Darting to the floor, I retrieved the weapon and had it levelled at him before he had a chance to recover.

'Now,' I gasped, trying with some difficulty to catch my breath. 'Start talking.'

'Go screw yourself,' he croaked, holding his ruined hand as though it didn't belong to him.

'Not on an empty stomach, thanks.' I sank back onto a bar stool. Volatile was out cold. 'I presume you're working for Mons's lot. You needed to rub out that fellah on the floor there before he told me all about your lord and master, eh?'

He might have talked. We shall never know. Because I was just conscious of a vague movement behind me as someone emerged from the back of the drugstore, a small pinprick of pain on the back of my neck and then a warm, fuzzy, muffled darkness as I crashed to the floor.

My tongue felt like a stick in my mouth. I blinked a couple of times and focused on a tobacco-soiled ceiling and bare bulb hanging from wire that looked like a string of liver. Turning my head slightly, I found that I was resting on a rough candy-striped pillow that had seen infinitely better days. I turned my head the other way and sat up with a yell.

Sal Volatile lay naked in bed next to me, three holes in his chest leaking unhealthy gouts of blood onto the stained mattress.

I blinked and stared at the body, my bare back hitting the cold plaster of the wall behind the bed. The Webley lay on the carpetless floor, and as I moved to get out of bed, I noticed that a man was sitting on a nearby stool, arms folded, smiling over at me with an infuriating insouciance. It was Percy Flarge.

'Oh, Lor,' he said, pulling a face. 'Got ourselves into a bit of a pickle this time, eh, old fruit?'

I didn't move but glanced quickly around the grim, bare room. 'What . . . what the hell's going on, Flarge? Where am I?'

'You tell me. Favourite haunt of yours, by all accounts. We got a tip-off from the owner. You and the stiff came in some time ago, high as kites by his account.'

'He's lying—'

'Checked into your usual room. Started getting up to . . . whatever it is you chaps get up to,' continued Flarge, hatefully. 'Lovers' tiff ensues and . . . well . . .'

He gestured towards the corpse. 'Funny thing,' he grinned suddenly. 'My Pa always said he supposed men like you shot themselves. Turns out, you shoot each other!'

I tried to keep my temper and got to my feet, glancing down at Volatile's stiffening form. 'What the hell are you on about? Listen, Flarge. *Percy*. I was approached by this chap in connection with an assignment for the RA. We arranged to meet earlier this evening. Well, someone must've been onto him, because it was a trap. He was shot – but only wounded – and I was drugged . . .'

Flarge took out a pipe and began to fill it. He looked thoroughly sceptical.

I felt suddenly hot with rage. 'Look here. We can sort all this out. Would you mind awfully if we get out of here and leave the Domestics to clear things up?'

Flarge shook his head. 'No can do.'

The door to the squalid room suddenly flew open and a skinny man in the uniform of a police captain emerged. He looked at my

pendulous, swinging tackle, swore under his breath and then, turning back to the open door, beckoned. A chattering flurry of people suddenly piled inside, two of them photographers. Flash bulbs zinged and whined in my face. I threw up my hands to shield myself.

'I suggest we make a move, sir,' said the captain.

'I was just making the same suggestion,' I said, looking about for my clothes. 'Move where?'

'To the station house, sir. Where you'll be charged with murder.'

8

The Buttons Come Off the Foils

This was a new and peculiarly horrid sensation. As long-term readers may recall, I've been in at more kills than the average Scotland Yarder has had bully beef, the victim usually having been knocked off by yours truly. And always – barring the odd assignment well away from civilized society – things have been hushed up nicely by the Royal Academy. True, I had once spent a night in the cells of a filthy Chinese nick when some over-zealous Cantonese mandarin (or a Mandarin Cantonese) threatened me with seven kinds of hell for despatching his Warlord chum with an ornamental tooth-pick. On that occasion, though, the Domestics simply missed their train and glided in smoothly the very next morning, apologizing profusely and leaving the mandarin red-faced and cursing over his stringy moustaches. I was on a fast boat out of there before the sun was over the old clay tiles of the cop-shop.

Now dressed and sitting in the police car this time, I knew I was in real trouble.

Percy Flarge slipped onto the seat next to me, his long blond fringe bouncing into his eyes, a delighted smile on his lips. Both doors of the motor remained open and bitter night air bled over us from the white street.

The police captain – inevitably Irish – was squawking orders to his subordinates, who were pushing back the eager crowd of ghouls that'd appeared around the entrance to the flophouse.

'Look here, Flarge!' I hissed. 'This is insane! What the hell are you up to?'

I flashed a look through the back window of the motor. The captain would return any moment. I didn't have long. 'Come on, man! This isn't how we do things! We look out for each other in the RA. There's a system! Why haven't you called the Domestics? Or Reynolds?'

'I'm merely helping the police arrest the guilty party.'

'There's more to this. You know there is. I've been – what do they say here? – framed up!'

A thought suddenly struck me. Hubbard had said the same thing. That he was a patsy. I decided to risk showing my meagre hand. I was pretty much out of options. 'Listen,' I whispered urgently, 'I've got what you're looking for.'

'What?'

'That "lamb" or whatever the hell it is. I found it on Hubbard's body.'

'You found a lamb on Hubbard's body? Taking it home for Sunday lunch, was he? Hmmph. Nice try, old thing.'Fraid I searched him thoroughly. No livestock to be seen.'

'You weren't told, were you?' I persisted. 'You weren't told exactly what you were looking for?'

Flarge looked momentarily nonplussed. 'My orders were to bring back everything he had on him—'

'You missed his top pocket, *old boy*,' I mocked. 'A small square of silk like a handkerchief. I know it's important.'

'You're running away with yourself, old sport,' said Flarge smoothly.

I looked wildly about, anticipating with dread the approach of the police captain and the disappearance of all my long-held privileges. I'd be down in the cells with a copper's boot in my guts and that'd be the end of old Lucifer.

'I'll tell you where it is,' I said at last. 'Then you can claim all the credit. Just get me out of this hell.'

Flarge glanced over his shoulder. The captain was still talking, his flashlight bobbing in the darkness.

'All right,' he said. 'I can't promise anything, but . . . Tell me. Quickly.'

He leant forward.

I moved like a panther, jerking back my neck and then ramming my forehead into his nose. There was an awful crack and I felt warm blood jet onto my face. Flarge shrieked in agony but I was already smothering him, muffling his cries with my body as my hands moved expertly over his chest to where I knew he kept his pistol. It was out of its holster and in my hands before Flarge could get his bearings. I swung the butt up against his chin and he grunted into rapid unconsciousness.

Letting him slide sideways onto the sweaty upholstery, I melted out of the motor and onto the road, flattening myself against the freezing tarmacadam and risking a look under the vehicle. I could see the captain's steel-toed boots crunching their way towards me. Scuttling like a cripple, I moved across the roadway and within seconds made the safety of a pitch-dark alley.

Huge black apartment blocks reared up on either side. It was nigh on impossible to make out anything in the darkness but I caught a suggestion of spindly fire escape and reeking bins as I pelted on.

And suddenly there were yells and whistles and I knew they'd found friend Flarge. I ran on – and came crashing to the ground as

I smacked headlong into a mildewed wall. The alley was a dead end!

There wasn't a moment to be lost so I sprang onto the nearest of the metal bins and used it as a vault, finding purchase on the bottom rung of the fire-escape ladder and swinging myself up and onto it.

The metal was wet and cold and smelled rusty. I managed to get some little way up it and onto a kind of gantry before the alley was lit up like a talkie premiere, police flashlights swooping over the black bricks.

The gantry ringed the building, acting as some kind of balcony for the apartment block's residents, and upon it squatted big, ugly plant pots full of withered shrubs.

I looked down at my pursuers. Perished though I was, I knew I had to take a chance, so, shrugging out of my overcoat, I wrapped it around the nearest of the plant pots and hung my trilby onto the drooping remains of a neglected olive tree. I peered at my little decoy, pleased by its resemblance to a crouched man trying to hide himself. Then I jumped back onto the ladder and positively swarmed up it to the roof.

It was flat and asphalt-covered. I heard clanging footsteps, harsh voices challenging the olive tree then I turned on my heel and skittered across the roof towards the far edge of the block.

Glancing across at the neighbouring building gave me pause. My decoy would be discovered at any moment and my only chance lay in a jump across the giddying void.

Queasy street light from far below silhouetted strings of washing that hung between the windows, shirts and trousers made stiff by the frost looking, rather disquietingly, like strung-up felons.

As must now be clear, I was no longer in the first flush of youth but needs must when, appropriately enough, the Devil drives. I shot a last look over my shoulder – flashlights were already bobbing over the edge as the police clambered upwards – then took a running jump and launched myself into space.

I make no claims as to my dignity, scrambling through the smoky

night air like a novice swimmer, limbs paddling frantically until, with a winded grunt, I hit solid brick. With one elbow firmly over the lip of the roof, my other hand splayed out in a desperate effort to find purchase, I hauled myself up and heaved my aching chest over the edge, legs dangling below, shoes scraping off the upper edge of a bricked-up window.

My jacket ripped as I kicked upwards and fell, breathless and bruised, onto the roof. I'd made it.

There was little time for celebration, as one look back the way I'd come showed that the roof of the first block was now dotted with pursuing rozzers. If they were bright enough, it would only take one shouted command and they'd have the neighbouring building – upon which I now stood – surrounded and I'd be back in the police motor double-quick.

I could taste iron in my spit and a crippling stitch was already making merry in my gut but I ran on, reached the edge of this new roof, judged the distance – slightly less this time – and once more flung myself across.

This time I only just made it, my chest slamming into the edge of the neighbouring roof. I hooked my hands over the lip and some-how found the strength to haul my exhausted frame to safety, curling into a ball as I struggled to get my breath back.

A huge rectangular area with canvas stretched over it occupied most of the space. The tarpaulin was knotted around a series of stanchions and I realized absently that it must be a swimming pool wearing its winter finery.

I know what you're thinking. Why's old Boxy staying skywards? There's only one way down from there, chum, we've seen it at the pictures. Spreadeagled and strawberry jam-like on the damned pavement. Well, I was thinking along just those lines.

My injured hand was bleeding again – I could feel the bandage growing heavy and wet – but I stumbled forward towards a non-descript hut-like structure. Yanking open the door, I looked down

into a cold, dark stairwell. My ears pricked up at once at the muffled yells from below. They were on to me!

Slamming the door shut, I looked wildly around the roof for some hiding place but it was bare and totally exposed. Except for the pool!

Skulking low in the darkness, I raced to the perimeter and searched for an opening in the stretched covering. The tarpaulin, tied off with great knots of nautical rope, was rigid with ice. My hands were already numb and I clawed uselessly at the nearest, mind flashing back briefly to games lessons at school and the almost impossible job of rebuttoning one's shirt after a wretched cross-country run. Still I persevered, fingernails splintering as I worried and tore at the looped rope.

I brought down my shoe onto the stretched canvas, hoping that it might slacken the knot, but the material hardly gave, as unyielding as the dirigible skin I'd seen arching over the dance floor of the "99".

Finally, desperately, I dropped onto my chest and began to pull at the knot with my teeth. And suddenly it began to give!

A rush of hope flooded through me, followed almost immediately by a hollow dread as I heard the sound of footsteps pounding on the stairwell. Grabbing at the rope with useless fingers, I managed to prise the knot apart. The covering slackened, the tarpaulin crumpled and a narrow space opened up, showing up black above the empty pool.

Thanking the stars for my lithe frame, I slid through just as the door to the stairs flew open with a crack like a thunderbolt.

Keeping hold of the loosened rope, I tumbled down the rough render of the wall. I scraped my backside painfully, and was immediately assailed by the foetid atmosphere, somewhere between the grassy pong of a tent and the sickening odour one sometimes finds at the bottom of one's toothbrush mug.

But this was no time to spare my finer feelings. I held onto the rope for grim death, my already-bleeding nails flaking hideously on

the frayed end as I tried to make the tarpaulin tauter lest my hiding place be discovered.

From my vantage point beneath the canvas, all I could see were the haloes of my pursuers' flashlights. I held my breath. Through the gap, I saw a familiar pair of two-tone brogues the colour of café-au-lait. Percy Flarge had joined the hunt, no doubt in a perfectly foul mood after my distinctly un-Queensberry dodge.

Flarge's shoes came closer, crunching on the asphalt chippings that covered the roof. I could see tiny droplets of blood from his smashed hooter hitting his creamy leather uppers. He didn't move. A flashlight flared in my eyeline and I looked down at the bottom of the pool. Something I saw there gave me crazy hope.

There was a shout from close by and finally Flarge was on the move. I waited until his shoes were well out of sight and then let myself tumble down the wall, splashing into the inevitable puddle on the pool floor.

What I'd noticed in the momentary gleam of the flashlight was a huge monogram made out in coloured tiles. Some cod coat-of-arms cobbled together by Yanks desperate for historical roots, of course, but, more importantly, the emblem of my own hotel! Somehow or other, after all the shenanigans of the evening, I'd managed to vault onto the roof of my own residence. This had both advantages and disadvantages. In a hotel I could certainly move about less conspicuously, but at the same time they'd be bound to have my room – and probably the whole place – under observation in case I came back.

I scolded myself. It was imperative to keep focused! All that depended upon whether I could get off this damned roof alive. Had Flarge really assumed I'd already made my escape? Or was he lying in wait?

The crunching of boots on the asphalt had died away but there'd been no corresponding sound to indicate the door to the stairwell had been closed behind my pursuers.

I waited a further five minutes and then decided to risk it. Leaping for the trailing end of the rope once more, I hauled myself up and poked my head through the gap in the tarpaulin. Not a soul in sight. With one last effortful grunt, I pulled myself out from under the canvas and lay panting on the poolside, my hand hurting like blazes.

Then, with a great sigh, I jumped up and sprinted back towards the entrance to the stairwell, giving not one thought to the notion that the roof might have been left guarded.

I was down the concrete steps in moments and emerged into the beautifully carpeted uppermost floor of the hotel, a cocoon of mint-green and black elegance after the freezing outdoors. There was no one about so I made straight for the next stairwell, clattering down five floors until I reached my own. Emerging into an almost identical corridor, my heart leapt as I spotted the door to Room fifteen-o-eight. The unguarded door.

It could be a ruse of course but there was also the possibility, the *wonderful* possibility, that Flarge hadn't thought to put a man outside my room. Furthermore, to employ one of the hoariest clichés of cheap thrillers, it might well be the last place they'd think to look for me!

Giving up a silent prayer of thanks to hoary clichés, I padded down the corridor towards my room. My bandaged hand, with newly bloodied fingernails, was almost upon the shiny brass knob when the door began to open.

I spun on my heel, tottering like Chaplin in one of his sentimental two-reelers, and immediately bent low, retrieving the keys from my trouser pocket and scrabbling at the lock of the room opposite.

Now Dame Cecily Midwinter (under whom I'd trained more years ago than I cared to remember) had always advocated hiding in plain sight. Thus, rather than trying to blend into the wallpaper, I began to sing at the top of my voice, feigning a look of pie-eyed incoherence which I hoped might explain away my tattered appearance.

'Come on and hear!' I belted out. 'Come on and hear Alexander's Ragtime Band!'

Out of the corner of my eye I saw the blue of a policeman's uniform as he emerged from my room.

'Come on and hear! Come and . . . hear! It's the best band in the land . . .'

I fumbled with my key and turned to face the copper with a stupid grin on my face. 'Dashed thing won't fit,' I slurred. 'Must've . . . must've picked up the wrong one at recep— reception.'

I threw in a hiccup and a modest belch. The policeman looked mildly disgusted at the sight of this idiotic Britisher three sheets to the wind. He narrowed his eyes and I suddenly remembered that it probably wasn't terribly wise to pretend drunkenness in a city where Prohibition still reigned. 'Sorry,' I stage-whispered. 'I'll get out of your way.'

'I'd advise that, sir,' he said darkly.

I nodded at his sagacity and shuffled towards the elevator. 'Just pop downstairs and get the proper key.'

Jabbing at the brass button I prayed the lift would come with all due dispatch before my law-enforcing friend decided to take a closer look.

The arrow on its luminous dial crawled round to fifteen with wretched tardiness. I gave the officer one last dim grin and then turned back as the lift doors sprang open.

My heart dropped into my boots. Half a dozen uniformed policemen were revealed, crowding the lift. Thankfully I was still wearing my idiot grin otherwise I'm sure my face would have given me away. My luck held and, incredibly, the entire phalanx didn't spare me a second glance, merely peeling out of the lift in two lines, leaving me stranded on the carpet like a gasping salmon.

And then I had an even better piece of luck. For inside the lift, revealed by the exiting coppers, was Rex the bellhop, his hand already on the display of buttons.

'Going down, sir?' he said, automatically.

'Not just now, sugar.'

He turned his big green eyes on me and gawped. 'Mr Box! Jeez! What happened to—'

I stepped across and jabbed at a button. The lift shuddered and began to descend. 'Never mind,' I barked. 'I need your help, Rex.'

He chewed anxiously on his pouting lip. 'Is this something to do with the cops that're here? I heard there's a guy they're looking for. Killed someone and – oh my gosh!'

I clamped a hand over his pretty mouth and nodded. 'Yes. It's me they're after. But I didn't kill anyone, Rex. Not today, anyway. And you're going to help me get out of here, you understand?'

He nodded mutely, his eyes bulging in fright.

I glanced at the floor display glittering prettily like Japanese carp in a pond. 'We'll stop at the second floor. Then you need to find me a cupboard . . . um . . . a closet, all right? And don't do anything silly. It wouldn't be wise.'

He nodded again and I removed my hand. The poor boy looked badly frightened. The lift doors pinged open and we stole out onto the second floor of the hotel, Rex leading the way. His bum looked dashed appealing in those tight blue trousers so I gave it a little pat to show we were still friends. Carnality seemed far from Rex's thoughts, however, as he jangled a bunch of keys from his pocket and unlocked the door to a linen cupboard.

I slipped through, grabbing him by the lapels and pulling him in after me.

'Jeez, Mr Box!' he piped. 'If they find out I been helping you—'

I ignored him and felt for the light cord that was tickling at my face like a cobweb. With a click, a dim, bare bulb struggled into life. I looked about and groaned in dismay.

'What's up?' quizzed Rex.

'Nothing but towels!' I muttered. 'I was hoping for, you know, a waiter's apron. Spare commissionaire's uniform. Anything!'

'You asked for a closet . . .'

I sighed. 'Look, there's no time for this. I have to get out of here.'

I looked Rex up and down. He looked awfully dishy in that nice blue uniform. I gave him an encouraging smile and, not for the first time in twenty-four hours, asked him nicely to take it off.

9

All At Sea

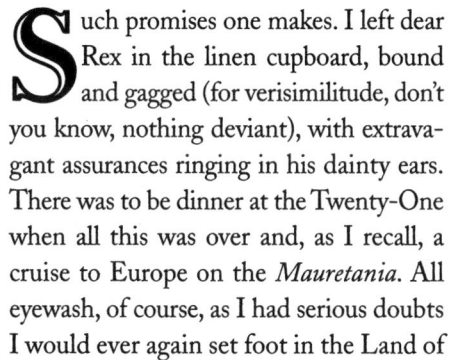

Such promises one makes. I left dear Rex in the linen cupboard, bound and gagged (for verisimilitude, don't you know, nothing deviant), with extravagant assurances ringing in his dainty ears. There was to be dinner at the Twenty-One when all this was over and, as I recall, a cruise to Europe on the *Mauretania*. All eyewash, of course, as I had serious doubts I would ever again set foot in the Land of the Free, always supposing I escaped in the first place.

I emerged into the hotel lobby wearing Rex's uniform and feeling indescribably foolish, my shins showing bare where the lad's not-quite-long-enough trousers exposed my disguise. Pulling the little pillbox hat as far down my forehead as I could without drawing attention, I crossed towards the front doors with the easy swagger I'd seen Rex and his kind adopt on many occasions. I could only pray that as usual the clientele wouldn't spare the staff a second glance, otherwise the sight of a middle-aged man in blue and gold brocade might excite unwanted comment.

Policemen were dotted discreetly around the palm-fringed lobby.

I hovered near the lift for a few moments, patting, for reassurance, my money-belt, where Hubbard's silk relic now reposed. I watched the activity at the front desk with keen interest. A dwarfish fellow in a tailcoat and derby was trying to check in for a night of illicit thrills with a gum-chewing young lady in white furs. The weary-looking concierge looked ill-disposed to help.

Next to them stood a pile of orangey-leather cases, shiny as fresh conkers, awaiting collection. With complete nonchalance, I sailed past the desk, picked up a pair of the cases and glided out through the revolving doors into the street.

More coppers were walking up and down in the brilliantly lit forecourt. Heart pounding and resisting the urge to run for it, I walked as casually as I could around the side of the hotel until the darkness closed about me. Under this blessed cover I took to my heels, gripping the suitcases and emerging onto the neighbouring block, where traffic streamed by in a great blaring confusion.

Stepping boldly into the fray, I hailed a yellow cab and ordered him to take me to Pier Thirty-Nine down by the river, pulling a couple of greenbacks from my money belt to show I was in earnest.

I sank back, utterly spent, and cast an anxious glance through the rear window. All seemed well.

Allowing myself a moment to gloat, I pulled the first of the cases onto my lap and clicked it open. A wave of cheap perfume overwhelmed me. I reached inside and lifted out a negligee decorated with pink Malibu feathers. Not quite the thing for the journey I had in mind. The rest of the case proved equally barren and I moved onto the smaller one, hoping that it belonged to a chap of a similar build to me.

The locks yielded to my thumbs with two satisfying clunks. I stared down at the contents and let out an audible groan.

The driver's inquisitive features appeared in the mirror. 'You OK, bud?'

I sighed. 'Just not my day. Not my day at all.'

I held up several pairs of tiny, gaily checked trousers, garishly coloured waistcoats and bow ties. Tipping back the lid of the case, an old poster that had been pasted into it was exposed.

Adolph the Little Atom, I read. *Mimicry. Minstrel songs. Tumbling.* I recalled with a weary smile the dwarf at the hotel reception.

Well, that's where gloating gets you.

The old tub *Stiffkey* lay at her berth at the pier just as I'd seen her only that afternoon, black water lapping at the rusted plates of her creaking hull and looking comprehensively unfit for an Atlantic crossing.

Having paid off the cab, I crept down a set of rotting wooden stairs and hid myself on the jetty behind two great coils of weed-smeared rope. As female drag or midget's stage-wear were unlikely to prove useful to me I was still squeezed into the bellhop's ludicrous get-up, though I threw the pillbox hat into the Hudson where it sank into the freezing water as though swallowed by tar.

Taking Sal Volatile's envelope from my pocket, I took stock of the situation. The dead man's exit strategy was completely open to me and, as my presence on the bitterly cold pier indicated, it was currently my only option. What I wanted very much to avoid, though, was falling into a trap. Did those intent on framing me know about Volatile's plan to substitute me on board the *Stiffkey*? Had I come all this way only to find Flarge's men waiting for me in the rusting old ship?

As far as I could tell, the tub was under no observation save that of an old tramp in a battered pilot's hat, sitting on the edge of the planking and very much at peace with the world. I gave it a few more minutes, eyes keenly scanning the shadowed docks, then, taking a deep breath, I strode swiftly up the rope-banistered gangway and onto the deck.

The pounding of the engines set my already strained nerves on edge.

A woolly-headed sailor in a sweater spat tobacco juice at my feet and eyed me with interest.

'Volatile,' I muttered, handing over my documents.

'Are you now?' he said, smiling in cheeky fashion. 'We shall have to watch you, then, eh?' The accent was thick Norfolk and the sudden sound of home was as comforting as if I was being wrapped in a Union flag.

He nodded towards a stairway and we passed from the darkness into a gloomy corridor, feeble electric bulbs strung down its length. Hooking a thumb over his shoulder, he indicated a battered cabin door. There was a small brass frame inset in it, presumably meant to bear the name of whichever unfortunate soul was travelling on the mangy old ship. I'd taken the *Stiffkey* to be some kind of trawler or merchant vessel with passengers a rare commodity. No doubt Volatile had paid a princely sum for this discreet exit from America, no questions asked.

The sailor flattened himself against the buckled wooden panelling of the corridor so that I could pass. 'When do we cast off?' I said.

'Half hour, ducks,' he replied with a funny little smile.

'Won't the captain want to see me?' I asked, trying not to sound too plaintive.

He let out a gurgling laugh. 'Cor, blast me! Ha! That'd be a turn-up and no mistaking. Ha, ha! Want to see you? Mr Volatile, he don't give a cuss for nothing 'cept getting here to ol' New York and then gettin' home. Now if I were you I'd keep my head down, eat your grub and not go for any long turns on the deck.'

I nodded. 'Very well.'

A slim shape in a white sweater and woollen cap flashed past us – a cabin boy, I supposed – and the sailor caught his arm. ''Ere! Hold you 'ard! You take care of Mr Volatile 'ere!'

The sailor gave me another queer look, tapped his tobacco-yellow fingers to his cap and vanished into the gloom, leaving me alone with the boy, who stooped at once for my cases.

Dog-tired, I ignored the lad and shouldered open the cabin door,

revealing a tiny, airless room, very close to the engines judging by the constant drumming that set the brass ring of the porthole rattling. A simple bunk with a grey army blanket slung over it comprised the only furniture.

The boy let the suitcases tumble to the floor and went out. Kneeling on the bunk, I peered through the porthole. Outside the sea stretched like a black sheet towards Manhattan island, the ship's ancient propeller churning the icy water at her stern a startling white as the engines ticked over.

I glanced at my wristwatch. If we could only get going soon, if Volatile's escape route really hadn't been discovered, I might just be in with a chance.

With nothing else to do but wait, I stripped off Rex's jacket and sat there in my under-vest – stained black with grime and perspiration – and opened the two cases again. A more thorough check was in order.

The dwarf's case proved as useless as it had appeared save for some pornographic postcards of dubious titillation and a coral-pink cigar case containing a brace of fine-looking Havanas. I decided to save the smokes until I had something to celebrate.

Turning my attention to the girl's case I was delighted to find not only a roll of ten-dollar bills tucked inside her underwear but (God bless fashion!) a pair of wide-legged culottes that might just about pass muster as a gentleman's trousers. I was just slipping out of Rex's when we suddenly started moving. I moved to the porthole again and watched the blessed sight of the New York skyline begin to slip away into the night.

With a groan of exhaustion, I sank down on the bunk and closed my eyes.

I'd made it.

Poor old Lucifer has always been a rotten sailor, and waking in a fug of engine fumes, I greeted the new day with a dry heave, swung my

legs off the bunk and sat up, coughing like a consumptive. I needed some fresh air sharpish.

Tottering into the culottes, I made my way across to the door and stumbled into the corridor beyond but that stank of oil and provided scant relief. As the *Stiffkey* plunged through the sea, I swayed towards the stairwell, only to walk, face-first, into the massive aproned chest of what could only be the ship's cook.

I took an involuntary step backwards and looked up at all six foot six of the brute. Built like the proverbial brick garderobe, this mulatto's ears were bright with silver rings and one hand – in appropriately piratical fashion – was replaced by what looked like a tin-opener.

'So sorry,' I bleated. 'Just . . . just on my way to the deck.'

Sweat rolled in great glistening beads over his bricklike brow. He made no move to stand aside.

'Not feeling too bright,' I managed, putting on my best silly-ass voice again in order to defuse any potentially violent urges he might have. 'So if you'd just let me pass . . .'

A strange guttural croak was his only answer.

Then, rather unexpectedly, he drew out a tin from the ruddily stained pocket of his apron, proceeded to spear it with the end of his harpoon-hand and, with astonishing delicacy, to open it up. Within a very few moments, he was scooping out pinkish meat – corned beef by the look – and stuffing it into his mouth. I shuddered briefly at the sight of his tongue. It had evidently been sliced clean off long ago, and the remains clacked about over the wet meat like some ghastly earthworm.

He croaked again, glared down at me in an openly challenging fashion and held the sharp end of his harpoon close to my perspiring face.

'*Bullfrog!*'

The cry was unexpected as it was welcome. The cabin boy from the previous night came running down the pitching corridor. In the

queasy light I could still make out little of his face but I grew suddenly alert at the very noticeable protuberances in the rough fabric of his sweater. The very noticeable and *breast-shaped* protuberances.

'I am Aggie,' said the cabin 'boy', with great gravity. 'Do not mind Bullfrog. He is harmless. Welcome to the *Stiffkey*.'

She was duskily skinned, petite and devilishly exotic, her coal-black hair cut into a manageable crop under the cap. Her eyes were like polished jet and there was the light of another race in their depths. She set up a rather pleasant little fluttering in my churning innards.

'Isn't it meant to be unlucky?' I ventured.

'Sir?'

'Girls on ships?'

'They do not think of me as a girl,' she said, again with a kind of uncalled-for seriousness. 'So I do not either.'

Aggie's voice had a vaguely Indian inflection. Despite feeling as sick as a dog I attempted a ravishing smile. 'What a silly way of thinking. I'm sure if we become acquainted, I should like very much to think of you as a girl. Often.'

Such drawling charm never fails.

Except this time.

She stared at me with what looked very much like concern. 'You are sick. You must get air.'

At an impatient gesture from the girl, the brutish Bullfrog finally stepped aside and clumped off into the innards of the ship. With both hands on the rope banisters I hauled myself on deck, Aggie close behind.

The day was dark and oppressive, the sea like a greasy grey blanket, and I found, much to my distress, that I felt no better. The waves battering at the creaking ship's plates were deafening.

'How do I look?' I cried.

'You are green,' shouted Aggie, with wounding directness.

I swallowed a mouthful of bile and made my way towards the rail, my feet dragging as though they were stuck in glue.

Aggie's hand on my elbow was a great comfort. She narrowed her eyes against the spray. 'I could, if you like, prepare something for your condition. It is not exactly unknown aboard ship.'

I nodded, salty water dribbling down my face. 'You old sea dogs have a dozen tried and tested remedies, eh?'

'Sea dogs?'

I heaved again and put a hand to my clammy forehead. 'I'd be most grateful.'

'Come, then,' she said with impeccable manners. 'It is senseless to linger here when it is doing you no good.'

Aggie began to steer me back towards the stairwell then pulled up so sharply that I almost fell forward. A stout fellow with a liverish countenance had swung into our line of sight. I felt the girl stiffen as he strode with perfect composure over the soaked planks.

'It is the captain,' she hissed in my ear.

So here was Captain Corpusty again, whom I'd glimpsed only briefly when he stood deep in conversation with Mons a mere twenty-four hours before. At close quarters, his face was like a battered sail, strung tight across his bones as though against a force-ten gale. And just as the sailmaker might have patched and worried at the old canvas, so Corpusty's flesh was uneven and terribly scarred. Jaundiced eyes popped out from sweaty, shadowed flesh. He glanced at me for the briefest of moments and was about to resume his patrol of the deck when he suddenly swung back round.

'This our passenger, is it, Aggie?' he rumbled.

'Yes, sir.'

'Sal Volatile,' I croaked, holding out a trembling hand that the captain declined to shake.

'And how are you finding us aboard the *Stiffkey*, Mr Volatile?'

'Well,' I said airily, 'I've only just become acquainted with your friend here, though we did run into a charming one-armed fellow who seemed awful anxious to serve up corned beef for breakfast.'

Corpusty's disastrous face twisted into a semblance of a grin.

'Oh, old Bullfrog's bark is worse than his bite. But then, since I cut his tongue out, he don't have much of a bark.'

'You . . . ?'

'I prize loyalty above all things, sir. Bullfrog got himself soused one night in 'Frisco and fell to telling tales about me. He won't never tell those tales again.'

I swallowed another gobbet of bile. 'Expect not.'

'But he's loyal now,' continued the captain. 'And he keeps a watchful eye on things for me.'

I nodded breezily. 'Right-oh! Well, I must be getting below. Haven't found the old sea legs yet. Good day, Captain.'

Aggie helped me towards the steps. I was aware of Corpusty's eyes on my back the whole time.

10

A Guest Of Captain Corpusty

By the next day, after some food and a modicum of hot water, I was feeling a little better. Aggie and I had become sufficiently pally for me to enquire as to the possibility of getting some togs more suitable for the crossing and I was sitting on the bed that night, the ship pitching horrendously in a gale, grey water slapping at the porthole, when her light knock sounded.

'Yes?'

The girl's head appeared around the jamb. 'I have them,' she said solemnly.

I jumped from the bed and relieved her of a pile of clothes, shaking them out and holding them up to the dim light. A cable-knit sweater, moleskin trousers, thick socks and stout boots comprised my friend's booty yet I fell on them as though they were treasure. I swore a secret vow never again to be so damned fussy about my appearance, knowing that I would recant on such a promise at the first sight of a decent bit of Jermyn Street.

Without a thought to my modesty, I stripped off the wretched

vest and culottes and shrugged on the new clothes.

Aggie cast her gaze at the floor, blushing.

'You're a miracle worker, Aggie,' I enthused, pulling the sweater onto my bare torso.

'You must not say such things,' she muttered.

'It's the exact and literal truth.'

'No, no,' she cried, earnestly. 'I am only a foolish girl and miracles are not performed by the likes of me.'

I stopped in the process of putting on my new boots. 'What a queer thing to say. Did someone tell you that?'

Aggie looked at me searchingly for a moment, then cleared her throat. 'It was not too hard to find the clothes. There is much clobber' – she said the word with utmost care – 'aboard the *Stiffkey*. They will not be missed.'

She cleared her throat again, lifted off her woollen cap and scratched her head.

I caught her meaning, nodded and reached into my money belt. As I handed over some dollar bills I saw Aggie's gaze stray to the belt. Hurriedly, I pulled down the jersey. We might be getting on well but I could hardly trust her. I might yet wake in the night to find her pretty face looming over me and a dagger in my ribs.

She put away the money in her back pocket. 'Is there anything else I can do for you, sir?'

'Yes. Why not stay awhile? Have a drink.' I gestured to the small bottle of Scotch I'd liberated from the blonde's suitcase.

She shook her head. 'I must get back. The captain says there is a storm brewing.'

As though to emphasize the point, the vessel gave a great roll and Aggie and I almost toppled to the floor. She fell into my arms and I laughed, but the girl looked confused and hastily got to her feet.

'I can only apologize,' she said quietly.

'For what?' I cried. 'I'm not an ogre, you know, my dear.'

'This I know.'

'Well, then. What say you and I become better acquainted?'

Aggie looked shocked. I had meant what it sounded like I meant, naturally, but I quickly converted my statement into something far more innocuous. 'Tell me your story.'

'No, no. I must go. I shall . . . I shall see you tomorrow.'

She averted her eyes again and slipped out into the corridor, closing the door behind her with a soft click.

I'd discovered from the girl that the *Stiffkey* was heading for Norfolk, swinging round the south coast of England and putting in at one or other of the tiny harbours that pepper that haunted coastline. The thought of home, however straitened my circumstances, was like a balm. Flarge would ensure I was a wanted man but I felt that the reassurance of British soil would do me the power of good.

But what exactly was I to do when I got there? Continue with my mission to investigate Mons? Plead my case with the frankly unsympathetic Joshua Reynolds? Or piece together whatever strange clues linked the silken relic (presumably the 'lamb' of which Volatile had spoken) and the dead man's reference to the Convent of St Bede?

I lay back on the bunk, luxuriating in the relative freshness of my linen. The old divine's name, of course, suggested some northern locale, possibly as far as Northumberland, but I had a vague intuition that the *Stiffkey* had been chosen for a reason. After all, Volatile was desperate to find safety. It wasn't in his interests to go tramping across half of England when he felt sure his life was in peril.

But all that could wait until I was on terra firma. For now, I had the *Stiffkey* to investigate. The ship was apparently carrying dry goods – a description that might cover a multitude of sins. I knew Mons had some interest in the old bucket, but what? He and Corpusty had been thick as thieves when I'd seen them on the quayside what seemed like weeks before. A spot of rooting about was definitely in order.

I waited until the ship had settled down for the night before slipping out of my cabin.

Keeping snug to the stained woodwork of the corridor, I crept into the old tub's bowels, passing the captain's door – no sign of life – and the galley. I peered into the gloom. Bullfrog the cook lay in a stained hammock that creaked back and forth with the motion of the ship. But he wasn't alone. His good arm was draped over, of all things, a salted pig. It nestled alongside him in the hammock, glazed eyes seeming to watch me as I slipped past the door. These voyages do get awful lonely, don't you know?

There was even less light down here but I knew I was getting close to the engine rooms. Sea water sloshed about my ankles and there came the constant tattoo of shifting cargo, banging about in the hold.

I chose the closest door and stole inside. The hold was foetid and in total darkness so I lit a match, trusting that Captain Corpusty's 'dry goods' were not sticks of dynamite. In the brief flare of light, I saw that I was surrounded by about a dozen crates, each branded with what looked like a Maltese cross. I used the remaining light to position myself by the nearest crate and then, as the match spent itself, began to wrench at the lid in the darkness.

The wood protested as I managed to force my ruined fingernails between the slats and then, with an astonishingly loud *crack*, the lid broke open. I felt about inside the crate and was answered by a curious dry, stirring sound. I fumbled in my trouser pocket and drew out the matchbox, lit another lucifer and stared down at the treasure. I laughed lightly. Of the things I thought I might see . . .

The crate was full of Communion wafers.

'*Hosts* of them,' I grunted to myself.

I turned in shock as the door to the hold swung open and a figure was revealed, silhouetted against the dim light from the corridor.

'Mr Volatile?'

It was Aggie. I breathed a sigh of relief, got to my feet and stepped back into the corridor. Taking the girl by the arm, I flashed her my most endearing smile. 'Best not say anything about this, my dear. I lost my way, you see, and was so damned curious about what this old wreck might be carrying—'

But Aggie had a puzzled look on her face as if my sneaking about was of no consequence. 'I beg your pardon, sir,' she said with her accustomed gravitas, 'but the captain asks if you would be so good as to join him for a *nightcap*.'

I straightened up in surprise. 'Eh?'

Aggie nodded. 'You are privileged, Mr Volatile. Captain Corpusty does not usually find time for such pleasantries.'

That was what worried me.

Nevertheless, I closed the door to the hold and dutifully followed Aggie out into the listing corridor. Another set of steps and we were at the captain's door.

A barked '*Come!*' was the response to Aggie's knock and I was ushered in.

The cabin was a riot of disorder; charts and books lay everywhere, drawings and photographs had been tacked to the wooden walls and there were grotesquely carved African masks and a guitar made from alligator-hide slung lazily from the ceiling.

Captain Corpusty was of a piece with his room. He looked up from his contemplation of a book and the lamplight flashed in his yellowish eyes.

'Ah, yes. Mr . . . Volatile.'

I shook his hand. 'At your service, Captain.'

'No, no. No indeed. It is I who should be at yours, sir. I'm heartily sorry not to have properly extended my hospitality earlier in the voyage but I'm a busy man, as you can see.'

He gestured about at the disarray and gave a helpless shrug. His gaze flicked over my shoulder. 'That will be all, Aggie.'

The girl flashed me a worried look and slipped out, the door

clicking behind her. Something about the captain's manner and the memory of those eyes boring into my back made me extremely jumpy all of a sudden. Why had the previously unresponsive Corpusty suddenly turned so friendly?

'Drink?'

I accepted gratefully and relished the grog, though the captain knocked back his own measure of brandy in one go. I cradled the chipped custard glass and smiled warmly at him.

'I'm very grateful for your expert seamanship, sir,' I began. 'I know the Atlantic can be treacherous and—'

'Now, then,' he cut across me abruptly, 'let's not waste time.'

'How's that?' I queried.

Corpusty glanced idly down at his book and I caught sight of the lurid, hand-coloured illustrations. 'It's a rum old life out here on the seas,' he grumbled, like some old-world pirate, 'but we're more up to date than you might expect. The *Stiffkey*'s got many of the modern conveniences.'

I found this very hard to believe. 'Really? Don't tell me that cook of yours is a maestro trained at Delmonico's?'

He gave a throaty laugh and his grey skin puckered unpleasantly about the eyes. 'No, sir. But we do have wireless. And we picks up all kinds of chatter on a lonely night. All kinds of chatter . . . *Mr Box*.'

I felt suddenly cold. As cold as though I'd been standing on the prow of the rusty old vessel and Atlantic spray had covered me head to foot. 'Aha,' I said at last.

Corpusty rubbed at his chin and it made a sound like sandpaper. 'Fact is, there's all hell broken loose. The Yanks are after you and have put out a description and a mighty big reward. All I have to do is wire them and the British coppers'll be ready with a nice welcoming party when we pitch up in Norfolk.'

I looked levelly at him. 'So why haven't you?'

'P'raps I've got a natural sympathy for those a little outside the law.'

Oh, Lor, I thought. It can't be my body he's after, can it? Bullfrog's porcine pal showed how lonesome these jack tars could get but surely there were nicer sprats to be landed? And, if like me, he travelled on the number 38 bus as well as the 19 (you get my drift) then a comely little piece like Aggie was surely more in the grizzled old fellow's line? Perhaps it was the novelty he craved. Able to take his pick of the fresh-faced young'uns, Corpusty had long ago tired of feeling the hot, quick breath of the cabin girl as she slipped onto his grimy mattress.

An extremely unpleasant vision leapt into my mind and I hastily banished it. Corpusty seemed to read my thoughts and slammed his meaty fist onto his desk. 'I'm not a savage, sir!' he barked. Then he gestured around the squalid cabin. 'As you can see.'

For the first time, I looked in some detail at the pictures that had been tacked to the walls. To my utter astonishment, I now saw that they were, to a man, photographic representations of Old Masters. Here was Velázquez sharing a warped beam with a Venetian Madonna. An unfinished Romney overlapped the capacious bosom of a flabby Rubens. And dotted between them, Sargents, Whistlers and . . . me! I recognized in quick succession the portrait I'd done of Lloyd George just after the end of the last show that the House of Commons had commissioned, then refused to hang, and an earlier picture of a lovely girl with cornflowers in her hair, which had first brought me to the world's attention.

Captain Corpusty nodded solemnly. 'As I say, Mr Box, I am not a savage. If fate had conspired otherwise, I might have made a living from the canvas and the brush as you have done, but I wasn't so lucky. But I've a brain in my head and a keen eye for beauty. And I should deem it an honour, an *honour*, sir, if you would consent to cast an eye over my humble scribblings.'

I blinked in absolute astonishment.

'Good God,' I breathed at last. 'You're a fan!'

11

A Whiff Of Brimstone

I have known, in my time, many species of praise. The charming art mistress who initiated me into the ways of the world – and of, incidentally, oil pastel – was very fond of the little hollow at the base of my throat just below the Adam's apple. Many a lazy summer afternoon was passed with waxen fruit un-rendered and her pretty, heart-shaped face nestled there, beads of sweat rolling like pearls from her brow.

Then there was the renowned critic with morbidly unruly chest hair who, seeking to make up for his withering of my doodles, chased me around a slipper bath with his tumescent member poking from his pinstripes.

And then there was the boy with the very blue eyes who smelled of honey and stayed by my side for almost ten years until . . . ah, well. *C'est la vie. C'est la guerre.*

Captain Corpusty's effulgent response to my presence, however, counted amongst the best.

'I don't care what you've done or not done, sir,' he announced. 'Far

as I'm concerned you're a genius of the first water and that's' – emphasized with slap on corduroyed knee – '*that*.' I had been starved of appreciation for so long I almost wept.

Thus passed the next few days of the voyage, yours truly casting a practised eye over the smelly old pirate's artwork in return for a faithful promise to set me ashore at some unknown spot where the peelers wouldn't find me.

My habit was to rise early and then make my way down to Corpusty's chaotic diggings, where he'd be waiting with a pot of stewed Darjeeling and another of his rather ropey canvases in which the sea, would you credit it, featured heavily. So heavily, in fact, that I began to grow weary of its crudely executed form, ladled onto Norfolk landscapes or Atlantic storm-scapes in thick grey impasto resembling sea-gull excrement.

The routine was enlivened by the captain's occasional foray into portraiture, mostly wretched, though he'd caught something of friend Aggie's impish charm in a pencil sketch that appeared to have been executed during a typhoon.

'Don't spare my blushes, Mr Box,' Corpusty would cackle. 'I can take criticism.'

He couldn't, of course. Who can? So I was extremely careful to lard him with praise for his amateurish efforts lest he think twice and ditch me into the rollers.

Of course, I could see where all this was leading, and the fatal moment arrived one evening after dinner when Corpusty was treating me to a not-indifferent Amontillado. 'I don't suppose,' he said, screwing up one eye as he lit a cigar from the candle, 'you'd ever consent to making a picture . . . of me?'

The old fellow asked it as shyly as a school-girl. Eager to please, I pooh-poohed my talents once more, made a show of resistance but then grudgingly consented. A portrait in oils was completely out of the question given the incessant pitch and roll of the *Stiffkey*, but I would just about be able to manage a creditable pencil sketch.

Mon Capitaine said little during these sittings but simply sat and smoked, occasionally outlining his plans for my disembarkation, which consisted of plonking me in a rowing boat just off the coast whilst the *Stiffkey* herself steamed onwards to Cromer. According to the wireless, all the main ports were being watched, but Corpusty was confident the route he'd dreamt up would put me out of harm's way.

Once or twice I gently probed him as to the nature of his business, hoping that Olympus Mons's name might pop up, but the leathery sailor seemed to be keeping those particular cards very close to his tattooed chest.

As we churned through the leaden Atlantic towards England I actually found a measure of peace in my scribblings. Corpusty's ravaged countenance with its heavy lids and ragged, gin-blossomed nostrils provided real inspiration. Of one thing I was extremely conscious, though: the *Stiffkey* was possessed of a most peculiar atmosphere that hung about it like a noxious cloud. It wasn't just the hissing and chuffing of the ancient engines, nor yet the stifling fug of the airless passageways. There was about the ship a sort of dread, drear gloom, a feeling that something malign lay at its very heart, like the shuttered door to a secret room in some Gothic romance.

I am not a superstitious man. The closest I had ever come to encountering the other side was during the lurid business of the Cardinal's Windpipe. I dare say you read about it in the picture papers. A decrepit Stuart pile (a house, you understand, not a person) was being 'haunted' by a ghastly apparition in a tricorne hat. Turned out to be a doe-eyed youth trying to frighten a hated cousin out of her inheritance. After much kerfuffle, I'd done the decent thing and well, *laid* the ghost.

So, naturally, I shrugged off the curious atmosphere aboard the creaking old tub until an incident occurred that could not be so easily dismissed.

During an afternoon sitting for Corpusty's portrait, I ventured to

enquire how he'd managed to come by such a lovely creature as Aggie for a crew member.

He pulled at his pipe and gave a throaty chuckle. 'Wondered when you'd get round to that. Quite the peach, ain't she?'

'Indian?' I asked, coyly, rubbing at the paper with my lead-darkened fingers.

'Yar. With a dash of Swiss, so I'm told.'

'My ears pricked up at this mention of the land of cantons and holed cheese. 'How exotic.'

Corpusty's addled eyes twinkled naughtily. 'You fancying a bit of a Swiss roll, eh, Mr Box?'

I laughed lightly. 'What *can* you mean, Captain?'

Corpusty settled himself more comfortably in his chair. 'Can't say as I blame you. But you'll get nowhere. Aggie Daye's as pure as the driven. On account of her upbringing.'

'Oh yes?'

'Yar. *Nuns*,' he said, pointedly, coughing up a ball of phlegm and spitting it against the cabin wall.

My ears pricked so far they practically grazed the tobacco-glazed ceiling. 'Nuns?' I watched the phlegm roll over the Madonna of the Rocks and Whistler's mother before disappearing behind a cracked lampshade. 'This was in Switzerland, yes?'

Corpusty shook his head, jabbing his pipe in my direction as though scoring a point. 'No! You'd never believe it, but she's local to Norfolk. Settled in my neck of the woods when she weren't no more than a mawther.'

'Hm?'

'A young girl,' he translated.

I affected nonchalance, concentrating on the drawing for a full minute before asking: 'In a convent, you mean?'

Corpusty nodded. 'Funny old place. Out on a causeway.'

My heart thumped in my chest. 'St Bede's?'

Corpusty frowned. 'Dunno. Least ways, don't ring no bells.

Though, if it's a convent, I s'pose it does! Rings bells, that is! Ha ha! *St Bede's.* Suppose it could be. Why? You heard of it?'

'Read about it in some gazetteer or other,' I said with a dismissive shrug.

Corpusty folded his arms and looked up at the low ceiling, where a hurricane lamp swung restlessly to and fro. 'Funny to recall how I first clapped eyes on one of them holy sisters. All black and white like a puffin bird. I wor only a boy and I thought it wor a spook! I says to old Ben – he wor cap'n of this ship afore me – just put that thar crate down, Ben, and lookee yonder, for there's a ghost a-drifting 'cross the pier towards us or I'm a Dutchman.'

I nodded indulgently.

' "Well," says he. "Reckon you'd better break out your clogs, young'un,'cos that's one o' them bloomin' brides of Christ!"'

Corpusty slapped his thigh again, then drifted off into a brown study. 'Poor old Ben. Basking shark took him. Funny, that. I mean, they's harmless creatures and I ain't never heard of no one dying 'cos of 'em, but this shark sort of *sucked* him to death and . . .'

He roused himself. 'Funny buggers, in't they?'

'Basking sharks?'

'Nuns! Fancy wasting their lives on that all that tosh. I ain't never had much truck with Jesus.'

'You do surprise me.' I shaded in the shadows beneath the captain's drooping earlobes. 'So how did Aggie get from being lodged at the convent to sitting below decks on the *Stiffkey* darning your socks?' I continued. 'Ran away to sea, did she?'

Corpusty smiled, relishing the pleasure of slowly unfolding the tale, like a grandfather telling ghost stories round a Christmas fireside.

'Not quite,' he said at last. 'Not quite. I was . . . approached one day. On the quay. The Mother Superior it was, and . . .' He clapped his pipe into his mouth. 'Well, that's another story.'

Feigning indifference, I yawned and stretched. 'I'm done for now, Captain. Might snatch a nap before dinner.'

Corpusty nodded and, with a contented hum, absorbed himself in some chart or other.

I had retreated to my cabin, somewhat fagged out, when Aggie's familiar light knock sounded at the door.

'Come!'

Ribbons of fog drifted inside with the girl, creeping around the jamb like the tentacles of a spectral sea-beast.

'A bad fog is coming up, Mr Volatile,' she said, shaking her head.

'Well,' I said cheerily. 'Don't fret.'

There was no response. Clearly the vernacular hadn't penetrated the walls of the convent. 'You'll be glad to be getting home soon, I expect,' I continued at length.

'Home? Norfolk is not my home,' she replied, mournfully, like something out of Chekhov.

'You favour New York?'

She shook her head, still glum. 'The *Stiffkey* is my only home.'

I sat down on the bunk, gesturing round at the grim interior. 'I can understand that. I mean, why would you want to live anywhere else?'

She looked at me with her huge, tragic eyes. 'Yes. I would miss the bright lights.' Suddenly she grinned and her melancholy beauty was instantly transformed into something altogether delightful. The smile was infectious and I returned it with enthusiasm.

Aggie knew nothing of my planned escape – as far as she was concerned I was simply a fare-paying passenger to be landed at Cromer with the rest of their cargo. Yet at that moment I had a tremendous urge to confide in her. I simply didn't want to say good-bye to this fascinating creature. As I've already indicated, and happily for me, I've always taken whatever's pretty whenever it comes along. Makes life so much more interesting, don't you know?

'Look,' I said gently, 'you've been awfully good to me these last days. Before we part forever, isn't there something I can do to say thanks?'

Her eyes bored into mine, suddenly serious again, then she bounded onto the bunk, knocked me flat on my back and kissed me with somewhat startling fervour.

I hardly had time to respond when she pulled away, licking her lips thoughtfully, and frowning.

'So. This is how it is to kiss a man. I think it is disappointing.'

She began to move off but I grabbed her arm to pull her back. 'Hang on!' I entreated. 'You caught me off guard, my dear. It's really much nicer if we both have a go.'

So saying, I let her crumple into my embrace and planted a long, lingering smacker on her dark lips whilst running my hand over the knotty tufts of her cropped hair. She relaxed a little, then stretched out like a cat, pressing her body tightly to mine.

After the appalling stresses and privations of the past weeks, I felt a kind of fuzzy warmth flood through me like an infusion of sunlight, and my hips moved instinctively forward to grind against the girl's, our belt buckles scraping together. Then Aggie pulled away, giggling.

She flopped back onto the pillow and leant her head on her hand, gazing at me, searchingly. 'I have never in my life thought to do such a thing before.'

Hang on, I thought, there's plenty more still to do! One chaste kiss isn't the bally be-all and end-all.

I stroked the creamy curve of her jaw. 'Aggie Daye,' I murmured. 'Short for Agatha, is it?'

The girl said nothing but languorously closed and re-opened her eyes.

I decided to press my advantage. 'The captain tells me you were raised in a convent—'

She sat up with an angry hiss. 'He had no right to tell you that! No right at all!'

'Hey, hey, hey!' I soothed, slipping an arm round her waist. She resisted and wriggled towards the edge of the bed, trying to plant

both feet on the cabin floor. 'It's all right, Aggie,' I cried. 'This isn't an interrogation. I'm just interested, that's all.'

She turned her flushed face towards me, her lip turned down petulantly. 'They did not raise me!' she said proudly, sinking back against the wall, arms folded. 'They imprisoned me!'

'What do you mean?'

Aggie looked glum and her eyes suddenly swam with tears. She let them roll over her cheeks, then impatiently wiped them away. 'All I wanted was to be like them. As good as them. But the sisters told me it was impossible. I was *special*. So special, they kept me locked up!'

Gently, I pulled her back so that her head lay on my chest. She suddenly gave in to racking sobs and I stroked her head, making the soothing sounds one does on these occasions. I said nothing for a long time.

This was all terribly mysterious. Sal Volatile knew of the Convent of St Bede. Indeed it was the only place he said he'd feel safe. But why? And was this beautiful girl somehow caught up in it all?

I was mulling this over when I suddenly became aware that Aggie had stopped crying. At first I assumed she'd drifted into sleep but then I felt a soft fumbling at my fly buttons and an immediate tumescence in my moleskins.

Aggie's neat little hand slipped inside my trousers and I felt a thrill of desire as her cold fingertips connected with my thighs, instantly prickling the skin into goose-flesh.

Lifting her head from my chest, I gazed into her night-black eyes and then leant to kiss her once more, my stubbly chin scratching her soft, downy face. Her lips parted with sudden ferocity, like a snarling lioness, and she bit at my face and tongue. I pushed her down onto the bunk and dragged the sweater from her body, revealing a long, marble-smooth neck and perfect, pert breasts, the nipples huge and brown as toffee.

With practised ease, I slipped out of my trousers and wrenched

down Aggie's own till they reached her knees, passion preventing any further undressing.

Must I burden you with the details of that night? Of how we thrashed about in the none-too-clean sheets, plunging towards ecstasy till almost dawn? Of my lean and lithe body (it still was, I swear!) conjoining with hers, our legs intertwining, our mad kisses, locked in a fevered embrace that for a few sweet stolen hours banished all thoughts of Sal Volatile, Percy Flarge, nuns, lambs and mysterious Cabalistic handkerchiefs?

Well, it was shaping up to be a dashed good shag, is all I can tell you, when something rather uncommon occurred.

Quite suddenly, the incessant pounding of the waves against the rusty hull fell quiet, as though I were in a kinema and the sound had suddenly shut off. Even the constant asthmatic grumbling of the ship's engines stilled. I glanced down at Aggie's face but her eyes were screwed tightly shut in pleasure, fully absorbed in the matter in hand. Yet I knew in my very bones that if I opened my mouth to cry out, not a sound would escape me.

And, all at once, the air in the cabin began to thicken. A strange bluey haze, like wood-smoke, began to bleed through it, hanging in trailing threads, one layer overlapping another like a formation of storm clouds. Deep, deep within the smoke there was a noiseless detonation, as though I was looking down the twin barrels of a shotgun, and two points of red light, glowing hellishly like coals, blossomed into life.

I knew even before the smoke that surrounded them began to take on the vague, ectoplasmic structure of some nightmarish face that these ghastly, glowing embers were *eyes*.

I choked in shock and ceased my coupling. Aggie stirred beneath me, and as I felt cold sweat trickle down my neck, the spectre began to take on more solid form, the blood-red eyes leering out from a long, goatish face, crazed with deep lines, black as gunpowder. There was no nose, only a hellish, skeletal hole edged about with

scraps of mouldering fur. As for the mouth, it never seemed fully to form. Only a terrible, gaping, indefinite maw occupied the lower half of the face, the bluey smoke drifting in and out of its orbit like rank breath. But in its baleful black emptiness I seemed to see all the dismal, hateful things of the world distilled. I was seized by a sudden, blank terror, rolled off Aggie and curled up into a ball.

I could feel the girl's hands shaking me by the shoulders but still there was no sound.

I glanced fearfully over her shoulder and the goatish face broke into a filthy heathen grin.

Then I screamed.

12

Troubled Waters

The pounding of the waves and the wheezing of the engines crashed back into my consciousness with the force of Dempsey's right hook. I recall opening wide my eyes and calling out, before sinking into the cool embrace of the pillow, where I must have fallen into a deep, deep sleep.

When at last I awoke, there was no sign of Aggie. Lord knows what she must've been thinking, *pauvre petite*, choosing me as her first tumble only for yours truly to screech into her lovely face some little way from any kind of, shall we say, resolution.

My thoughts, though, were somewhat disarranged. I own I was in a total funk, trembling all over and covered in a sheen of cold sweat. What the hell had I seen? Or, indeed, what *from hell* had I seen? It could only have been some fevered hallucination. Perhaps the noxious fumes from the ship's engines had finally taken their toll?

I shuddered at the memory of that dreadful apparition and tried to dismiss it, yet even as my eyes closed the hateful, bestial face

sprang back into my mind. Further sleep seemed impossible and I'd pretty much made up my mind to track Aggie down in order to apologize when I heard heavy footsteps in the passage outside.

Staggering unsteadily from the bed and opening the door just a fraction, I caught sight of the woolly-headed sailor who'd taken my papers when first I'd come aboard. He was carrying one of the crates I'd seen in the hold, branded with a Maltese cross, though this one was small and knotted with tarry string.

I let him pass from view, took several deep breaths to right myself, then slipped out of the cabin and followed.

The corridors of the vessel were as stifling as rabbit warrens, swirling with oily vapour and shaking incessantly with the drumming of engines. Passing door after closed door, I suddenly flattened myself against the wall as Woolly-Head gave a stealthy look back and crept into the crew's quarters.

I waited a few moments, then bobbed my head around the jamb.

It was almost completely dark inside but I could make out the sound of stifled giggles and, as my eyes grew accustomed to the murk, the Behemothal form of Bullfrog the cook, squatting on the floor clad only in his shatteringly awful underwear. Above the perished elastic waistline hung ropes of flabby flesh.

Bullfrog was concentrating intently on something at his feet. I strained to see. It was the crate! The string had been sliced off and his meaty hand and rusted hook were busily scrabbling about inside. I could hear vague grinding sounds and for one crazed moment assumed he was preparing supper for his pals.

Woolly-Head was giggling with a kind of manic glee. 'In the name of the father,' he said between hyena laughs. 'And of the son . . .'

'And of the holy ghost!' chorused the others, Bullfrog making a horrible wet response as though swallowing a live eel.

To my astonishment, I saw the mute lift a Communion wafer from the box and break it in two. Then he dropped the two halves into a little pot and began to grind up the stuff with a pestle.

I looked on in fascination as he tipped the powder onto a tin tray and proceeded to divide it into neat lines.

And then I understood. I'd seen Corpusty deep in confab with Olympus Mons and now here was the connection that bound them together! Mons was behind the massive influx of cocaine into Manhattan – smuggled innocuously across the Atlantic in the form of Communion wafers!

And now the *Stiffkey*'s crew were presumably enjoying the left-overs, the last few crates left unsold to Mons's New York supplier. Woolly-Head, Bullfrog and the others bowed their heads as if in prayer and partook of the cocaine in a great snuffling orgy, like sweaty pigs round a truffle-rich tree.

I used the distraction to creep past, but had gone no more than a few yards when a door flew open and Captain Corpusty was revealed, his bulk silhouetted against the glow of the hurricane lamp within.

'Trouble sleeping?' he said, cocking his head to one side.

''Fraid so!' I extemporised. 'Martyr to insomnia, alas. Do you . . . do you mind if I carry on with the picture?'

The old bruiser didn't seem more than faintly surprised and hap-pily consented to this evening shift, busying himself with brewing tea and pouring booze as I sharpened my pencils with a pearl-han-dled knife.

We sat in silence as I laboured steadily away, my mind racing the whole time, only Corpusty's breathing and the scratch of the lead pencils disturbing the stillness. I had fallen into a kind of trance when there came a light double knock and Aggie's be-capped head appeared around the door.

I flashed her a reassuring look but she completely ignored me, merely announcing we would be in sight of the eastern coast of England that very night. Through busy contractions of my brows, I tried to telegraph my profoundest apologies but the girl didn't even favour me with a glance as she ducked back into the corridor.

Grumpily, I hastened to finish my picture of the captain, ending with a hasty flourish around his wiry eyebrows of which I wasn't particularly proud. I called to the fellow and he craned over my shoulder, nodding appreciatively as I laid down my pencils for the final time.

'Marvellous!' he cried. 'Marvellous, Mr Box! A ruddy triumph. I never dreamed I'd see this day! But there's a little something you've neglected.'

I frowned, looking the portrait over. 'I don't think so.'

Corpusty chuckled. 'Why, your signature, sir! Just scribble it at the bottom there.'

'I thought you a student of my work, Captain,' I said lightly. 'Don't you know I never sign?'

He laughed and rubbed at his chin. 'Of course, of course! I just wondered, perhaps this one time. As a special favour . . .'

'It would be very odd to make an exception, even for you.'

Corpusty nodded, grunted and gestured helplessly with both hands. 'But how else is it to be . . .?' he began. Then, with a sudden burst of energy, he clapped one hand on my shoulder. 'Forgive the hasty words of a mere amateur, Mr Box. For genius is visible in every line, every battered old contour you've rendered of this old mug o' mine! And I shall treasure it, sir. Treasure it as long as I live. These past few days have been a joy to me. Now, let's see about getting you home and safe.'

He gave orders for the rowing boat to be prepared for launch just before dawn, we shook hands and I left him sizing up the sketch, pride lighting up his ravaged features. I made my way back, a mite unsteadily, to my own cabin and began to make ready for disembarkation.

Firstly, I made sure the precious silk relic was still safely stowed within my money belt, then I turned my attention to Percy Flarge's stolen automatic. I was wrapping it in oilskin and secreting it in a pea coat (another treasure the lovely Aggie had procured) when I

straightened up, convinced that someone was standing on the other side of the woodwork. Throwing open the door, I revealed Aggie crouched low, her eye level with the keyhole.

She turned at once on her heel but I dashed forward and jerked her back.

'Now you wish to touch me!' she cried. 'Before, I disgust you so much that you flee from my embrace!'

'No, no, no,' I insisted. 'It wasn't like that at all—'

Aggie wriggled about as I tried to restrain her. 'Get off me! I do not wish to see you—'

'Then why were you spying at my door, hm?'

'I was not!'

'Look!' I yelled with finality. 'Just listen for a moment, damn you!'

I dragged her further into the cabin and kicked the door shut. Aggie looked a little shocked and fell silent.

I rubbed my weary face. 'What happened before, it was nothing to do with you. You're divine, my dear, really you are. The cat's pyjamas. But something dashed odd happened. I . . . I saw something. In the air above us. A . . . a sort of face.'

Aggie stiffened in my arms. 'Face?'

I led her back towards the bunk, more or less content that she wouldn't flee. 'It sounds like utter rot, I know. But it was like some demon had appeared. Scared the bloody life out of me.'

Aggie's smooth brown cheeks had drained of colour. 'You have seen it too!'

'You mean—?'

'Yes!' cried the girl. 'Perhaps three or four times since I came to live aboard the *Stiffkey*. At first I thought it was a dream, but . . .'

'No dream,' I insisted. 'But maybe it's some foul concoction Bullfrog puts in the ship's grub? There's narcotics aboard, Aggie. Cocaine. Perhaps there might be other stuff. Heady stuff from Kingston or Shanghai intended to dope us. But why?'

Aggie's countenance resumed its solemn aspect. 'I do not believe this to be true. I have long felt that there is something strange about this ship. The face of the demon – that was just one more part of it. But then I began to feel . . .' She shook her head dismissively.

'No,' I urged. 'Go on.'

'I felt that it was watching over me,' Aggie bit her lip. 'Like . . . like a guardian.'

She turned her fathomless eyes towards me and then, like a child needing reassurance, draped her arms around my neck and we slid back onto the bed.

Though my first instinct was to take advantage, like the good Christian I'm not, I let the girl fall asleep with her head on my chest. With nothing to do until my dawn departure, I attempted to fall into the arms of Morpheus myself.

Yet sleep stubbornly refused to come. I tried to concentrate on the rhythmic motion of the ship and the familiar chug of the engines, yet still I lay awake, my eyes burning.

At first my brain fizzed with chaotic thoughts. Why was I being falsely accused of Volatile's death? He'd been alive, if injured, when last I'd seen him, so what had happened whilst I was drugged? Who had put three bullets in his lungs? Who stood to gain? Was Flarge so ludicrously jealous that he was behind the whole mad scheme?

There was something else, though, something the captain had said, and it kept jabbing at my thoughts like a fat bluebottle banging against a windowpane. That little exchange of ours after I'd completed his drawing. What had he muttered when I'd refused to sign the damned thing?

But how else is it to be . . .?

To be *what*?

I sat up in my bunk, making Aggie stir. How is it to be *identified*?

I knew all at once, with terrible certainty, that I was about to be betrayed. Looking down at my wristwatch I saw that it was twenty minutes to four.

As carefully as I could, I disentangled myself from Aggie's embrace, reached down for my discarded coat and carefully removed Flarge's pistol from its oilskin wrapper.

I glanced quickly towards the bunk – the girl was still sleeping peacefully – then creaked open the cabin door and stole out into the darkness.

The old ship rolled unsteadily beneath my bare feet as I padded through the dinge.

An irregular electronic bleeping told me I was nearing the *Stiffkey*'s radio room. I crouched down in the shadows of the weird greenish aura given off by the dial. Inside the room, Corpusty and Woolly-Head – acting as operator – were conversing in low voices.

'Understood,' said the Captain. I could see his great thick bonce, nodding in silhouette. 'Rendezvous oh-four-thirty hours,' he continued, the sharp, insistent bleep of the Morse telegraph sending out his message into the ether. 'Package to be taken off and . . . disposed of at your discretion.'

Woolly-Head laughed his hissing laugh and Corpusty joined in, throatily.

So there it was! The jolly old smuggler was trying to have his cake and eat it. He meant to turn me in, collect the reward and then, at some later date, flog off the picture I'd done of him. The provenance would be impeccable and my price was bound to rocket once I'd been hanged as a murderer.

I cursed the talentless booby. I'd steal a march on him yet!

There was very little time, though, before the rendezvous. I was supposed to be roused just before dawn for my pretended escape, Corpusty evidently bargaining on catching me asleep.

Feet slapping against the rotten old planking, I dashed back to my cabin. As quietly as I could, I crept back inside – to be met by the blade of a knife jabbing at my cheek.

Aggie sighed with relief and let the weapon drop. 'It is you! I am glad. I woke up and was afraid – what is wrong?'

I stuffed away the pistol. 'Change of plan. Corpusty's trying to double-cross me. I'm off.'

'Double-cross you? But why?'

I decided against putting on my boots. There might be swimming to come and I didn't much fancy being dragged down by the steel toecaps.

'Long story, my pet,' I said with a smile. 'You coming?'

'What?'

'Are you coming with me?' I said, crossing to the cabin door and swinging it open.

Aggie violently shook her head. 'No! I cannot do that!'

'Why ever not, for God's sake? What is there for you here?'

'The *Stiffkey* is my life. I owe everything to the captain.'

'The same captain who's about to give me up for filthy lucre?' I whispered.

She looked pained and confused. 'These people are my comrades. My world.'

I sighed. 'Listen, I need to tell you something. My name's not Volatile, it's Box. Lucifer Box. I'm on the run from America because someone's accused me of murder. Your precious Corpusty is even now arranging for the police to meet this ship and take me away. I'm completely innocent. Well, not completely. There'll come a reckoning outside the Pearly Gates, I shouldn't wonder. But if you like me and you want to help, I'd be most awfully grateful. Are you game?'

Aggie dipped her head, evidently shocked by this revelation. I ruffled her jet-black hair. 'Listen, Ishmael, you can stay. Of course you can. But do you really think your life'll be worth a fig once Corpusty realizes you helped me escape?'

She looked as grave as ever.

'Then there's this convent of yours and the smuggling operation and that devilish face. Don't you want to get to the bottom of it all?'

The girl looked far from certain.

'And then,' I continued. 'There's that private business of ours that was so rudely interrupted—'

Aggie suddenly flashed me a winning smile. 'I shall come!'

'I'm so glad! Now, let's not waste any more time. Come on.'

Tucking in at my elbow, Aggie stepped with me into the corridor. It was ill-lit and suddenly seemed threatening as the pair of us stole quickly along its rocking length, making our way up the rusted stairs to the deck.

At once, I saw that Nature was on my side. The fret that Aggie had earlier complained of had matured into a dense and oily fog, slowing up the *Stiffkey*'s progress and giving us a wondrous cover for our escape.

Aggie and I crept across the deck, treading carefully to avoid the creaking boards, until we reached the rail, the paint all blistered and rusted like that on a seaside pier. The boat, as leaky and unpromising as her parent craft, lay alongside. Corpusty had no doubt ensured it was prepared as planned in case insomniac old me had smelled a rat.

Swiftly, I put a leg over the side of the rail and glanced down at the little boat, swaying in the fog-shrouded swell.

Aggie held back.

'Don't fail me now!' I cried. 'You deserve a better life than this, Aggie! You know you do.'

I put my hand on the rail, preparing to vault over, when there came the harsh clang of metal on metal. Next to my hand had appeared Bullfrog's tin-opener appliance, ringing off the rail by my own vulnerable digits.

My head snapped up and there he was, a great Buddha in his stained underwear, towering over the two of us, his boiled-egg eyes alive with dope-fuelled malice.

13

Flight Across the Marshes

'Hell!' I cried, pulling my leg back over the railing and dodging the mulatto's claw as he swung it towards my head.

It was no good simply trying to make our escape by boat, the cook would raise the alarm and we'd be done for. The only solution was to silence the bugger − if a mute can be silenced − and in as permanent a fashion as possible. Taking advantage of Bullfrog's unwieldy bulk, I put my head down and charged him, connecting with his massive gut and sending him staggering backwards.

Bullfrog let out a guttural rasp, his half-tongue shifting in his mouth like a flayed thumb, then raised his metal claw to strike again.

Aggie was everywhere at once, raining blows onto the side of his head and kicking at his calves until he roared with fury, spit gushing from his lips. He lashed out as though swatting at a bothersome fly and I grabbed one of his massive arms, straining to keep the deadly barb from connecting with anything fleshy of

mine. Jabbing my elbow backwards into his face, I felt his nose break with a satisfying crunch but the beast was so powerful that he scarcely flinched and simply tossed me and Aggie aside like limp dolls.

Skidding over the slippery deck and almost toppling into the freezing sea, I saw Bullfrog stomping towards us again, looming out of the fog like a ghoul from an old sea yarn and waggling his tongue in fury.

Fumbling for the pistol, I tried to take aim but Bullfrog was too swift, smashing me to the deck with one great paw and then raising his harpoon-hand to impale me. The gun went sliding across the decks and vanished over the side.

This pleased Bullfrog, who set up a slobbering chuckle, sweat dribbling from his brick-like forehead and collecting in the pouchy bags beneath those manic, glittering eyes.

Then, all of a sudden, he came crashing down beside me with the force of a felled tree. I slid out of the way just in time. Aggie had clamboured onto the fo'c's'le behind him and swung a fire extinguisher against his temple with every ounce of strength she possessed.

Bullfrog shrieked in pain and put his good hand up to his face. Recognizing that we meant business, he began to stagger back towards the stairs, evidently intent on raising the alarm.

I scrabbled forward on my elbows, grabbed him by the ankles and yanked backwards. It was like trying to topple a block of granite. Aggie appeared at my side with the extinguisher, ready to swing again, but the brute lashed out and speared it with his hook.

At that moment, a terrific wave hit the *Stiffkey* and the vessel bucked violently, knocking the cook off balance.

It was all the chance I needed. Leaping up, I pulled his absurd chef's hat over his eyes and, as he struggled to see, I grabbed him by his filthy neckerchief and wrenched him down onto his knees.

He toppled over and, metal claw rendered useless by the impaled extinguisher, rolled like a carpet towards the railing. For a moment he lay like a crab on its back, flailing and gasping, then I skittered over the saturated boards after him. Planting my feet against his side, I gave a mighty kick and propelled the great monster over the side.

He gave one last strangled cry, there was a brief splash and he was swallowed up by the waves.

A strange quiet fell, disturbed only by the chugging of the engines.

'All right?' I gasped, turning to Aggie.

The girl looked a little dazed but then nodded quickly and jumped to her feet. 'Come!'

Incredibly, our desperate fisticuffs hadn't disturbed a soul. We climbed silently over the rails into the swaying dinghy, slipped from the capstan in seconds and began to row away from the ship for dear life.

The girl stayed at the stern, looking anxiously over her shoulder, expecting, as did I, that we would be discovered at any moment. Yet still I pulled at the oars, with no sign of life from the *Stiffkey*. The old ship gradually vanished into the fog as we struggled towards the mainland.

Aggie wanted to relieve me (from the rowing, you understand) but I demurred, although my arms seemed to have turned to jelly and I could scarcely feel my frozen feet. I prayed we would make landfall with all due despatch.

I rowed until I was sick with fatigue. Then, just as I felt my head nodding on my breast, there was a percussive explosion and the livid glow of a flare overhead. I sat up at once, rubbed my dry, exhausted eyes and looked for Aggie. She was staring upwards at the flare blossoming above us, briefly turning the fog-bank a hellish red.

'They're on to us!' I hissed. Aggie peered into the fog, looking for

the first sign of the *Stiffkey* in pursuit. I could only hope we were on the right course. For all I knew I was pulling out to sea, possibly into some hazardous shipping lane where we would be crushed to matchwood.

Fear of capture gave me renewed energy. In my school days, despite my detestation of all forms of exercise, I'd been quite a dab hand at rowing, although I'd only joined the team in order to get closer to a chap called Reggie Side. He was a smasher with a cheeky grin and thighs upon which you could've landed a small aeroplane. Hey ho. Happiest days of your life, what?

Those days were long past, however, and my middle-aged muscles shrieked for release from this unexpected exertion.

Aggie's impish face was suddenly illumined ghoulishly by a yellow glare as she clicked on a flashlight. 'There is a promontory – a kind of spur – hereabouts,' she whispered. 'That is what we are heading for. But the fog . . .'

She trailed off, biting her lip anxiously and staring out into the solid wall of swirling moisture. I strained to hear the noise of the *Stiffkey*'s engines but there was only the steady splash of my oars in the water and the creak of the old boat.

Then, all at once, another sound intruded on my numbed senses: a steady, metrical *thrum*. A ship's engines, no doubt, but not those of the fagged-out old rust-bucket from which we'd escaped.

Suddenly, a big searchlight crackled into life and swung in our direction, throwing out a snow-white beam that bobbed and shifted over the surface of the sea.

'Police launch!' I yelled over the racket of its engines.

Aggie stood up in the boat, taking advantage of the sudden illumination to get her bearings. The craft rocked perilously. As the searchlight struggled towards us, she sat down heavily and pointed starboard. 'There! There!'

I needed no prompting and sculled feverishly in the designated direction. The searchlight, infuriatingly, found the retreating prow

and we were suddenly blinded as its glare flooded over the boat.

A voice barked out, muffled by both fog and megaphone, and it was startling in that oppressive murk. 'This is the police! Prepare to be boarded!'

'Not bloody likely!' I muttered, wrenching at the paddles and craning my neck to spy out the elusive spur of land.

Not a moment too soon, the boat bumped against sand and I fell back, the oars skewing crazily and almost catching Aggie on the side of her head. She somersaulted over the side, the water coming to her waist. 'We've done it!' she cried. 'Quick! Ashore!'

I stumbled to my feet, then immediately ducked down as a bullet sang off the boat, sending splinters into the air in a little cloud. They were shooting at us. By James! Was this England?

More bullets hit the water – *ploop – ploop* – as I vaulted into the sea. The cold was intense and took my breath away but I knew we hadn't a moment to spare. Grabbing Aggie's hand, we waded ashore, hopelessly encumbered by our heavy clothes.

I dragged myself onto the shingle, weary to the very bone. Aggie followed suit and stood up, just as the damned searchlight swung round and lit her up, bright as day.

Another shot rang out. She looked briefly astonished, then fell back into my arms.

From somewhere, as though in a dream, I heard more barked commands from the police launch but paid them no heed. Aggie crumpled into my arms and went limp.

The huge dreary sky was beginning to streak with crimson as the dawn took hold, and in the rosy light, I could clearly see the hole in the girl's coat where the bullet had struck her.

'Aggie!' I whispered urgently. 'Are you . . .?'

'I am all right,' she whispered back. 'Please do not concern yourself.' But her eyelids were fluttering weakly and she sagged in my embrace. I yanked the coat from her back. The sweater beneath was darkening with blood. She'd only been struck in the

shoulder, I was hugely relieved to see, but it was clear she could go no further.

As if reading my thoughts, she tried to focus on me, her eyes rolling in her head. 'Go! You must go!' she sighed, shakily batting my arm.

She was right, of course, and I had no intention of giving myself up to the bobbies just for her sake, but I nobly shook my head, striking my most heroic pose. 'I'm not leaving you like this,' I breathed, like an overwrought Ivor Novello.

'You must!' she cried. 'I will be all right.' She turned her head towards the sea, where the sound of the approaching police launch was growing louder. 'They are coming! Go, my dear, dark man! We shall meet again soon!'

'Right-oh!' I cried, brightly. Well, chivalry's all well and good but when a chap's liberty is at stake . . .

I laid her gently on the cold sand. Normally, I'd have been confident that, whatever charges were laid against her, we were no longer in America and she would at least be treated well. But the trigger-happy antics of our pursuers gave me pause.

'I'll find you,' I gallantly whispered in her ear. 'I promise.'

She nodded absently, already slipping into unconsciousness.

Taking to my heels, I didn't look back as I hared across the beach, my bare feet sending up sprays of shingle.

It was devilishly hard going. The 'spur' was scarcely more than that, a narrow strip of land with the dark sea on both sides and, as I ran, I willed it to become wider and more solid so as to provide me with at least a scrap of cover.

Perilously exposed, I risked a glance backwards as the sun rose like a dull guinea amidst the cloud. The police launch had beached and I could see a cluster of men around poor Aggie. There was a brief pause and then three of them began to pelt in my direction. I didn't wait for the next bullet but dashed on, clutching my clammy coat around me against the bitter, howling wind.

All at once, the shingle suddenly gave way to marshland but this provided scant relief. Exhaustingly, for every stretch of firm, reed-covered ground there was another of swampy morass. Time and again, I wasted valuable minutes tugging my frozen feet from the ground, the saturated soil gripping leech-like to my shins and only giving them up with a horrible, sucking belch.

I was conscious of little save the huge, cold sky and the smudge of land at the horizon. The bleak landscape was dotted all over with boats, stranded by the low tide, their rudders projecting in ungainly fashion from every limpet-encrusted stern.

Staggering on, I tripped and fell head-first into the reeds, sending a pair of geese clattering and squawking into the air. Lungs aching appallingly and with the familiar taste of iron in my mouth, I lay there for a long moment. I watched the geese flap off into the reddening sky, their path crisscrossed by a ragged 'V' of other birds winging south.

Utterly spent, I could hardly bear to raise my face from the embrace of the soaking soil and took long, laboured breaths, inhaling the scents of the marsh, the musty stink of the reeds, the distant aroma of woodsmoke.

Cracking open an eyelid, I suddenly saw salvation. Lying abandoned and almost completely covered in the long grass was the wreck of a fishing boat. It was upturned so that the peeling planks – Wedgwood blue and positively festive in that desolate landscape – faced the sky. It was exactly what I needed as a hiding place and I crawled towards the wooden shape hoping against hope that the interior was dry.

The knees of my trousers were soaked through to the skin but I inched onwards, pulling myself through a ragged hole in the disintegrating planks and into fusty but wonderful darkness.

I sank down, breath coming in great whooping bursts. It was hardly a permanent solution, but this shattered hull at least gave me room to think.

I could head for the nearest town. Despite my state of déshabillé, I'd pass for a sailor and I still had cash, tucked away in the soaking money-belt. But, of course, the place would be crawling with rozzers. I might as well turn up and bang a gong, announcing the arrival of the celebrated Lucifer Box: artist, bon-viveur, sexual athlete and wanted felon.

An uncontrollable shivering took hold of me and I hugged my knees in a vain effort to keep warm. I knew I should move on, find somewhere genuinely secure to rest, but I felt my head nodding again as the strain of the past few hours began to take its toll.

I snapped suddenly awake at the dreaded sound of baying hounds. With renewed desperation, I felt in my pocket for matches, hoping against hope that they were sufficiently dry to be of use. I stiffened as, below the noise of the pursuing dogs I became aware of another sound. Close to. A sort of *shuffling*.

At once, I tried the matches. Once, twice, three times, I rasped at the sandpaper without result until, suddenly, the little stalk flared into sulphurous life.

I grinned happily at my success until I saw what the match had illumined.

It was as though the whole of the stern of the ruined old boat were encrusted with jewels. Bright, shining shapes glittered at me like rubies in the darkness.

Eyes.

I gawped as the match spent its little life and then an horrendous squealing confirmed what I already knew. The place was alive, was *boiling* with rats.

Scrambling backwards on my rear, I made for the open air just as the mass of rodents exploded outwards and I was overtaken by a torrent of stinking fur. I cried out in sheer horror as they overwhelmed me, their teeth sinking into the fabric of my coat and trousers, their scaly tails, thick as my numbed fingers, thrashing

about my face. Gagging with disgust, I tried to scramble under the rotten planks and out into the daylight but the tide of rodents overwhelmed me. I positively *swam* through the onslaught of fur and teeth, my arms flailing as I clawed at the wet ground and dragged myself through into the open air.

Then, all at once, as though obeying some silent command, the rats streamed away into the marshes like a trickle of oil.

Flat on my back, I looked up at the vast expanse of sky, chest heaving.

A strange quiet had descended and I sat up, looking about me. There was absolutely no sign of the pack of rats and not a sound to be heard: no curlew winging through the morning sky, no frog paddling in the soaking ground at my feet. Even the icy wind had dropped completely. I got to my feet and looked about, conscious of the same curious feeling of dread that had come upon me in my cabin on the *Stiffkey*. I felt with absolute certainty that if I stamped my foot it would make no sound whatsoever. It was as though the whole world had been smothered in cotton wool.

And then, as before, the clear air began to blur and change.

I froze in absolute terror as the dreadful, goatish face began to form once more, pitiless eyes shining redder and more lurid than those of the slavering rats. Closer to, the creature's flesh seemed like some horrid mixture of animal remains, squashed together beneath the wheels of a motor car.

As I watched, transfixed in absolute sweating terror, the tendrils of smoke drifted into the marshland and, with a horrible, shrieking peal, the pack of rats appeared once more, spilling out of the grass in three distinct lines, then merging into one. I steeled myself for their attack but the great charcoal-black phalanx took off across the wetland at a rate of knots. My skin crawled at the awful sight of them.

Yet this was nothing compared to the frightful apparition

hovering in the air beside me. I tried to look away but it was as though some queer magnetism were working on my strained frame. My eyelids quivered and my face glowed with cold perspiration as a sense of utter despair took hold of me and I sank to my knees on the spongy ground.

Then, as suddenly as if I'd been slapped across the face, the spell was broken. I cried out in horror, shocked by the sound of my own voice – but of the apparition there was no sign. Instead, I became fully aware of the rumbling bark of the police dogs. Struggling to see into the middle distance, I could make out the bent shapes of men being dragged through the marshland by their excited hounds. They were moving in completely the wrong direction!

I knew at once what had happened. The dogs were in full pursuit of the filthy pack of rats. In which case the hellish ghoul I had seen – had I seen it or was I merely delirious? – *had come to my rescue.*

I thought back to what Aggie had said. That the thing she'd seen was her guardian . . .

'Yet this was nothing compared to the frightful apparition
hovering in the air beside me.'

14

Tuppence For A Bloater

N ot wanting to waste a moment, I assumed a low crouch and scarpered, keeping out of sight of the men and their dogs, now little more than vague silhouettes on the horizon.

There wasn't time to consider the insane events I had just witnessed. I could only thank my stars that Fate had granted me a chance of escape. Now I had to find proper shelter and food and give some thought to rescuing Aggie.

I rounded a kind of crescent-shaped outcrop that might once have been a harbour, though it was now silted up and choked with marsh grass. Slowing to a brisk walking pace, I almost immediately spied a structure projecting from the landscape like a broken tooth. Tarred and tumbledown, it had evidently been cannibalized from driftwood and resembled nothing so much as the ribcage of some fossilized giant of the Jurassic. In sharp contrast to this, the front door, salvaged, it seemed, from a luxurious Portuguese vessel, was of gorgeous teak and bore the legend *Capitão* in beautiful copperplate script. The door was slightly

ajar and the somewhat overwhelming strains of *Don Giovanni* were blasting through it.

Tacked to the outside of the shack and swaying gently in the breeze were dozens of smoked fish glinting like gold leaf, woodsmoke swirling about them. My stomach cramped painfully and I realized, with a jolt, how utterly ravenous I was. Inhaling the bluey smoke until I felt my eyes beginning to sting, I let the music flood over me.

Worn out and ragged since that night in the Manhattan drugstore – how long ago? – it was no wonder I'd started seeing things. What next hove into view seemed merely one more part of my delirium.

There was no sign of life save for the sound of the scratchy gramophone and I was just reaching over for one of the smoked fish when the teak door flew open and an old, old woman came out. With my senses stunned to buggery, I thought she was a witch.

Bent almost double, she leant heavily upon a gnarled stick only a foot or so long, had virtually a full white beard of a rather frightful wispiness and a heavily tanned face resembling a long-perished fig. Her black bonnet, as crow-black as the rest of her apparel, was in the style of forty years back. She fixed me with eyes as moist and clouded as the sky.

'Tuppence,' she cawed, chewing gummily at her lips.

'Pleased to meet you, Tuppence,' I said with more gaiety than I felt. The crone stared at me. I coughed as the woodsmoke caught in my throat.

'Bloaters is tuppence,' insisted the contorted old thing in a strange Australian squawk. 'I'm Mrs Croup,' she said with a laugh. 'Wanna come in?'

'Madam, I could kiss you.'

She looked me up and down and gestured towards the teak door.

Introducing myself as Sal Volatile, lately of New York and now tramping about the countryside in search of work, I was ushered

into a wonderland of curious relics, mostly, I presumed, reclaimed from the sea. All the furniture was slightly crippled, a missing ball and claw foot here, a patched-together cane bottom there. The tarred walls had patterned fabric pinned to them and, though filthy, the whole place had a sort of weathered charm that well suited its owner.

The principal decoration, however, consisted of newspaper clippings, seemingly hundreds of them, though my exhausted eyes couldn't make out the details.

In one corner, in pristine nick, was the gramophone, with a vast yellow trumpet like a daffodil. Neatly stacked records abutted it, a spidery scrawl identifying them. Mrs Croup plunged me into a disreputable old armchair whose burst cushions sprouted straggly hair as freely as her chin.

'Well!' said the old woman, bending over the dirty old stove and tossing a fish into a pan. 'Mr Volatile of New York, is it? Strewth, you must've seen some of the best'uns out there.'

'Best'uns?'

'Did you see Stanford White shoot Thaw? Or Leopold and Loeb? No, that was out in Illinois, wasn't it? Did you ever go out West? That's where they done for Fatty Arbuckle.'

My face must've been a picture. What the deuce was the old dear banging on about? 'Umm . . .'

'I slipped away from the old man once and caught a peek of Robert Wood. He'd been fingered for the Camden Town business, if you remember. But then the buggers only went and acquitted him!'

My eyes scanned the newsprint-plastered walls and suddenly all became clear. For every yellowing clipping, every carefully scissored paragraph, every damp-mottled photograph related to a notorious murder trial.

'Oh!' I cried, settling back in the chair and anxious to curry favour. 'Oh yes, I've seen some corkers. Both here and in the States.'

Mrs Croup's gums worked feverishly. 'Christ, what I wouldn't give to travel again. The Old Bailey! Manchester Assizes! Too crooked now, though. Almost got to the Bailey when they strung up Thompson and Bywaters, but . . . well, Mr Croup was very strict on these matters.'

I settled my hands on my lap, knowing I could warm to the theme. 'I saw Crippen and Le Neve back in '10—'

'No!'

'. . . and my father knew Dr Neil Cream . . .'

'Never!' she almost screamed. 'Cream? The boss-eyed Canadian strychnine poisoner? I'd have hacked off me arms and legs to have caught the merest glimpse! Strike me down, leave me a limbless torso and stuff me in a trunk at Charing Cross Station if I wouldn't. Cor!'

She gazed at me, from my wet hair to my clammy feet, and blow me if she didn't whistle. 'Strewth. You're a man after me own heart. And a looker too. Just like Mr Croup was. But he wasn't a kind man. No, sir, not kind at all. You can overdose me with hyoscine, steam across the Atlantic and get caught by electric telegraphy but I won't say he was a kind 'un. No I won't.'

What a queer old egg she was. I cleared my throat. 'Any tea on the go?'

Mrs Croup shuffled towards the gramophone, wound it up with great energy, then pulled out a big black disc. 'Murder a cuppa, eh?' she cackled. 'I'll get the kettle on. First though, a bit of "Carmen" Caruso recorded, in San Francisco, night before the 'quake. It's a beaut.'

She proceeded to stuff a quantity of woollen knickers into the trumpet of the machine to muffle the sound, then swilled out a cracked Dresden pot. 'You look done in, mate,' she observed. 'Never mind bloaters. I'll fix you some proper breakfast. Agreed?'

'I must bow to your wisdom. You're an angel.'

She cackled and rubbed her chin. 'With these whiskers? Hee-hee! Reckon you've been at sea too long, mate! It's a long time since

old missus here turned any feller's head, unless it was to turn away and spew up his dinner! Distil arsenic from me wallpaper and poison me kiddies if I tell a lie.'

I threw myself with gay abandon into a plate of thick gammon, eggs and sausages, washed down with strong tea that ran like quicksilver through my being. I closed my eyes in unadulterated joy.

As I ate, Mrs Croup sang along with Don José in a cracked warble and gave me a neat précis of the illustrious career of the great barrister Marshall Hall. That got us through pudding. I was just belching behind my hand as we reached the Green Bicycle Murder and the old bird paused to smile benevolently at me. 'Enjoy that? Don't you fret about letting your wind out, neither. I hear tell it's a sign of appreciation, somewhere out foreign'

She plonked herself in a shipwrecked deckchair and, rolling a thin cigarette, fixed me with a twinkling stare.

'Still, 'spect you didn't come here just to hear about sundry hangings and gougings and suchlike.'

I returned her frank gaze. 'Then why am I here?'

She shrugged her bony shoulders. 'Reckon you're looking for something. Reckon we're all looking for *something*.'

'I've found everything I could possibly want in your larder, my dear,' I said, folding my arms over my stomach. 'But if you could help me with a little information, I'd be inordinately grateful.'

She spat into the fire. 'I'll help if I can.'

'Is there a convent hereabouts called St Bede's?'

Mrs Croup pulled the fag from her mouth with a pronounced *pop*. 'Like the Venerable?'

I nodded.

'Oh, yeah. There's one. It's out on an island close by, mate. There's a causeway at low tide, otherwise it's a boat trip. You taking holy orders?'

I yawned expansively. 'Not quite.' The cosy room and the crackling fire were beginning to lull me into exquisite slumber.

'You want to get your head down?' she murmured, her hand toying with the ragged hem of her skirt.

I swallowed, nervously. 'Hmm?'

'I can make you up a beautiful little camp bed,' she said, to my relief. 'Then we can head out to the island tonight, if you like. What d'you say?'

I don't think I've ever been so glad to flop my head down onto a pillow. If Percy Flarge and Olympus Mons and the Mongol hordes of Genghis Khan had descended on the old woman's hut I don't think I could've stayed compos.

'That's it, dearie,' cooed Mrs Croup. 'You drift off now. Old Mother here'll look after you. Slice out my guts, throw 'em over my shoulder and leave me in a Whitechapel slum if I don't.'

With which charming send-off, aware only briefly of the rough pillow-ticking in my face and the faded blankets slung about me, I sank into the sleep of the blessed.

When finally I stirred, waking to the muffled strains of 'La Boheme', I felt wonderfully refreshed. Stretching out my long legs under the blankets, I gave a little yelp as my foot hit something cold and hairy.

I cracked open a sleepy eye. A rheumy grey one looked back at me.

Lying on the adjacent pillow in the hastily improvised bed was Mrs Croup!

She was grinning suggestively, a blanket pulled up over her withered — and naked — dugs.

'What . . . what are you doing?' I swallowed.

'Protecting me modesty,' she wheezed. 'What does it look like?'

My toes still lay against her own horribly hairy specimens. I attempted a smile. 'Your . . . um . . . your tiny foot is frozen.'

Mrs Croup seemed pleased with my *bon mot*. 'I can't offer you no artificial flowers, only smoked fish.'

I shuffled backwards on the mattress. Happily I was still fully clothed but my decrepit antipodean Mimi, taking advantage of my exhaustion, had stripped completely. It was rather like waking up next to a quantity of brown tissue paper and it was not a pretty sight.

'Madam,' I said, sounding like an affronted parson, 'I'm very grateful for your charity—'

'Ain't charity,' she grinned, sucking on her lower lip. 'Tuppence for a bloater, as I say. Gammon and eggs, though' – at this she winked suggestively – 'they might be a little more expensive.'

By Jove, this was a pickle! 'What. . .um. . .what would *Mister* Croup say?' I managed at last.

'He's dead,' cried the hag. 'God curse him. Dead as if I'd bashed a chop-axe twenty-three times into his face!'

I went quite cold. 'You didn't, did you?'

'*No!*' she cried, sounding disappointed. 'I only wish I had! The bastard ran off with a winkle-picker from Blakeney! I heard the 'flu took him just after the War. Serves him right. Anyway, I'm alive! I'm here, now! Nice and warm to the touch of your lovely nimble fingers!'

My mind raced. *I'm married, I couldn't possibly, it's against my religion, I'm a Uranian outcast, I'm a eunuch, I prefer goats* (no, that one might not help).

I think I was on the point of smothering her with the pillow when the old girl saved me, creeping out from beneath the covers and pulling on a tattered nightdress that might as well have been a shroud. 'No,' she said, shaking her head. 'I'm moving too quickly for you, ain't I? It's always been my curse. I frighten off the fellers 'cos I'm so eager. There's plenty of time, eh?'

I gawped at her. She'd been an invaluable help and I'd need her to find the causeway so, somehow, I found myself muttering, 'Ye-es. Plenty of time.'

Mrs Croup dragged on the rest of her ancient garments, smiling

to herself. 'Jesus, but you're a handsome bastard. Don't get many like you washed up on this old beach.'

I clambered from the bed, stretched, and rubbed my hands together in cheery fashion in an effort to reassert some form of normality.

Night showed through the ragged curtains as an indigo rectangle. I pushed aside the dirty netting and gazed out. The beach was utterly deserted.

'Anyone been . . . hanging around?' I ventured.

Mrs Croup shook her filthy old bonnet and it rustled like newspaper. 'Funny you should say that. It's been quiet as the grave round here for longer than I can recall. Suddenly there's a great hooplah about some escaped convict or other.'

Before I could react, the old woman's leathery face creased into a tortoise-smile. 'We'd best keep an eye out for him, eh?'

I nodded, immensely cheered. Keeping the old bird on a promise might help me out of a multitude of sticky situations.

From somewhere in the recesses of the hovel, Mrs Croup managed to find a pair of boots and some thick socks that I hastened to pull onto my still-frozen feet. I wondered what other relics of male company she kept hidden away. A grisly image of a spider's web dotted with flies' wings sprang to mind.

'Are we ready for the off?' I cried, clapping my hands together enthusiastically and hoping to dissuade her from any more carnal thoughts.

'Almost.' As she rooted out a muffler and gloves, I spotted a stack of cardboard boxes. Noticing my interested expression, the crone smiled slyly and lifted one of the lids. 'What d'you think to these, then?'

I peered down at what at first I took to be cigars. Then the veil lifted. 'Dynamite?'

Mrs Croup gave a chuckle. 'Herring don't catch themselves, you know. Not at my age!'

She carefully replaced the lid, then nodded her bonneted head

towards the window and snuffed out the lamps. 'Tide's just about low enough now. We can cross by the causeway.'

Outside it was a startlingly cold, clear, moonless night. The stars shimmered overhead like splinters of exploded champagne bottles. As we made our way across the rocky beach, I cast nervous glances over my shoulder.

'Tide turns about midnight,' croaked Mrs Croup from the recesses of her black bonnet. 'If you're not back by then, you're stuck out there for the night. There'd be no one to save you. Put thirty grains of antimony into me laudanum and leave me to die in shrieking agony if I tell a lie!'

'I'll be fine,' I cried. 'I'm sure the . . . um . . . sisters of St Bede's will give me a bed for the night.'

The causeway was suddenly visible, projecting straight out from the beach and uncomfortably reminiscent of the narrow spur of shingle where I'd first come ashore. Though the tide was low, black water still sloshed over our booted feet.

'On second thoughts, I reckon I'd best come with you all the way,' said my guide. 'Since you keep getting into trouble.'

Fearing the loss of her best chance in years, the old girl clearly didn't want to lose sight of me.

'There's absolutely no need, my dear,' I cooed. 'You get yourself home now.'

At this, she swung sharply in my direction. The starlight glinted off her bloodshot old eyes. 'You want to pack old Mother off to the Land of Nod just when things is getting interesting?' she squawked. 'The bloomin' ingratitude! Youth! I've a good mind to flay you alive and pull off your—'

'Now, now!' I interrupted, hastening to still the cracked voice that was carrying startlingly through the still, freezing night. Taking her by her knobbly elbows, I beamed appreciatively. 'Mrs Croup, I've offended you. I apologize unreservedly. You're clearly made of stern stuff and I absolutely owe you my life. But I have to go alone. I've no

idea what I might be facing and I simply won't have you risking yourself for my sake.'

The crone considered this, sucking noisily on wizened gums that pressed together like pencil rubbers. 'I could wait and keep a look-out—'

'These are desperate men—'

'My favourite kind!'

'– who'll stop at nothing. It's too dangerous, my pet. Now I'll be back by midnight, I promise. Have the kettle on ready.'

She sniffed and heaved a sigh. 'All right.'

I turned her about and she began to retrace her steps, though with markedly less enthusiasm.

'Oh, by the way!' I whispered at her retreating back. Mrs Croup turned. 'Thanks for thinking of me as a youth. Does wonders for one's confidence!'

She held up a withered hand and was gone.

What a dear, terrifying thing she was. Still, if I couldn't be considered young next to a witch of eighty-odd then I truly was ready for the knacker's yard.

I put on a real pace now, having had to hang back somewhat to make allowance for Mrs Croup's ancient gait, and sloshed through the water, the insecure causeway shifting beneath my boots.

There was something uncanny about the sight of the wind-chopped sea stretching on either side of me and I hastened to cross, not liking the look of the salty depths and the mysteries they might contain. I was across the causeway in about ten minutes, suddenly finding myself on a soft beach, littered with dark, jagged rocks.

Some way ahead, an imposing Gothic building reared up, utterly black against the starlight save for a single electric light burning in a high window. There was about it the familiar musty smell of a church building; a mixture of damp-foxed books, incense and rotten nosh.

I padded across the sand until my feet hit surer ground. There was a kind of cobbled driveway stretching for about five hundred yards towards the convent's arched porch and I could see at once a canvas-covered lorry – such as the army might use – and a rather smashing silver-coloured motor parked up outside.

Utilizing an old trick, I carefully removed my boots and socks, then put the boots back onto my bare feet and the socks over *them*. I was now free to clump about on the cobbles with impunity.

Obviously in no position to go knocking on the front door posing as an itinerant archbishop, I reasoned my best plan was to try to see what was going on behind that lighted window. Happily, a great verdant bush of waxy ivy was sprouting from beneath the stony crenellations and, grabbing great handfuls of it, I made my way by degrees to a spot just under the windowsill.

I don't know what I expected to find – a studious nun looking like the penitent Magdalen, perhaps, crouched over a sputtering candle and mumbling a catechism. What I certainly didn't expect was to see my sister Pandora, legs neatly crossed ankle over ankle, smoking a cigarillo and pointing a gun at what was evidently the Mother Superior.

15

Whatever Possessed You

The aged nun, her huge white wimple still perfectly ordered like the bowl of an orchid, sat bound to a rickety chair, a desk lamp blazing in her face. Pandora was regarding the woman with detached coolness, her black hair glossy in the reflected light.

I was still hanging there on the ivy. The window under which I perched was old, the lead sealing the diamond panes un-repaired for donkey's years, so I was afforded a pretty good chance to make out what they might say.

Suddenly the door opened and Olympus Mons strode into the room, his face buried in some sort of file. He'd abandoned his absurd uniform for a well-cut dark pinstripe and neatly knotted tie, collar pinched into dimples by a golden pin. He gave the nun a warm smile as though he were a genial solicitor about to tell her she'd come into money, and then fixed Pandora with his penetrating stare.

'Anything?' he said sharply.

My sister shook her head. 'Still refuses to admit there's any such thing.'

Mons put down the file and folded his arms. Again, the dazzling smile flitted across his saturnine features, but this time the scarred lip curled up, exposing the full length of his dog tooth.

'You're not being very bright,' he said directly to the Mother Superior in his light Yankee accent. 'As I've explained, I'll do whatever it takes to get hold of the Lamb. My fellows downstairs will start shooting the first of your order in . . . oh . . . about thirty minutes. So, as the gangsters say in the flickers, "Start talking, sister."'

He giggled at his own witticism and it had the uncomfortably shrill ring of a child's laugh.

The Mother Superior's face was ashen but she raised her chin with dignity. 'I've nothing to say to you. I can only repeat that here at the convent we have little or no interaction with the outside world. Why you think that—'

Mons's hand lashed out with terrible suddenness, catching the poor old girl across the face. His signet ring must have torn her skin because a little teardrop of blood rolled like sap down her withered cheek.

'You're trying to make a monkey out of me,' he said in a low, threatening tone. 'It's awful inadvisable.'

He began pacing the room, arms folded, his chin sunk onto his breast. It put me in mind at once of that strutting popinjay Mussolini and I had a sudden vivid impression of Mons studying hours of newsreel footage in an effort to emulate the Duce.

'We happen to know that the Lamb was bred here,' he went on. 'Was sent out from here. It's a secret your order has been guarding for years.'

'Nonsense!'

Mons swung round to face the nun again, his eyes flashing like beacons. Then his heavy lids closed and he was all sweetness again.

'I'm a reasonable fellow,' he purred. 'I don't expect a Christian lady such as yourself to betray her vows just like *that*.' He snapped his fingers. 'But think of the alternative. All those poor girls downstairs.

They've not done anyone any harm. They're good, studious, pious kids.' As if a switch had been flipped, his face hardened and his voice took on a lethal seriousness. 'And they're all going to die,' he hissed. 'Unless you tell me what I want to know.'

The Mother Superior bowed her head, tears welling in her red-rimmed eyes. Mons approached her and raised her chin. 'Now. Where is she?'

I frowned. What had he said? Where is *she*?

The nun slowly shook her head. 'God forgive me,' she murmured. 'But I must serve a greater good. I will not tell you. I will not!'

Mons's face twisted with rage and his hands flew to the nun's neck. She managed one rasp of shock as his fingers sank into the wrinkled flesh, then only a horrid squawking was audible as she struggled desperately for air.

The American's dark rage grew upon him like a storm, his face growing almost as black as his victim's, oiled hair bouncing forwards into eyes that bulged like pickles.

'You fool!' he hissed. 'You stupid pious fool!'

'*Olympus!*' cried Pandora shrilly.

Still Mons throttled the unfortunate nun, his fingers almost meeting as he grasped at her neck.

'*Olympus, please!*' Pandora raced across the room and tried to prise Mons's hands away. She pawed at him ineffectually and actually hung off his arm but he showed no signs of giving way, standing stock-still like an electrocuted man.

I was about to smash through the window and come to the nun's rescue when my sister saved me the bother, shrieking: 'She's all we've got!'

At this, Mons seemed to come to his senses. He suddenly threw up his hands and stepped back, breathing raggedly.

The Mother Superior slumped forward, gasping for breath, her black-garbed chest heaving, livid red weals already showing up on her throat.

Mons smoothed back his hair, twisting his neck in his tight collar and adjusting his tie. 'You're right. We need this one.'

Then he swivelled sharply round on his heel, his face right by Pandora's, spit flecking his scarred lip. 'But don't ever touch me like that again, do you hear me? *Ever.*'

Pandora positively wilted before his words, her hair falling forwards like curtains over her face.

Mons swung back and addressed the recovering nun. 'I warned you', he said, producing a slim, long-barrelled foreign pistol from inside his jacket. 'I shall shoot the first of your order myself. And you will watch me.'

With that he hauled the unfortunate creature to her feet and began to drag her from the room. She dissolved into bitter tears, her whole frame shrinking, hands wrenching uselessly at the coil of rope that bound her.

Pandora gave the old nun a push in the small of the back, as though blaming her for Mons's response, and then the three of them disappeared into the corridor, slamming the door behind them.

I wasted no more time. Taking the silk 'handkerchief' from my money belt, I wrapped it around my fist and, with a precise punch, knocked out two panes of the diamond-shaped glass, then reached inside to unhook the latch. In seconds I was through and skittering across the stone floor.

The door hadn't been locked and I crept out into a narrow corridor, down which a tomb-cold draught was creeping. Happily there was no guard awaiting me and I was able to move swiftly, keeping close to the scarcely lit walls, until I reached a sort of minstrels' gallery that projected out over a large central hall.

Under a beamed ceiling there was a festive glow of candle sconces: beneath that, a sea of black-and-white-garbed figures. Forty or so nuns had been rounded up into a square formation before a massive fire-blackened stone hearth, penned in like sheep with amber-shirt guards at each corner. Each guard carried a Tommy gun.

There was an air of scarcely suppressed hysteria, although some of the older nuns retained a serene calm, as though above the threat of imminent extinction.

Mons was pacing up and down in front of them, waving his pistol, grinning crazily and seemingly feeding off their distress. Pandora stood to one side, twisting a lock of her hair, a childish gesture I knew very well. She was anxious.

At last, Mons raised the gun and fired into the air. It echoed with a terrific report and splinters tumbled down from the beams.

'Listen to me!'

There was silence, save for the odd whimper of distress. Or the odd wimple, I suppose.

Mons smoothed back his boot-polish-black hair. 'Your illustrious *superior* refuses to tell me what I need to know. So, I shall kill one of you in –' he glanced at his wristwatch – 'two minutes. Unless—'

There was a fresh outbreak of terror amongst the nuns and Mons raised his voice to compensate. Its already high timbre reached a hysterical pitch, the veins on his neck standing out like whipcords. 'UNLESS,' he yelled, 'one of you can help me!'

The Mother Superior, partially recovered from her near throttling, moved swiftly towards Mons, floating like a ghost over the flagstones. 'You silly little man!' she croaked. 'You really think your brutal tactics will—'

Mons blinked, staring down his nose at the woman as though she were an insect who'd suddenly acquired voice. A shot rang out and the nun standing closest to the Mother Superior simply crumpled into her robes as though she'd fallen through a trapdoor.

The still-smoking gun in his outstretched hand, Mons spat on the body. 'You were saying?' he screeched.

The Mother Superior blanched, her hand flying to her mouth.

I looked down grimly from my hiding place. What the deuce could I do? There were too many of them for me to mount any sort of attack. Any advantage I had would be instantly forfeited.

The nuns were positively screaming now and Mons revelled in the sight, darting in amongst them like a fox among sheep, giggling nastily as they veered out of his path, several tripping over their long robes and falling heavily to the flagstones.

'That one,' he yelled, pointing to the dead woman, 'doesn't count. So. Who's going to be next?'

To my horror, the gun spoke again and another nun was sent splaying to the floor.

'Stop this!' screamed the Mother Superior. 'Oh please! Stop this I beg you!'

Suddenly I felt a sharp pain in the ribs and swung round to find a broken-nosed amber-shirt thug jabbing his Tommy gun at me.

'Sir!' he cried and Mons looked up, his face glowing with blood-lust.

Heaving a heavy sigh, I was soon padding down stone steps and across the floor towards the fireplace, hands above my head.

Pandora ceased her hair-twiddling and gasped.

'I say, sis,' I said cheerily, 'I'm not up on the old-time religion and all that but isn't nun-murdering a little. . .beyond the pale?'

Pandora groaned, as though we were children again and I'd kicked over her snowman. 'Olympus, I'm so sorry. I don't know what he's doing here.'

Mons broke into a slightly hysterical laugh. 'But I do, my dear. I do. Would you care to enlighten us, Mr Box?'

I gave a casual shrug. 'I'm on a brass-rubbing holiday, would you believe?'

Mons's face fell. 'I wouldn't.'

'Didn't think so.'

Pandora strode towards me, hands on hips. 'What is this madness? Why the hell have you followed us?'

'I didn't exactly follow *you*, my dear.'

Mons folded his arms and planted a booted foot on the back of one of the dead nuns, like a great white hunter posing for a picture with a recumbent tigress.

'I'm afraid you must prepare yourself for a shock, Pandora,' he oiled. 'You see, my sources have been telling me some interesting things about your dear brother. He isn't quite the gentleman he appears.'

'Oh, I've always known that,' said Pandora with a sour look.

Mons was relishing every moment. 'Whilst presenting the world with the image of a successful artist – well, a *once*-successful artist—'

'That was low,' I said.

' – and fixture of the London demi-monde, your sibling has been, for many years, an employee of His Majesty's Government.'

'A civil servant?' said Pandora, thickly.

Mons shook his head. 'A most uncivil one, I fear. He's an assassin, aren't you, Mr Box?'

'Don't be ridiculous!' chuckled Pandora.

Mons flashed her a dangerous look. 'Be careful what you call me, my dear.'

Pandora flushed anxiously. 'I'm . . . I'm sorry, Olympus. But I simply can't credit it. My brother a . . . a hired killer?'

The Mother Superior was sobbing now and I moved towards her, only to find the Tommy gun rammed sharply in my side. Mons scowled at the old woman. 'Shut up,' he spat.

I plunged my hands into the pockets of my moleskin trousers. 'Your boyfriend does me a disservice, Pan. I do the lot. Sleuthing, derring-do. The assassinating's just part of it.'

Mons clapped his hands together. 'Oh! So your other profession is as workmanlike as your painting. How neat.'

'Now you're just being nasty.'

Still the Mother Superior sobbed, burying her face in her hands. Mons's eyes grew large again, glistening with fury.

'I'm afraid I can't help myself,' he said, between gritted teeth. 'Pandora here will testify to it. I'm a very nasty fellow.'

So saying, he suddenly loosed off a shot and the Mother Superior fell with a sharp cry of surprise, her robes suddenly splashed with scarlet.

As one, the other nuns let out a groan of distress.

'Look here, Mons,' I yelled, 'there's no need for this slaughter!'

'Oh, don't bleat, Mr Box,' he said sourly. 'I'd hate to think that anyone called *Lucifer* could be so feeble.'

Alone and helpless, the poor Mother Superior lay gasping her last on the cold stone floor. She managed to mutter some prayer and then, with a gentle sigh, passed away, a great pool of dark blood expanding like the tide beneath her.

'That was stupid,' I shrugged. 'Now how're you going to find out what you want to know?'

Mons watched the white smoke curling from the end of his pistol, fascinated. 'I have my methods,' he muttered at last. A cracked smile lit up his features, his dog tooth protruding like a glittering fang. 'Yes! After all, why not? I have access to these powers. Why not use them?'

He gestured impatiently to two of his armed thugs and pointed at the corpse of the Mother Superior. 'Pick her up.'

The amber-shirts obliged, dragging the dead woman from the flagged floor and dropping her onto a chair with brutal casualness. Then, stripping the wimple from around her head, Mons pushed back the body so that it sat up straight. The old woman's shorn white hair almost glowed in the crypt-like atmosphere.

Mons stood for a moment, his face raised to the ceiling, swaying slightly on his feet like a dancer picking up a rhythm. He began to mumble in a low, guttural tone. It was impossible to make out his words, but every now and then he would pause, listening, and make some curious sign or other, turning through all points of the compass and raising first his left then his right hand. He crooked his middle fingers so that they dug into his palm, leaving little white half-moon impressions in the flesh.

Then, in one quick movement, he jerked his body round, leant directly over the dead Mother Superior, and pressed his fingers to her temples. The intonation bubbling in his throat grew even deeper and more sonorous.

The effect on all concerned was utterly mesmeric. I, the captured sisters and even the guards had become spellbound. Pandora stared at her leader, twisting her hair with almost feverish eagerness.

Then the atmosphere in the room suddenly changed. The temperature plummeted and I glanced nervously over my shoulder, quite convinced that we were being watched by some new presence. The place was so wreathed in shadow that one might imagine all kinds of terrors lurking there but we could all see that the air was thickening queerly. I found that I was shivering inside my thick coat and sweater.

A kind of miasma began to form on the stone floor of the chamber as though mist were creeping in from the grey sea beyond, and I again had that weird sensation that time had somehow stopped.

At first, I couldn't see what had happened. But then one of the nuns screamed and backed away, revealing the impossible sight of the dead Mother Superior sitting bolt upright, her face tipped up as if staring at the ceiling, her eyes perfectly white and opaque.

And then she spoke.

'*Who has summoned me?*'

The voice was dreadful, low, cracked, flat.

Mons strutted before the woman, his features contorted with hellish triumph. 'I! Olympus Mons! In the name of Asrael, Baralamensis and the Chief Princes of the throne of Apologia! I command you to answer me.'

The late nun twisted in her chair, her chalk-white face screwing up as though in distress. Then some higher authority seemed to overwhelm her and she sagged once more into a waxy death mask. '*As I am commanded, so must I speak.*'

Mons thrust his face towards hers. 'Then tell me! Where is the Lamb?'

A playful half-smile crept onto the nun's face, the weird force within her taking command. '*You parley with dark forces to find the Lamb of God?*'

The corpse's words nudged a fragment of memory somewhere in my overheated brain. The Lamb of God?

'You know why she is important!' thundered Mons. 'I seek to do the Devil's bidding. I command you to aid me!'

The nun's head fell back, a terrible, gargling moan erupting from her throat and she spoke for a moment in her old, gentle tones. 'I cannot tell! I must not tell!'

Mons pointed his bony finger at her. 'I command you! By Him who spoke and it was done! By the most Holy and Glorious names Adonai, El Elohim, Elohe, Zabaoth . . .'

'No . . .'

'Elion, Escherche, Jar and Tetragrammaton . . .'

'*No!*'

Mons wrenched the dead woman by the throat and shook her. 'Tell me! Tell me! I command you!'

Suddenly, as though all resistance had been overcome, the woman went limp in his grip and a torrent of words began to tumble from her slack, dribbling mouth. Mons dashed to her side so as to hear.

'*Bred here. Bred here but sent far away,*' murmured the un-dead nun. '*Far away. She travels by sea. But now she's landlocked again. Haha! They sought to hide her from the likes of you. She is dangerous. A gentle, gentle girl. But so dangerous to the world! To us all! Agnus Dei, qui tollis peccata mundi, miserere nobis! The Lamb. The Lamb of God.*'

I felt cold all over.

An image of the beautiful cabin girl suddenly swam into my mind. Aggie!

Not short for Agatha but Agnes. Agnes Daye!

Agnus Dei: the Lamb of God!

16

Further Adventures Of A
Fallen Angel

I stood in wretched impotence, frozen by the terrible knowledge I possessed. All the attention I'd squandered on that ruddy 'handkerchief'thinking *that* was the elusive Lamb! And it was sweet Aggie they'd been after the whole time!

What part could she possibly play in Mons's nefarious schemes? My mind raced as the garrulous corpse cheerfully spilled the beans.

'Where is she now?' demanded Mons, his hands dancing about the nun's throat as though he were tempted to have at her again. 'Where?'

'Where the blue lamp glows and the red church looms. And only a friend stands watch over her.'

'Where is she, damn you!' screamed Mons.

'Ask him who is fallen,' smiled the dead Mother Superior. For one last time, her face assumed a look of serenity, then distorted again as though in torment. 'God forgive me!' she shrieked, then slumped to the floor, her dead face smacking on the flagstones. The séance was over.

'Why do they always do that?' raged Mons. 'I hate it when they

do that! They talk in damned riddles and I'm left none the—'

'Him who is fallen,' murmured Pandora.

Well, I knew what that meant, all right. Curiously, though, no one seemed to be taking the hint. But what of the blue lamp and the red church? And a friend standing watch?'

Pandora's face creased into a puzzled frown, like a schoolgirl sucking thoughtfully on the end of a pencil. 'Him who is fallen . . . him who is fallen.'

Mons seemed stumped. He gave the Mother Superior's body a swift kick in frustration.

I was finding this difficult to credit. Didn't Mons's mob know their Bible? Particularly the bit about the battle between God and the most comely of his angels? And who had got his comeuppance at the hands of the Almighty?

'Someone who's had a nasty fall recently?' mused Pandora. She snapped her fingers. 'You jumped off that pier, Olympus! Would that count?'

'Unlikely,' mused Mons. 'I'm the one asking the question.' He cracked his knuckles and frowned. 'Perhaps that nun I shot first. She could be said to have fallen—'

'IT'S ME!' I yelled, unable to bear their lack of erudition a moment more. 'For Christ's sake, what did you *do* at school, Pandora?'

My sister swung round. 'You, Lucy?'

Mons brightened up at once. 'Of course! The fallen angel! Lucifer!'

'*Yes*,' I said patiently. 'Really, you're not being awfully bright.'

Mons fixed me with his arc-light stare. 'You know her, then? You know this woman, this Lamb of God?'

I whistled nonchalantly. 'Perhaps. Say I do know her . . . what do you want her for?'

'That doesn't concern a bungling amateur like you!' Mons positively spat. 'Just tell me where she is!'

I folded my arms. 'Or what? I suppose you could shoot me and

then try that trick with the hypnosis or whatever but I rather get the feeling it's not something one can just do at the drop of a hat. You do look a mite peaky, if I might say so.'

Mons's hand flew unconsciously to his face. The séance did indeed seem to have taken a great toll on him. His skin had assumed a greyish pallor and his eyes were heavily bloodshot.

He marched right up to me, mouth curling into a snarl. I could smell the tobacco on his breath. 'You'll tell me, Box, or by God—'

'By God?' I queried. 'I rather thought He was out of the picture.'

Mons's reddened eyes bulged beneath his heavy lids and I could see he was building to another of his rages. Thankfully Pandora stepped in.

'Can't do any harm, Olympus,' she drawled, inhaling deeply on a black cheroot. 'After all, he's not leaving any time soon, is he?'

Mons held my stare. 'He's not leaving here at all.'

I gave Pandora my sweetest smile. 'How does the old saying go? One can choose one's friends . . .'

'Don't you dare bring family into this!' she hissed. 'There's nothing left between us! Nothing! What kindness or family loyalty have you ever shown me? You selfish, arrogant whoremonger! For the sake of the Tribune I would cut you down without a second thought.'

She dashed her cheroot to the flagstones and stubbed it into oblivion. A flurry of ash, picked up by the draught, whispered away into the shadows.

I shrugged. 'Well, at least I know where I stand. You were about to outline this great plan of yours.'

Mons clasped his hands behind his back and began his Eyetie strut again. 'Oh, it's nothing much really. I merely wish to summon the Devil himself and use his power to perpetuate my own.'

'Oh, *that* old plan,' I mused, stifling a yawn. 'Well, best of luck, old darling. Where does the girl come into all this?'

'So you do know her!' cried Pandora triumphantly.

I held out my hands, palm upwards, ceding their point.

Mons stroked his waxed moustache. 'There is an invocation. An ancient, ancient thing. It's called the Jerusalem Prayer and it's mentioned in heathen writings and diabolistic tracts going back as far as you can imagine. It shows how not just some minor demon but the Dark One himself, the Goat of Mendez, may be summoned back to hold sway over his earthly kingdom.'

'Rot,' I said simply.

Mons seemed rather pleased by my scepticism. 'Many have doubted as you do, Mr Box, only to find their cherished and simplistic view of the world turned upon its head. But let us return to the Prayer. It describes how, if a chosen one is sacrificed to Satan, he will be released from the supernatural bonds with which he is restrained. That sacrifice is a Perfect Victim, a woman with holy blood running through her veins, descended from an unbroken line of such anointed ones—'

'I've heard of such a legend!' I gasped. 'A child descended from a union between Christ and Mary Magdalene!'

'Don't be so fucking stupid,' snorted Mons. 'There's *hundreds* of those! No, this one is *really* special. In a designated place, at a designated hour, she must become his Bride. It has taken me a long time but finally I tracked her down. To the Convent of St Bede.'

I thought of what Captain Corpusty had said. Aggie had been brought up by the sisters but then placed in his care. But why? Then Sal Volatile's words came back to me. He'd found the Lamb, he said. Hidden under Mons's very nose. The sisters must have seen that Mons was getting close and so secreted the precious girl on the *Stiffkey* as a crew member, never realizing that the ship was already bound up in Mons's drug-smuggling schemes. She'd been hidden in plain sight, indeed.

'Doesn't do you much good without this Jerusalem whatsit of yours, though. Or have your clever boys found that as well?'

Mons nodded excitedly and let out another of his childish

giggles. 'I've spent several fortunes in the hunt but I finally traced it to some filthy little fence back in the good old U.S. of A.'

Hubbard the Cupboard, of course. Pennies, as you can imagine, were now dropping all over the shop. 'But he got greedy, yes?' I speculated. 'Removed part of the Prayer in order to hold out for more money?'

Mons's face darkened. 'To find myself held to ransom by scum like that! After all those years of fruitless searching.'

I grunted unhappily. So Mons had managed to infiltrate the RA and had used his acolyte, the odious Percy Flarge, to rub the fellow out. But Flarge hadn't found the square of silk, the 'handkerchief' that obviously contained some vital missing part of the ritual! The part dealing with the sacrifice of the Lamb of God!

My hand stole to my trouser pocket where the wretched thing now nestled. 'So now you're going to kill this girl – stab her with an ornamental dagger on a stone altar or some such tosh, I'll wager – just to fuel your insane fantasies about black magic?'

Mons seemed surprised. 'You've seen what I can do!' he cried. 'I made the dead speak! I am as one with Banebdjed!'

I glanced down at the motionless form of the Mother Superior. 'A conjuring trick. Some form of deep hypnosis. I wouldn't be at all surprised if she were simply in a deep sleep.'

'She's dead!' he yelled.

'I doubt it.'

'She *is*!' he squealed, like a petulant child, reaching down and grabbing the Mother Superior by the arms.

Suddenly, she let out a dreadful groan. Whether it was the last residue of air in her leathery old lungs or the vestiges of the demonic possession I cannot tell, but Mons stepped back, startled, and the assembled nuns set up a terrible caterwauling. It was all the distraction I needed.

Swinging round, I socked the amber-shirt guard on the jaw and grabbed his Tommy gun, immediately turning it on Mons.

His hands flew up and I yanked him towards me by the lapels of his expensive suit. The other guards rushed forward.

'Not one more step,' I yelled, 'or I'll spray his brains all over the stonework! You understand?'

'Get back!' hissed Mons. 'Get back, you cretins! He means it!'

Pulling Mons to me and wrapping my arm around his neck, I jerked him backwards so he let out a little squawk. Then, pressing the gun to his temple, I looked wildly about for an exit.

Despite the shadows, I could see a huge iron-banded wooden door in the wall behind me and I shuffled slowly towards it, Mons's boots dragging over the flagstones.

'Don't be an idiot, Lucifer!' sneered Pandora. 'You know you haven't a chance. Give up now and we'll be merciful.'

'The quality of your mercy, dear sis, is somewhat strained, I fear,' I cried, eyeing the doorway. 'You!' I jerked my head towards one of the guards. 'Get the door open.'

The pale-faced thug looked to his master, who said nothing. I jabbed the gun into Mons's face to encourage him and he nodded hastily. The guard unlocked the great door and it swung open with a dreadful, protesting shriek of rusted hinges. The outside showed as an arched black silhouette. Freezing air poured inside and over us.

'I could kill you now,' I hissed in Mons's ear. 'Bring this whole thing to an end.'

He swivelled his dark eyes towards me. 'Then why don't you?'

That was obvious. If I cut down Mons, his followers would have no compunction in taking me down with him. He was my guarantee out of there.

Mons laughed mirthlessly. 'And where do you think you're going? We're on an island, Mr Box. There's no hiding place.'

It was true. I hadn't thought much past getting out of the convent in one piece. I glanced feverishly around the chamber. Each of the guards was poised to spring should I put a foot wrong.

I renewed my grip on Mons's throat and hauled him backwards through the doorway and out into the night.

It was good to breathe clean, fresh air after the horrible frowst within. I glanced at the black water lapping close by, whipped up by the breeze.

Right by us was the lorry, and next to it the sleek silver motor that must be Mons's car. The man I was semi-throttling seemed to read my mind and giggled his little boy's giggle. 'High tide, my friend. No one's driving out of here for a while yet.'

I cursed his smug face. The amber-shirts and Pandora had formed a semi-circle just outside the convent doorway.

'Stay back!' I yelled, then aimed the Tommy gun and a spray of bullets ate up the shingle on the threshold.

In answer, a bullet whistled past my cheek – so close I could feel its scorching heat – and I saw that Pandora had let fly with a pistol.

'Don't try that again or I swear I'll cut you down!' I bellowed.

A wonky smile lit up my sister's features and I saw that she was about to take aim, calling my bluff. 'You won't shoot me and you won't shoot him,' she called, calm as a snake.

'Pandora!' hissed Mons. 'Don't risk it.'

'It's no risk,' she said, coolly cocking the gun. 'My brother's a coward. Always has been.'

I chanced a look behind me at the short distance to the sea. The swim back to the mainland seemed to be my only option. My mind was made up, quite suddenly, as Pandora let fly with a couple more shots. I dived to one side, taking Mons with me, then sprayed the whole of the facade of the convent with sub-machine-gun fire. The night lit up like a fireworks display as the bullets sang off the stones.

Mons let out a kind of croak of fear as I dragged him into the shadows. An amber-shirt came pelting towards us and I loosed off a round, smashing his jaw. A spray of blood showed up, black as ink, against the light pouring through the open doorway. The poor

fool crashed to the shingle but Mons took advantage of the distraction to twist round and ram his head into my solar plexus. I crumpled backwards, all the air knocked from me, and strained weakly to pull the trigger of the Tommy gun.

Mons scrabbled to his feet, shingle jumping everywhere, and yelled for assistance. I lashed out at his shin and he fell heavily on top of me. I managed a couple of sharp jabs to his face but he was strong and fought back, wrestling with the icy steel of the weapon in my hands. Still winded, I could scarcely retaliate and I felt my grip slackening on the machine-gun. I was done for unless I could pull one last trick. Mons was dragging so desperately at the gun that when I suddenly let go, he toppled over with a cry of surprise.

In the instant before he got up and trained the weapon on me, I scrambled frantically into my pocket and pulled out the silk handkerchief.

Mons loomed over me, outlined against the starlight. 'You'll pay for this little display, my friend,' he raged, spraying my face with his spittle. 'You'll pay right now!'

'Wait, wait, wait!' I gasped, catching my breath at last. 'Recognize this?'

I lifted the square of silk and felt it flapping over my sweat-drenched face. Mons sat back, reached into his suit and flicked open a cigarette lighter. In the long, narrow yellow flame I saw his pitiless eyes widen.

'The missing piece!' he croaked. 'The Jerusalem Prayer!'

With a great cry, I grasped hold of his wrist and pulled it back so that the flame caught him on the cheek. He shrieked with pain and dropped the lighter. I lashed out desperately with my boot, kicked him in the gut, threw off my coat, rammed the silk into my trouser pocket and, without another thought, hurled myself into the icy water.

The waves closed over my head, there was a sharp, piercing pain in my ears and the world vanished into confusion.

I swam downwards with frantic energy, dimly aware of bullets sizzling through the dark water. Weighed down by my heavy clothes, it was a titanic struggle simply not to drown then and there, but I kicked and thrashed at the current, trying desperately to put some distance between myself and the island.

At last, lungs afire, I propelled myself upwards towards the air and emerged, gasping for breath, still perilously close to my tormentors. Amidst the splashing came the sound of yelled orders and a fresh spurt of bullets bit the water. Mons screamed at his men to cease firing. My gamble had paid off. He couldn't risk me dying and taking the fragment of his precious Prayer to the bottom. With the unpredictable current, my body might never be found.

I'd bought myself some time, at least until they managed to launch a boat and come after me. I trod water for a few moments, then began to flog my way through the sea with a steady rhythm. How far was land? It had taken me ten minutes to walk swiftly across the barely exposed causeway. Could I possibly manage to crawl all that way in this bitter weather?

The water slapped and churned about me and I could already feel numbness tingling in my feet and hands. Suddenly I stopped swimming and, chest heaving, trod water again as I became aware of the soft plashing of oars close by. Surely they couldn't be on to me already!

Looking about desperately for the source of the sound, I realized that it came not from the island but from the darkness ahead. And as I paddled, legs heavy as lead, a wonderful sight hove into view. It was a rowing boat and at the oars was a familiar crook-backed personage.

'Didn't I say you'd get yourself into trouble, mate?' said Mrs Croup, reaching out a withered hand for me to grasp. 'Drown me in the bath and claim on me life insurance if I didn't say so!'

I swam with new vigour towards the boat, grinning madly and hauling myself aboard to sprawl like a landed fish onto the

weathered planks. They were wonderfully dry and comforting as my cheek pressed against them.

At once, though, the illusion of security was shattered by the roar of an outboard motor. I craned my neck and spotted a sleek wooden shape racing across the waves towards us. Mons had a speedboat on our trail!

17

In Pursuit Of The Lamb

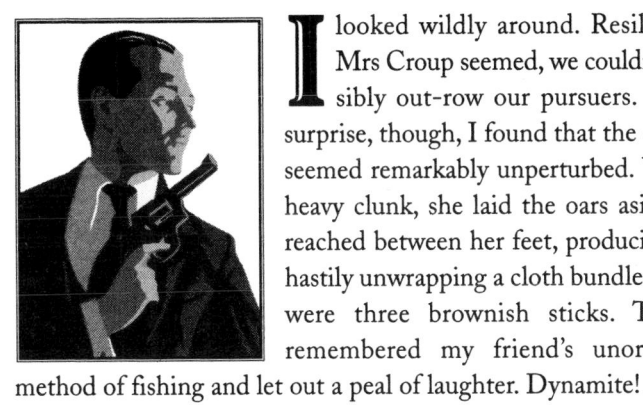

I looked wildly around. Resilient as Mrs Croup seemed, we couldn't possibly out-row our pursuers. To my surprise, though, I found that the old girl seemed remarkably unperturbed. With a heavy clunk, she laid the oars aside and reached between her feet, producing and hastily unwrapping a cloth bundle. Inside were three brownish sticks. Then I remembered my friend's unorthodox method of fishing and let out a peal of laughter. Dynamite!

Mrs Croup's boat began to rock precariously as it was hit by waves from the approaching motor-craft. Calmly, the old woman pulled a quiver of matches from her skirts, lit one on a serrated silver fob at her waist, applied it to the fuse of the first stick and hurled it into the darkness. It span end over end, fizzing like a roman candle and leaving a spiralling pattern on my retina.

I was conscious of the roar of the motor, the lapping of the water and of my own urgent breathing, then the night split apart in searing white flame.

The dynamite had detonated above the sea, and by its sunburst of

light we were able to see our pursuers taking desperate evasive manoeuvres.

'I have me target in sight now!' cackled Mrs Croup, lighting the second stick and hurling it towards Mons and his men. There was a desperate scrambling on board the speedboat and the hollering of frightened souls as the dynamite came cartwheeling towards them. There was an immensely satisfying *whoomph!* and the black water erupted, spraying us with foam.

I grabbed at the oars to make for the shore, peered through the smoke to assess the damage to our hunters and let out a spontaneous cheer. The front of the boat was gone, smoke hanging over it like mist, the sea a mass of splintered wood. Coughing amber-shirts were already in the drink, treading water and scrabbling towards the wrecked boat for safety. I couldn't see if Mons was among them but we had bested the swine and I pulled at the oars with a new impetus.

Mrs Croup let out an asthmatic chuckle. 'That should do it. Laws of maritime combat and all.'

I reached down for the last stick of dynamite. 'Bugger that!' I cried. 'Let's finish 'em off!'

With great delight, the old bird lit the fuse and chucked it with main force at the ruined speed-boat. An anguished screech arose from the survivors as it approached but this time the explosive went off early, merely detonating in midair and doing little more than temporarily deafening us both.

My saviour took the oars again as I shrugged a filthy horse-blanket onto my shoulders, willing the elusive shore to come closer.

'I sat there and thought long and hard,' Mrs Croup chuntered, wheezing at each stroke of the oars. 'That young fellow needs me, I thought. Strangle me with a silk stocking and stuff me under the floorboards, he *needs* me and there's an end to it. So I put out my old boat and I come looking for you.'

'You are, quite simply, a life-saver,' I beamed. 'How can I ever thank you?'

She turned a twinkling eye on me and my heart sank. Oh, Lord. I'd forgotten about *that*.

It wasn't long before the old boat bumped into the shingle and I staggered onto terra firma, my exhausted legs quaking like a newborn pup's.

Gripping the blanket tightly about me, I shuddered with cold. 'And now I must be off, my dear,' I chattered. 'I'll make good use of the head start you've given me—'

'But you can't!'

I looked at her with all the earnestness I could muster. 'You know how I long to enfold you in my arms, my sweet. But there isn't a moment to lose!'

She nodded unhappily, seeing the truth of it. 'But you must dry off at least! Some hot tea, eh? And then a steaming pot of my famous porridge! That'll put the bloom back in your—'

'No time,' I protested.

'But you'll catch your death!'

I smiled grimly. 'Save the hangman a job.' Then I glanced down at myself, a shivering ruin, and realized she was talking perfect sense. I'd simply freeze to death out on the open roads in my soaked togs. 'Very well. But I can't linger.'

We crunched swiftly over the shingle towards the rough little cabin. On the higher ground above it was parked a large and rather distressed old motor car, engine ticking over, the beams of its headlights piercing the dark like beacons. Suspicious, I slowed my pace but Mrs Croup merely took my arm and steered me on. 'Midnight fishermen,' she whispered. 'They'll pay us no heed.' As we approached, the door of the motor opened and two bulky silhouetted figures clambered out, rods over their shoulders.

Mrs Croup pushed open the door of her lovely little hovel and I rushed inside to warm myself before the blazing fire.

'Here you are, my pet,' cooed the old woman, handing me a rough towel. I stripped at once, without a blush, though I was

conscious of the old girl's eye upon my frankly smashing physique.

Mrs Croup was everywhere at once, brewing tea and rustling up hot porridge whilst simultaneously rooting out a variety of fresh duds for me. I'd been right about the amount of male attire on the premises, though, judging by their age, it was safe to assume she hadn't been 'entertaining' for some years.

Eventually, I found myself in a flannel shirt, plimsolls and a rather nasty late-Victorian tweed suit. But beggars can't be choosers.

I smoothed down the musty-smelling material. 'How do I look?'

Mrs Croup twinkled and looked down shyly. 'Very handsome. I could hide you here, you know. They'd never find you.'

'It's a very tempting offer, but—'

She hushed me, placing a gnarled finger to my lips. 'Tuppence for a bloater, that's all, remember? God speed, now.'

I stooped to kiss her on the cheek but the old minx swivelled round so quickly that I caught her a smacker on her cracked and flaky lips. Then I felt her tongue worm its way around my mouth like a bobbing apple! A little shiver of disgust rippled through me. Well, I *was* grateful, of course, but gratitude has its limits.

Mrs Croup seemed to mistake my revulsion for emotion and turned me towards the door, wiping a tear from her rheumy eye.

I closed the Portuguese cabin door behind me, breathed deeply of the freezing night air and took to my heels. It was perhaps the narrowest escape of my career.

Close by I could make out the silhouetted shapes of those oh-so-keen fishermen as they tramped towards the sea. A sudden inspiration seized me. As quietly I could, I raced across the pebbles, crouched down behind their stately old motor and reached out for the door handle. The metal was freezing to the touch. I clunked it downwards and was thrilled to feel the door swing slowly open.

I slipped inside, conscious at once of the reek of fish and old leather, and felt about the dashboard, praying that the keys had

been left in. My fingers found the blessed little piece of metal and I twisted it clockwise.

The engine whirred, turned over and died. At once, I tried again. The headlamps flared into life and I cursed my own stupidity at not deactivating them. There were angry voices coming from the beach and the crunch of feet on the shingle. Still the engine refused to start. I tried once more and, with a bucking, wheezing splutter, the ancient thing roared into life.

In the blaze of the lamps I could see two elderly men, swathed in tweeds, stomping towards me. Abandoning all attempts at concealment, I threw the car into reverse and the still-open door caught one of the poor saps across the legs as he launched himself at the side. The motor chugged backwards, sending a spray of stones into the air. I span the wheel, crunched the squealing gears, slammed my plimsolled foot onto the pedal and roared off.

The beach gave way to a rough road almost at once and the motor bucked as it hit the smoother surface. Peeking into the mirror I saw the unfortunate owners rapidly disappearing behind me.

Gripping the cold Bakelite of the steering wheel, I threw back my head and laughed. By God, I'd see that blessed old woman right when all this was over! Well, I might send her a postal order, at any rate.

Swinging the car from the beach road onto glorious tarmacadam, I found myself tearing through a little village, suggestions of lobster pots and upturned boats all that were readily visible in the white cones of the headlamps. In minutes I was through it and dipping down a steep hill, then up again and onto the first of many twisting country roads. Windmills and pubs flashed by, lying under a countryside hush.

Mons, I knew, would waste little time in procuring transport and would be after me post haste. The question now was, what to do with my head start? Thanks to Captain Corpusty, the British police were already aware of my return. I could head for London,

where I was at least assured of help from old friends but the vital thing to me seemed the rescue of Agnes Daye. The nun had spoken of a blue lamp and a red church. It seemed safe to assume the former referred to a police station and the odds were on that my poor wounded Aggie was being held locally, charged with aiding and abetting a wanted felon. I hadn't the faintest idea where this station might be but vaguely planned to find the nearest and bluff my way into discovering the girl's whereabouts. After that, it was simply a question of getting her as far away as possible from these fanatics. In this regard I was definitely ahead. Mons and Pandora knew that *a* girl, originating in the Convent of St Bede, was the Lamb they sought but only I – so far – knew her identity.

I motored at high speed through half a dozen tiny outcrops of houses that hugged the coastline, scarcely passing a single other motor. Just when it looked like I would never hit anything remotely like civilization, another steep dip brought me out into a larger conurbation, dominated by a big ugly church and a rambling inn ablaze with electric light. In the glow from the windows, I could see that the church was clearly built of weathered red sandstone. I could hardly believe my luck.

Slowing down as I drove down the main street, I craned round to look about and gave a grunt of satisfaction at the comforting sight of a blue lamp outside a large, modern-looking police station. So here was the red church and the blue lamp. I glanced at my wristwatch. It was a little after six in the morning.

Parking the car by the edge of the village green, I crept out into the bitter night. There wasn't much of a plan in my exhausted brain. I was conscious that I must look like an escaped lunatic and my description – probably even my photograph – had been circulated to every cop-shop in the land. But the Mother Superior had said Agnes was being watched over by a friend and from this I took comfort. As an innocent man, the police could be said to be my true

helpers against the forces of darkness. Nevertheless, I was placing a deal of trust in the dead woman's riddle. Daniel was truly entering the Lions' Den.

I mounted the steps to the station, the facade stained blue by the lamplight as though I was standing in a cathedral transept. Pushing at the frosted-glass door, I was surprised to find it unlocked. But then they were ever so trusting out there in the sticks, I assured myself.

Moving swiftly inside, all seemed absolutely dark but, as my eyes adjusted, I found I could make out the shape of the main desk and a couple of chairs. A door to the side of the desk was ajar. As I'd hoped, barred cells, lit only by starlight, were visible beyond. If the Mother Superior – or whatever possessed her – had been speaking the truth then poor Aggie was inside. And, if my luck held, the foolish local bobbies had left her unguarded!

'Aggie!' I whispered.

No reply. Probably sound asleep, poor thing.

'*Agnes!*'

There came the sound of stirring, the creak of a stool perhaps, and the folding back of blankets.

Then there was movement in the darkness and a flashlight in my eyes. I squinted and held up my hand to shield my eyes.

But it wasn't Aggie who spoke. It was a man's voice, oozing malice. 'Oh, happy day. I knew you'd come.'

The newcomer held the torch under his chin. His nose was almost completely obscured by sticking plaster and both his eyes were black and bruised. It was only the shock of blond hair sticking out like damp straw from beneath the brim of his trilby that told me Percy Flarge was back on the scent.

Even beneath the bruising and the bindings I could see the look of utter hatred he had assumed.

'The fox run to ground at last,' he seethed, brandishing his revolver. 'You've made quite a chase of it, Box, but it's over now.'

Electric lights rattled into life around me and I squinted at the unaccustomed brightness. Uniformed shapes darted from the corners of the room and I found myself suddenly restrained.

Flarge looked at me with utter contempt. Next to him stood an excited-looking local bobby of almost unbearable youth and the weasel-like form of 'Twice' Daley, the American Domestic I'd encountered back in the Manhattan church. He held up a hand and gave me a cheery wave. I felt quite sick.

'We seem to be making a habit of this, old man,' said Flarge, his voice rendered somewhat nasal by the sticking plaster.

'Look, Flarge, I don't give a pin for myself,' I announced heroically. 'But tell me the girl's all right.'

'Formed a little attachment, have we? How sweet. Look behind you.'

I whirled round. We were standing before the cells, and curled in the bunk that lay alongside the wall was Aggie, sound asleep. Her face was pale beneath the crop of dark hair. I moved towards the bars but the policemen held me back.

'She's fine,' cried Flarge. 'Flesh wound in the shoulder. But the charge of aiding and abetting a wanted felon might be more difficult to shrug off.'

'She was coerced,' I lied. 'You can let her go.'

'I might at that. She was useful as bait to trap you. Beyond that . . .'

My spirits rose. Like his odious master, Flarge couldn't know of her importance. Aggie might be freed and could simply vanish, thus depriving Mons of his 'Perfect Victim'.

'Alas,' said Flarge, 'I would be exceeding my powers. She's to be taken back to London to be properly questioned by the RA. You too, of course. Now. We must be off. Daley, get those derbies on nice and snug.'

'Sure thing, Mr Flarge,' said Daley with unpleasant relish. 'Nice to see you again so soon, Mr Box.'

I ignored the tick.

The coppers pinioned my arms roughly behind my back and the little Domestic clapped on handcuffs that pinched pinkly at my wrist. The other end he clapped onto his own arm.

'I believe,' I said at last, 'that I'm entitled to telephone my solicitor.'

'We'll arrange that whilst you're on the train to London,' snapped Flarge.

I shook my head. 'Oh no. There's no telling what you chaps have got cooked up for me. I'd rather do it here, in front of this honest yeoman.' I nodded towards the fresh-faced constable. 'I am only asserting my rights, am I not, officer?'

The constable glanced over at Flarge. 'He is right, sir. I can soon get a call through the exchange—'

'No, that's perfectly all right. No decent solicitor will be up at this hour.'

'Mine will,' I urged. 'He won't mind getting out of bed, at any rate.'

Flarge shook his head. 'Out of the question.'

'It would be the proper procedure, sir,' murmured the boy. 'I shouldn't like to have to face the sergeant when he gets back and—'

'All right, all right!' barked Flarge. 'Just get on with it.'

Daley took me by the elbow towards the desk where, with considerable gentleness, the noble copper asked me to furnish him with the number of my solicitor. I gave it to him and he wrote it down with infinite slowness using a blunt pencil. The figures were rounded and childish. He glanced nervously at me, clearly overwhelmed by the big case that had dropped into his lap, his cheeks flushing in the way only a boy's can.

Flarge threw himself down in a big swivel chair, arms tightly folded, glaring at me until the call was put through.

The constable handed me the cold black receiver. There was a crackle on the other end and then a familiar voice.

'Hullo?'

'Box here,' I said crisply. 'Look here, old thing, I seem to have got myself in a bit of bother. Oh, read about it, have you? Yes, well, all a lot of nonsense of course but I'd be rather glad of your . . . representation. Uh-huh. Somewhere in Norfolk, I think.'

My solicitor's voice sounded as though it were coming from several fathoms beneath the ocean. 'London train,' I said in response to the solicitor's question. 'Well, any minute now.'

I was conscious of my captors listening to every word. I flashed them a pleasant smile. 'Right-oh. Thanks. Yes, thanks awfully. How's Ida? Oh, *really?*'

Flarge rolled his eyes and began to get to his feet.

'Yes, well, I'd bring her, certainly. And try prunes. They always do the trick.'

Flarge's hand came crashing down on the telephone. 'No more chit-chat. You've been indulged long enough, Box. Come along.'

Daley began to drag me towards the doors. The boyish constable moved to the cell door, unlocked it and shook Aggie by the shoulder. She groaned and feebly attempted to push the lad away.

I glared at his back but refrained from speaking. Flarge stood back, made an elaborate bow as Daley yanked at the cuffs, hustled me out of the station and into the bleary dawn.

It was a wonderful sky, black night splashed with pink like an unknown Whistler, and I wished I could have seen it under kinder circumstances. As Daley pushed me down the steps, I spotted the owners of the stolen motor, still brandishing their fishing rods, standing before the rust-coloured church and deep in conversation with another policeman. One of the anglers, a great red-faced walrus of a chap, pointed at me as I emerged onto the steps and there was much swearing and muttering about my 'bloody cheek'.

To my horror, there was also a knot of be-trilbied reporters, and as I was led in cuffs to Flarge's waiting car, a cascade of flashbulbs went off in my face. I held up my free arm to shield myself but the

ravening mob got exactly what they wanted: 'noted painter arrested for murder after daring Atlantic flight'. Mrs Croup would be thrilled. I was the new Crippen!

I glanced round and saw the ghastly look of satisfaction on Flarge's bruised face. The door to the station swung open and the policeman emerged, holding by the arm a dazed – and possibly doped – Agnes Daye, her pretty face slack with sleep. Then I felt Daley's gloved hand on my head, the girl and I were pushed into the motor and we were off.

Percy Flarge had got what he wanted. All I had to look forward to was the gallows.

18

Night Train To Death

The railway station we puttered into was large and busy, enveloped in billowing steam from numerous clanking engines, glimpses of gay livery visible between the clouds, pistons flashing like horse-brasses.

With alacrity Flarge and Daley pushed Aggie and me through the crowds. The poor girl didn't seem to know where she was and offered no resistance, shambling along like a zombie, her arm in a neat sling.

If anyone noticed I was cuffed they didn't show it. Scarcely looking up from my shoes, I was only aware of a cloying mass of snow-wetted coats and pale faces beneath dark hats. We passed a couple of steam-shrouded carriages until we reached an old chap, his uniform bright with buttons, his hand on the handle of the train door. Like the constable, he was clearly relishing his moment in the sun helping out what he took to be Scotland Yard.

'Mr Flarge, sir?' he cried, touching his cap. 'All's prepared, sir, as per your instructions.'

'Thanks,' grunted Flarge. 'Let's get them in.'

Flarge stood guard as the door to the carriage was hauled open and Daley stepped inside, pulling me up after him. I made no attempt to resist, merely glancing around at the bustling station. This was the rummest set-out imaginable. It was all so impossibly normal! How could these people be going about their daily business whilst I was being led away to face arrest and probable execution for a murder I had not committed? Even more startling had been those snatches I'd seen of another world, a shadow world of spirits and such that I could scarcely conceive as possible in the twentieth century. And yet here were these worthies, these bankers and clerks and type-writers boarding the same train that would lead them to mundane routine.

The compartment was dark and stank like damp dogs. There were six seats and Daley and I took up one pair, the short chain between the cuffs that bound us catching tight over the armrest. Flarge and Aggie settled into the green upholstery opposite, the girl drifting immediately into unconsciousness. She was very pale and there were unhealthy dark rings under her eyes.

The railway official shot me once last look, a queer mixture of awe and disgust, then slid the glass door to.

Flarge crossed his feet one over the other and opened a news-paper. 'Well, isn't this nice?'

I heaved a deep sigh. 'Why are we taking the train, Flarge?'

'Speed is of the essence, old thing,' he said, snapping the paper outwards so that it billowed like a sail. 'I say, you're all over *The Times*. Would you care to see?'

'No, thanks. Any chance of a cigarette?'

He smiled nastily from beneath his bindings. 'If you're very good.'

All four of us lurched forward slightly as the train began to pull away from the station. Aggie stirred and groaned. Flarge looked her up and down.

'Quite a dish, old man,' he said, hatefully. 'Dear me, I wish you'd make up your mind which way you incline. A chap struggles to keep up.'

'Story of your life, Percy,' I retorted.

He grunted mirthlessly.

Putting my free hand to the window, I rubbed at the steamed-up glass, the condensation squeaking beneath my fingers. The terminus – and freedom – slipped away as we steamed out, melting into a blur of colour then a monotonous succession of telegraph poles.

I pretty soon fell into a reverie, rocking from side to side as the train crawled south.

Aggie, looking very beautiful and vulnerable, curled into a tight ball on the fusty upholstery, a little pulse beating in her slender throat. I'd promised her a better life away from the *Stiffkey* yet all I'd succeeded in doing was thrusting her into the hands of her enemies.

'Twice' Daley fell into a doze, his yellow-gloved hands folded over his belly, his ferrety face occasionally enlivened with little twitches like that of a sleeping puppy.

After a few hours, Flarge relented and allowed me a smoke. I inhaled deeply on one of his expensive Turkish numbers and felt heaps better, though it made me slightly dizzy after so long without. The short winter day faded with miserable rapidity and electric light suddenly sprang into life above our heads.

Daley's eyes flickered open and he looked about as though unsure of his surroundings. I gave him a cheery wave with my free hand and he shot me back a look of undiluted East-Coast venom.

'Don't suppose you'd care to chat?' I opined to Flarge, picking shreds of tobacco from my teeth.

My nemesis was invisible behind the paper. He seemed engrossed in the football scores. 'What about?' he said at last.

'About this trumped-up bloody charge, of course,' I cried. 'And why you seem so keen to believe in it.'

Flarge collapsed the paper onto his lap and I saw fragments of lurid headline. Humming a little tune – he seemed in a very gay mood – he began filling his pipe. In a short while, a haze of

cherry-smelling tobacco smoke conjoined with the harsher stuff from my fag, hovering over us all like ectoplasm.

'I just do as I'm told, old boy,' said Flarge blandly, jamming the pipe into the corner of his mouth. 'Something you should have considered doing a long time ago. It was inevitable you'd get tripped up.'

'I had nothing to do with Sal Volatile's death!' I insisted.

'That's not what the evidence says, old dear. Wouldn't be the first time a chap from the RA has abused his privileges, of course, but I think it's the only time anyone's tried to cover up a domestic murder as being all in the line of duty.'

'Must we play these games?' I sighed. 'I'm not really in the mood, to be honest. I could pretend I don't know what you're up to, we could exchange quips and *bons mots* till the cows come home, but we both know what's going on over on that island.'

Flarge's brow wrinkled. 'What?'

'Don't let him bamboozle you, sir,' muttered the Domestic.

'Shut up, Daley.' Flarge looked irritated from beneath his sticking plaster. 'What're you talking about? What island?'

I sighed wearily. 'The convent! Your chum Mons and his fascist goons. I didn't realize you'd added Satanism to your list of hobbies.'

Flarge bit on the pipe with an unpleasant clack. 'You really are raving. Perhaps the papers have it right. Balance of the mind disturbed, and so forth.'

Daley liked the sound of that and chuckled, raising a gloved hand to his tiny teeth.

I suddenly remembered the fragment of the Jerusalem Prayer and my hand flew to my trouser pocket. Daley twisted in his seat to stop me but Flarge didn't flinch. 'It's all right,' he said mildly. 'It isn't there.'

'What isn't?' I said.

'The relic, of course! Worth a king's ransom, so I'm told. Ah!' He snapped his fingers. 'Got it! You were in league with that fellow

Volatile. You both conspired to get the silk whatsit off that Hubbard chap and divide the spoils. He tried to double-cross you so you shot him. Good job we searched you thoroughly or we'd have missed the damn thing.'

'As you did last time.'

Flarge dipped his head. 'As you say. The first and only time you will best me, Box, old chum.'

I dragged on the stub of my cigarette. 'That blasted hankie's only part of the puzzle, Flarge, and you know it!'

'Charmin' little thing, don't you think?' continued the blond nit. 'All those doodles embroidered on. Like that ruddy Frog tapestry. What's the one? With poor old King Harold gettin' his daylights poked out.'

I looked hard at Flarge. Did he really know nothing about the truth behind this? Could he possibly be as silly an ass as he appeared?

'So where is it now?' I asked.

Flarge sucked on his pipe and let his gaze drift to the ceiling of the compartment. The tobacco smoke was shifting restlessly above the luggage rack like a restless spirit. 'Mr Daley here has it nice and safe. Until it can be returned to its rightful owner.'

'Mons?'

'Now there you go again. You're quite fixated on that fellah. What on earth makes you think it belongs to *him*?'

I had no chance to enquire further. There was a terrible, tortured screech of metal on metal and I pitched forward, my face almost burying itself in Flarge's lap. Daley fell forward, his knees thumping against the uncarpeted floor of the carriage, and he uttered an unmentionable Yankee oath.

The screaming of the brakes continued for a full minute as the train ground to a shuddering halt. Aggie didn't even stir. The lights flickered, then died.

Flarge pushed me off him and leapt to his feet, cocking a pistol.

179

Daley got up and twisted the handcuff chain painfully as he forced me back into my seat.

'You all right, Daley?' said Flarge, outlined starkly against the bluey light coming through the fogged-up window.

The flunkey nodded. 'Shoo-er, Mr Flarge.'

With a stuttering crackle, the lights came back on. Flarge looked about, weapon raised. 'I don't like this. Wait here.'

Great plumes of steam were hissing past the window as the stalled train marked time. Flarge slid back the compartment door, stepped out into the corridor, glanced quickly up and down it, then pointed the gun at my face. 'If you try anything,' he warned, 'anything at all, Daley will you shoot you down, you understand?'

'You make yourself abundantly clear, Perce,' I cried.

The door crashed shut over Flarge's scowling face.

I glanced over at poor Aggie, still curled up in her seat, then shrugged and smiled cheerily at my guard. 'Well, Mr Daley. It's just the three of us now—'

'Shut up, you lousy faggot,' he began – then his head snapped round at the unmistakeable sound of gunshots from outside the train. 'You heard what Mr Flarge said. I'll blow you away if you get clever.'

'Charmin',' I retorted. 'But I can't *get* clever, Mr Daley. I *am* clever.'

And the lights winked out again.

In the sudden darkness, I was instantly all over the little creature, battering the heel of my hand against what I took to be the fleshier parts of his face as he struggled to aim his Colt.

We toppled over Aggie – she merely grunted – and onto the floor. I fell awkwardly and Daley's whole weight hit me square in the chest, the dusty carpet scraping at my cheek as I struggled to get back my wind. Daley succeeded in raining several solid punches into my gut, whilst my fists met merely empty air.

Scrabbling desperately at the upholstery, I failed to raise myself

up and was beginning to funk when, remarkably, I found salvation. I spotted a little red glow and my splayed finger-ends touched Flarge's pipe, forgotten in the crisis, the bowl still warm and smouldering with tobacco.

More shots rang outside. Daley's knee found my crotch and he leant heavily forward. It was agonizing.

'Now I got you, Mr Box,' he spat.

I could smell the sharp metallic tang of his Colt as he jabbed it into my face. I tugged at the old upholstery, sending up clouds of dust as I struggled desperately to roll the pipe towards me. At last I gained purchase and grasped the blasted thing. I settled the bowl in my palm and then lashed out with main force towards my assailant.

My weapon met almost no resistance and I would've assumed I'd missed had it not been for Daley's sharp, surprised cry. I moved the pipe a little and there was a dreadful soft, wet sound.

He fell forward and, in the pitch blackness, I touched his face. The still-warm bowl of the pipe was projecting from his left eye socket. I'd driven the stem of the pipe right into his brain.

Oh, Christ, I thought. That's torn it.

There was no time to hang about. Reaching out towards Aggie, I felt for her face and slapped at her cheeks.

'Aggie!' I urged. 'Aggie, my dear. Wake up!'

There was no response. I tapped her face again, gently at first then gave her a good crack across the chops. She moaned and stirred, but clearly whatever Flarge had doped her with was infuriatingly efficacious.

What the hell to do?

With athleticism born of desperation I dashed to the exterior carriage door, dragging Daley's dead weight still chained to my wrist. More cries and whistles and gunshots sounded from outside. I pushed down the window, leant out, grasped hold of the handle and swung open the door.

Clambering down into the freezing night, my boots crunched on

the chippings of a parallel rail line. The handcuff chain was stretched taut over the threshold of the doorway, Daley's corpse still slumped on the carpet within. I knew I couldn't linger – Flarge might be back any moment – but I obviously wouldn't get far with this great lump attached to me.

First of all, I leant back in and scrabbled in the dead man's pockets in search of the key. But trace of it there was none. Instead, I found the silken relic – even in the dark I could feel the familiar ragged edges – and stuffed it into my trousers before grabbing Daley's gun. Could I blast off the chain, freeing myself? Hardly. In the pitch blackness I would be more likely to shoot Aggie or myself in the foot. If a train came along, the perfect solution would present itself, the lumbering rolling stock making short work of the chain. But I could hardly hang around all night waiting for the blasted eight thirty-eight to Cromer to flash past and, besides, my own wrist would have to be uncommonly close to the rail.

No, there was only one thing for it. In my adventures I've had to do a lot of unpleasant things – in amongst the fun and frolics – but this one is up there with the grimmest.

The night was briefly lit up by more gunfire.

Panting hard, I hefted Daley's body forward until only his hand projected. Carefully, I let the carriage door creak closed, the cuff and chain that connected him to me glinting in the starlight. I took a deep breath, grabbed hold of the brass door handle and slammed the door with all my strength. It met the dead man's wrist with a sickening splinter.

I couldn't see anything much so I traced the chain from my own handcuff to Daley's. My fingers came away warm with blood. I'd felt tendons and smashed bone but it hadn't been quite enough. I repositioned Daley's wrist as best I could and swung the door shut again. There was a softer percussion, as though I were chopping on damp green wood. I tried to open the door again but it had fully closed. Pulling backwards, I felt the last sinews snap and suddenly I was

free, the corpse's hand – still firmly gripped by the cuff – dangling and dripping in ghastly fashion from the chain at my wrist.

There was no time to think about this latest act of carnage. With tremendous effort, I managed to lug open the carriage door once more and pull myself back inside. In once swift movement, I picked up Aggie and threw her over my shoulder then, knees almost buckling, jumped back out onto the tracks and slammed the carriage door closed.

Aggie was light but in my exhausted state I could hardly manage to carry her. Just as I was about to set off away from the stalled train, I almost leapt out of my skin as the carriage door flew open and a shot rang out. In the brief, flaring illumination I saw Percy Flarge framed there, his face contorted with fury. I reached for Daley's gun to reply in kind but Flarge gave a startled cry and I heard him pitch forward out of the carriage. Evidently he'd tripped over the late Domestic's prone form.

Taking to my heels, I lumbered as swiftly as possible alongside the train, expecting a bullet in my back at any moment, the still-unconscious girl draped over my shoulder.

Suddenly, I was clear of the train and crunching over the exposed tracks. A flashlight snapped into life and I was momentarily dazzled.

'Mr Box, sir?'

I staggered towards the figure, shielding my eyes with the back of my hand.

'Turn that ruddy thing off, Delilah,' I commanded. 'What kept you?'

The massive, squarish form of my devoted servant loomed up at me, swaddled in greatcoat and balaclava.

'Motor's just halong 'ere, sah,' she said efficiently. 'Sorry to take so long but you didn't give much notice to get the obstruction set hup.'

'Not to worry. Would you be a dear?'

I set Aggie gently down on the ground and Delilah scooped her

up as though she was a child. We ran swiftly towards a waiting car, engine turning over, its headlights masked by slitted baffles.

Delilah threw open the door and settled Aggie inside. I slumped in gratefully after her, the severed hand flapping horribly against my leg.

'Let's go!' I yelled.

But Delilah merely peeled off the balaclava, revealing a blotchy, weathered face like Christmas-turkey giblets left to linger until New Year.

She sniffed, miserably. 'Begging your pardon, sah, but there's ha gentleman 'ere what wants to see you.'

'Gentleman? What gentleman?'

As you can imagine, I'd had quite enough surprises for a while.

Delilah shook her head, as though saddened.

I heard two delicate coughs and a figure leant forward out of the shadows of the car's interior.

'So sorry, Mr Box,' said the figure. 'But there's no time to explain.' He seemed to be holding something in his hand. Darting forward, he pressed it to my face. I was very much surprised to find it was chloroform . . .

19

Eastwards By Monoplane

To long-time readers, this will come as a blow to make their whole fabric shiver. Has the faithful Delilah, stout companion of the Adventure of the Palsied Alienist, the Wakefield Thumb Murders et al, turned her outsize coat? Was the ugly old thing in the pay of Mr Percy Flarge?

By that stage in my career, my pleb of a factotum was retired from the Royal Academy's Domestic staff and employed full time as cook, butler, valet and bottle-washer to yours truly. She had never let me down in all the years I'd known her and she wasn't about to start doing so now.

We'd executed an existing plan (all that blether about 'bringing Ida' and the 'prunes', you understand, being code for the stopping of the train and my rescue), and as I emerged from my drugged state, I was confident she'd have an explanation for this latest turn of events.

Awaking from fevered dreams of goatish pandemonia, I found myself looking out through a little squarish window, a bar of

brilliant sunlight across my face. I was airborne, don't you know, and could see the fuselage of the monoplane glinting like tin.

Far, far below, snow-capped mountains glittered in the rarefied atmosphere, looking for all the world like a three-dimensional map rolled out for my benefit. I craned forward and a beautiful landscape of lush green firs sprang up, dusted magically with snow that draped every branch and trunk. I was at once overwhelmed by an odd sensation. I knew with absolute certainty that I'd seen such a landscape before.

Before I could contemplate further, a shadow fell across me and Delilah's ugly mug loomed into view. She gave me the dubious benefit of her smashed-tooth smile. 'Morning, sah.'

'What the hell's going on?'

Sinking to her knees – they cracked like pistol shots – my menial began to fiddle at my wrist with a hairpin. Glancing down, I shuddered as I realized I still had 'Twice' Daley's severed hand flapping from the chain. It gave off a queer smell like a butcher's shop at closing time.

"Ave that hoff in a jiffy, sah.'

I looked behind Delilah at the length of the cabin. 'Where's the girl?'

Delilah sighed. 'She's hall right.' With a cry of satisfaction, she un-clicked the handcuff and tossed the grisly relic of my railway adventure onto the seat across the way. 'We his honly minutes off hour destination,' she concluded.

'And where's that?' I steadied myself in my seat as the aeroplane gave a lurch.

'Switzerland,' said a new voice. I turned my head.

Sitting behind me was a small man in a serge suit. He was as pale as his own hair and, rising, he gave a couple of tiny coughs behind his gloved hand. 'It's good to see you again, Mr Box. We have much to discuss, you and I.'

So this was Delilah's mysterious 'gentleman': Professor Reiss-

Mueller of the Metropolitan Museum, the curious fellow who'd given his expert opinion on the hankie back in New York. He sat down opposite me, a chrome-bordered, blond-wood table between us.

'I'm sure we do,' I rejoined. 'Care to start with why you've kidnapped me?'

The aspirin-white expert gave a helpless shrug. 'Time was of the essence, friend. Once I'd contacted Delilah here and came in on the plan to liberate you, it was essential we get on our way forthwith.'

I threw an unimpressed look at Delilah. 'Hi didn't know what to do, Mr Box, sah!' she shrugged helplessly. Her face brightened. 'Hi saw your picture hin the paper!' she cried happily, rather as though I'd been snapped opening the Chelsea Flower Show rather than caught in a flophouse bed with Sal Volatile's naked corpse.

'Hi knew something must be a bit rum,' she continued, chewing her lip. 'What the 'ell's the hacademy hup to, I thinks, letting Mr Box take the drop for this? Hand then the Prof 'ere got in touch and it all started to make sense.'

I scratched at my unshaven chin. 'And what's your story?' I said to Reiss-Mueller. 'You got in touch? How? And why drug me?'

The Professor put his hand to his pursed lips like a coy child. 'I had to do that! We'd only have wasted time on tedious explanations in the back of a freezing English automobile! Whereas now we have the luxury of our Armstrong Whitworth Argosy –' he patted the sleek upholstery of his seat – 'and can chat at our leisure.'

'I happen to like tedious explanations,' I protested. 'What the deuce is going on? Where's Aggie?'

Reiss-Mueller gestured towards a royal-blue curtain that divided the cabin. 'Through there, enjoying two boiled eggs. Three and one-quarter minutes. Just the way she likes them, apparently. She'll join us presently.'

'All right,' I said with an exhausted sigh. 'Explain.'

Reiss-Mueller gave a funny little laugh that dissolved into a

double cough. 'I'm afraid I haven't been fully frank with you, Mr Box. Or, rather, my government hasn't.'

'Meaning?'

The little man balanced his homburg on the table and moved it round in a clockwise direction, contemplating it like an indecisive shopper. 'Well, let's just say that the Metropolitan Museum and the Royal Academy have more in common than you might think.'

I frowned. 'You're not . . .?'

'Agents of a secretive bent, yes!' he giggled. 'Nothing for the FBI to get their pretty little heads worried over. But like you at the RA, we like to think we keep a more watchful eye on things than the headline-grabbers.'

'But that's impossible. We'd know!' I felt a sudden lack of confidence in my country's intelligence network. 'Wouldn't we?'

'We're *very* discreet, is all I can say. I'm afraid I wasn't at that party at the "99" by coincidence. I was tailing you.'

I raised an eyebrow.

'Just routine, you understand,' he continued. 'And then I saw the relic and couldn't help asking. It's not just a pose, you see. I really am an expert.'

'But not enough of one to recognize the Jerusalem Prayer?'

He sat up at that. 'You know what it is?'

I waved an idle hand. 'Oh, just the most powerful occult object of all time, or some such.'

'Quite.' Reiss-Mueller took off his glasses and polished them with his colourless tie. 'Things have changed so much since we last met. I didn't realize the importance of it at the time. I've seen a lot of fakes and what-have-you so I've learned not to get too excited. But then I did some more research. Talked to other experts. When I realised the fragment must be genuine, I nearly had a fit.'

He cast a glance towards the window. As the 'plane banked to the right, a little patch of sunlight climbed the curved wall of the cabin and ignited the lenses of his spectacles. 'The prayer's been lost for so

many centuries,' continued Reiss-Mueller, 'that many believe it to be mere myth. I never dreamed' – cough, cough – 'I'd get to touch it . . .'

His watery gaze settled on me. 'The most powerful occult artefact in history,' he repeated.

The curtain was suddenly thrown back and Agnes Daye raced through. She was flanked by two well-built men in pork-pie hats who, although not laying a finger on her person, were clearly guards of some species. Each was glowingly tanned and white of teeth as though they'd stepped from the pages of a Sears-Roebuck catalogue. They didn't try to prevent her from throwing her uninjured arm about me.

'You are awake!' Her lovely face lit up but there was real worry and exhaustion behind her eyes and egg yolk on her neat little chin.

'Hello, there,' I said chirpily. 'You all right?'

'It is not for me that you must be concerned,' she cried, with her customary gravity, stroking my cheek. 'My poor Lucifer. You have been through so much. When the police took me, I thought I would never see you again. And then that terrible man put me to sleep. Now there is this fellow with the spectacles. What is happening? Will you tell me what is to become of me?'

'I think that rather depends on the Professor here,' I mused, turning to the little fellow. 'Perhaps you could explain more fully to Aggie and me – any Scotch on the go? – why this Prayer thing's so powerful?'

Reiss-Mueller nodded vaguely to one of his pork-pie hatted chaps, who scurried off behind the curtain, reappearing moments later with a decanter. Delilah, whose department this was, gave a low growl and took it off him. The fella didn't argue.

The Professor took off his glasses and rubbed at heavily bagged eyes.

'There's a legend,' he began at last, leaning forward, 'old as Mankind but long forgotten. In the time after the Flood, Satan's

power on Earth grew so strong that God was forced to rejoin battle. The Devil was eventually defeated and God imprisoned him in a kind of living death, trapped like a fly in amber . . .'

Delilah handed Reiss-Mueller a tumbler and I mixed one for myself and Aggie.

The little man downed his in one. 'Such was Satan's malign power that not even this could keep Evil from the world, but so long as the Dark One himself remains thus bound, Mankind is safe from ultimate destruction.'

'I have heard this story,' Aggie piped up, wincing a little as she moved her shoulder. 'The sisters taught it to me when I was small.'

I sipped my Scotch. 'And the Jerusalem Prayer . . .?'

Reiss-Mueller shrugged. 'Is the key to unlocking the enchantment that chains the Devil. Almighty God, it is said, granted us free will and so the means of releasing this horror have always been available. The Prayer was separated into fragments and hidden around the world. That square of silk is one of the fragments.'

I turned to the window and allowed myself a moment to contemplate the beautiful and serene landscape below. 'And it could really happen? It's not just all purple robes, black candles and how-d'you-do?'

'I know it might be hard to believe—'

'Not so hard as you might think, my friend,' I sighed, thinking back to the horrible visions I'd endured on the *Stiffkey* and the Norfolk marsh. 'You don't know what I'd give to believe Mons was using it all as an excuse to seduce a lot of nubile Swiss serving girls. But I've seen things in the past few days that make me doubt every one of those cosy little certainties that make life tolerable.'

Reiss-Mueller nodded slowly, then brightened. 'Luckily Mons had only the fragment. And he doesn't even have that any more. My orders are to take him . . . um . . . out of the picture, as it were, and return the relic to the US.'

I thought for a moment. I knew a few things that the Professor evidently did not.

'And you've not involved the Royal Academy? They don't know anything about this?'

Delilah shook her head determinedly. 'The Prof 'ere don't want 'em to know. 'E don't trust 'em. That's why I took 'im in on hour little scheme.'

Reiss-Mueller picked a thread from his sleeve. 'This is an entirely independent operation. You've nothing to fear.'

'So why all the hoo-hah? Why not just take the relic off me?'

Reiss-Mueller looked hurt. 'Take it off you? We're not thieves, Mr Box. You and I are partners. Once we're safe, you can fully debrief me.'

I grimaced inwardly, a horrible picture of a naked Reiss-Mueller popping into my overheated brain. I'd much rather de-brief Aggie. 'Where exactly are we heading, by the way?'

'One of the Met's safe houses. On the Franco-Swiss border. We'll hole up there and keep an eye on Mons's activities.'

'Is he in Switzerland?'

'Oh, yes. Our sources tell us he's returned to his schloss within the last day or so.' Reiss-Mueller's mouth turned down. 'I suspect he thinks he's found the Tomb of Satan but the exact location is contained in your fragment so he's digging in the dark, as it were.'

I took out the silken object and smoothed it over the arm of my chair. 'I think I have a surprise for you too, Professor Reiss-Mueller,' I said, choosing my words with care for maximum dramatic impact. 'You see, it's not just a question of arresting a deluded fascist bully and hiding away this little rag in our communal attic. Olympus Mons has the rest of the prayer. Every last fragment. And he intends to use it.'

Reiss-Mueller's milk-white face turned paler still. He leant across the table and pawed at my sleeve. 'You've got to be kidding me?'

'I rarely kid. Brings me out in hives.'

His plump hand shot to his mouth. 'But do you know . . . do *they* know . . . what power the prayer possesses?'

'I think I have some notion.'

Reiss-Mueller straightened up in his seat. 'If the Prayer is performed, the Dark Powers invoked and the Horned One released from his bonds, then chaos will engulf us all as surely as night follows day.'

With perfect timing, the 'plane suddenly began to descend. It was as though the bottom had fallen out of the world.

20

Memento Mori

We dropped in wide, looping arcs, the plane's engines groaning, and I gripped the arms of the seat to steady myself. As the craft finally thumped down, my stomach gave a great lurch and only settled itself as, with a last shudder, we slowed to a halt.

I sank back as the machine taxied along, sun-glinted snow already settling wetly on the glass of the portholes, the flickering shadows of the slowing propellers crisscrossing my face.

Aggie was gazing thoughtfully at the relic, her dark brows drawn tightly together. 'Why do we not just destroy it?'

'Hmm?'

'Destroy this thing, then the Prayer can never be complete and the . . . evil . . . will never be released!'

Reiss-Mueller shook his head. 'It's not so simple.'

'Why not?' I cried.

'No, no.'

'Look—'

I lifted up the Prayer fragment and, producing my cigarette lighter, struck my thumb off its stiff wheel. A neat yellow flame jumped into life only inches from the ragged cloth.

'No!' cried Reiss-Mueller. 'It's priceless!' His hands danced about in the air in agitation.

I waved the flame closer. 'Wouldn't you destroy the *Mona Lisa* if it meant saving the world?'

'No! I mean, of course, yes, but there's no need. Mr Box, please! There's another way!'

'Sure?'

'Yes!'

Relenting, I let the silk flop back onto the arm of the chair.

The Professor sighed with relief and ran his palm over his suddenly sweaty brow. 'What you've told me changes things somewhat. I'm minded to follow the course of one of your illustrious predecessors. That hunchbacked fellow who gave the Gunpowder plotters enough rope to hang themselves? Or so they say. Why don't we let Mons's plans mature then grab him red-handed? If he's taken *in flagrante* trying to summon the Devil then we'll get him and all his crazy followers at the same time. We can pump him for everything he's got on the Anglo-American fascist network, and with the world situation brewing up the way it is, that'll be pretty hot information. After that, we'll nail him with something commonplace. The IRS are trying a similar dodge with Capone. Tax evasion, would you believe?'

Armed with one of my few scoops, I decided to show off a bit. 'You could try this. Mons makes his moolah from smuggling cocaine into New York.'

Reiss-Mueller gave a low whistle. 'You don't say?'

'In the form of Communion wafers.'

'How very enterprising. That's sure good to know. You see, my dear sir, this partnership's going to go splendidly! Now, tell me what you've learned about Mons's plans—'

I yawned expansively. 'Details later. Are we to be fed and watered?'

'So Hi am hassured, sah,' put in Delilah, pushing aside the two pork-pie-hatted chaps and stooping to open the door. Cold, crisp air and sunshine immediately flooded the cabin.

I got up, hooked my arm through Aggie's and popped my head through the hatch.

We'd landed on a private airstrip, bordered on all sides by dense green forest with snow-bright peaks bobbing above the treeline. I froze on the steps, not because of the temperature but because, as I'd suspected from the view above, I *had* been there before.

I recalled Christopher Miracle's warning and a kind of numb misery washed over me. 'What did you say this place was called?'

'I didn't,' said Reiss-Mueller, appearing behind us and popping his homburg onto his neatly parted hair. 'Little village called—'

'Lit-de-Diable?'

Reiss-Mueller looked surprised. 'How did you know that?'

I gazed around at the airstrip. It was much changed but I knew every inch of the wretched place. 'I've been here once before. A long time ago. Lit-de-Diable.' I laughed mirthlessly. '"The Devil's Bed". Never realized its significance at the time.'

'When was that?' asked Aggie, gently.

I closed my eyes as though against the glare of the sun but, for a moment, that still and beautiful morning dissolved into a shrieking nightmare of remembrance, the air red as Hell, rain pounding like a hail of bullets in the mud, dying men strewn over the barbed wire, screaming and screaming . . .

I snapped open my eyes, shook my head. 'It's not important.'

Looking above the tree-line, I oriented myself. 'Mons has taken over the castle, then?' I said at length.

'See for yourself,' said Reiss-Mueller, producing a pair of brass binoculars and pointing towards the snowy peaks.

Above the forest loomed a familiar mountain, its surface dotted

all over with searchlight housings. It was, of course, identical to the image sewn into the silken fragment of the Jerusalem Prayer.

At the mountain's peak, like something from Hans Andersen, stood a huge fortress, two of its smooth-faced stone walls towards us, a massive tiled keep projecting from the centre.

I'd known it under different circumstances and, clapping the binoculars to my eyes, strained to make out a new addition. For a moment, the view swam about, like trying to focus on a distant star through a cheap telescope. Then I caught one of the castle's absurdly spindly turrets and suddenly made out the strong lines of steel cables heading from it towards the ground. Seconds later, the gondola of a cable car trundled into view. I watched its progress downwards with keen attention, noting that, at several points, the vehicle came close to touching the rock face.

'Suits his dreams of grandeur, I guess,' said Reiss-Mueller, giving a short wave to the pilot, who was just a blur of goggles and flying coat behind the glass of the cockpit. 'Pilot'll stay ready till we need him again. Now, if you and the young lady are okay, Mr Box, it's only a short walk.'

I shrugged, knocked somewhat for six by the strange co-incidence of finding myself once more in the quaint Franco-Swiss town of infamous memory. For the moment I was content to give myself over to the Yank's plans, and draped an arm around Aggie's waist, taking care to avoid her be-slinged arm, as the four of us walked slowly off the airstrip towards the woodland.

I tried to banish the memories and enjoy the sunshine on my face. After a time, I began to feel a little more chipper. Reiss-Mueller's chloroform may have been an unorthodox sleeping draught, but at least I'd had some rest.

A short walk off the tarmacadam over snow peppered with pine needles and Reiss-Mueller came to a halt. Delilah, Aggie and I pulled up too, gazing in unconcealed delight at the sight before us. It was a cottage so idyllic that it could have been the castle's

fairy-tale twin. Its weathered blue door was bordered by hoar-bush, berries sparkling as the frost that rimed them melted in the sun. Mullioned windows were set deep in the thick old stonework and the high, tiled roof could have been made of gingerbread and icing.

Fiddling with a key, Reiss-Mueller swung open the door and ushered us over a doorstep worn with a deep groove by the passage of centuries.

Inside, it was every bit as cosy and delightful as we could've wished for. I received a hurried impression of pale yellow walls, flag-stones and rustic furnishings. A huge stove dominated one corner. Hugging herself with happiness, Aggie scurried over to a plump armchair and threw herself into its downy embrace.

'Hi shall hattend to lunch at once, sir,' said Delilah, clicking her heels together like a maître d'. 'There'll shortly be 'ot water and food has well.'

As the Professor and I seated ourselves, Delilah got the stove blazing and soon after began filling the tub upstairs with buckets of steaming water. There were plenty of togs in storage and, after a brief, heavenly soak, I changed into canvas trousers, soft-collared shirt and pullover. Immensely comforted, I settled down for Reiss-Mueller's questioning. Aggie, meanwhile, prepared herself for the next bath.

The Professor steepled his fingers as he relaxed into the chair. 'So Mons has the rest of the prayer,' he mused. 'How'd he come to lose the most important piece?'

'Mustn't ever have had it, surely? Otherwise he'd know the loca-tion of the . . . um . . . Devil's tomb and wouldn't be digging up half his estate.' I smoothed back my still-damp hair. 'No, it seems a chap called Hubbard was trying to extort millions from Mons for that last piece. He must've known how much it was worth, but Hubbard reckoned without an agent called Flarge.'

'Flarge?'

'Percy Flarge. A swine of the first order of merit. He's the one out to frame me up. Whether it's just him or the whole of the Royal Academy, I simply don't know. All that's clear is that I got the drop on the brute. Found the one thing they'd been searching for just tucked into Hubbard's breast pocket.'

Reiss-Mueller contemplated his nails and gave his double cough. 'But all this is academic, anyway, unless Mons has found the Perfect Victim.'

'Well, she was hiding in plain sight just like the relic. That cocaine-smuggling business I told you about? Leaky old crate called the *Stiffkey*, operating out of Norfolk. Among its crew members was a girl brought up in the Convent of St Bede. A girl descended from an unbroken line of such victims, all waiting for the appointed hour.'

Reiss-Mueller looked at me steadily over the top of his spectacles. 'You know where she is?'

'She's taking a tub upstairs right at this moment.'

At this, the little chap positively exploded in staccato coughing. I told him everything about Aggie's identity, how Sal Volatile had discovered her location and then attempted to prise himself away from Mons's clutches and frustrate his schemes.

Finally, after Delilah had served us with a deliciously simple lunch of hot rolls and ham, we fell to examining the Prayer again. I peered at the embroidered mountain and at the lamb burning on the spit. Then I remembered our previous conversation and turned my attention to the dense, crabbed text.

'These other specialists,' I said to Reiss-Mueller. 'Did they have any clue about the words? How did they go again?'

The Professor tilted back his head and contemplated the low ceiling. 'That there will come one who is spoken of. All unknowing will he come. And only he who makes himself alone in the world can defeat the Beast.'

My eyebrows rose interrogatively.

'Not a clue, I'm afraid,' sighed the Professor.

I straightened up, stretched and popped the relic into the pocket of my new trousers. 'Well, Devil or no Devil, I need a kip. If you'd excuse me.'

Reiss-Mueller bobbed his head. 'Of course. I'll leave my boys on guard so you've no need to worry. Get some shut-eye and I'll join you later. I need to speak to the Met as to how to proceed.'

We rose to our feet simultaneously and briefly banged into one another, the Professor's glasses dislodging. He mumbled apologies and went out. Once upstairs, I looked in on Aggie and found her sound asleep, still wrapped in a huge rough towel. I carefully unwound it from her and she murmured something, one slender coffee-coloured arm flopping carelessly behind her head. The other was still in its sling, the bandage wet from the tub.

Then, languorously, Aggie opened one eye. 'Can I help you?'

I gazed down at her frankly wonderful form and smiled as a droplet of water slid from my hair and splashed onto her exposed tummy.

'I'd better dry that off,' I murmured. 'You'll catch your death.'

Pressing my fingers to her smooth skin, I wiped away the moisture. Aggie reached out and gently grasped my hand, moving it to touch her lips, her throat and then to cup her breast. Her wet hair was plastered to her forehead and, for once, her curiously serious expression was mingled with something altogether more naughty.

I slunk in beside her, the rough towel strangely comforting as I stripped off my clothes and nuzzled my freshly shaven face over her firm nipples. She clasped her free hand behind my head and pulled me closer, tighter as I thrust forward, the terrors and privations of the last weeks melting away into a glow of pleasure.

She fell to biting my ears and murmuring in a low, low fashion that prickled the hairs on my neck.

'Keep me safe,' she sighed. 'Promise me you'll keep me safe.'

I promised. I promised many things as we plunged wonderfully on. It seemed of suddenly vital import that I celebrate my existence, my life force, there in Lit-de-Diable, that place of dead and dread remembrance. And, as the girl and I conjoined in bliss, I decided there was some unfinished business I had to attend to.

Afterwards came the glorious lull of lovers' sleep until, with the winter day fast waning, I crept from Aggie's room and sought out my own. I was just lacing up my boots when the door opened and Delilah entered.

'The Prof's not back yet, sir,' she announced. 'So hi was wondering, hif we is not likely to storm Mr Mons's barricades any time soon, sah, what you and the young lady might want for your tea, sah.'

'Miss Daye is sleeping,' I said. 'And I have to go out.'

'Go out, sah?'

I nodded. 'There's something I have to do, Delilah. I'll be back before nightfall.'

The drudge looked worried. 'You sure, sir?'

'Absolutely.' I gave her a warm smile. 'Don't fret, I know this place like the back of my hand. Look after the girl, won't you?'

I found a long leather flying coat hanging on the back of the door, slipped it on and headed out of the cottage, straight into the path of one of the Professor's horribly healthy, pork-pie hatted friends.

He seemed in no mood to let me pass.

'Just going for a stroll,' I said airily.

The po-faced fellow shook his head. 'I don't think the Professor would like that, sir.' His accent was as regulation as his regulation American suit. 'We have your welfare at heart.'

'My welfare? Look here, you're supposed to be our guards not our gaolers.'

'Of course, sir. And that's why it wouldn't be wise to let you go

wandering off. Surely you see that?' He flashed me his dazzling pearly whites.

I looked him up and down. Definitely not the type to be won over by friendly persuasion, I decided. Instead I nipped back through the doorway. 'My dear chap, of course! Quite understand. Night night.'

Closing the door behind me, I leaned back against the woodwork and frowned. No doubt Reiss-Mueller had the best of intentions but I've never liked being fenced in, as you may have noticed, and instantly made the decision to break free of my friendly confinement. Unfinished business, as I said.

Creeping softly back up the stairs I emerged onto the landing and made my way to a small sash window. Peering out, I saw Delilah in the snow-blanketed garden, chopping wood for the stove. A short distance away, arms neatly folded, sat the second of the Professor's Metropolitan Museum pals, his hat pulled down over his no doubt frost-nipped ears. I moved swiftly to the other end of the landing, where there was an identical window. This one looked out onto a neglected-looking roadway, and scrambling at the insecure lock, I heaved it open and slipped through onto the slippery drainpipe.

In moments, I had shinned down and landed with a crump in a thick drift. Keeping low, I crept along a hedgerow bordering that side of the cottage and was soon out onto the roadway and free.

The village of Lit-de-Diable was only marginally Swiss – as I knew to my cost – and had been fought over by various factions for centuries. It was little more than a couple of streets of quaintly cramped houses, inns and a pretty, onion-spired church. As a result, it took me only minutes to move through it towards the airstrip and across the un-patrolled border into France. I could have walked the way blindfolded.

Just past the airstrip where our plane was still parked, an area of

woodland turned into a neat avenue of poplars. This in turn led, after some five hundred yards, to a small stone memorial that was quite lovely and glowing like coral in the pinkish light of evening.

My boots crunched through the drifts as I made my way towards it, then I paused, gaze averted, letting the memories wash over me.

I circled the memorial, the names standing out clearly.

PTE JOHN ROPER (small, keen, delightful), PTE SAMUEL FORTUNE (gloomy, Welsh, loyal to a fault), SGT JEREMIAH FORRESTER (good man in a tight spot), PTE INNES COPELY (no, didn't remember him) . . .

The next face of the stonework ran on in the same fashion, the inscribed names picked out by the fading light of the setting sun.

CAPTAIN WILLIAM BUNSEN . . . PTE DAVID HENDRIX

In all those years, I'd somehow never managed to make the short journey. I could have come at any time but now, in the teeth of this strange adventure, fate had conspired to return me to that little place on the Franco-Swiss border.

LT HAROLD LATIMER (ill-tempered, drank), SGT GABRIEL BOOTHE (Yorkshireman, prim, humourless), PTE PETER HOLLIS (a real smasher. Made good grub) . . .

The names began to blur as I moved round the snow-covered stone. And then I saw it. The last simple inscription amongst all the others.

PTE CHARLES JACKPOT

I plunged my hands into the deep pockets of the flying coat and wished I had a cigarette. Charlie was always good for a gasper. I would've liked to have smoked one for him at that moment.

There was no body under the French turf, of course. Like so many others, the young man's corpse had never been recovered. He was listed as missing. Forever. And we'd been so close to the Swiss border and freedom . . .

There'd been many an adventure since we'd first met in that bizarre brothel in old Naples but, perhaps, none so bold and terrifying as the mission in '17 that finally parted us.

'A neat avenue of poplars led to a small stone memorial.'

I briefly touched my fingers to the cold stone, then turned on my heel.

Plunging my numbed hands into my trouser pockets, I suddenly panicked. The Prayer was gone! Oh Lor!

Taking to my heels, I pelted towards the airstrip. As Reiss-Mueller had promised, the pilot of our 'plane was sitting on a low wall, awaiting our instruction. He held up a hand in greeting, then slid the same hand into his jacket and pulled out a pistol.

I stopped dead.

The pilot reached up and hauled off his goggles and flying helmet in one smooth movement, revealing a shock of blond hair and a very bruised and broken nose.

'Don't say a word,' said Percy Flarge, between gritted teeth. 'Just come with me.'

21

Devil's Bargain

I followed meekly but my mind was afire. It was imperative I get away from Flarge and retrieve the fragment of the Jerusalem Prayer! Everything else – my life, Aggie's safety – was mere beer and skittles in comparison. And I would destroy the cursed thing if it meant saving the world from eternal darkness.

I crossed without fuss towards the aeroplane, which was now shining like a toy in the last beams of the purple sun. The cabin door was open and Flarge prodded at my side until I clambered inside.

'Don't gloat,' I muttered. 'I can bear anything if you don't gloat.'

'Shut up,' snapped Flarge.

I flopped down into my old seat, gaze flickering towards the door. Could I overcome him and get back to the cottage? 'Neat trick, that,' I murmured with faux nonchalance. 'Substituting yourself for the pilot. How did you cotton on to us?'

Flarge seemed anxious, his usual smug smile replaced by a sort of blankness. 'You're joking, aren't you?' he scoffed. 'The Metropolitan

Museum is wide open. We know about almost everything they do. Standing joke at the RA.'

I refrained from mentioning that I didn't even know of the Metropolitan Museum's espionage credentials. Dear me, I *was* getting too old for this lark.

Flarge waved the gun about. 'What we've certainly known for a long time is that chap Reiss-Mueller's as leaky as a sieve. Whatever discretion he once possessed has flown out of the window. He asks questions a bit too loudly these days and people listen. Didn't take too much to penetrate his plans. I reckon the Met want the Jerusalem Prayer for themselves.'

Something about Flarge's tone disquieted me and thoughts of immediate flight subsided. 'There's something wrong, isn't there, Percy?'

Flarge scowled. 'Yes, there's something wrong! There's something bloody wrong! You smash my face in, escape capture, escape again, kill my Domestic and then slice his blasted hand off!'

I shook my head. 'No. Something else. By now you should be thumping me and swearing seven kinds of vengeance for all I've put you through.'

'I should!' he rasped. 'I know I want to. Ever since I joined the RA I've had your ruddy name and reputation rubbed in my face. I thought I'd never get one up on you. But then I saw a little chink. Just whispers from on high. Scribbled notes from no one in particular telling me to shadow you because you weren't up to it any more.'

I would normally have bristled at this but bristling didn't seem called for. Something interesting was up. Instead I shrugged. 'You saved my life back in that church tower. I'm very grateful. But why the hell are you persecuting me? Because I found that blasted silk rag and you didn't?'

'I knew it was there!' protested Flarge. 'I saw it. But my orders . . . my orders didn't mention it. I was to keep an eye on you and on no account let you get hurt.'

'What?'

Flarge put his foot up on the chair in front and chewed his lip. 'Look here, Box. I was thrilled when I got the tip-off to come to that flea-bitten hotel and I found you in bed with the corpse. I was even more thrilled when the Academy told me that normal rules didn't apply. That the Domestics would not be called, and that you would have to face the full rigour of the law. It was perfect. Lucifer Box reduced to this! Caught with his trousers down in a sodomitic bloodbath. In *America*! As I say, perfect.' He heaved a sigh and let the barrel of the pistol droop slightly. 'Too perfect.'

Flarge cleared his throat and stared into space. 'I know what you think of me and I dare say you're right. I've admired you, resented you, wanted to see you utterly smashed so that I might advance but one thing I'll never do. I'll never see you go down for something you didn't do. I may be a swine but I'm not a traitor.'

With which remarkable statement, he took out a small and ancient-looking book and tipped out a folded piece of foolscap that lay within.

I read it over and then read it again. My skin grew clammy and I felt sick to my stomach. 'Where did you get this?' I managed at last, my voice reduced to a croaking whisper.

'It was inside Daley's coat,' said Flarge. 'Inside this book. I found it when you escaped from the train. Looks like the draft of a cryptogram. Makes things pretty clear, what?'

That it did. The thing, scrawled in Daley's untidy hand and annotated with various jottings showing where words would be substituted in a cryptogram, ran this way:

'Planted the rag, as requested. Box took the bait. Took him down in the drugstore and interrogated Volatile re: Lamb. Subject died during process. What should I do?'

I looked up. 'Daley set up that little charade in the hotel so that I'd carry the can?'

Flarge nodded. 'There's more. A reply.'

He tossed over an actual cryptogram on thin yellow paper with Daley's patient decoding in pencil beneath.

'Box will find the Lamb for us. He's still the best we have. He must have the Prayer. And Banebdjed shall rise! . . .'

Clearly, then, 'Twice' Daley and not Flarge was in league with Mons – but who else had betrayed us and fallen in with the fascist's diabolical schemes?

One thing I still failed to understand. The cryptogram reply had said 'Box must have the Prayer'. But didn't they already know that, having given Daley orders to plant it on Hubbard's body?

'And all this time I thought it was you,' I muttered.

'What?'

'This will sound crazy—' I began carefully, but Flarge held up his hand and contemplated his pistol.

'I know,' he said flatly.

'Hmm?'

Flarge scratched at his flaxen hair. 'All the Satanism stuff. Efforts were made to initiate me. All dark rooms and hooded robes. Never found out who was at the root of it. They were very subtle at first. Told me there were ways a chap like me might gain advancement, not just in the Royal Academy but in life. There's a route to true power, they said. Power over the wills of others.'

'What did you have to do?'

'The whole caboodle. Bell, book and candle. I mean, at first I took it for first-class tosh, but. . .whatever it might take to get on, you know? Then it got more serious and I . . . I saw things. Terrible things. And I wanted out. They seemed disappointed but agreed. I'd thought I was clear of the wretched business. Now I know I've been their damned pawn all this time! The question is, now we're on the same team, what're we going to do?'

I nodded towards his gun. 'We *are* on the same team, then?' I said.

Flarge stood up and his face was grim from beneath his sticking

plaster. 'We might never be best pals, Box, but we can rub along for as long as it takes to sort out this mess, can't we?'

I looked the fella over. I'd loathed his very guts for so long it was going to take an effort of will not to knock him down where he stood. At last I got to my feet, put out my hand and Percy Flarge gripped it, firm and almost painfully.

'Chums?'

'All right, *old boy*,' I said. 'Chums. Now let's get the hell back to the cottage.'

As we opened the plane door, it was clear the weather was worsening. The day had faded in a riot of crimson and purple but there were huge, fat storm clouds lowering on the horizon. Snow was already falling thickly. We raced from the airstrip and onto the practically deserted streets of Lit-de-Diable as though afraid of the creeping dark.

The wind was roaring down the narrow streets and I'd stopped to catch my breath by a charmingly tumbledown inn when the brick just by my face shattered into fragments. Whirling round, I'd hardly managed to register the shot when another rang out, slicing into the ground at my feet and sending up a great plume of snow.

Flarge – slightly ahead of me – span on his heel and replied in kind over my shoulder. I had a brief flash of receding pork-pie hat in the fading light. Snow was pelting down in a great rushing fall.

'It's Reiss-Mueller's men!' I hissed.

One of the beggars was right behind me, concealed behind a pale yellow cottage. The location of the other was confirmed at once as his pistol rang out, shattering the window of the inn. Weaponless, I was helpless to respond, but my new ally Flarge was on blistering form, sending round after round our enemies' way.

We took immediate shelter behind the old market cross but we were hopelessly pinned down. The snow screamed in our faces.

'What the hell are they playing at?' snapped Flarge.

'Damned if I know,' I shouted. 'But the world's gone so corkscrew I half expect to be double-crossed every minute of the day!'

Flarge fired off three shots in rapid succession and was answered by two single bullets from opposite directions. 'Why would the Met want you dead?'

My mind raced. 'They could've killed me any time. Instead they brought me all the way over here. Why?'

Flarge pulled the trigger again but nothing happened. He slammed the weapon against his palm.

'Damn it all! Jammed!' He shot me a defeated look.

'All out for a duck, old boy?' I cried.

A bullet whined past, a great splinter of stone erupted from the market cross and the fragments caught me in the eyes. I threw myself to the ground, getting a mouthful of snow and lay there, utterly helpless. Then I lifted my head, eyes stinging and quite unable to get my bearings.

'Look out!' cried Flarge.

I tried to clear the snow from my eyes but was only blurrily aware of a figure stepping into my line of sight, the yellow flash of his revolver and a deafening percussion. This was it.

I waited for the bullet to hit me but something very queer happened. I was vaguely aware that the freezing night air had turned yet colder but the wind dropped suddenly and then that awful low depression gripped my guts like a cramp. There was a strange choking gasp from Flarge kneeling at my side.

'My God, Box,' he cried. 'Look!'

Great dusty tears were welling in my eyes, and as I rubbed desperately at them I saw the bullet hovering in the air right by my face.

As I watched incredulously, the damned thing simply faded away. Blinking stupidly, I looked up to see Reiss Mueller's men gazing down on us in unfeigned shock. Then, as if on cue, Flarge's pistol made a

little clicking sound. He looked at it, raised it and, in one swift movement, put two bullets into our enemies' regulation suits.

The Men from the Met crumpled into the snow, wearing looks of complete bewilderment in addition to the new blood-blossom buttonholes in their lapels.

The wind suddenly rose up again like an unstoppered genie.

'What the deuce happened there?' squeaked Flarge above the din.

I shook my head. Once again, it seemed some supernatural power had come to my aid. And I didn't want to dwell on it. 'Don't ask,' I yelled, 'let's go!'

We were back at the cottage in minutes but, as soon as I saw the half-open door, I knew something was horribly amiss. Keeping close to the wall, Flarge moved to the worn step and kicked the door fully open. There was no one inside.

Flarge and I exchanged glances and I crossed swiftly to the back door. There was no sign of Delilah.

With a horribly heavy heart, I began to mount the stairs, Flarge following closely behind, revolver cocked. I moved swiftly across the landing and threw open the door to Aggie's room. Expecting to find her dead, it came as something of a relief to find the bed merely empty, the blanket I'd so carefully pulled over her gently sleeping body wrenched back like the snarling lip of Olympus Mons himself.

Sinking down on the bedspread, the full horror of the situation dawned on me. And I'd promised to keep her safe.

'What now?' said Flarge glumly.

'They've got Agnes and they've got the Prayer,' I sighed. 'What else can we do? We've got to get into that castle.'

Outside, the weather had closed in, transforming the night into a howling maelstrom. The sleet-choked wind shrieked through the bare trees and I clutched my leather coat about me as we set off towards the mountain. The cold was simply appalling, snow lashing at our exposed faces like a shower of needles.

Keeping to the Swiss side of the border, we soon cleared the tiny airstrip and found ourselves enveloped by dense forest, trees looming up like soldiers in our flickering flashlight beams. It was fearfully hard going, the drifts underfoot had refrozen and were treacherous, the snow that fell thickly onto our shoulders only added to the slog.

Pretty soon I was spent. Merely keeping from falling on my arse was hard enough, but the trudge upwards soon began to tell on my protesting leg muscles. Neck and face swamped by the upturned sheepskin of the flying-coat's collar, I strained to see the mountain through the black curtain of the forest. For a very long time, though, there was only the dreary regularity of the snow and the trees.

Then, all at once, a small, rectangular building seemed to spring up out of nowhere and we emerged into a clearing to find ourselves facing the departure point of the cable-car. Flarge and I exchanged glances and then trudged swiftly and noiselessly towards it.

Closer to, I could see that the terminus was divided into two so that, as one carriage arrived another set off upwards in the opposite direction. To my delight, I saw that a car was rapidly approaching.

Crouching in the snow just outside of the pool of electric light thrown from the station, Flarge and I watched as the vehicle clunked downwards. A shadow flickered in the window and I breathed a sigh of relief. The car sliding down the wire towards us was empty and there seemed only to be a single fellah on guard in the station itself. Flarge and I hastily devised a plan and then waited for the cable-car to come to a halt.

I signalled to my new ally, who nodded and covered me with his pistol as I crept forward, boots crumping through the impacted snow. Marching boldly to the steamed-up glass door of the terminus, I knocked and plastered a pleasant smile onto my face. Through the fog of condensation, I watched the guard frown, unshoulder his Tommy gun and slide back the door.

'*Pardon,*' I cried. '*Je suis un peu perdu.*'

Like a flash, Flarge leapt from his hiding place, reared up and

plunged a knife into the guard's sternum. The unfortunate chap slid noiselessly to the floor.

Flarge dashed inside, studied the controls for a moment and then set the opposite lift moving. Without hesitation, the pair of us ran across and piled inside.

The car rocked and then began to lurch upwards and I let my gaze drink in the huge spotlit carpet of snow that illumined both the mountainside and castle with a bone-white glow.

Within the car, the atmosphere was pretty stifling: melted snow puddling on the wooden floor and rising off our clothes in great steaming clouds. Flarge was watchful as a hawk, gazing down at the glittering landscape below as we shuddered heavenwards on the narrow steel cable.

I was silent and anxious. The situation could hardly be more grim. Mons had both his Perfect Victim and the completed Jerusalem Prayer. My only hope lay in his not knowing the exact location of the 'Tomb' – the place where Aggie's sacrifice was destined to occur. That at least might buy us some time. I caught sight of myself in the glass, reflection distorted and ghastly-looking, my face clammy and beaded with sweat that stood out on my forehead like diamonds on cloth.

Still the lift clanked onwards, a persistent squeal coming from the steel wheels as they trundled over the cable. I watched as the ground disappeared into the inky darkness below and the jagged, snow-streaked rocks of the mountain reared up before us.

'All right,' said Flarge at last. 'Any bright ideas? We'll be arriving at Mons's castle in a few minutes and there may well be a welcoming committee—'

'Look!' I cried suddenly. 'There! Down there. Do you see them?'

'What?'

I dashed across the cabin and hauled open the sliding door. A wild and chilling wind immediately whipped at our hair and clothes. 'Come on!' I called.

'Don't play games, Box!' cried Flarge. 'What did you see?'

I glanced outside and saw that the trajectory of the cable had brought us within six feet or so of the mountain's jagged surface. Clambering over the lip of the car, I swung like an ape, jumped into space and landed softly in the snow. I beckoned urgently to Flarge, who calmly dropped onto his rear, pushed himself off and fell into the powdery drift.

The now-empty cable-car continued at once on its upward ascent, but I was already striding forward towards the two shapes I'd espied from the cabin, screwing up my eyes against the snow that lashed at my face. From the deeply drifted ravine on which we'd landed, I led the way towards a track that wound around the mountain.

And suddenly, there they were. Two huddled human shapes, snow already piling over their prone forms.

'Who is it?' cried Flarge, racing to my side.

I turned over the first: a massive, familiar bulk, still breathing – thank the Lord Harry. Delilah!

'Out cold,' I muttered, examining her pallid features. Reaching inside my coat, I pulled out a hip flask and managed to get some whisky past my old friend's frozen lips.

Flarge had bent to uncover the second body but suddenly cried out, stumbled onto his rear and, with a guttural retch, vomited copiously into the drift.

I trudged towards him and knelt before the second body, knowing from its size and clothing that it was Professor Reiss-Mueller. In all honesty, I was grateful for these clues, as what lay before me was scarcely recognizable as human.

Reiss-Mueller's skin was shiny and black as rotten fruit, his eyes – fixed in an expression of absolute terror – rolled up horribly into the very limits of their sockets. His nose and mouth, merely flayed holes now, ran with a dreadful green pus that steamed in the frozen air.

And, tucked neatly into his breast pocket, was the silken fragment of the Jerusalem Prayer.

22

The Tomb Of Satan

I whipped the relic from the corpse and plunged it into my coat pocket. The unfortunate Reiss-Mueller must have swiped the wretched thing back in the cottage when he'd 'stumbled' against me. Well, much good had it done him.

Flarge staggered to his feet, wiping the bile from his chin and studiously avoiding the dreadful sight before us. 'What the deuce happened to him?' he croaked.

There was a low groan from Delilah's prone form and I hastened to her side. Despite the thudding snowfall, I could see from the tracks that surrounded her that she and Reiss-Mueller hadn't been alone. There'd been a third party – Aggie, of course – but from the agitated state of the snow, clearly others had arrived.

Delilah suddenly sat up and yelled in absolute terror.

'No! Ho Gawd!' she cried. 'Ho my ruddy Gawd! No! No!'

I tried to push her back down with a soothing hand. 'It's all right, Delilah. It's me. It's Mr Box. You're safe now.'

She looked wildly about then grasped my wrist, her ravaged

countenance streaming with sweat. 'Mr Box, sah!' she rasped, swallowing repeatedly. 'Hif you'd honly seen it!'

I detached myself from her grasp with some difficulty. 'Now just take it easy. Tell us what happened.'

Delilah collapsed onto her back, breathing stertorously and shaking her massive head in disbelief. 'The Professor,' she gasped. "E come back, hout of the blue. 'Ad words wiv 'is boys and sent 'em horf. Then 'e pulls a pistol on me and says, "Get the girl."' Delilah flashed me a look of desperate appeal. "E'd've shot me down then hand there, sah, Hi swear it!'

'It's all right,' I soothed. 'I understand. What happened then?'

'Well, Hi 'ad to drag Miss Haggie downstairs, sah, and we set horf for the castle. Hi thought we'd perish out 'ere, sah, but the Professor – blast 'is heyes – 'e says 'e 'ad heverything 'e needed now hand we must get to the tomb come 'ell hor 'igh water.'

She grabbed the hip flask from me and drained it dry. Whisky bubbled over her cracked lips. '"Hit's my time," his what 'e said. "I shall be the one the Prince of Darkness favours."'

I nodded slowly to myself. Flarge crouched down and tried to get his arm around Delilah's waist in order to help him up. To my astonishment, the old girl lashed out and clocked him on the side of the head.

'What the hell!' he ejaculated.

Delilah rolled over and began to box poor Percy about the ears until I dragged her off by the shoulders. 'No, no! He's with us now. It's all right, believe me!'

'But you said 'e was trying to—'

'I know, I know! But things have changed, Delilah. Please. Let go of Mr Flarge's head!'

With great reluctance, my wonderfully brutish slavey did as she was bidden and Flarge flopped into the snow, spluttering and heaving up a little more of his lunch. Delilah shook herself all over and then continued her tale. 'We got up 'ere, hand then . . . then . . . something awful odd 'appened, sah.'

'Go on.'

Delilah rubbed her jowls. 'Miss Haggie sets up ha terrible crying, sah, and the Professor tells 'er to shut 'er noise. But she says, "Can't you feel it? Can't you feel it?", and that's when I gets this 'orrible feeling. Like when Hi gets one of me black dogs, you know, sah.'

I knew what was coming.

'Then Miss Haggie points a'ead through the snow. Hi thought someone was coming to meet hus, sah, but the Prof just let out an 'orrible moan and fell to 'is knees. There was somebody there, Mr Box. But it weren't 'uman! This terrible face! And the eyes on it!'

I patted her hand. 'I know, I know.'

'What happened then?' said Flarge, keeping a wary distance from Delilah.

My servant stared into the falling snow, almost unable to bear the recollection. 'The Professor pulls out that blessed 'ankie,' she whispered, 'and waves it habout. "Hi'm 'ere!" he shouts. "Hi 'ave come!" But the thing just glares at 'im and its eyes glowed red and the Professor started screaming and . . . I don't remember no more. Hi'm sorry, sah.'

She sank into herself and began to sob uncontrollably, something I'd never seen in all our years together. Giving her a reassuring pat on the shoulder, I rose to my feet. 'I reckon Reiss-Mueller was operating on his own. He kept me alive just long enough to find out the identity of the Perfect Victim then pick-pocketed the relic from me and went in search of his destiny. He was a real expert, as he said. Crazy about the occult. And he wanted the evil power for himself. Unfortunately for him, old Nick seems to have had other ideas.'

Rubbing his near-throttled neck, Flarge came closer, gingerly retrieving the brass binoculars from Reiss-Mueller's mangled corpse. 'And the girl?' he said at last.

'From the look of these tracks, Mons's men came along and took Aggie away, leaving Delilah to freeze to death.'

'And the relic? Why the hell would they leave that?'

I shook my head. Flarge cast a longing glance at the cable above our heads. 'Well, it's a dashed hard climb for us now. Night on a bare mountain, what?'

I waved the silk under his nose. 'What you don't know is that this thing is also a kind of map. And what the late Professor and I discovered some time ago is that the location of the imprisoned brimstone-lover is located halfway up this mountain. We're almost there.'

Which was an optimistic statement, to say the least. With the exhausted Delilah slowing us down, it was terrifically hard going, the startling white of the snow coupled with the deep, deep shadows of the treacherous rocks conspiring to confuse our every step.

Trudging on regardless, the snow buffeting us in swirling eddies like miniature cyclones, we made our way up the mountain track as it began to level out.

Machine-cut chips of rock littered the drifts beneath our boots like black threads in ermine and, as I peered through the white curtain of the weather, I made out, just ahead of us, the semicircle of a tunnel entrance.

'Mons's work, you reckon?' I cried.

Flarge frowned, then advanced and began to rub with a gloved hand against the rock wall. A rusted metal sign emerged from the peppering of snow, bearing the letters *PTT*.

My new ally let out a little laugh. 'No, old boy. This is something far more powerful. Its pernicious tentacles spread across the globe!'

'What do you mean?'

'*PTT!* Postal Telegraph and Telephones! It's the Swiss Post Office! Clearly they had cause to dig into this rock long before Mons did!'

'Very handy for the bugger, I'm sure.'

'Look 'ere, sah!' called Delilah, beckoning me over.

I hauled my way through the drifts and looked down to see where Delilah had brushed away the snow, revealing the rusted tracks of a

narrow-gauge railway leading into the cave. Dear me but the Swiss were funny beggars. Why the hell would they build a post-office railway inside a mountain? Nevertheless grateful for their eccentricity, I led our little party through the narrow entrance into the tunnel and it was a huge relief to be out of the howling gale. Pushing down the snow-soaked scarf from over my mouth, I took in our new surroundings.

From somewhere close by there came a repetitive throbbing beat, reminiscent of the pounding drums at the F.A.U.S.T. rally. But what drew our attention at once was the ruddy glow coming from up ahead. Gingerly, the three of us advanced until we reached a much more ragged archway, which, judging by the great piles of dusty rock that surrounded it, had only recently been excavated.

There were voices coming from within. As if the place weren't uncanny enough, it sounded for all the world like a sermon in a country church; low, monotonous grumbling followed by hushed responses. Well I knew, though, that it was some hideously bastardized version of the familiar ritual.

We listened for a time, Delilah getting her breath back, Flarge concentrating on reloading his pistol. At last, I signalled them to follow and we crept stealthily forward to spy out the unfamiliar territory.

The tunnel opened into a cathedral-like chamber, its ceiling festooned with stalactites that dripped like the venom-laden fangs of some great serpent. The place exhibited the signs of its hasty excavation, though vast black drapes had been strung from the rock walls, their surfaces beautifully worked in diabolical designs of crimson, azure and gold. At the centre of the chamber stood a big stone altar, draped in black cloth.

I swallowed hard. Agnes Daye lay sprawled nude on her belly on that altar, seemingly insensible, her arms bound behind her back. Even at that distance I could see the ugly wound in her shoulder, black against the burnt-sugar brown of her smooth flesh. Around

her, wreathed in smoking incense, were scores of equally naked men and women, their faces covered by grotesquely carved animal masks. Pigs, wolves and bug-eyed insects leered out of the miasmic gloom, chanting, writhing and wildly gesticulating.

Only three faces remained uncovered: my sister Pandora, swamped by a floor-length robe of Roman purple, Olympus Mons, who stood at a sort of lectern, and a corpulent figure clothed in black, his multiple chins wobbling over the tight collar. It was Joshua Reynolds, his eyes shining with depraved joy. Once Flarge had told me his tale I'd suspected as much but here was the living proof. Who was better placed to lure Percy Flarge into his nefarious schemes than the head of the Royal Academy himself!

I thought back to that fateful meeting in the Moscow Tea Rooms. Of how he'd taunted me, dismissed me as a relic of a bygone age – whilst all the time I'd been vital to his terrible plans. He'd counted on my skills to hunt down Agnes Daye and return the relic to its rightful place. Rage boiled within me but I tried to suppress it and concentrate instead on the lectern before which Mons was standing. Upon it was stretched what I knew at once to be the remainder of the Jerusalem Prayer, patched together like an exquisite quilt. The left-hand corner was missing.

Mons was naked save for his own black robe, embroidered all over with slithering serpents, chased in silver and bronze. There was a wildly triumphant look in his searchlight eyes as he intoned his blasphemous verses. 'He comes! He that is Spoken Of! As it is written, so mote it be!' he bellowed. 'The Prayer speaks truly! All unknowing he returns the last piece to the whole!'

I was so absorbed by this performance that at first I didn't notice the cold barrel of an automatic pressing into my neck. Whirling round, I groaned at the sight of amber-shirt guards depriving Flarge of his pistol and others training their machine-guns on Delilah.

With a sharp jab in my side, I was propelled through into the incense-soaked chamber beyond.

Mons paused in his declamation, his ruddy face suffused with delight.

I smiled in clubbable fashion. 'Oh. You've started without us. And I thought I was being fashionably late.'

Mons seemed amused and rubbed his hands like a genial host. 'Very good, Mr Box. Ever so good.'

'Welcome Box!' cried Reynolds.

'Welcome brother!' giggled Pandora. 'At last you're here. And you've fulfilled your side of the bargain admirably.'

Delilah stumped to my side. 'What the 'ell do they mean, sah?' she grumbled. 'What bargain?'

Reynolds rubbed his massive belly in delight. 'What other kind is there, Box? A Devil's bargain!'

Pandora licked her carmined lips. 'Oh, poor Lucy, you *have* been naive!'

A cold wave of sickness passed over me. What had I done?

'Haven't you read your fragment of the Prayer?' cried Mons, smiling. 'It was written there the whole time.'

'Didn't I say he was getting slow?' cackled Reynolds.

I gazed around the chamber, feeling utterly hollow. '"All unknowing will he come,"' I quoted in a dull whisper.

Mons nodded feverishly. 'The Prayer has been separated into fragments all these years but the text itself decrees that the last piece must be restored by one who comes all unknowing. You, my friend, you!'

'No!' I cried. '*No!*'

'We've been leading you here all along, Box,' sneered Reynolds. 'Why'd you think we made it so damned easy for you to escape?'

'Easy!' I exclaimed. 'I could have lost your blasted relic half a dozen times. Along with my ruddy life!'

Mons shook his head. 'You were watched over all the time,' he said, troublingly.

'Watched over?' I whispered, voice cracking. 'By whom?'

Mons stroked his waxed moustache. 'By the Prince of Darkness himself. Knowing how close we had come to releasing him, he stretched out his terrible influence to ensure you came to no harm.'

As disquieting thoughts go it was up there with the best. But now I understood why that frightful apparition had sent the police off on the wrong trail back in Norfolk, why the bullet had melted into air before my face and why Professor Reiss-Mueller had been rejected by the Dark Master he so longed to serve. It was essential that I, thick-headed dolt that I was, bring back the last fragment of the Prayer without ever knowing I was being used as its hapless courier. What had the cypher said? 'Box *must* have the Prayer.'

'So you've put me through all this, *all this*,' I seethed, 'just to bring back that bloody dish-rag for you?'

'It was ours all along,' laughed Mons. 'But the ritual is clear. One of those annoying little codicils that were meant to stop us from raising the Beast. Only one all unknowing could restore the final piece.'

My mind raced back to Hubbard the Cupboard, scrabbling between the bells in that clapboard church what felt like months ago. He'd told me then and there that he was a patsy. Suddenly my mouth was bone dry. 'You . . . you planted the handkerchief on Hubbard? You meant me to find it?'

Reynolds nodded gleefully. 'Oh yes! I must say you've more than lived up to the reputation I sought so hard to debase for young Percy there.'

Flarge looked suitably miserable and shook his fist at his former boss. 'Gad! You utter swine! How could you?'

Reynolds gave an idle flick of the hand. 'You were useful, Percy, that's all. You added – what's the word? – *verisimilitude*. Box had to believe he was a wanted man so that he wouldn't suspect for a moment that, all along, we were leading him here.'

Mons took up the tale. 'We made it a fascinating journey, as full of surprise and co-incidence as any tall tale. There were even surprises for us! Like discovering that the smuggling operation I'd been

running across the Atlantic was rather more important than I thought.'

I felt dazed and nauseous. It was all I could do to stay upright. 'Sal Volatile found the girl, didn't he?' I murmured. 'Hidden away on that rotten old ship of yours. But he kept it a secret. Kept it until—'

'Until Daley tortured the truth out of him,' said Mons, evenly. 'But he'd only got as far as naming the convent of St Bede before he. . .expired. I must say, it was a most hair-raising time for us. All our plans tottered on the brink of collapse. For without the Perfect Victim, the Prayer was useless.'

I looked over at poor Aggie, naked and insensate on the cold stone of that profane altar. 'And I brought her to you, didn't I?' I whispered, utterly demolished.

'Practically gift-wrapped,' tittered Reynolds. 'With a little help from Professor Reiss-Mueller. Poor sap. He thought he could leap-frog the competition. But it doesn't work like that. One must play by the rules.'

Pandora straightened up, clearly enjoying the pantomime bold-ness of her luxuriant gown. 'We've wound you up like a little clockwork mouse, dear brother. And now you've come home.'

My sister stepped forward and, after rifling my coat pockets, took the last fragment of the Prayer and handed it with great ceremony to Olympus Mons. He smoothed out the ancient silk, placed it on the frame alongside the rest of the heathen text and, sweeping back his hair, advanced towards the altar where Aggie lay on cold stone.

'It begins at last!' he cried. 'The Devil is loose!'

23

The Sabbat of Olympus Mons

Amber-shirt thugs swooped on Flarge, Delilah and myself, rapidly binding us at the wrists and pushing us down onto our rumps, Pandora supervising.

'Don't want you to miss the show, Lucy,' she said, cheerily, tying off the knots before slipping back into the throng.

'Damn you,' I hissed.

'Too late for that,' she cried gaily, smoothing some strange and noxious brown unguent onto her chest and calves.

A shattered cross had been rammed, upside down, into the stone of the altar and close by stinking candles fizzled and flared. From their stench I reckoned them to be made from corrupted human fat.

Mons's acolytes, all of them naked save for the amber-shirts who guarded us, began to sway and rock on their heels as the filthy incense took hold, a low murmur bubbling in their upturned throats. Pandora thrashed about amongst the throng, grunting horribly, her hands held aloft in gleeful ecstasy, her bare feet scuffing over a carpet of broken Communion wafers – real this time – that

had evidently been looted from some church. I saw, to my disgust, that several of the masked lunatics were busily urinating on the Host.

We could only gaze on in absolute horror as the obscene ritual was enacted before us: the most finished piece of blackguardism since Caligula ran amok. Poor Agnes lay sprawled on her belly, rump in the air, whilst Mons pushed back his cape, revealing the strongly muscled contours of his body and intoned his hideous inversion of the Mass, kissing her all over at the points where a congregation would normally have muttered the responses.

As the animalistic grunting and snuffling increased to shattering volume and Mons's hissed repudiation of Christ and the Virgin topped even that, I became aware of a piercing cry that turned my blood to ice-water.

'Oh God,' whispered Flarge. 'Not that!'

'What is it?' I cried.

I could feel Flarge sagging right by me as his head sank onto his chest. 'It's all in the rituals they told me of. The slaughter of the innocent.'

I jerked my head around. A slim naked youth of perhaps fifteen years, his head disguised by a wolf-mask, was dragged forward by two of the amber-shirts. Evidently the news that he was to be sacrificed to his Nibs had been only recently relayed. He was jabbering in terror, trying desperately to convince his captors that they must choose another. But the burly guards merely scooped him up and, with awful strength, held him upside down by his shins. His hair, ringing wet with cold sweat, flopped towards the dusty floor and the wolf-mask fell with a sharp clatter, revealing a flushed face red and contorted with fear.

'For God's sake, Mons!' I yelled. 'Think what you're doing!'

Pandora was at my side in an instant and I felt her hand crack across my cheek. 'Silence!' she shrieked. 'The Dark One must feed! He must *feed*!'

The amber-shirts staggered slightly under the youth's weight but still they held him firm, like a trussed chicken. Despite the terrible rapture that seemed to be consuming Mons, he spared a moment to glance aside and wink at me. I whimpered with sheer impotent fury, calling upon all the saints to help me.

For answer, Mons produced a tiny silver blade, like a fruit knife, and slipped it quickly across the youth's throat. The boy made no sound at all and the commotion in the chamber suddenly ceased. The heavy wet bubbling of arterial blood from his throat was the only noise to be heard, splashing horribly to the floor of the chamber in a great, frothing rush.

Mons stooped to catch the blood in a chalice, then, lifting it to his lips, he drank deep.

'Oh my Christ,' groaned Flarge.

Mouth befouled with the boy's blood, Mons suddenly flung the remainder in a wide arc over the curve of Agnes's smooth backside. At this, the girl began to stir and turned her face towards us three bound together. I prayed for her to remain insensible but she seemed to take in the full dread of her situation all at once and let out an awful scream.

Two more animal-masked followers leapt forward and, grasping her by the wrists, swung her over onto her back. From the blond braids of one and the flabby little body of the other, I knew them to be the amber-shirt elite who had stood with Mons on his Manhattan platform.

The 'congregation' responded to Aggie's scream and the grunting, squealing and frenzied dancing took up again, a pounding drum-beat sounded from close by.

I turned away in disgust at the dark rime of blood that clung to Mons's black moustaches. The dead body of the sacrificed youth was dropped to the rocky floor and then, with a whoop of bacchanalian delight, Mons gestured towards the corpse, inviting his acolytes to rub the foul substance onto their naked torsos.

Pandora rushed to the altar and dipped her hands into the ghastly wound on the youth's throat that gaped like an empty sleeve. She smeared blood carelessly over her breasts and face and then reached out for Mons as though seeking praise – but he pushed her aside with some violence. Appallingly, I could see that beneath his black robe, Mons had become as priapic as a goat. Pandora fell back, looking, I have to say, a little put out.

'Choose me!' she yelled. 'Why can't it be me?'

Mons glared at her, apoplectic with rage. 'Get back! Get back, you worthless drudge!'

Pandora wrang her bloodstained hands. 'I know she's the Perfect Victim, but, please, after the ritual's done. You know how I feel—'

Mons's face was growing black with fury. 'You bother me with such trivia now? At the very moment of my greatest glory? You loathsome sow, do you think I could ever, ever even spare you a solitary thought?'

Pandora looked as though she'd been cracked across the chops.

Mons shook his head and laughed. 'You were only chosen to join my side after your luckless brother was selected to be the one. He Who Comes All Unknowing. You pathetic parasite! Now get back amongst the rest of my worthless slaves and keep your mouth shut.'

Pandora literally staggered where she stood.

'Oh, crumbs,' I cried. 'Boyfriend trouble again, sis? Just like old times.'

Expecting the usual scowl, I was shocked to see the utter blankness in Pandora's face. She looked completely undone and her skin showed waxy and deathly pale beneath the streams of blood and stinking unguents that covered it.

Now Mons returned his attention to poor Aggie. He moved slowly, almost reverently towards her, his hands gory with haemoglobin, his cock twitching in anticipation of the diabolical coupling to come.

But it was not to be. I was suddenly aware of a muttering voice

from close by. At first I assumed that some hellish ritual was to accompany the dread moment, but to my astonishment I saw that Pandora had moved to one side, bending over the Jerusalem Prayer on its frame, her lips moving quickly as she declaimed the ancient and forbidden text.

Mons span round, appalled. 'What are you doing? It's too early! Too early, you senseless fool!'

He threw aside the little knife he'd used on the poor boy, sending it clattering down the steps of the altar as Pandora's voice raced on, chattering through the ritual with almost supernatural speed. Mons dashed towards her, his fist raised to strike, but then stopped dead and whipped about as all the flaming torches and the beastly candles in the chamber suddenly. . .winked. . .out.

My scalp prickled and I felt as though a great weight were pressing on my chest.

'Bloody 'ell,' gasped Delilah. 'What's going hon?'

'Yes,' whispered Flarge. 'I feel it too.'

A freezing draught crept through the darkness, colder than the snowy journey to the mountain, colder than anything I had ever known.

'My God,' I hissed. 'Something's coming!'

'*He* is coming,' croaked Flarge, his voice tiny and broken in that dreadful, dark place.

And then I felt once again that curious blanket of silence, as though we were all spinning in the total vacuum of space. In the sepulchral blackness, there was suddenly a form of light, a dreary, ghastly light like something rotten and long buried that has been unwisely disturbed. In this greenish phosphorescence, I became aware that all of Mons's acolytes were silently creeping closer to the altar. Despite their ambitions, they were as terrified as us. In the shadows, though, something else was approaching. At first I took it to be more of the naked, animal-masked throng, but even in that weird luminescence I could see that the flesh was somehow *wrong*.

What I took to be several people was in fact one great lumpen thing, its pale and spindly body thrashing about as it slobbered and crawled its way towards us. It was covered all over with eyes, tiny black orbs like those on a spider, yet somewhere in that mass of disgusting tissue there was the semblance of a human mouth. And to my unutterable horror, it was *singing*.

It was some kind of bastardized plainsong, rather like a gramophone record of monks chanting that has somehow gone awry. And between gasps of this foul cacophony, the thing began to giggle.

As I looked, a second creature shuffled and crawled towards us, extruding itself from the darkness like an obscene sausage skin. This one had a vast maw that sparkled with filth and spit and waves of corruption seemed to spill from it. It was a thing of the grave, a thing of utter and profound darkness, and I shuddered to my very soul in its presence.

Something moved behind me and I yelled in terror – but it was only Flarge. 'Shh!' he hissed. 'If you value your life, Box, silence! We haven't much time!'

I thrilled with shock as I saw that the enterprising chap had managed to grasp the sacrificial knife – abandoned by Mons – between his heels and was dragging it towards him.

Delilah and I, with our backs towards him, could be of little aid but I was grateful for any distraction from the grisly apparitions. In seconds, Flarge's straining hands had grabbed the knife and we had it between our hands, sawing desperately at the ropes that bound us.

"Ow we gonna get out hof 'ere?' hissed Delilah.

'We can't escape,' said Flarge flatly. 'But there is a chance, a *chance*, we might be saved.' To my surprise, he waved the little old book he'd retrieved from Daley's pocket on the train. 'It's a dangerous business, this. None more dangerous. So there are safeguards. In *here*.'

I felt him jerk away and realized he was suddenly free. He looked wildly about but the entire wretched coven had eyes only for the filthy, squealing beasts that were undulating towards them.

With the book in one hand, Flarge got into a crouching position and grasped a small, powdery rock. In seconds, he had made a circuit of me and Delilah and I realized that he was scrawling as though with chalk on the rough floor of the cave. But it was a five-pointed star that he drew, not a circle as I'd expected. Flicking through the brittle pages of the book, he muttered under his breath and then frantically scrabbled some words and symbols that it was impossible to make out in the queer light.

'If only there were more time,' cried Flarge, hoarsely. 'It's a bad job! *Hod, Malchut, Kether, Binah, Cerburah*! A bad job. But the best I can do. You see, your sister's intervention means the invocation hasn't been properly performed. Like the cad Reynolds said, there are rules – and that might give us hope.'

He froze and I too turned to see that all of us, Mons, Pandora, the acolytes, were completely surrounded by legions of the unspeakable creatures, rolling and slobbering over one another like maggots in a fisherman's basket. The stench was so overwhelming that I gagged.

But it was not this that arrested us. For over the altar, forming in the very air, was the strange, hazy smoke that I had seen out on the *Stiffkey* and again on the Norfolk marsh. Just as before, twin points of red light suddenly blazed into life but this time the apparition rapidly assumed a terrible solidity.

The thing was gigantic. The wreaths of smoke wound round and round each other like the bindings on a mummy until massive furry haunches, greasy and bestial, emerged from the murk. As though for dramatic effect, the flaming torches and candles relumed and an awed gasp rippled through the assembly.

The great muscular legs of the creature terminated in hooves, black and smeared with filth that was even now creeping upwards in concert with the pall of strange smoke. This too began to solidify and a great human torso rose up above the legs, the skin oily with sweat, yet the stomach was covered all over in lurid green scales like those on a fish.

Now, with great rapidity, the rest of the monstrous beast took shape. Mammoth female breasts, firm, ripe and *blue*, rose from the torso, the swollen nipples dripping with black milk. At last the head was revealed, resolving itself around those pitiless red eyes in the shape of a sheep's head, vast shining horns projecting from the furrowed brow, patches of bare bone showing through amongst the long, lank human hair that spewed from its scalp.

'Oh, God!' gasped Flarge. 'He's free! Banebdjed! The Witch Lord! He comes to conjoin with the Lamb in mockery of God!'

The creature – this devil, whatever it was – began to turn its head. It was such an uncanny sight that my guts turned absolutely to water. The furious eyes blazed within its withered, skull-like face, a face covered in matted hair, fur and feathers. Immense leathery wings projected from the shoulders.

I was stupefied with terror and almost didn't notice as Delilah suddenly seized my hand as the pentagram was completed. Flarge did the same, his own palms pouring with sweat – and put his mouth right by our ears. 'If you value your souls, don't look in its eyes. We're face to face with the very Devil himself. Keep hold of each other's hands and pray. Pray as you've never prayed. And believe! *Believe!*'

I needed no urging. What I had considered lunacy only scant days ago was there before my eyes: profound, abject, undiluted evil. I strained to recall every schoolboy prayer, every catechism, but my mind was like a stone, refusing to dredge up even the slenderest memory.

Mons alone seemed not to fear the apparition. Stretching to his full height he strode towards it, cape billowing behind him, his handsome face alight with energy and triumph. As he smiled, his lip curled up over his fanglike tooth.

'Lord of the Sky! Banebdjed! I, Olympus Mons, have summoned thee back from the darkest place. I shall shatter the bonds that have laid thee low these past millennia. And in return you will

grant me power! Power over these feeble scum and millions like them! This world shall be mine! Everything refashioned into my image! Nothing will live, nothing will think without my granting it leave to do so. I have made all this possible, Banebdjed. I am *your* saviour!'

Still I struggled to remember anything even vaguely holy. *Jesus' hands were kind hands*, ran a ludicrous voice in my head. *Onward Christian soldiers!* insisted another. But then something did come to me. Not a half-remembered prayer from schooldays, nor any invocation to the forces of light. It was something from that wretched silk relic. The part that Reiss-Mueller could not fathom. 'And only he who makes himself alone in the world can defeat the Beast'.

The ram-headed creature had dropped its mighty head to gaze with horrible, patient desire at the prone body of Agnes Daye: the perfect victim whose sacrifice would release it from its earthly prison. Putrid saliva coursed from its wet mouth as it reached out one vast, human hand towards her. The unholy conjunction was only moments away. Then this force of destruction, this rampant evil would be once more unleashed upon the world.

And only he who makes himself alone in the world can defeat the Beast.

I stood up within the five-pointed star. Flarge grabbed at my ankle but I shook him off.

'What are you doing?' he hissed. 'Sit down! Sit down, you fool!'

'Mr Box!' gasped Delilah.

I stepped out of the pentagram and immediately felt that awful, draining misery that I had endured before, as though every depressive thought, every wasted moment had been condensed into a liquid transfusion that now crept into my very bones.

But I fought back, struggling towards the terrible monster, my every step weighted down as though my shoes were made of oak.

'Banebdjed!' I gasped. Then, louder – 'Banebdjed, hear me!'

Mons turned in surprise then let out a peal of laughter. 'Oh, you really are persistent, Mr Box! Well, then, Lucifer. Meet LUCIFER!'

I ignored him and turned my face towards the creature, averting my eyes from its own and focusing instead on the abomination that was its body. 'Banebdjed! I don't care what this . . . specimen here says. *I* have brought you back. *I* was the one who transported the last fragment of the Jerusalem Prayer to this unholy place. *I* am the one spoken of in the forbidden texts. I brought it here, all unknowing, as the prophecy states!'

'Box! Box, what are you doing?' screamed Flarge.

Pandora jerked towards me, the tendons on her neck standing out like cords. 'Get back! Get back, you pathetic little man! This is our moment! The glory is ours!'

I didn't even look at her. 'I am the one who found the Lamb of God! I am He That Is Spoken Of! Is this not so?'

Mons shrugged. 'I cannot deny it. This man has done all these things. But I am the one who seeks your freedom! I am the one!'

'Banebdjed!' I yelled. 'Do you acknowledge that I am He That Is Spoken Of? DO YOU?'

The ram-headed abhorrence seemed to consider for what felt like hours, rancid breath streaming from its nostrils and the black, black hole of its poisonous mouth. At last, the great head inclined downwards just a fraction.

Adrenaline surged through my body. I felt a kind of thrilling victory.

'Then!' I bellowed. 'Being thus, I claim the right to send you back whence you came!'

Mons laughed again. The creature made a low, grumbling roar that ran through me like an earth tremor.

Now Pandora was chuckling. 'You fool! You blind fool! You don't even know what you're saying. Only one who makes himself all alone in the world can do that!'

I looked at her. 'And I'm not alone, am I? I have *you*!'

My hand flew to my coat and I whipped out the knife that Flarge had used to slice through our bonds. Pandora's carmine smile fell. Then I dashed forward and with one smooth action cut a new and redder smile in her throat.

24

The Charm's Wound Up

Well, we'd never got on, had we?

Hell, having already broken loose, was content to bide its time at this singular intervention. Pandora slipped to the rocky floor, her neck fountaining blood and soaking her hair, a last look of complete surprise on her cruel, pallid face.

Mons staggered backwards, his bare feet clapping on the cold stone. 'What have you done? What have you *done?*'

Then a strange primal howl began to escape from his breast, immediately silenced by the shattering and ghastly cry of the foul sheep-headed monster that towered above us all. Its great red eyes rolled in its head, and stinking black smoke began to billow from its nostrils and vast mouth, filling the chamber as though a four-alarm fire had broken out. Then the Beast's hooves began to beat an enraged tattoo on the floor like a Spanish bull venting its spleen, and the whole chamber shook with the percussion.

Behind me, Flarge was frantically intoning prayers but I found myself filled with renewed confidence. The game was up. I'd played this Devil by his own rules and bested him.

The creature's dreadful maw fell open and a hideous belching moan erupted from deep within its cavernous chest, great ropes of saliva hanging like slug-trails from its cracked and blackened lips.

Mons pushed me aside and staggered towards the abomination, his hands plucking at its rancid fur. Already it seemed to be diminishing, as though it was being propelled backwards down a long, fathomless tunnel.

'*No!*' screeched Mons. 'Come back! You must come back!'

The creature's body was unravelling, great strips of flesh and bone turning once again into the strange wispy blue smoke. One by one the dreadful crawling horrors that surrounded the creature were absorbed into it as though sucked up by a hurricane.

'You!' raged Mons, pounding up to me and pummelling at my chest with his bare fists. 'You have done this! After all these years of planning and hoping and—'

Suddenly he caught sight of the Jerusalem Prayer, still on its frame, and his face lit up as he raced towards it.

'It's not too late! Of course it's not! I shall simply summon him back again!'

Grasping the edges of the frame he bowed his head and began rapidly to intone the forbidden text.

I was on my feet at once and haring towards him but Flarge was suddenly at my side, laying a restraining hand on my arm. 'Let him finish, old boy.'

'Are you insane?' I yelled. 'I've just slit my bloody sister's throat so that he couldn't unleash that blasted monster—'

Flarge shook his head. 'The Jerusalem Prayer has already been misused once. For the same person to try again is suicide. *One must play by the rules.*'

Joshua Reynolds seemed to know this too. He raced to his master's side and tried to drag him away from the lectern. 'You mustn't!' he screeched. 'You know what will happen!'

But Mons grabbed at the silver chalice and smashed it across Reynolds's face. He crashed to his gargantuan belly, then, staggering to his feet, tottered from the chamber.

I goggled at Mons as he raced feverishly through the ritual, glancing every now and then over his shoulder, willing Banebdjed to reverse his trajectory.

'He's crazy!' yelled Flarge. 'We've got to get out!'

Suddenly a lurid light began to infuse Mons's features. He grinned, obviously confident that, great all-powerful sorcerer that he was, he alone had managed to confound the rules and resurrect the Beast once more. But the light was coming from the Prayer itself. Its edges were on fire.

Mons gasped and looked down as the strange, almost liquid flame licked across the silk. In seconds it had caught the trailing sleeves of his black cloak and was running over his hands like quick-silver.

He screamed and looked wildly around him, looking for support from his loyal acolytes who, like loyal acolytes across the ages, were running to save their skins.

'Banebdjed!' he screamed. 'Save me!'

Staggering towards the satanic creature, his arms ablaze, Mons collapsed onto his knees. Banebdjed, its ghastly ram's head twisting and writhing in agony, was vanishing fast, darkness enveloping its rancid fur and scaly flesh. Flames burst into life under Mons's jaw and his lips drew back in one last snarl. There was a great whoosh of air and orange fire exploded within his skull, belching from his open mouth and sending his eyes shooting out of their sockets. Like twin comets they flared across the cavern, exploding against the rock wall. Then the rest of Mons collapsed into a ball of flame that span round and round before hurtling straight

into the maw of the creature, its jaws snapping shut with terrible finality.

There was a final, almost pathetic sigh and then, as if I had emerged from a dip underwater, everything sprang sharply into focus. The temperature rocketed and that curious sensation of muffled sound vanished on the instant. Naked amber-shirts were fleeing in droves from the chamber, leaving only Flarge, Delilah and me standing as the place shuddered to its very foundations.

Clearly, Banebdjed intended to take down the place with him. I raced towards the altar and scooped up Agnes in my arms.

'Lucifer!' she cried, tears streaming down her beautiful face. 'You have saved me?'

'I promised, didn't I?' I breathed. Delilah was by me in an instant, draping her own heavy coat over the poor girl.

'Let me take 'er, sir,' cried my servant. 'You and Mr Flarge concentrate on getting hus outa 'ere!'

I nodded dumbly, passing Agnes into Delilah's massive embrace. The girl managed to stand, Delilah's coat completely encasing her.

Rocks were tumbling all about and the way out was simply stuffed with screaming, desperate Satanists who'd seen their dreams turn to ashes and now cared only for themselves. We'd never get past them and would in all probability be crushed to death if we tried.

Then my eyes alighted on a wonderful sight. It was a little metal sign bearing the legend *PTT* and, right by it, the arched entrance to some form of maintenance tunnel. Blessing the Post Office in all its forms, I hared forward and popped my head inside. The tunnel was narrow and cramped but looked wholly sound.

'This way!' I yelled. 'Come on!'

Delilah and Agnes moved first and I waved them through.

Flarge paused at the entrance and I urged him on with a thump on the shoulder blades.

'What if it just leads further into the mountain?' he yelled.

'We've no choice!' I cried. 'Get moving!'

He nodded dumbly, then held out his hand. 'Look here, Box, I've got to say this. I'm sorry for everything that happened. If I could undo—'

'Buy me lunch at the Berkeley sometime, eh? Now, go!'

I pushed him in the small of the back and then crumpled to my knees as the floor shook. Enormous chunks of the cavern were coming loose now, peeling from the walls and ceiling, and the black Satanic drapes that had decorated the place billowed and were torn asunder like the sails of a doomed pirate ship.

The fang-like stalactites cracked and fell, spearing amber-shirts with deadly accuracy. There was no time to linger and I staggered through the archway into the Post Office tunnel where all was hot, oppressive darkness.

Crook-backed by the low ceiling, I stumped forward only to run headlong into the rest of the party. I felt my guts revolve as the tunnel shuddered about us, Delilah's sweaty bosom stuffed into my face and Flarge's bony elbow jammed into my side as I tried to get my bearings.

'This way!' gasped Aggie through clouds of choking dust. I groped for my cigarette lighter and flicked it into life. Rock particles glittered in the sudden yellow glow but I could see that Aggie was on the right track. The tiny tunnel snaked round to the left and the flame of the lighter suddenly sputtered as it met a cold breeze.

I could feel Aggie's hot breath against my cheek as I inched forward on my knees, clearing away rubble and then rising once more to a semi-crouching position as I moved, crablike, towards the tantalizing night beyond.

I felt queasy with bending so low, my legs cramping appallingly

and the rough tunnel mortar scraping against the nape of my neck, but all at once I was through and breathing stunningly fresh air.

I turned round at once and dragged first Agnes, then Delilah, then Flarge after me.

We lay dazed for a long moment, retching and coughing and shaking our heads. Above us, the star-packed night sky was immense and wonderful.

There was a distant percussion from inside the mountain and a billowing cloud of choking smoke puffed from the tunnel exit like a dragon's last breath.

'Cor!' croaked Delilah. 'What a night!'

I got to my feet and sighed heavily. Agnes Daye bounced nimbly to my side, her lithe form all but invisible within Delilah's enormous trench-coat.

I ran my hand over her hair and smiled warmly. 'We'd better get you warm, eh? You'll not last long in the buff.'

She chewed her lip and shuddered. 'Is it really over?' she cried, plaintively.

About to reply, I took in a great lungful of the blessed Swiss air, then looked up suddenly, hearing the sound of grinding gears and metal on metal. Flarge was by me in a flash and both of us craned our necks to see the cable cars from Mons's castle stirring into life.

'Capital!' I cried. 'We hopped off when it came close to the mountain. Perhaps we can jump back on board and get a lift down!'

The carriage was blazing with light and I kept my eye on it as the four of us raced through the snow. To my surprise, the light in the car was momentarily blocked by a bulky shape and I realized the thing was occupied.

Flarge whipped out the binoculars he'd taken from Reiss-Mueller's corpse. 'Probably just one of Mons's guards fleeing the castle – hello!'

'What is it?' I cried.

Flarge slowly lowered the glasses. 'It's Joshua Reynolds,' he grinned. 'Fatty Reynolds, trying to save his worthless skin.'

I felt a surge of new purpose rush through my veins. 'I see,' I said calmly. 'Percy, do you reckon you can see these ladies safely to the village?'

'Nothing to it, old sport. Got something to attend to?'

'You might say that. You might very well say that.'

Aggie cocked her lovely head to one side and frowned. 'Lucifer?'

I bent to kiss her on the forehead and then took to my heels, racing through the powdery snow and casting rapid glances at the descending cable car. Within minutes I'd reached the rocky point where the car would come close to the mountainside. Crouching low lest my treacherous chief spot me, I watched as the metal box slid downwards on its steel wire, hovering only a foot or so above my head.

Summoning my last reserves of energy, I hurled myself upwards and grabbed hold of the bottom of the car, swinging up my legs and nestling within the metalwork. The car rocked slightly but there was otherwise no sign that I had thus stowed away. My old injury suddenly flared back into life, however, and I hissed in pain at the renewed agony in my palm.

As the cable-car trundled away from the mountainside, dizzyingly empty air opened up below me. I took a deep breath and concentrated on the matter in hand, probing with my fingers at the housing above my head and soon locating the edges of the hatch. Electric light showed through in a thin yellow rectangle. Planting both feet firmly into the recesses of the undercarriage, I pressed my hands to the hatch, counted to five and pushed upwards with all my strength.

Taken aback by how easily it shifted, I suddenly found myself looking into the car at floor level. The light was blinding after the

darkness outside and the hatch clattered backwards with a noise that would've woken the dead. Reynolds, still in his absurd black costume, span round from the window and gawped down at me.

Before he could move, I put out both hands and hauled myself into the cabin, leaving the hatch wide open. 'Evening!' I cried. 'Going so soon?'

Reynolds's paunchy face was utterly ashen. 'You!' he squealed. 'How did you—? What . . . what happened back there?'

I settled back against the glass and folded my arms nonchalantly. 'Oh yes. I forgot. You didn't stay for the Main House, did you? Scuttled up to the castle, eh, and decided to take the posh way down?'

Reynolds's great pale paw flashed into his robe and pulled out an automatic. 'You'll tell me, Box, if it's the last thing you do,' he snarled. 'Which, incidentally, it will be.'

I shrugged. 'I'm content. I've done my duty. The Devil has been trapped once again and the Jerusalem Prayer destroyed.' I turned to the window and watched our swift progress down the mountain.

Reynolds chins quivered alarmingly. 'And Mons?'

'Gone to Hell.'

Passing a shaking hand across his face, Reynolds heaved a great, shuddering sigh, then seemed to recover himself. He levelled the gun at me and there was black vengeance in his hooded eyes. 'No matter,' he whispered. 'Who knows of my role in all this save you and your amusingly motley band?'

'I wouldn't underestimate any one of us.'

'No? I'm disappointed with Percy, I must admit. He showed great promise. I'm afraid the tales of one obese Domestic and a callow girl with a shade too much of the tar-brush about her won't hold much water back in Blighty.'

'What about me?'

Reynolds's face turned sour. 'You? Didn't I tell you a long time ago that it was time for you to retire?'

He cocked the automatic. I held my breath. And in the blink of an eye, stepped forward and dropped through the open hatch.

My belly lurched horribly as I met empty air but I struck out at once, grabbing hold of the undercarriage of the cable-car and swinging myself back into my previous position. Reynolds's pistol appeared through the open hatch like a rat out of a drainpipe, his hand twisting uncomfortably round as he loosed off a random shot.

The bullet sparked off the metal right by me and I ducked as it whistled past my cheek. I caught sight of Reynolds's eye as he pressed one flabby cheek to the floor and then poked out his hand once again, determined to get a clear shot at me.

The fat man's exposed eye swivelled in my direction and the corner of it creased into a smile as he spotted me, skulking amongst the metalwork. 'I've got you, Box, you interfering bastard!' he screamed, blasting off another bullet.

I dodged out of the way but the shot was true, searing a neat hole through the flapping tail of my leather coat. I wasted no time, swaying from metal strut to metal strut so that I was on the other side of the hatch – behind Reynolds – and out of his firing line.

His plump hand scrabbled about the rim of the open hatch as he tried to reorientate himself but I moved like lightning, grasping his thick wrist and trying desperately to wrestle the gun from his grip. But he was a tenacious bugger, and try as I might I couldn't get him to relinquish it. Twisting round his wrist, I yelled as the pistol spoke again and a bullet smashed through the floor of the car above my head.

Without warning, the whole vehicle lurched and there was a curious, tortured whipping sound from somewhere above. I looked down and saw, to my intense relief, that the station was now only a hundred or so feet below us. If I could only hang on and avoid getting shot, I'd be able to drop off into the snowdrift. The strange

lashing sound came again and the car suddenly dropped fully two feet. I fell forward from my place of safety and found myself hanging onto Reynolds' wrist for grim death. The fat man tried desperately to shake me off and he dropped the automatic. It fell like a stone and I grabbed at Reynold's arm, trying to haul myself up.

'Let go!' he gasped.

'No thanks!' I cried.

The car rocked again and I realized with horror that Reynolds's last shot, the one that had penetrated the car, must've struck the steel wheels that attached the car to the cable above! If they sheared away now, the gondola would be literally hanging by a thread! My own grip on my boss's sweaty arm was fast loosening and I scrabbled frantically at his sleeve, trying to get a purchase on the thick black fabric. Reynolds howled in pain and fought back with the tenacity of a tiger, wriggling his arm back through the hatch and evidently attempting to slip out of his costume to free his put-upon limb.

Then, with the cable station only twenty feet below us, the car gave a great lurch and Reynolds himself fell halfway through the hatch. I clutched at his collar to stop myself from falling and he cried out in frustration and terror. The mechanism above us was disintegrating fast and the air was alive with a metallic splintering sound.

I locked my arms around Reynold's great thick neck, and blow me if he didn't try to bite me! I glanced below again and suddenly knew I was safe. The car dropped one last time. Above us, the steel wheels fell apart and suddenly the car was falling free. With a delighted laugh, I kissed Reynolds on the forehead and let go, falling only ten feet or so and rolling expertly into the snowdrifts.

I looked up as the cable car plummeted towards earth, Reynolds jutting from the hatchway like a cork in a bottle. Shrieking, he tried to force out his massive body from its confinement but it was too late. Like a yo-yo snapped from its string, the cable car went smashing

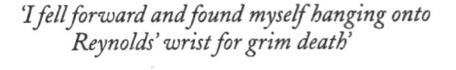

*'I fell forward and found myself hanging onto
Reynolds' wrist for grim death'*

into its station, shearing the corpulent chief of the Royal Academy neatly in two.

As the car came to rest amidst the tangled machinery it burst into flame and I averted my face, taking solace in the freezing snow in which I lay half buried.

I walked slowly back towards Lit-de-Diable, the cable-car terminus blossoming into flame far behind me, but the roar of the explosion was almost blotted out by the sweet pattering of snowflakes. Down here, snow blanketed every wooden gable, every glowing gas lamp.

As I neared the inn, the door flew open and Delilah, Flarge and Agnes emerged.

'Good to see you, sah!' cried Delilah. 'Hi trust everything's been sorted out to your satisfaction?'

'Rather,' I cried as Aggie slammed into me and threw her arms about my neck. 'Have you got us all beds for the night, Percy?'

Flarge grinned hugely. 'Naturally. No flies on me, old thing. Could I buy you that dinner now, do you think?'

I thought of warm food and wine and a downy bed and sweet Agnes Daye and suddenly I was the happiest of men. I kissed the girl full on the mouth and then whistled at the rather fetching Swiss peasant costume of gingham dress and tight blouse that she seemed to have acquired.

'Glad you've changed, my dear. You'd've frightened the yodellers!'

She gave a glum look and plucked at the pretty frock. 'That was shaming. I must have looked indecent.'

'Nun's training kicking in again, eh?' I shrugged. 'Well, it was nothing I hadn't seen before.'

She batted me playfully on the arm. 'Brute. You are a beast and I cannot think why I like you.'

'Well,' I said, putting my arm around her shivering shoulders and leading her towards the warmth of the inn, 'better the devil you know, eh?'

SIMON &
SCHUSTER

Mark Gatiss

Black Butterfly

LUCIFER BOX. He's tall, he's dark and, like the shark, he
looks for trouble.

Or so he wishes. For, with Queen Elizabeth newly
established on her throne, the now elderly secret agent is
reaching the end of his scandalous career. Despite his fast-
approaching retirement, queer events leave Box unable to
resist investigating one last case...

Why have pillars of the Establishment started dying in
bizarrely reckless accidents?
Who are the deadly pay-masters of enigmatic assassin
Kingdom Kum?
And who or what is the mysterious Black Butterfly?

From the seedy streets of Soho to the souks of Istanbul and
the sun-drenched shores of Jamaica, Box must use his
artistic licence to kill and eventually confront an enemy
with its roots in his own notorious past. Can Lucifer Box
save the day before the dying of the light?

ISBN 978-0-7432-5711-4
PRICE £15

POCKET
BOOKS

Mark Gatiss

The Vesuvius Club

Lucifer Box is the darling of the Edwardian belle monde:
portrait painter, wit, dandy and rake – the guest all
hostesses must have. And most do.

But few of his connections or conquests know that Lucifer
Box is also His Majesty's most daring secret agent, at
home in both London's Imperial grandeur and the
underworld of crazed vice that seethes beneath.

And so, of course, when Britain's most prominent
scientists begin turning up dead, there is only one man his
country can turn to.

Lucifer Box ruthlessly deduces and seduces his way from
his elegant townhouse at Number 9 Downing Street
(somebody has to live there), to the seediest stews of
Naples, in search of the mighty secret society that may
hold the fate of the world in its claw-like hands – the
Vesuvius Club.

ISBN 978-0-7434-8379-7
PRICE £7.99

**POCKET
BOOKS**

Mark Gatiss

The Devil in Amber

Lucifer Box – the gorgeous butterfly of King Bertie's reign, portraitist, dandy and terribly good secret agent – is feeling his age. Assigned to observe the activities of fascist leader Olympus Mons and his fanatical Amber Shirts in snow-bound 1920s New York, Box finds himself framed for a vicious murder.

Using all his native cunning, Box escapes aboard a vessel bound for England armed only with a Broadway midget's suitcase and a string of unanswered questions. What lies hidden in the bleak Norfolk convent of St Bede? What is 'the lamb' that Olympus Mons searches for in his bid for world domination? And what has all this to do with a medieval prayer intended to summon the Devil himself?

From the glittering sophistication of Art Deco Manhattan to the eerie Norfolk coast and the snow-capped peaks of Switzerland, *The Devil in Amber* takes us on a thrilling ride that pits Lucifer Box against the most lethal adversary of his career: the Prince of Darkness himself.

ISBN 978-0-7434-8380-3
PRICE £7.99

POCKET
BOOKS

Mark Gatiss

The Vesuvius Club
Graphic Edition

The first adventure of Lucifer Box is rendered in
every detail in this special graphic novel edition of
The Vesuvius Club.

Lucifer Box, the greatest portraitist of the
Edwardian age and England's most dashing secret
agent, investigates a series of bizarre disappearances
and plunges headlong into low life and high society.

Who is killing Britain's most prominent vulcanologists?
What secrets lie beyond the grave?
And which tie goes best with a white carnation?

ISBN 978-0-7432-7600-9
PRICE £12.99